AMOK

AN ANTHOLOGY OF ASIA-PACIFIC SPECULATIVE FICTION

Edited by Dominica Malcolm

SOLARWYRM PRESS

2014

Published and produced by Solarwyrm Press
http://www.solarwyrm.com

Amok: An Anthology of Asia-Pacific Speculative Fiction

Cover design by Jun Hun Yap
http://www.junhunyap.com

Production by Dominica Malcolm

ISBN: 978-0-9805084-4-4

CONTENTS

Tom Barlow | North Pacific Gyre

INTRODUCTION

Dominica Malcolm

As an Australian who knew a number of excellent Australian short story writers, in the early stages of conceptualising my first anthology, my instinct had been to have a collection of speculative fiction set in Australia. Then I had a request to include New Zealand as a setting, and once that door opened, it occurred to me that living in Malaysia and sharing my writing with those I met in Kuala Lumpur meant I at the very least had some connections to help me spread the word within the region. It then ended up being no surprise to me that the majority of submissions came from and/or were set in Australia and Malaysia.

When I put up the call for submissions, I was specifically looking for the kind of diversity that doesn't seem so common in mainstream fiction. Not only is the Asia-Pacific region home to a vast number of races—which are captured very well in this anthology—but I was also hoping to find more characters both young and old, from non-Western religious backgrounds, women, LGBT, and disabled characters. I am thankful to say all of this diversity is represented in this collection.

Whilst the stories feature settings in Australia, China, Hawai'i, Hong Kong, India, Indonesia, Japan, Malaysia, New Zealand, the Pacific Ocean, the Philippines, Singapore, South Korea, Thailand, and Vietnam, the authors are also diverse, living across the globe in Australia, Canada, China, England, Japan, Malaysia, New Zealand, the Philippines, Vietnam, and the USA.

As well as diversity, I was naturally also looking for good quality speculative fiction, which I generally define as "real world settings in the past, present, or future, with science-fiction or fantasy elements." The stories I selected range from using traditional mythology of the country or region they're set in, re-imagined mythology or other fantasy, and possible futures, which includes both new technologies and dystopias.

I'm really proud of the selection of stories I was able to include. I hope you enjoy them as much as I do!

THE DONOR

Brett Adams

~ Australia ~

I wasn't born blind.

At least, that's what my mother told me.

My sight was stolen by a man calling himself Doctor Fletcher. He gave me the wrong drops—the wrong treatment entirely—for swollen eyes, and ran away when the shit hit the fan. Left me blind at six months, when I was just beginning to drink in the kaleidoscope, only to have it wink out in the time it took to draw breath.

That's the gist of what Mum told me. I don't remember any of it.

As I grew, it fell to my remaining senses to give me a kind of sight. With my ears I learned how to map a room by the subtle play of echo from texture. With my nose I fixed upon a thousand different scents undetected by mere mortals. With my fingers I grasped the Elephant—hide, tusk and trunk. And so I saw, after all.

At least, that's what my teachers told me.

But the sense I held most dear is the common sort. It's a pity it kept silent on that fateful day in August all those years ago, instead of screaming how crazy it was for three kids—one blind, one deaf, and one... other—to be on the cliffs of Blackwall Reach just shy of midnight, winter's breath heavy on our necks, hunting for a missing man.

Did I mention we were twelve? Three boys of twelve at Blackwall Reach in the witching hour. Not very Disney. But we figured we had the pooled resources of a thirty-six year old man. Treble the feet and hands in any case. Funny to think that thirty-six was the missing man's age.

Why Blackwall? That had been Barny's idea.

I remember it vividly. Earlier that day he'd said, "Paahlie," (my name is Paulus) in that voice of his, which sounded like a crow in flight. I liked Barny's crow's caw. It had a singsong quality. The other kids might have liked it too if they'd shut up long enough to listen, instead of gibbering to each other to bugger up his lip reading. That was before we changed school, mind you. But I'm getting ahead of myself.

"Paahlie," he cawed, "Let's go."

We were killing time in a foodhall after school, and I thought he meant we should leave. I sucked harder on my shake and made to get up.

"No." He laughed in that breathy way of his. "Not here. Blackwall."

He was a brave bugger, Barny. I could have travelled the world if I had a fiver for every time some well-meaning adult told me how brave *I* was. So independent, so 'autonomous'—and blind!

But Barny had it worse. His dad had belted his hearing from him when he was six. He didn't have a mum. No one else knew how he'd lost his hearing. He told only me, and that's the other reason I harboured a special fondness for Barny.

Me, brave? It was Barny who walked home from school every day after he lost his hearing, just like normal. Home to that man. To his *Guardian*. Barny went home to his father every day at 3.30 on the dot, and sat with him on the couch and watched TV and fetched his poison from the fridge. And as the years passed and Barny's legs lengthened and his dad's gut grew, Barny loved him until he crawled out of the hole and into the sun.

I had the first inkling the day he told me all this that giants walked among us.

So it was brave Barny's suggestion to go to Blackwall Reach.

And it was Nate who seconded it.

He was with us in the foodhall. He stood so quickly his chair squealed on the tiles. "Yeah," was all he said, and I heard him stuffing his things back into his bag.

"Nate," I said, "There's no way my parents, or yours for that matter, are gunna buy that."

"We'll go tonight," he said. He was standing now. There was a finality in his voice that sent a shiver down my spine.

Why the fuss about Blackwall Reach? Well, for that we need to go back a little further than that day in August, to January of the same year.

But first let me set the scene.

Come with me. Shut your eyes for a moment. Turn out the lights if you can, and let even the after image fade.

Black, right? Empty? Think you're going cross-cultural with a blind man?

You're not even close.

Forgive me. I was being a little insincere when I said 'come with me'. You see, you can't.

But go ahead and picture as best you can the inner world of the man for whom the photon has been forever banished. This is immediate living. No time lag here. No awaiting that neural zap of the universe's synaptic pathways to carry the sensory payload to your brain. No Neo-Kanto-Einsteinian phenomenological distance here: The thing beheld is the thing. It is the desert of the now.

People often ask me what a blind person sees. If I'm in a surly mood, I'll say floral wallpaper themed sub-cranial pink. Otherwise, I'll explain that it's different for everyone. Some get fireworks, some get phantoms. Me, I get jet black. Once in a blue moon, and for no reason I can discern, I'll get sable. But uniform, liquid jet velvet has been the order of the day for as long as I remember.

Now imagine on that January day, as a freak summer storm raged outside my window, how it felt to see that first *glimmer*. It came while I lay on my bed, the faintest flicker of light. There and gone in the same breath.

Was I dreaming? Had my mind torn this ember of memory from my primordial past?

Perhaps I was having an aneurism.

I waited to die, and when I didn't, I fell asleep and forgot the episode altogether.

But it was not *altogether*. Because I remembered, sure enough, when it happened again, and this time with a searing clarity by contrast. The second time it flared into being in the vault of my mind as I lay in bed, smelling the frangipani through the window. I'd tossed and turned on my sheets, and now was well and truly into turning and tossing. I had no idea how late it was, as my sweat-slicked fingers on the talky clock's button had yielded only a drunken buzz.

In that melancholy moment a visitor entered my world and drew aside the curtain on a bonfire-blaze of a face. It was all fuzzy, smudges of dark and light, but it was a face, I was sure of it. A woman's face.

Over the next days and weeks the visions came again and again, with growing clarity. Sometimes they would begin as a faint haze, snowy static in blackness. Other times they would slam into my head with a force that shocked my balance. But all the time, after those first few, they came with such detail, such presence, I could have reached out my hands and *felt*. I was seeing, but it was someone else's world; It was stolen vision.

These images were disjointed mostly. Wooden bars. Wind billowing gauze curtains. Goldfish gobbling at fingers. And the woman. More than once I must have looked a fool, standing in the school hall, my hand outstretched mutely to trace the crows feet beside her thick lashes and the contour of her cheek bone.

As I said, these visions—*memories*, I'll call them—were disjointed in time. I knew this after the sudden appearance of a man. One day he bundled into my thoughts clean shaven and blowing raspberries on my stomach. The next, he wore an inch of black-grey mottled beard, and the skin beneath his eyes had pouched and gone dull grey. But his eyes still smiled.

I didn't tell Barny about my 'vision' until well after we'd moved to Bungaree Special School. The move had been 'to a more appropriate learning environment,' which was short for Mrs Yates had gotten fed up writing twin syllabi for her year 8s—normal and other. It was my fault. I'd failed to assume an appropriately remorseful demeanour following an incident of culpable boredom. Barny came with me without a fuss, but I didn't tell him right away. Not that I didn't trust him. But I—we—had only just become happy, faceless amoeba, and I was loathe to rattle the petri dish so early on. I had just for the first time in memory been stamped 'normal'. I wasn't keen to go freak-squared so soon after.

But tell him I did, and Barny, in characteristic fashion, just silently soaked it up and gave me a pat on the back. Then my deaf friend said those words that spring to life every so often and ricochet around inside my head to this day: "I've been hearing."

We sat there and I don't remember hearing anything but his voice until the end-of-lunch siren rang. He told me how these sounds had intruded first as a low *thump thump* that had sent him scrambling onto his knees in the middle of the night. He thought he was dying. I believed him too. He sniffled it out to me and I could feel him shaking as he recalled it.

So you can guess what the topic of conversation was pretty much for every moment we were alone together from then on. There was no draining this cistern. Imagine it!

That's how we were the day Nate came. Barny was saying, again with tears, "Paahlie. Last night my ears travelled to a symphony. A symphony!" He struck my shoulder in faux outrage. "Why didn't you tell me that something invisible could be so beautiful?"

I had no reply. And neither did I hear the newcomer, Nate, approach through the leaf litter beneath the oak at the far angle of the playground. Because Barny had just derailed my train of thought and sent it crashing into icy water.

I had been to the symphony too. The previous night as I lay on bed and gave full attention to my stolen sight. My eyes had drunk in rows of flashing, duelling violin bows, fingers flickering along slender flutes, and the mad gesticulations of the conductor—a magician with fly-away hair whose wand brought to life the chimeric beast before him.

Barny had heard a symphony; I had seen one.

It was a coincidence that stretched credulity.

And when I cast my mind back to examine each conversation since Barny's confession of hearing, every instance of stolen vision and sound, I discovered they fit, tooth to ward, like a key in a mile-long lock. For a month Barny had been hearing what I was seeing.

In hindsight it was so obvious. But what did it mean?

A nudge from Barny finally alerted me to the arrival of Nate, who for some inscrutable reason, had picked us to make his first introduction. And it took me no time to sense that Nate was not like any other student at Bungaree Special School.

I said Barny was a giant, and he was, God rest his soul. But Nate—Nate was a dragon, or a genie, or a fey elemental. I just didn't know it at the time.

He wasn't one to talk about why he was at Bungaree. Most of the other kids were happy to. We did it with a cathartic rush, similar I imagine to the confessions of an AA meeting. Not that we accepted the world's labels, mostly. In talking there came understanding, pride even. But Nate was different.

My first impression of Nate was strengthened by the attention he attracted from the visiting medicos. He was forever joining us at break time surrounded by the cloying odour of the infirmary, almost as though he were a specimen they unbottled, shocked into life, and sent shambling into lunch and recess to observe the customs of the living.

So, I guess, they poked and prodded him. And then there was the media on occasion, who poked and prodded him in their own way. Perth, Western Australia, was a small place—the end of the world, really. When there wasn't something as galaxy shaking as a football hero running from a booze bus or a model's pants falling off (imagine the apoplexy if it had been the football hero whose pants had fallen off), there was always the 'Unfeeling Boy' to fallback on. 'Case follow-up' they called it. Serialised reality soap opera way before its time.

But we didn't bug Nate about it. I think we were kinder than your average twelve year olds, and perhaps that's why he had come to Bungaree in the first place. It had been his decision. When you're the only known case of a medical condition in the world, I guess being surrounded by others of some condition at all, regardless of the ilk, rendered living more tolerable.

As near as Barny and I could tell, Nate *felt* nothing.

I don't mean he lacked any sense of touch. If he stepped on a tack, he knew about it. But only in the sense that a computer knows if you type at its keyboard. The tack was just data to Nate. Nothing penetrated. He heard, he saw, he smelled and he tasted, but nothing *moved* him. Like dropping pebbles on a frozen lake, there were no ripples.

All of this took time to nut out. At first we thought he had a skin disease or neural trauma. He even called himself 'the Leper,' the nearest he ever went to talking about his condition. He joked about the possibility of sitting on his hand at the cinema, and leaving it there like a half-eaten box of popcorn for the next session.

But he was no leper. His nerves were fine. So too was his brain, apparently. It's just that some connection between the two had gone missing, or dropped acid.

So there you are. We three became a coterie. The blind, the deaf, and the feel-less? Nate hadn't been put off by what probably looked like an icy reception on my part, and he was a welcome companion. He became the extra leg I sometimes needed to prop up the conversation with Barny. I'll be the first to admit I get moody at times, but often I just love to sit and listen to people shoot the breeze. Let my mind wheel freely, shuttle back and forth and weave my own tapestry from their words and my thoughts.

I forget when we let Nate into our little secret.

Nate had his rapid mood swings though. I vaguely recall Mr Crossman listing such as a fixture of the tortureplex of puberty, but I'm half-convinced he was referring to girls at the time. (I refrained from plugging Nate with that one.) The clearest I remember came one humid March day. Summer hadn't really bothered that year and appeared to be making a late push for its reputation. We slapped our bums down in the shaded part of the quadrangle, my starched shirt stained with drinking fountain water and clinging coolly, deliciously to my chest. Nate said something about Miss Turner's nose looking like a turnip and wasn't that a coincidence and wasn't that argument for a Creator. Barny chided him in his gentle way, and I wished I could see so as to look at Miss Turner's turnip, when Nate swore and laughed in the same breath, muttered that it was too bright, and strode off.

His mood swings weren't always so explosive. Often—I'm sure I was the only one who heard it—I noticed something in him change, as if a dimmer switch had been turned down inside him. Other times it was as if a signalman in his brain threw a lever, causing his conversation to rumble off in a new direction. He would be talking about a stereo he wanted to buy, then clouds would move in, and suddenly he was talking about speakers and the way their carbon cores sucked and pounded like a heart.

So when, in that foodhall in August, Nate seconded Barny's idea about going to Blackwall Reach, I thought it merely another freak weather change in the fickle atmosphere of planet Nate; It would blow over and Barny would locate his temporarily misplaced sense.

But it didn't blow over, and Barny, apparently, hadn't sent out a search party.

We weaved a web of half-truths among our parents, and later that night there was seen a line of three quiet boys hopping penguin-like onto the last-chance 377 from Southlands Shopping Centre to Attadale.

I could imagine the bus driver's eyes on me as I scrabbled through my wallet for the tokens that would buy me passage. Nate passed me, pausing only to buzz-click his multi-rider. When I finally yielded the coins to the driver, I caught the whiff of Betadine, and felt the brief touch of his hand, which was leathery like a gardener's glove. He must've been an old-fashioned sort, and if he suspected there was some mischief afoot, he didn't let on.

Nate made a b-line for the back seat, apparently, and I uncharacteristically kicked every other seat leg or floor rivet on my pilgrimage to the back of the swaying bus. When Barny and I plopped down next to Nate, he was poking about in his backpack.

We were silent for a time, until Nate pressed two objects into my hands. "Bread. Juice," he said. "Rations," followed by words I couldn't make out above the sudden roaring whine of the bus as it geared down. I heard Barny murmur thanks from the other side of Nate.

We bit and munched in silence and then Nate began plugging us with questions—questions about what we had seen and heard that day. Ever since we had told him our secret, he'd been intrigued. But lately his interest had hit some sort of critical mass—become a neutron star of fascination. That night in the bus it burned such that I fancied I could feel it radiating from within him.

"What has our friend been up to?" he said, and by that he meant the man on whose vision and hearing we had been eavesdropping.

Yes—Barney's new ears, and my new eyes, came from the same man. This much we knew, and more.

"Burning his fingers," I said nervously. The rattling cage of the bus was making me edgy. The whole thing was not right, but I couldn't put my finger on it.

I took Nate's silence to mean go on. "Just a pulse today. An image. He snuffed a candle with his fingers," and I pressed my thumb and forefinger together to indicate. The man's fingers had looked dry.

'The man' was pale and thin. He had brown hair that was curling at the edges for want of cutting. Sometimes I glimpsed him as he stared, motionless into a mirror. Sometimes I would catch a shard of his reflection in a window or the blade of a knife. His name was Stephen Brand, age 36, 6'11" as it turned out.

"Shouting," said Barny in a low voice. I felt Nate's attention leave me.

"Shouting what?" said Nate. "Was the woman there?"

"I don't know. Not words." He paused. "Words on groans. It made me feel sick in the stomach." Barny fell silent. Nate grunted with strange satisfaction then.

The woman seemed to go with the man. She appeared in many of my visions—was perhaps in half of all the things I saw. Not the woman of early on, when I first began to see. No, she had gone, as had the other man, the one with the smiling eyes. This lady was different altogether. She was slim, with blonde tresses, and had about her a nervous air, as though she were a penned animal who now and then sensed the hidden bars. She appeared often, smiled often, or had done. I saw her in ways that made me blush, but—and this will sound weird—I was not ashamed. Those visions came like especially gleaming gems among other pretty stones, lovingly, gently gifted to me.

The bus rattled on toward Blackwall as the night drew down, and its motion lulled me. But there was no fader knob at play in Nate that night. The further we went, the more the cyclones tore through him, as though time were compressing to the end of all things and each maelstrom was eager to spend its strength before it lost the chance. One minute he was probing us for information, the next he would slap the window or thrust his head between his knees.

We got off the bus, same penguins, same order, and in the wake of the rattle and sway of the bus, it felt as though the cool air settled on my shoulders like a shawl. We walked down a road that Barny said looked over the river and, in the distance, the alien lights of Perth's pocket of skyscrapers. A breeze was stirring, and it brought up the tang of salt and river-weed.

I guess you're still wondering what we were doing there? Well, it has to do with our man, Mr Stephen Brand. For all I know, his mug shot was plastered on the back of our bus, which whined its way off into the dark streets as though it had never been there. You see Mr-Stephen-Brand-age-36 was a *missing* man.

That had taken a bit of figuring out. Barny must have seen Stephen's face on TV in the missing person's slot before Law & Order many times and, likewise, I had heard his name each time before the show's trademark *dun dun* percussive. But had it not been for the wiles of serendipity, we would never have made the connection, and might have been at home that night, tucked up in bed.

Brand had been missing since January, his wife also. No family contactable. The details given in the missing persons blurb had the feeling of flotsam and jetsam, the detritus of unknown lives, stumbled on by investigators and yielded up to the public almost apologetically. Mr Brand, said the blurb, was an amateur musician, and collector of rare and exotic instruments. We knew *our* man was a musician. I had watched his hands dance, and sometimes trip, across fretboards and frames, and Barny had heard snatches of alien sounds. But we would never have made the connection if the blurb hadn't mentioned one harmless little detail. It had noted one instrument in particular, a sitar. Neither of us had a clue what a sitar was—until a classmate show-and-tell'ed his specimen at school. I felt the thing, Barny saw it; and that was the spark to the tinder.

Our man had a sitar, there was no doubt, and being boys this meant the missing man might be one and the same. It didn't take long for us to marry the other clues up to this hypothesis, his apartment, rented with the tiniest sliver of a river view, his job as a nurse, and in no time, as far as we were concerned, his identity was a fact.

Barny, bless him, had blurted that we should tell the police. I replied caustically, "Yeah, right. 'Officer, my deaf friend here and I have recently received second-hand hearing and sight, respectively, and as a consequence, and quite coincidentally really, have come to believe that we may be able to tell you more about Mr-Stephen-Brand-age-thirty-six, maybe even find him.' Come off it, Barn." Nate kicked me. I apologised.

But the more I thought about it, the more I came round to the view that maybe we did have something to offer the police. Who was better placed than Barny and me, who were privy to the memories of his eyes and ears? Who knew his habits and haunts?

One such haunt was Blackwall Reach. It recurred much in my mind's eye. Each of us has a quiet place, I think, a place to sit, to put out the clamour of the world (or bathe in it)—its demands, its temptations, its despairs—and just be. And Mr Brand's was Blackwall Reach, I was sure of it. Like a lodestone in my mind, the needle of my thoughts was drawn to it, and the idea that the mystery of Mr Brand might be revealed there. Pity I didn't know his compass sported a many-coloured feather of needles.

As we crossed the threshold into the bush hugging Blackwall's cliffs, I yearned for the predictable footfall of the asphalt we'd left. Barny came behind me, and Nate led, holding my arm. I could feel him straining against it, eager to press forward. In his haste he almost pulled me down onto the dewy ground. A spider web clung to my face, and when I wrenched my arm free to pry it away, Nate went on.

In that moment I felt my blindness keenly. I remembered a passage from the bible that Barny had told me. In it a fellow named John, who had lived on locusts and honey—spiders too perhaps—sent word from prison inquiring if Jesus was the One. John had thought so, but in the cell's darkness his doubts had grown. Jesus's answer began, "Tell him this: The blind receive sight..."

How I yearned for that. True sight. Sight to see what made me stumble. Sight to see it, name it, and go around it. That verse rang in my head in the tangled gloom of the bush that night. But I remembered too that John's head had ultimately rolled at the word of a girl probably no older than some of the kids he'd been baptising weeks earlier.

Then I felt Barny's hand on my arm, and I recovered my courage.

And suddenly, as if my face had broken though a wave, I was free of the bush. We had reached the cliffs. Unfettered air caressed my skin, and the sound of the suck and spume below swelled.

Then it happened.

If I'd had the presence of mind in the minutes before to think clearly, I would have known what was coming. Perhaps it wouldn't have mattered.

I would have felt the terror in Barny's clutch, for that's what it was. I'd have asked, and he would have wailed at the maelstrom of groaning and crying that had made his head ring the nearer we went to Black-wall.

I would have seen that as I fought my panic on Nate's trail, images peppered me like never before, of Stephen Brand beating his way to the cliff's edge, and noted it for the path of a madman, a pioneer, a zealot.

Instead, all I experienced was the totality of sense that encom-passed each of us, three-and-one, at the cliff's edge, past and future combined: A stark vision of a woman standing there, dripping at the bush's edge, for it was raining, and in her hands a gun. Pointed at me. At Stephen Brand. A flash of fire at its muzzle, and the oddly surprised, wondering "Uh." This last not from the mute memory, but from Nate's own mouth.

Then Nate fell.

And in my mind's eye I fell too. I saw water and rock fly toward me, and then utter dark. It was the last vision I ever had.

A kindly wave swallowed the sickening crunch as Nate met with the jagged limestone below. He was dead. I knew it without asking.

I don't remember for how long we stood and cried at Blackwall Reach.

Given Nate's 'special' status, and his parents desire to clear his name of any shadow of suicide, there was a post-mortem. I read the report. Naaman Gould, age twelve, suffered a heart attack, whereupon he fell to his death on the rocks beneath Blackwall Reach. His heart stopped, he fell, and his adolescent body crumpled like a soft drink can on the rocks below. That was forty-three years ago. And in another forty-three, if you so happened to pull up the report, you'd find it read just so, printed matter-of-factly in black and white.

But I don't think that's what happened.

I'm speculating, of course. But you be the judge.

You recall I likened Nate's condition to bubble wrap for the soul? "The Unfeeling Boy" Can you imagine what it would be like one day, one nominal day—nothing to mark it different from the other four thousand odd lived in sense-stasis—to feel a pin prick through the blanket? It would hurt, yes. But would you call it pain? A sliver of metal to rouse the sleeping monks to the ropes to ring the bells in that inner, fog-shrouded city. That peal came and told Nate 'pain,' just as hearing and sight came to Barny and me, and ushered us into a new world. 'Pain,' they rang out at Lauds, 'Heat,' at Sext, 'Smoothness,' at Vespers, 'Pleasure,' at Matins.

But I say pain first, because this I think bit deepest, bit most often, if I am any judge of men—and particularly for Stephen Brand, who loved and lost more than the average.

I have researched his life so much so I confuse it with my own. Those of his classmates who remembered him at all, remembered him well, or rather, remembered a crystalline memory of some kind act. Invariably, when I pressed further for observations of the man, their eyes would glaze. It was hard to find memory of him distinct from his deeds. He tried and failed three times to qualify for Medicine at the University of Western Australia. At last, he settled into nursing. He graduated, worked shifts at Hollywood Hospital, or Greythorpe, and then at a hospice that was pulled down in the early 80s. The hospice was one of those put up just after WWII, one of those laced with asbestos.

It took a while for the time bomb to hit Stephen Brand, but when it did it worked a curious kind of torture on him. It began with spasms that took his job, let loose micro-storms of agony, shattered his nervous system, taking with it the solace of his music, and ultimately undid his marriage thread by thread until it gave in one cataclysmic tear at the seams.

And it was this pain—compressed and magnified—that was Nate's introduction to the world of feeling. The memory of Mr Brand's private Gulag. And it spat at him like a sewing machine. Like a junkie, Nate couldn't get enough of it. If I'd known then, as a twelve year old, what I know now, I'd have seen the monkey slapping out the tune on Nate's back and I'd have offered it a cyanide banana.

That night at Blackwall, Nate wasn't looking for any missing man. He was after the ultimate fix, the ultimate burn. He knew Brand was going to Blackwall to suicide—and on that, he was way ahead of Barny and me—and he wanted to share it. He must have sensed that the flame thawing his senses to life was the very one that was burning Mr Brand to the ground. His days filled with physical torment, his friends driven from him, pausing for a time to stare at the proverbial car crash of his life, but leaving before the real, bloody work of love began. His job taken from him. His wife fleeing to hers. Nate knew this through our answers to his questions and the filter of his pain, and knew the only conclusion would be Stephen's decision to end all adventures. And as Nate contemplated the extinguishment of his wonderful drug, he hit upon the idea of the greatest adventure of all: He reached out, as it were, across such a tiny span of time—a mere handful of months?—linked, and walked hand in hand to the brink.

Nate knew the big one was coming that night, and from what he gleaned from our talk, he knew it would be Blackwall Brand would choose. Brand had grown up there, chasing possums and playing spotlight in the warm evenings of Summer holidays there as a child. He and his parents had lived there before his father had died. To die there would be symmetry. Full circle.

What Nate couldn't have known was that Brand would not complete his plan.

It was no silent, brief flight through the air for Mr Brand. Instead, it was the alien snap of gunfire. For Nate was not the only person to feel the force of Brand's pain. His wife also suffered, but she warped under the strain of it.

Again, if I had had an adult's wisdom in my twelve-year-old body, I would have understood why her mood in those last days swung like a wind-chime in the tempest. One day spilling tears into immaculately folded laundry. The next gliding through a house full of revellers, her eyes and teeth shining. She was everywhere at that party, and Mr Brand's eyes followed her. But nobody looked at me—Mr Brand. And then finally there had become violent. Thrown plates and slammed doors. Then tears, and laughter and distance all at once.

I guess somewhere in there she decided to kill him. For it was she who stood there, dripping, pale, and vacant-eyed, the night Stephen Brand went to take his own life. I can imagine her pulling the car to a stop not so far from where we marched off the bus. I can see her slipping through the rain-slick bush, see her pausing for only a moment as she saw the silhouette of her husband, an inky statue against the rich, festooned houses of Peppermint Grove across the river. There she administered not only the brute lead projectile that killed her husband, but the fatal echo of its shocking impact that, months later, would stun Nate's heart to a stand still, and send him tumbling over the brink.

It was when the police came to recover Nate's body that they found the horribly decomposed remains of Brand wedged into rock at the base of the cliffs.

I have no proof for my theory, none that would stand up in court at any rate. But on the strength of it I have spent my life. I am this day a detective with the West Australian Police Force, have gathered to myself considerable resources, and have spent every ounce of energy I could spare scouring Australia, and any land holding the faintest glimmer of hope, for a woman who the records hold guilty of one murder, which I know to be two.

I write this now at the end of my quest. Do not misunderstand me. I never did find Mrs Brand. She may be dead now for all I know. I retire from it. The badge given me all those years ago is pitted and lined like the face I see staring back at me in the mirror above the washbasin each morning. I've known for some time now this unending search has drained me, left me a wasted and weary man. Again, I wish I had known something sooner.

There is another verse in the bible that Barny shared with me before he died. Stroke at age thirty-nine. He must have sensed it coming. Caring to the end.

It says: "I desire mercy, not sacrifice."

Mercy? I so took the image of that woman, her selfishness, that the only consolation she had for the hell her husband was going through was a bullet—and this for a man who I think did everything in this power to stem the flow of it outside himself—that it came to live and breathe. It began to walk beside me, and lay its burning hand on my shoulder, and yearn for a setting aright.

Barny knew this. Perhaps he felt the heat upon my shoulder when his own hand found its way there in his characteristically physical connection. He wondered in his still strangely stressed syllables if she had not suffered much already. Perhaps he had heard something in her voice all those years ago that spoke of her love for Stephen. A deep, true love, strained beyond bearing. "Who really knows all that is needed to pass judgment on her?" he had gently probed. At what cost to myself was I pursuing it to the bitter end? These words I endured and let pass in debt to our friendship.

Of all the witnesses pertinent to the case, the one not able to be summoned by any human court, Stephen Brand, perhaps has the most valuable testimony. It strikes me now he has given it. More than donating the memory of his senses to three boys who lacked them—a philanthropist to his final moments—he may also have given us the only testimony that could shed light on the inner dimension of this tragedy. That in doing so yet another life was lost only bears further evidence to the tangle of human motive and circumstance in this broken world.

Below me the river still sucks and slaps on the same rocks it did that night all those years ago, but this place no longer remembers Stephen Brand. Or Nate. We really are flowers of the field, here today and gone tomorrow, the dream that vanishes when the sleeper awakes.

I have wasted my time here on vengeance. The wind carries the cries of yachtsmen bustling to tack, and, faintly, I can hear cars thrumming around the riverside road on the far bank, straining to 'do the view' in under a minute. As I rake across the stations on my portable trannie and hear the spitfire of beat and talk—a thousand different voices speaking to millions more—and imagine that multiplied ten thousand-fold, I have the feeling the sky above, the one Stephen Brand showed me, is made of some material impervious to any technology we here possess.

Maybe earth itself is wrapped in Nate's bubble-wrap for the soul. But if so, who will give us to feel?

ABOUT BRETT ADAMS

Brett Adams is the author of two novels, *Dark Matter* and *Strawman Made Steel*. He has a PhD in Computer Science that taught him to love puzzles, and a family who taught him to love stories—or vice versa. He lives in Perth, Western Australia. Find Brett at http://dweomingwell.blogspot.com and Twitter: @dweomingwell

MOON RABBIT

Jo Wu

~ China ~

Every day, in every waking hour, and all through the evenings when earthlings are tucked away in deep slumber, I am forever chained to the stone mortar and pestle on the moon. You may know me as the Moon Rabbit, the "companion" to the moon goddess Chang'e. I trust you have heard of the tale of Chang'e and how she came to be the moon goddess. She was once a mortal, and her husband, the great archer Houyi, shot down nine of the ten suns that were burning earthlings to death. As a reward for his great deed, the Emperor gave him a pill of immortality. Houyi was hesitant to ingest the pill, unsure if he wanted to be immortal. He stored it away in a box, and warned his wife to never open it, without explaining to her what it contained. His warning backfired. As all young women are apt to do, Chang'e became curious and opened the box. Fearing her husband's wrath upon discovering that she disobeyed him, she swallowed the pill, and due to the overdose, she began floating into the sky and eventually landed on the moon.

Living on the moon for the rest of eternity would surely be mind-numbingly boring. That's when I came in. The Dragon God moulded me, the Moon Rabbit, out of evening clouds and pieces of jade. He manufactured me into an adorable rabbit companion for the silly Chang'e. Of course I was physically endearing. How could I not be, with my soft, thick white fur, long floppy ears, and round little snout?

Oh, I was a good little companion, alright. That is, if you take the word "companion" as a code word for "slave." I wear heavy steel chains that shackle me to my stone mortar and pestle. Lilac fumes rise from my beatings and poundings as I produce the Elixir of Life, hour after hour, just so that Chang'e could survive on the moon. Does she enjoy her life on the moon, you ask me? Well, if you enjoy the pastime of weeping over a possessive ex-husband, admiring your ebony tresses and silk hanfus in a handheld mirror, and ordering me to pound my mortar faster and faster while you pet my fluffy fur, then sure, her life is considerably decent.

"Faster, faster!"

I pounded and ground powder, and poured water over the paste, creating a more viscous, fluid mixture.

Chang'e collapsed on her divan, which sat within a pagoda the Dragon God had built on the moon's surface for her. "Oh, what a bore it is! Serves Houyi right that he had to be deprived of me as his wife! I stay eternally young and beautiful, while he grew old and crippled and is nothing but dust now! But oh, I adored him dearly. He was so handsome!"

I ladled spoonfuls of the finished elixir into a goblet and held it out. "For you, Mistress."

As she guzzled down the beverage, I gazed down at planet Earth, a blue-green globe that looked like a jewelled marble from where I'm perched on the moon. How beautiful the Earth must be. Sometimes, when Chang'e chose to engage in more active conversations with me (after all, there was no one else to talk to on the moon), she would tell me about life on earth. She told me of the invention of paper and compasses, of the four seasons of the year, of valiant warriors who died for the love of their families and home countries, and of tragic love stories between concubines and emperors, among countless other topics.

"I wish I could travel to Earth!" I sighed. "How fascinating life there sounds!"

"Oh, Yue Tu, Earth is a dangerous, horrible place," said Chang'e. "A rabbit like you would be devoured by giant beasts, or even shot by human arrows and put into a stew!"

In response, or lack thereof, I continued pounding away at the next batch of the elixir. I waited until Chang'e retired to her bedchamber before I relinquished my hold on my mortar, flopped onto my back on the moon's surface, and sighed.

"If only I was a human on Earth!"

"Do you really wish that?"

Out of the blue, a golden glow appeared before me. It was a glowing ball, morphing and unfurling into a snaking line until a great dragon with scarlet scales that shimmered with gold undulated before me. He surveyed me with green eyes, as a mentor would do when measuring a student's willingness to engage in education, and pulled on one of his long whiskers between two of his claws.

"So, Yue Tu, I heard that you wish to be a human?"

"Of course I do!"

"Why is that?"

"It's terribly boring being a rabbit on the moon! And being Chang'e's servant!" I wrinkled my nose, mimicking my mistress's orders in a mocking tone. "'Yue Tu, hurry up! Yue Tu, pound faster! Yue Tu, bring the elixir to my bed!'"

"Let me tell you," replied the Dragon God, "many humans would love the life you have."

I jumped with disbelief. "Why?"

"The human world is a disgrace, full of misery and cruelty. You live a life of comfort compared to them."

"Well, I think it's adventurous! Better than the boredom here!"

Dragon God began to glow again, the gold light engulfing him. "Think on what you are wishing for." He disappeared into a shower of golden light and glimmers, leaving me alone in the cold starkness upon the moon.

My first sight of earthlings was when I saw a prince come travelling in a ship of gold while Chang'e was asleep. He soared through the sky, his ship in the shape of a great-winged firebird emitting flames from the engine at its tail. Through the glass window of his ship, I could see that he was young and handsome. He was dressed in blue robes, and had ambitious, dark eyes and long black hair. Many robots flanked him. Some of them accompanied him inside the ship and sat by him, while others flew along with him outside by the side of his ship. They beeped, they buzzed, and they emitted fuzzy transmissions of communication to one another, but I could make out one statement quite clearly: *Find the Elixir of Life!*

I leapt to my feet, pounding them against the moon's surface. Perhaps, if I gave him the elixir, he would bring me back to Planet Earth with him.

I bounced up and down, leaping as high as only I, a rabbit, could do. My ears flopped over my head, undulating like great waving arms, trying to signal to the ship. It never came sailing my way—it only glided around and around the moon. Neither the Prince nor his army of automatons turned their heads to see me, to turn the ship and come in my direction. My heart sank.

"As mythological creatures, we cannot be seen by humans, by these mortals."

Dragon God materialised by my side, unfurling from his golden ball of light.

"But, Dragon God, if I give him the Elixir of Life, perhaps he can take me to Earth with him in his ship!"

"Is that what you want?"

"Yes, Dragon God! If he could take me to Earth, I would gladly give him the Elixir of Life!"

Dragon God sighed. Smoke and flickering flames, like multiple serpent tongues, seeped from between his fangs as he did so. "It just seems as though you will never be satisfied until you have a taste of human life, I presume?"

"I want to be human!"

Dragon God shook his head. "I have warned you, Yue Tu. The human world is a messy tragedy."

"It is certainly better than a banal existence on the moon!"

"Is that what you really think?" Dragon God sighed again. "Then, I shall grant your wish."

"You will?" I began bouncing up and down upon my great, strong feet, as if I was a human child jumping for joy, trying to snatch a present. "You really will, Dragon God?"

"But not for free!" Dragon God pointed up one claw, as if to lecture me. "I will grant your wish if you give me your fur coat."

"My fur?"

"Yes. I will skin you, but during the transaction process, I will transform you into a human. Do you know how to concoct an anaesthesia?"

I nodded. "The Elixir of Life is not the only recipe I know!"

"Very well. Start concocting. Once you drink it, I will begin to grant your wish."

After imbibing the turquoise-coloured liquid I brewed, which tasted of tart ginger, I lay on my back.

With his knife-like claws, Dragon God skinned me, stripping me of my fur so that I was nothing more than muscle, bones, and running rivulets of blood. Drawing circles in the air with the very same claws, Dragon God conjured white light that swirled all around me. In a haze of stars and glowing warmth, the swirling energy levitated me into the air. My spine twitched and jerked with a sensation of poking needles, and my paws scratched for mere air, flailing at the spurts of slight pain that shot through me, for the anaesthesia was not able to deprive me of all of my senses.

Ebony hair sprouted out of my scalp like skeins of silk. My neck elongated as smooth skin stretched over my muscles. My whiskers shrank into a pointed nose, and my paws morphed into long-fingered hands and delicate feet. A silk hanfu the colour of peonies with a sash like the sky fluttered over my bare skin. As I was slowly lowered to the ground, Dragon God snatched a mirror from the sleeping Chang'e's boudoir. I gasped at my appearance: I was certainly human, with skin as white as my fur had been, sleek black hair that grew to my slender hips, large eyes that glimmered like simmering black tea, and soft lips like lotus petals. The only characteristic I retained from my rabbit form was my long ears. They grew from over both of my human ears and dangled down to my shoulders.

"Dragon God, I'm pleased with this transaction, but..." I stroked my ears, relishing the new sensation of long fingers against my soft fur. "Why do I still have my rabbit ears?"

"It is because that is your true nature. I am able to change your appearance in accordance with all of your heart's whims, but in the end, you cannot run away from the fact that you are a rabbit. That is your identity." Dragon God grinned, exposing all of his dagger-sharp fangs. "Do not fear. I have given you the guise of a ravishing young woman. He cannot resist you."

I smiled. But then, Dragon God quickly added, "One more thing. Because you are a mythological creature, you are unable to communicate with him by speaking. It will be as if you are mute."

Before I could shout another question to him, and just as he dissolved into light again, I saw the firebird ship return, with all the giant automatons travelling by the ship like a swarm of butterflies. They descended from the sky, blowing back the skirt of my dress and my long hair as they landed before me.

"A beautiful lady!" The Prince called from his window as an immense robot who towered over my mistress's pagoda came walking towards me. "Do you know where the elixir is?"

I opened my mouth to try to speak. However, my tongue froze when I tried. I opened my mouth again, but it was as if my tongue was paralysed when I tried to speak to him. I turned to glance up at the giant robot. He held out a giant metal hand, his open palm as large and wide as a comfortable bed. When I nervously placed a stoppered bottle filled with the elixir upon his palm, the robot straightened his back and marched back to the Prince. The Prince opened the bottle and took a sip. He smiled. I knew that the elixir was taking effect on him. He kept on smiling, feeling the tingling sensation that the sweet liquid gave him.

"How did you make this, my Lady?"

I pointed to my stone mortar and pestle. Dragon God had broken the chains that attached me to it during my transformation.

The Prince grinned at me. His ship sprouted wheels, and he came rolling towards me.

He parked by me, and kept smiling as his dark eyes met mine. "May I take you back home to my palace to be my princess? You may bring your mortar and pestle with you. I want you to make the elixir for me every day."

Here it was, my chance to go to Earth! Gathering my mortar and pestle in my arms, which felt refreshingly long compared to my rabbit legs, I took his hand, and climbed into his ship.

We flew through the stars, through the galaxy and cosmos. Again and again, I tried to speak to the Prince. Every time I opened my mouth, words lodged in my throat like pebbles. I gave the Prince a forlorn glance after my last attempt.

He stroked my thigh through my silk skirt. "Do not worry. You are beautiful. I don't mind you being mute. You are a prized treasure I found from the moon."

He let me lay my head against his strong shoulder as he continued navigating through the stars and purple clouds of evening expanse.

✍

The red doors of the palace burst open as the Prince eagerly carried me in his arms, whisking me through the corridors even though I was still dressed in the red gown I had worn for the very abrupt, but much-demanded wedding ceremony at the temple, for everyone was eager for the Prince to have finally found his Princess and bear his offspring and carry on his royal name. That he had been so eager to marry me was flattering. But as he carried me through the hallowed halls, the palace, though beautiful, was rife with concubines. They surveyed me like cats sizing me up as their potential enemy. Even the maids would take advantage of my muteness to belittle me.

"She's so ugly," the concubines remarked earlier behind the fluttering of their fans.

One yanked on one of my ears as hard as she could. "Rabbit ears? How could the foolish Prince have married a freak?"

"She's mute!" sniggered another concubine. "She won't be able to tell him of anything we've said about her."

I had no dowry, nor family to send a bride price to. If the court had any objections, they were all dissolved by my indispensable ability to brew the Elixir of Life. After the wedding banquet, the Prince tossed me onto the bed of our crimson wedding chamber before throwing his muscular body onto me. I squirmed, but my breath raced with curiosity and rapture as he peeled my gown off me. I cried in shock when he squeezed my breasts with his large hands. Was this how humans copulated?

He pinned down my legs with his hands. "As my wife, you must bear my sons for my lineage. And of course, you will concoct the Elixir for me everyday."

That was our wedding night. Everyday, I brewed him a draught of the Elixir of Life, much as I did for Chang'e on the moon. At least, life here was more interesting. The Prince often took me for walks in the majestic gardens, strolling by my side past turquoise waterfalls and blooming lilies and cherry blossoms. His robot attendants often accompanied us, buzzing and whirring with every little movement they made. But I did not bear only the duties of being his wife. I had to bear the tortures of his concubines as they sat sewing, plucking at their lutes, or simply gossiping.

They yanked on both my long hair and rabbit ears when the Prince was not present. It did not help that I was shorter than most of the concubines.

"What has the Prince seen in her? If she's part-rabbit, why hasn't she been sent to the slaughterhouse?"

"Has your husband gotten you pregnant, Rabbit-Freak?"

How could I answer? They laughed and pointed at me when I opened my mouth, but I could only force out coughs every time I tried.

"No?" They all tittered, their voices like the clanging of a thousand goat-bells. "You should get pregnant soon, stupid girl! If you don't, one of us will take your place!"

Had I still been a rabbit, I would have been able to bounce high, been able to come stomping down on them with my large, powerful, broad feet. By instinct, I pounced out of my chair, trying to kick at them. Although my small, delicate human feet was treasured and eroticised by my Prince, it only made a fool of me when I couldn't jump more than a few inches up in the air.

I collapsed onto my back.

As the concubines all tittered and jeered at my expense, an epiphany flooded through me. Without my services, my ability to concoct the Elixir of Life, my worth was nothing. I may no longer be in the form of an animal, but I was neither a human.

It did not matter how often my husband and I were in bed together. I remained barren because I am a rabbit by nature. Not just any rabbit, but the Moon Rabbit. The Prince did not understand why I could never conceive, but mythological immortal creatures, such as myself, cannot bear mortal children. When I could not have a son, he left me lying alone in bed for several nights, sometimes for weeks at a time. Although I welcomed the solitude of having the comfort of a bed to myself, I did hear moans and screams from neighbouring rooms. In these cases, I tightly pressed my large rabbit ears against my human ears.

Even when these concubines gave birth to sons, the Prince outlived everyone, due to my Elixir of Life. He saw every concubine and her offspring grow old and grey and die. On the other hand, the Prince and I continued to live.

He was obviously growing tired of me. He had the cooks in the kitchen plagiarise my recipe for the elixir. I could tell they attempted to make it because I could smell the slight scent of lavender from the liquids they were brewing. However, my Prince always complained of varying degrees of bitterness, and preferred the taste of my elixir. In addition, since the cooks were mortal, their attempts to sustain the Prince's eternal life failed.

"Why do you continue living?" demanded the Prince when he realised that I never grew a strand of grey hair. But then he would recline on his divan and heave a great sigh as he glanced out into the gardens from the window. "But then again, you are my lifetime companion. If you stop making the elixir, who else can make it?"

Even after he no longer demanded intercourse from me, at least I knew I was useful.

Due to longevity, the Prince continued to rule China for the next several centuries.

But one day, the Westerners came. They were big, bearded men in their giant ships, yanking treaties from thin air, imposing expectations on a culture foreign to them, and commanding for land. Even when the Boxers tried to eliminate them from the country, the Westerners only proliferated, luring and trapping many able-bodied men inside opium houses, and building great walled cities for themselves, which may as well be pedestals upon which they could jeer at the Chinese for not meeting their alien standards of civilisation.

"Well, wife, what do you think I can do to regain the glory of China?" The Prince would ask me this as we sat in the lounge. I felt his fingers slip beneath my chin. His eyes met mine.

"You were from the moon." His voice was gentle. "Tell me, when I met you, were you a princess there?"

I shook my head.

"Well, perhaps I should go imperialise the moon. Prove to the White Demons that I am superior to them."

My eyes widened at the thought of this. Chang'e was still on the moon. If he went to try and take over the moon, he would kill her!

I shook my head.

"No? Why not?"

I scribbled on a piece of paper that I extracted from a pocket hidden in one of the layers of my skirt. Notes were my method of communicating to him when my eyes and gestures could not convey what I thought.

It's impossible, I wrote to him.

"Impossible?" The prince shot up from his seat and struck me across the face.

I toppled out of my chair, a silent scream ripping from my throat as I clamped my hand to my cheek. I coughed and hacked on the shriek I could not produce.

"You have neither say nor opinions in what I do, wife!" yelled the Prince. "Whose side are you on? I will imperialise the moon and prove myself as a fine ruler and drive these White Demons out from my people's homes! Just watch! I will!"

As the Prince assembled a troop of robots to accompany him to the moon once again, Dragon God appeared by my side. "Look, Yue Tu, I have warned you that the world is a terrible place. Whatever crimes that humankind has committed, they will only repeat and repeat."

Tears dripped out of my eyes. I rubbed at them with the silk sleeve of my hanfu. "But, Dragon God, was it wrong of me to want a taste of a life more exciting than my own?"

Between his claws, Dragon God conjured a crystal ball. "Life will continue on. The Westerners will only continue imperialising China. Then, the Western World will fall crisis to its own trials. China will become divided amongst its people, and Japan will come to conquer China. China will go through great turmoil and disharmony, all while rebuilding itself, and will return as a world power. But then the West will come again, and the cycle will repeat, over and over."

"What must I do?" I continued swatting at my tears. "I only wanted to be human."

"Save Chang'e. And if you do, I will lead you to the path of Nirvana."

Clutching my mortar and pestle, I rode on Dragon God's back, and we flew to the moon, arriving there before my husband could reach it.

"Chang'e!" I cried out.

She was reclining on her divan in her pagoda. When she saw me, she sat up in a shock. "Yue Tu? Where in the world have you been for all these years, leaving me in such boredom? And why do you still have rabbit ears if you're in human form?"

"Chang'e, just shut up and stay in your pagoda! I'm trying to save you from a Prince!"

"Oh, a Prince?" That seemed to be the only word her ears perked up at. "Is he handsome?"

"No! He's coming to imperialise the moon and kill you! Now shut up and stay there! He won't be able to see you since you're a mythological creature! But if he takes over the moon, you're as good as dead!"

With my mortar and pestle, I concocted a poison for the Prince.

When he arrived, his eyes widened with surprise at the sight of me on the moon. I held out the glass bottle with the new, clear-coloured concoction for him.

"A new elixir?" sneered my estranged husband. "What makes this different from the others you've made me throughout hundreds of years of our marriage?"

I scribbled a note to him: *This is one you can drink, and you will never need another elixir.*

"Really? So I won't need the trouble of seeking you to concoct any more for me?" He frowned and crossed his arms. "Now, how do I know you are not poisoning me?"

I expected this question. After all, after falling out of love with me, with the invasion of the Westerners, the many betrayals left and right within the court, and the mass conversion of peasants to Christianity, he was expected to be paranoid. But I would end all of his paranoia with a single sip.

As a mythological creature, I would not be affected. I downed a gulpful and smiled at the foolish Prince.

I thrust the re-stoppered bottle into the iron palm of Prince's robot escort. Nodding with satisfaction, the Prince boarded his firebird-shaped ship. In a flame, he and his robots flew up into the air, turned, and launched off back to Earth, abandoning me on the moon's surface.

I felt cold, rather empty and blank now that he was gone. But at least I was not unhappy.

"That felt a bit anticlimactic to those many years of being a human," I stated.

Dragon God chuckled. "Is that a bad thing?"

I shook my head. "Not at all. It was quite an interesting experience."

"Well, now that you have known of human life, and understand the suffering underlying all of existence, I will lead you to the path I have promised."

Out of thin air, the Dragon God opened a portal for me. The stone stairs, surrounded by bamboo, lead up to a clear blue sky.

"Now, Yue Tu," said the Dragon God with a grin that showed how all of his dagger-like fangs glistened by the glow of the portal, "lead the way to Nirvana."

About Jo Wu

Jo Wu attends UC Berkeley, where she is majoring in molecular cell biology and minoring in creative writing. Her works have appeared in various magazines and the anthologies *Gothology II: Misery Loves Company*, *Thrones of Desire*, and *Underneath the Juniper Tree's Best of 2012*. She's also an internationally published alternative model under the alias Carmilla Jo. Please visit her at http://jowu-timeispoisoned.blogspot.com, and/or follow her on Twitter: @Jo_Wu_Author.

OPERATION TOBA 2049

Kris Williamson

~ Malaysia ~

The small events hall at the Putra World Trade Centre was packed. Few talked, but the various news broadcasts from tablets and phones created the sense that the room was full of conversation. Words bounced around the room—ultra plinian, tephra ejecta—the content of this digital conversation was largely lost on those listening but not the severity of the impending disaster.

Faridah sat near the back, scanning the crowd for any familiar faces. She had been waiting there for an hour already but had not heard her name called over the piercing intercom system.

"Yang!" Daus called after spotting her in the crowd. As he hurried over, Faridah stood to hug him, losing her seat in the process. "Hear anything yet?"

"No," she lamented while wearing a long face. "But Suzi, one of my coworkers, had her name called. I'm glad you're finally here. I can't stand this waiting around. I need to vent my frustration somehow!"

Daus looked at her momentarily before pulling her body to his. He whispered assurances into her ear, knowing full well that they would not be okay if her name was not eventually called.

✿

Ria flipped through the channels quickly before settling on TVPM, where the familiar face of the Prime Minister, Datuk Seri Hussein Tun

Khairy, discussed his government's plans for helping all Malaysians get through the crisis in a "fair, efficient, and impartial" manner. He closed his speech with his usual race-based refrain about Malays never disappearing from the face of the Earth, a reference to an old folk legend that took on a new meaning after nearby Sumatra Island became seismically unstable.

She rolled her eyes as he spoke, shouting back to the television set. "You're not even in Malaysia any more! What are you going to do from Australia? Send a team of kangaroos to save the rest of us? Coward!"

She turned off the television, cursing quietly about the hopelessness of the majority of Malaysians and Indonesians who had yet to be evacuated. From the other room, she could hear her two younger siblings playing *oo som*. Ria walked over and watched the kids momentarily before telling them to shower.

"Sis, why don't you go to school any more?" the youngest asked. After being ignored, other questions came to mind. "When will mommy come home tonight? Late again? Where is daddy?"

Ria shrugged her shoulders and helped her little brother to his feet. "Go shower now. But don't use too much water."

It was always an uncertainty when or if another water truck would replenish the public water tank that sat next to the neighbourhood playground. The filthy water was all they had since water services simply stopped several months earlier. Water interruptions had always been a regular part of life in Malaysian urban areas. But then, at least, there was always the assumption that eventually it would be restored after problems arising from political dramas and infrastructural failures were addressed.

Ria realised that she had not showered in at least two days. She was unmotivated, having lost her faith in people since the mass evacuations across the region began. Her boyfriend left with his family to Thailand before the border was sealed off. She only found out from the family's maid, who had been left behind.

Some of her more wealthy friends had managed to get out before the airports closed down. Others returned to their hometowns far from KL to escape the rampant crime that swept the city after the emergency had been declared. And her father simply disappeared one day, with no word from him in three weeks. With the police no longer handling missing-persons cases, there was nothing to do but hope he would return with a way out for all of them.

❧

Faridah dug through her purse and pulled out a pink phone with small rhinestones glued on to the casing. She called home.

"Sorry, tonight will be another late night. I've got some business to attend to. Can you make sure the little ones get something to eat? Don't try anything fancy. Just keep it simple. We need to save food for when the shortages at the grocery stores return. Okay. Kisses all around."

After hanging up, another woman turned to Faridah and asked her about the way the process worked, clarifying that it was her first time coming down to PWTC's government worker lottery draw.

Faridah explained as best as she could while looking around the crowd for Daus. "It's slow, but you don't want to miss your name. They will only call it once before moving on to the next name on the list. If you don't hear it or are in the toilets, then you will lose your chance and have to get your department to submit your name again." Faridah added somewhat wearily, "I've been coming for over two weeks now with nothing to show for it."

"I am so grateful to have my name entered. I will wait here every night if I need to. Or until it's all over, I guess."

"What department are you with?"

"Department of Child Welfare Services. You?"

Faridah's eyes widened briefly. "Uh, the Office of Cybercrime Prevention."

The lady nodded her head, acknowledging that she knew the division. "We have worked with your office many times. But I imagine cybercrime is not a very high priority now for the country."

Faridah looked back at the woman after finding Daus in the crowd. "And you, happy to leave your post? No more children to take care of, is it?" She walked away, not waiting for a response.

❧

The house was quiet except for the occasional slurp of a noodle. Ria and her siblings finished eating their instant noodle soup with fish balls. As she sat lost in thought, her brother repeated his earlier question that went unanswered.

"When is mommy coming home?"

She reminded him that their mother would be late again as she had been every night for the past two weeks. Ria changed the conversation to distract her younger siblings. "Why don't you go play your PS8 before bed? The electricity will probably be on for at least another hour. Hurry!"

Ria cleaned up the dinner mess by herself. She tied the trash bag tightly and headed outdoors to throw it away. The air was still but uncomfortable and foul. She had nearly acclimated herself to the acrid stench that sat atop the peninsula with the help of a cheap surgical mask she wore over her face anytime she went outdoors.

"Oh, Ria. How are you? Beautiful night!" It was the voice of her elderly neighbour, Ms Chu, who sat in a lawn chair outside of her front door each night.

"Hello Ms Chu. Fine, thanks. How are you tonight?"

Ria didn't care much for Ms Chu. Despite living side-by-side since she had been born, their conversations had always been devoid of any substance. Ria preferred to just ignore people unless they had something significant to say.

"Where are you going so late? KL is too dangerous to go out by yourself."

"No, Ms Chu. I'm just throwing out the trash. Not going anywhere."

"Silly girl. Already how many weeks nobody to collect the trash? Look at your pile there. It's rotten. Can't you smell it? You have to burn it or take it to the Ampang Hilir lake gardens landfill."

Ria looked at the mound of trash bags in front of her house. She threw the bag in her hand over toward the pile. "Later lah."

As Ria started to go back inside, Ms Chu asked her about her family, likely trying to prolong the conversation out of loneliness, not because she would actually care about them in reality.

"And what about the One-Malaysia rice allowance? Did you collect yours already? The truck was here earlier, but I didn't see you go and get it."

Ria did hear the truck come by earlier but was not in the mood to queue in the hot sun. "No, I think my mother would take care of that from the office. She has a government job, you know. They get extra benefits. Did you get yours?"

Ms Chu laughed. "I am not eligible. But for the better, I think. The government's rice gives me gas."

Ria nodded and walked inside.

✐

Daus held Faridah around her waist as they stood up against the wall. The room had gotten noisier despite the number of people who had already collected their lottery tickets and left the hall for the heavily-guarded buses parked behind the building.

"Faridah Hazmawi."

Daus poked her as Faridah realised that her name had been called over the cracking intercom system. She let out a small squeal as they hurried up to the counter. Faridah produced her government ID card confirming her identity and scanned her thumb print for secondary verification. The clerk asked her to sign the form and enter through the side door.

Once inside, the clerk told her to hold onto the pair of tickets and guard them with her life. Faridah grabbed Daus's hand and jogged off in the direction the clerk pointed to board the bus to the seaport.

❧

Ria and her siblings laid on the floor of the living room with their pillows and blankets in the pitch dark. The electricity had been cut for the night. The kids were a bit restless as Ria tried once again to call their mother.

"When is mommy coming home?"

With all the repetition, Ria began to wonder if she had a younger brother or a parrot. "She isn't picking up her phone, kiddo. So that means she is really busy with her work or maybe she is driving home now. When you wake up in the morning, she will be here. Just like every morning."

"But I want her home now," he whined.

Ria set her phone down nearby and rested her head on the pillow, hoping he would do the same. After a few minutes of lying with her eyes open, though, she grabbed her phone and tried to call once again.

❧

Daus gently took Faridah's phone from her as she tried unsuccessfully to fight back her tears. "You need to be strong," he insisted as he turned off the ringing device. "Their suffering will end soon. Days? Weeks? I don't know. But you can't fall apart now. We have the chance to start a new life."

"I know. I do want this. Us, Daus. But I didn't think it would be this difficult to leave everything behind."

"You don't have to do this alone. I'm here. And you will have me until the day I die. But that won't be for a long time. We will be safe in Australia," he smiled, trying to be as optimistic-looking as possible. "The clerk said the boat will depart in about an hour. By the time the sun rises tomorrow, we will be past Java already, far enough away from the blast radius."

"My kids..."

"Your kids would understand that there was nothing you could do for them. They won't feel a thing when Toba blows. Tonight, I want you to cry yourself to sleep. A good cry. And tomorrow when you wake up, your life in KL will be far behind you. Your future together with me lies ahead. It's what you want, isn't it?"

Faridah held her breath before bobbing her head up and down. She embraced her lover.

ABOUT KRIS WILLIAMSON

Kris Williamson is a publishing consultant and writer living in Kuala Lumpur. He is the editor of *Anak Sastra* literary magazine and has contributed short fiction, travel narratives, and poetry to journals, magazines, and anthologies. His first novel, *Son Complex*, was published by Fixi Novo in 2013. He can be stalked at kriswilliamson.com or on Twitter at @iramalama.

TARGET: HEART

Recle Etino Vibal

~ Philippines ~

"Hey, wake up lover boy."

A shake on his shoulders interrupted Damian's dreams. When he opened his eyes, white walls greeted him. His head pounded for a minute.

"Same dream? You were murmuring a name, I think," Umer said.

Damian preferred a long sleep and wanted to wake up on his own accord. Getting his sleep disturbed in the middle of the night was common after he took the oath. At least twice a week, his fellow brothers woke him up—sometimes for night trainings, drills, field exams, or, like this night, a mission.

"No. A nightmare. I can't remember." Damian lied. The love and break-up had haunted him for more than four years. He lied to turn the bad memory into a common dream.

"I want to learn all about that nightmare and maybe try to psycho-analyse you, but a customer needs to be happy tonight. Better dress up first and get Y," Umer tossed a sealed envelope to Damian. "I'll be waiting for you downstairs. You have ten minutes."

Damian memorised all the information about the target: his face, the specified place and time for the hit, and the instructions of the client. The client was a middle-aged woman, recently widowed, and had a son and daughter, both living and working outside the country.

This will be quick and easy, he thought.

Red flames, a sign of good luck for Damian, engulfed the file. Black smoke rose to the spot on the ceiling covered with soot. The only evidence about the transaction that remained was the white ash and black soot.

Damian took Y from his table drawer. It was common practice for agents to name their weapons. Damian named his slingshot for its shape.

Y was from a thick guava branch. The handle was long, thick, and sturdy enough for his grip. The cylindrical handle divided into thinner and shorter branches. Two arms extended, forming an approximate parabola. Time and frequent use turned the wood's colour from a pale cream to a deep, dark brown. A thick, red rubber band wrapped, coiled, and squeezed around each arm's upper half to secure a black rubber tube at each end. A thick small elliptical leather pocket joined the rubber tube and completed the slingshot.

Testing it, Damian pushed the handle forward while pulling the leather pocket backward. The sling stretched up to its limit. The tension and resistance in the wood crawled up his arms.

Slingshots fascinated Damian since childhood. Cans and plastic bottles arranged in a row on top of a low concrete wall or on low benches served as good targets during practice. Soon, he got tired of hitting stationary objects. To remedy that, he took his cans and plastic bottles, tied it to a rope and hung the free end of the rope on his mother's clothesline. Targets moved back and forth. It gave him the level of difficulty he wanted, but that got boring too.

Instead of plastic bottles, he shattered glass bottles with stones. His mother tolerated his slingshot fascination up until then. She said that the shattered glass flying everywhere should not be a part of Damian's excitement.

Kids who also enjoyed slingshots invited him to try shooting down birds. Those creatures were not stationary, and their movement was unpredictable. The bursting of feathers or sputtering of blood was also more fun than the shattering of glasses.

Damian settled for inanimate objects and in his creativity to make shooting more challenging, he threw his targets in the air as far and as high as he can and shot it before it reached the ground. Sometimes he asked one of his friends to do it so the target's movement would be more unpredictable. He avoided shooting birds lest he would have enjoyed doing it so much he might have resorted to shooting rats next, then cats, then dogs, and then humans.

Damian released the sling and the rubber snapped in the air in a split second. The pocket passed between the wooden arms and re-coiled. His wrist jerked forward for follow-through. If he had loaded it with one of his smooth pebbles, there would be another one stuck on his wall. A dozen small stones clustered on one side of the room that he used as target to release frustration.

Damian's pouch of ammunition was also in the drawer, small smooth stone pebbles, black, white and grey. One thing he liked about slingshots was that a stone is always ready to be a projectile. Any stone would do, but his job allowed him to be critical about his ammunition. Smooth, spherical stones have less air resistance to them during flight compared to sharp and irregularly shaped ones. The latter had a bet-ter chance of piercing skin and flesh with its pointy end. He could al-ways let a stone pass through anyone or anything if he wanted, too. He had the skill and strength to do it, but it was not in his job description. Smooth stones and a mild force would do.

Damian placed Y and his load in the right side pocket of his jacket. A pack of cigarettes and his lighter went in the left.

"Man, what took you so long? I said five minutes right?" Umer waited down stairs, outside the building's main door.

"No. You said ten." Damian went down the stairs.

"Whatever. We just need to hurry up. We need to be there 10 minutes earlier than the agreed hit time. Remember protocol?" Umer ushered him to a white car on a No Parking Zone and occupying half of the sidewalk. "Get in."

Sunet—the agency's informant, contact, recruiter, courier, and driver, an old wrinkled brown man in his late sixties—greeted them as they got in.

"Where to, Sirs?" Sunet asked.

"Books and Brew Cafe, 76920 J.P. Rizal St. corner T. Buenavista St., Los Baños City." Damian's voice echoed within the car. Umer's smile seemed to indicate both approval and mocking.

"That's far away, Sir," Sunet replied. "It'll be a long ride. About an hour at least, two if we get caught in heavy traffic."

"Make it at most an hour and half." Umer said as he looked at his watch.

"Yes, Sir."

"At least an hour? Great. I can sleep on the way. You wouldn't mind right?" Sleep, excluding cigarettes and the job, was Damian's only addiction.

"Sure. No problem. Sunet will keep me company," Umer said.

The driver looked on his rear view mirror and gave a smile to both of them.

Excitement and doubt no longer filled Damian's heart during the trip to the hit zone after 408 missions. He relaxed and went to sleep.

Across the street, the cafeteria's neon light signs were off, and the sign on the door said, "Sorry We're Closed". The trees and bushes surrounding the parking lot hid them.

"You were tossing and turning again," Umer said. "Better get that 'recurring dream' checked. Iñigo says he's good with interpreting dreams."

"I don't need anyone to interpret my dreams," Damian said.

The beer filled his stomach and woke his spirits. They arrived an hour earlier, so there was time for beer and dinner (fish balls, quail eggs, grilled blood, chicken intestines and barbecue).

"You can tell me what to eat, but you can't tell me what to believe," Damian said.

"We dream things we want to happen," Sunet said. "Dreams incorporate the past. Dreams can be confused as memories and vice versa. When you start having problems deciding which is which, you should already ask for help. In my opinion, the need is aggravated when you start denying truth as nothing but fantasy."

Sunet's eyes looked at Damian as if he knew the agent's secret. The old man recruited Damian to the agency, so he expected the old man did a thorough profile check. When one joined the agency, one gave-up privacy and personal relationships.

"But that's only my suggestion, Sir," Sunet added.

"And a good suggestion it is," Umer winked at the driver. "Go see Iñigo. He wants some action, or anything interesting. It's been a while since high profiled cases were assigned to him. Your dream may cure him of his boredom."

"I don't want anyone cigarpreting my dreams," Damian said. "For all I know, it's the only thing the agency can't mess."

"Okay man, suit yourself," Umer raised his hands in surrender. "Five minutes to hit time. Can you see our client yet? She should be here already. Else, we can't go on."

"She's here," Damian saw the client emerging from the underpass. "She's looking at the coffee shop."

"Is that in the plan?"

"Not that she mentioned it. Maybe she just wants to make sure that it's the right guy on the shift. She'll leave if she wants to call the hit off."

"That would be bad. There are no refunds."

"Okay. She's in position now, better take mine too."

"Hide us, Sunet. Make sure nobody notices Damian pointing his slingshot."

Damian focused his senses on the client and the target. Everything dimmed and hid in the shadows. Only the light from the cafeteria and from the streetlight entered his eyes. Three minutes to hit, his heart was pounding, and adrenalin rushed all over his body.

During Damian's first few weeks in the agency, the excitement would always make him miss thrice before he hit the target. That was four years ago. Everything became natural to him, as normal as breathing. The anticipation of fulfilling the task only enhanced his focus and determination to finish it in one shot.

Damian took one pebble from his jacket's side pocket. He kissed the pebble and kept it close to his lips while whispering an incantation. The stone's colour was ivory, but it glowed red after he kissed it. With every word he uttered, the stone's light intensified.

"In the name of love, I command you," Damian ended his prayer. The stone turned into a burning ball, red light escaping through the spaces between his fingers. Two minutes to hit, the target was closing shop; the client, acting innocent, was still in position.

Damian, tilting his head to get a better angle and better snipe, was ready to shoot at will. He waited for the opportune moment. One minute to hit, the target finished closing the shop and started to walk towards the streetlight about a meter from the client.

Just give the signal, Damian thought. *Just ask for it and I'll do it for you. Or call it off, I don't care, just don't make me wait.*

Thirty seconds to hit, the target was in the right position, his heart unguarded and unaware. The client took her eyeglasses from her shoulder bag, wore it, stared at the target, and smiled. That was the signal.

The pebble tracked its trajectory. A streak of red light crossed the street. Sunet made sure no one else saw it except members of the agency.

The ray of light struck the target's chest, never to leave his body again. The target held on to the streetlight to regain his balance. Shock filled his face, and his chest glowed bright red. The glow accumulated in the man's heart. It formed a silhouette of his heart, blinking in unison with its beating. The light dimmed as it penetrated his heart. Damian saw the heart resisting the flame of emotion engulfing it. The client swayed her hips when she approached the target. Her smile caught the man's attention.

Damian stood up when he saw the two talking and laughing. Mission accomplished. The target fell in love with the client, forever.

&

"So how are you, Sir?" Sunet asked.

"I'm fine." Damian replied.

"I'd say that's a lie by the way you look, Sir."

"Just couldn't get any proper sleep."

"Really? And Carmelo calls you Sandman for all the sleep you've been doing."

"I don't care what Carmelo says."

"Of course you don't, Sir," Sunet fixed the eyeglasses on the bridge of his nose, licked his hands, and turned some leaves of the record book. "But keep in my mind that he's your senior."

"For as long as I am in probation. I'll be a full Cupid after this."

"You think so? I see you're very confident, Sir."

"Why shouldn't I? I deserve it."

"Too cocky, Sir, but we'll see." Sunet skimmed through the log of Damian's missions, from those two elementary students to the old woman who paid a lot of money to secure the young businessman's love. Misses, failures, and delays gave him demerits and harsh criticisms. Perfect missions earned him nothing except the chance for immortality.

"Overall, you've done a good job, Sir," Sunet said. "We can forgive all of your previous mistakes and for staying stubborn about using a slingshot instead of the customary bow and arrow. But before you graduate, we have one more mission for you, just to make sure you deserve Cupidity and immortality."

"The big bosses won't make it any easier for me?"

"Never mind the big bosses, Sir. It's all for the agency's benefit." Sunet handed a sealed brown envelop to Damian.

The contents were the same for any mission envelope: a piece of paper and a 4R picture. On the paper were the target's basic information (name, age, height, complexion, occupation and present residence), additional details, and instructions for the hit. Information about the client was missing. He asked for anonymity, either for safety concerns or, most likely, for unbearable shame in dealing with Cupids.

"Is this the agency's idea of a joke." Once Damian saw his target's name, he did not need to see any other personal detail. Only the picture would do for she had changed after four years, a shorter hair, dyed reddish brown, and a more slender body. She maintained the beautiful face he had fallen in love with.

"Based on your reaction, Sir, I'd say it proves the agency is doing the right thing." Sunet smiled and waited for Damian to answer.

The silence turned to a high pitch whistle that almost made Damian's ear drums explode. One punch could split open Sunet's lips and destroy his devious smile. Damian kept his cool. Hitting an innocent messenger was useless.

"Your last mission is to make Sarah Cortez fall in love. Do it and the big bosses will raise you to a full Cupid. And, as we have agreed, you will be immortal," Sunet said.

"Part of our agreement was to take Sarah out of my life. I didn't want to remember her. But you failed." Damian slapped Sarah's photo on the table. The sound reverberated in the room and made Sunet jerk.

"Interesting. The dreams went not only to your head but also to your heart," Sunet said.

"How did—"

"I know everything, and I never fail, Sir. The moment I learned about your dreams I knew what the reason was. It's all because of this." The messenger pointed to Damian's chest. He whispered the words as if it was top secret. "You still love her."

"I don't love her," Damian's words were a futile and worthless attempt to deny his feelings.

"You do. And the big bosses know, Sir. This is the perfect mission for you. Make her fall in love, and you can move on. Forget about her, be a Cupid, be immortal. The agency can force love to any heart, but we cannot take it away. It's like death, only worse."

The words pierced Damian to the bone. Sunet's eyes sent a creeping fear all over his body. The old man's smile froze his heart and his soul. Damian always saw Sunet as an old man, but at that moment, he feared Sunet.

"You will do this, Sir," Sunet continued. "Because if you don't, you'll break our contract, and as you already know there is no place for an ex-Cupid, even one in training, in the world of mortals. The agency will make sure hell reserves a special place for you."

✑

"I want red wings when this is all over."

Rain poured down on the city. Ankle deep flood sunk the city roads. The water sliding on the windshields made the city outside appear it was under a wild current of ocean. Damian was getting bored waiting and had started talking about all the things he wanted as a Cupid.

"And no one can force a bow and arrow on me, I'll keep Y," Damian continued. "I'm more troubled with immortality. I don't know what I'll do forever besides missions."

"You'll soon figure that out," Carmelo replied. The senior would assist Damian in his final mission, but Damian thought it was more of a precautionary measure for the agency.

"There are a lot of things you can do," Carmelo said. "You'll live forever right? You can actually just keep on thinking what to do, and you'll still have infinity to do it once you've decided. In that aspect, immortals are blessed. Mortals need to rush and decide what they'll do. If they don't, they'll die the next day without even accomplishing anything."

"Really? Cupids have the luxury of not dying?" Damian asked. "Then I wonder why I'm here. As far as I know, the agency needs five Cupids. There are four of you, what happened to the one before me?"

"Look here kid," Carmelo said, "Cupids are immortal, but if you ever find forever to be overwhelming, you can always decide to spend eternity in darkness and silence, in short death. That happens all the time."

"So we have that choice, huh? I never thought of that. Why did the last one decide to die?"

"He never decided to. It just happened."

"He got killed? He's immortal. He can't be killed."

"Unless he falls in love, love for a day and death for eternity. Demetrio never regretted it though. I saw it in those dying eyes of his."

"Love and then death? Talk about going from bad to worse," Damian said.

Sunet laughed, "I think you got it the wrong way around, Sir. Although the sequence is right, the severity is wrong. Love is always worse than death. Dying is an escape from love's tortures."

"So that's why the agency is making me do this," Damian said. "I can't become a Cupid if I'm still in love with Sarah."

"Yes," Sunet replied. "You can lie all you want. If the agency turns you into a full Cupid even with a single hint of love for Sarah still in your heart, you'll die in an instant. And that would be just a waste for the big bosses. They need to be sure first. Finding new trainees are not hard though, so you better make this."

Sunet parked the car on the sidewalk. The wind blew rain to almost a horizontal. Gust shook the buildings.

"Make this quick, Sir." Sunet said. "You know where she is. Do it. Then go back immediately. This storm is not that much of a problem. Sir Carmelo, go to the skies when I signal all clear, and carry Sir Damian to the top of that building there. The view will be perfect for him."

"Okay, Boss," Carmelo replied. "I love rain. I like getting my wings wet."

After a few short breaths and a long blank stare ahead, Sunet told them it was fine to get out. A splash of water greeted Damian. The strong wind took his balance off, and the flood made it impossible for his feet to grip the pavement. He was falling down. Before Damian took the impact, the ground fell further from him.

Carmelo took Damian under the arms. They flew above Sunet's car. Dark purple wings almost twice Carmelo's span forced its way against the violent gust. Its thick feathers and frequent flaps broke the rain's continuous pour. No mortal noticed this; the surrounding was all rain for them, no flying man with big wings, no Cupids.

The building's rooftop gave a good view of the 32nd floor of the adjacent building where Sarah was working. Sarah sat in front of her computer. Men occupied each cubicle around her. If Damian shot her then, the first man she would see could be any of them. He had specific instructions on the hit time. Damian looked at his watch.

"Five minutes," Damian said, "I better get ready."

"I'll just watch here. I'm enjoying this storm in flight." Carmelo said.

Sarah's heart had a bluish glow that indicated she was not, at that moment, in love. It assured Damian of what he was about to do.

"Carmelo? Why are you here?" Damian asked.

"To look over you, of course," Carmelo replied.

"Don't lie to me Carmelo," Damian said and faced Carmelo.

The Cupid kept his head raised, looking straight to the sky, allowing the rain to wash over his face.

"You only accompany me on heart break missions," Damian continued, "I know why you're here."

"I am the heart break Cupid indeed," Carmelo enjoyed the shower heaven gave him. "Still, why would it matter anyway? Just do your mission, kid. Then you'll be like me. If you don't like my job then you can always turn down hits like this."

"What if I don't do it?" His hesitation contradicted the loaded and stretched slingshot aimed at Sarah's heart.

"Do you really have to be stubborn about this?" Carmelo's face was blank.

The Cupid slid his hand through his long dark hair and took a strand. After whispering a prayer, the hair curved and took form, spreading like a piece of darkness in Carmelo's hands. A dark bow as long as Carmelo's span materialised in his hands. It was not the first time Damian saw Shadow's Crown. Rain and wind dispersed as Carmelo swung his right arm and Shadow's Crown, the gust unable to withstand the force of the act.

Carmelo plucked a feather from his wings. Blood dripped in a diagonal line that ended to a sharp tip. He kissed the purple quivers and licked the red shaft of his arrow up to its tip then shook the rain off it.

"Three minutes," Carmelo notched the arrow, drew, and aimed for Sarah's heart. "If you don't do it, I'll do it."

"And that's why the agency sent you," Damian returned his attention towards Sarah's heart, "if there really is an agency. Next question, who is Sunet? Why did you call him Boss?"

"I was stupid to make that slip. You know he can hear our conversation, right?"

"Yeah. And I want him to hear all of it."

"What the hell; you'll learn it anyway. Sunet is the agency, the big bosses, everything."

"So he is the God of love?"

Carmelo's laughter drowned the roar of thunder, "That'll amuse him. Not really, he's just who he is, eternal and mysterious. He doesn't have a real name. He's everything, life, knowledge, love, despair, dreams, destruction, growth, and death. I have to tell you, he's enjoying this conversation."

"Who wants to break Sarah's heart?" Damian asked.

"I do." Damian recognised Sunet's voice echoing in his head.

"Why, Sunet?" Damian asked.

"To test you if you still love her. You can't be a Cupid if you do," Sunet said. "But don't worry. I'll assure you the pain of the heartbreak will not last long. I made arrangements with my Angels of Death to give her an eternal rest after a couple of months. I hope that doesn't complicate your mission."

Damian could imagine the devilish smile on Sunet's wrinkled face, "No. No complications whatsoever."

Damian's focus had never been so intense, only a minute left until hit. He needed his full concentration to make sure he would do it right, no mistakes.

Thirty seconds, Damian's heartbeat slowed. He could see every detail of the storm, the raindrops, the spaces in between, the amount of water in each, and the momentary crown of splashing water on the concrete rooftop.

Ten seconds, Damian could see Sarah busy with her work. From the corner of his eyes, he could see Carmelo's silhouette tensed and poised to take a shot the moment Damian failed to do so. Below, Sunet waited for the mission's completion.

In the last second, Damian bowed his head, lowered his arms, and loosened the sling. When Carmelo saw this, he let go of the arrow. It flew through the air unaffected by the rain and the wind's resistance.

The arrow broke in half when a pebble struck it in mid-flight. Damian turned to face the surprised Cupid, took a sharp stone from his pocket, loaded it in his sling, aimed straight at Carmelo's heart, and let the stone loose while he leapt backwards. The stone pierced through Carmelo's chest.

Damian was falling head first towards the pavement. The short glimpse of Sarah's smile was the best thing he saw before he died. She was safe from Sunet's grasp. The pavement and death approached him. His only wish was to embrace Sarah for one last time, even for a second.

Moments before the impact, Damian saw Sunet standing on the sidewalk, and shaking his head from side to side. *This is how I want to spend forever, old man*, Damian thought. *In eternal rest.*

About Recle Etino Vibal

Recle Etino Vibal (born in the Pispis, Maasin, Iloilo, Philippines) spent his childhood and currently lives in Mayondon, Los Baños, Laguna, Philippines. A son of an Ilongga and a Bikolano, he is proudly Filipino. He obtained the degree of Bachelor of Science in Chemical Engineering at the University of the Philippines Los Baños, but works with numbers that are zero percent chemical and 100% financial engineering. He balances reading, writing, and living, a daily juggling act on a high tension wire a hundred meters above the ground. He manages to survive such a stunt, read, learn, write, and live for another day. Learn more about him at ibongtikling.wordpress.com.

Dreams

Tabitha Sin

~ (New) Hong Kong ~

There is a new love in my life. When I place it inside me, its soothing touch lingers, coursing through my veins. It helps me sleep, humming white noise against my ears. I feel warm and sated, my limbs heavy, my breath even. It leaves me complacent, and when I curl into a foetal position, I start to dream.

There is a new love in my life because it helps me bring the old one back from the dead.

❦

I prayed every day to one of the gods, to any of them that would hear me. I prayed to the old ones from our past that the government had tried so hard to make its citizens forget, but our parents had kept them well alive within us. I prayed to the new ones who always promised salvation. I prayed: Please, please. Do not let the sun rise.

But gods never listen when you want them to. As the sun chased the moon from the sky, its rays peeking through the pale blinds of her hospital room, I knew she would be lost to me forever. She had never shown any improvement, but still I stayed with her, separated by the oblong glass case that held her deteriorating body. I tried to tell her of a story about everlasting love because that's what she enjoyed best.

"The ghost and human," I said, "had loved each other very deeply. But their love for each other was against the rules of nature. They tried to fight against those higher powers, but in the end, they had to say goodbye. The only way they could be together was to hope that one day, their reincarnated souls would find each other."

"Did they find each other?" she asked me.

She turned her head to face me, and the skin from her scalp laid limply on her pillow, black tendrils left behind. Nothing on her face registered pain.

"Of course," I said, steadying my voice.

She had lost half of her hair when we realised something was wrong with her.

The corner of her pale lips rose, her eyes rheumy. "You were always a terrible liar."

🖋

The designer drug offers a way for users to control their dreams. We slip into an almost catatonic state, one where nothing can hurt us, and we feel as warm as we once did in our mother's womb. It is the elixir of dreams that our country could never really let go.

I had navigated the streets of the floating city to get just a small dosage. The place that deals the new strain of opiate is as close to the edge of our world as we know it. The seedy building looks like it has been shabbily constructed, almost keeling into the waterfall that marks the edge. The boats are tethered to the ports of New Aberdeen so that it won't float down the waterfall and into what was the original Kowloon Bay.

I once looked out the window from their apartment and had felt sick. The building was built so high, trying to relive the glory of its past, that I could see the wasteland of the Old Territories. Almost nothing survived the Flood that took over a quarter of the world. The old skyline looked dead and charred, a city that housed hundreds of thousands of ghosts. Hong Kong was one of the first cities to construct a floating city with a protective dome against the poisonous sun. We hung in the clouds, building replicas of the once grand buildings from below.

The Ah-ma who gives me the elixir of dreams shakes her head at me as she opens her spotted hand revealing the vial. Her gnarled fingers and light eyes indicate her age and also lack of wealth. Someday, and I do not know how soon, but I will look like her. When I swipe the vial from her palm, her mouth twists in disapproval, but I don't care. The drug brings me one step closer to *her*, the only one I will ever need.

When I get back to my apartment, I pull the yellow moth-eaten shades down to avoid the blistering sun. Even with the tinted windows, I can still see dust motes rising and swirling. I unbutton my cheongsam, my fingers lingering over the flower stitching. I remember how she used to pull down the zipper slowly past my waist, her lips ghosting my neck and every expanse of skin exposed, helping me out of the dress. I bury myself into the bed, straightening the cotton sheets over my chest. With the drug in my system, my limbs become heavy, and with one last effort, I curl onto my side. I close my eyes and wait for her to appear.

On her last night, she said to me, "I wish I could feel your hand again."

Like a lovesick fool, not knowing that promises should never be spoken unless they could be kept, I said to her, "You will."

Still, there was the barricade between us. Not only did her glass cage keep her away from me, but Death and Start Labs had already claimed her as theirs.

Before I give into the drug, I always remember her the best way I can. I make sure she looks healthy like the first time I ever locked eyes with her. She was the most beautiful woman I had ever seen. I marvelled at her slightly darker skin, like the sun had kissed it graciously. I kissed it lovingly from her temples to the rounded tip of her nose, from her prominent shoulder blades to her hips, from her knees to the smooth insides of her ankles. Her eyes were smaller than the large ones that had become so popular, and her teeth were slightly crooked. She had thick and long black hair, usually piled high, and always smelling like roses.

When I open my eyes, she is here, lying next to me. Her fingers are soft and delicate like flower petals brushing against my skin. She is wearing a thin camisole, her collarbone straining against flesh and looking like it will break through. Her eyes are bright and her hair is loose around us. In this small sanctuary, we are perfect just like before.

"I'm not the only one," she whispers against my brow.

She starts to ashen, and I see flakes forming against her jutting bone.

"What do you mean?" My words fall flat as I try to hold onto her disintegrating body.

She isn't supposed to be like this. In these lucid dreams, I hold her and keep the promises I make.

I hear her laugh, the one that she was embarrassed about because she snorted like a pig. She palms my cheek and presses her mouth against mine. I feel her rubbery gums mash against my lips.

"There are others who are suffering from this, too."

We are no longer together in my bed. Instead, she is standing at the edge of New Hong Kong, her feet above the water. I try to reach out and grab her, but she is out of reach. She goes through the phases of her disease, the one that had caught everyone by surprise. The one that wasn't supposed to exist. The one that Start Labs products had promised to fight but instead accelerated the process.

Her skin turns bone-white and her eyes look bloody from popped capillaries. Her once healthy, red-and-pink muscles become grey. Her hair falls out, clumps floating in the air. The water spray from behind her doesn't get her nightgown wet. The skin I had once adored sags from her bones. It drops into the water unevenly like pale slugs losing grip. Her mouth gapes open, her lower mandible shifting lower and slowly dipping. I scream and scream because this isn't supposed to happen. Before her jaw disappears into the bay, I see her mouth form a word.

I wake up hours later, my throat raw, and my body clammy from cold sweat. My room is dark and filled with shadows, and I feel like the loneliness in my heart will kill me. I know she will never appear to me again, not the way I want to dream of her. I keep the empty vials on the window ledge. As I walk amongst the masses or when I am alone, staring into the darkest corners of my room, I hear her final whisper, like the way she told me she loved me:

Help.

✿

"What happens when the souls are reincarnated again?" she asked me once.

I could hear air rattle in her chest as she pushed out the words from her mouth. Her ribcage looked fragile like if I stroked the bone, it would turn to dust.

"They spend years looking for each other," I tell her. "Since she was a ghost, she was able to deceive Meng Po. But he drank the Five Flavoured Tea of Forgetfulness that was offered. A sip was all that was needed for him to forget his past lives. But the ghost was determined that her human would remember the only life that mattered to her."

I was looking into her glass cell as I told the story. My hand pressed against the bottom. With obvious effort, she strained and lifted her half-bone, half-muscle arm and tried to press her decaying palm against the glass. She didn't have much skin left on her fingers at that point, but I tried as hard as I could to have her feel my warmth. My breath fogged the glass. I wished I could hold onto whatever was left and clutch it against my heart.

"I won't drink the tea," she said; one of the last things she ever said.

ABOUT TABITHA SIN

Tabitha Sin enjoys stories that make her skin crawl. She has been published in Moonroot zine and Thought Catalog. She is currently working on a speculative fiction YA novel set in the same world as "Dreams" while occasionally dabbling in hybrid fiction-memoir pieces. You can find her at http://tabithasin.wordpress.com or follow her thoughts on Twitter: @tabithameep.

Bumbye! Said the Candelarios

Ailia Hopkins

~ Hawai'i ~

The change was so innocuous and most were too busy to notice it, but the beach had grown over twenty-two feet that night, and if Chandel Reyes, under the influence of a heady mix of beer and bootleg psycho-pharmaceuticals, had not been driving down a deserted strip of coastal highway that subsequent afternoon, she might never have alerted the town in time. Of course, this fact was soon forgotten.

She had dozed off, the beer cans on the passenger floorboard rolling out from under the seat, the automotive receipts on the dashboard flying, the Ocean-Air air freshener in the rear view mirror twisting like a breathless scream. She was slammed forward and awake, then back down and unconscious. She awoke to the sound of Spanish guitars. The hood smoked as the radio played on and Chandel, instead of sighting, or maybe because of sighting, the scarlet stream dribbling down the dashboard of her corvette, found herself mesmerised by what she was certain the foreign tongue over the trill of the band was singing. *You pursue me as if I were a dove you want to devour!* She peeled her face from the steering wheel and felt her head spin. The chorus faded and the voice resumed its inscrutable Spanish.

Chandel fell against the car door, popping it open. Oblivious to the heat, she slid from the driver's seat to the sand, sat up and caught another strain of the haunted radio, this time without guitars. *Torn to shreds like my fucking heart.* Chandel touched her temple to rub it sober. It was time for a tonic. Squinting ahead, through a patch of yellow light, she saw where the beach ascended, narrowed, and dropped to sheer cliff. If not for the crash she would had been headed straight for the ocean.

She stood up, her thick arms trembling like the strings of those Spanish guitars, which trailed her, ever so softly, as she made her way to the passenger side. She felt her ribs, then looked at the windshield, and winced. The tyre, its rubber caught on a heap of seaweed and rock, was another mess entirely. She stuck her hand through the passenger window and clicked open the glove compartment, spilling a carton of cigarettes and a hoard of paper napkins onto the seat as she fumbled for the smooth metal knob of her flask. The front surface had been etched prettily with someone's silver initial: another souvenir. In it was the last seven ounces of a prime-grade whiskey, which, unlike anything else she currently owned, including the car itself, she had in fact purchased.

"*Cariño*," she said, unaware she wasn't speaking in English, and threw her head back for two generous gulps.

A sudden gust blew the last smoke from the car.

Her t-shirt clung to her chest in darkening splotches. She took a deep breath. In one swoop she ripped it up over her head, tossing it along with her shabby cargo pants into the back seat of the car. She polished off the last of the Maker's Mark and set the empty flask down about five yards from the water, plenty of room for high tide to come in. She strode toward the tide, ignoring the feeling of being a body-sized bruise, and dove in. The ocean bloomed into one foaming mouth, rushing forward as if to form another body around her.

It was a long while before she felt half-way sober enough to turn back to the car, and by then, she was much farther down from where she had started. She walked, for what seemed like hours, letting her body dry in the sun, until a sharp glinting, like the pinnacle of a church, signalled the flask, the rest of it buried underneath sand. It, too, seemed much farther from the tide than she remembered. The sun quivered with the same level intensity, yet there was no trace of her footprints and the water had ebbed. She wondered how long she'd been in the water. Perhaps she had simply gotten the tides mixed. Even the radio was silent, in all probability dead. She slipped back into her blood-stained t-shirt and tattered pants, and finding a pair of slippers in the trunk of the car, turned for the road. By the time she passed the torn guard rail, the stand of blighted pines and the crumbling outcrop that did nothing to buffer her fall to the bottom of the beach, the ocean had retreated another thirty feet.

Back from the coastal highway on which our hero had just begun lay a dreamy valley of little wooden houses raised on little wooden stilts. Some of the houses sat perched before macadamia groves, or coffee. Some simply overlooked ponds. All of them stood above gardens—gardens of such lushness and variety as if to have bloomed in response to a prehistoric explosion. There had not been any volcanic activity for quite some time now. It is important to note these details, for at the end of this road, tucked into a grove of plumeria and pines, stands the centre of our story—an inconspicuous shop, more like a glorified shed, in which three women in faded, slim-fitting dresses have just banged through the door, the copper bell nailed above ringing in irritating succession.

"You Candelarios need to stop bangin' that blessed door." The man behind the counter, his coarse hair clipped close above his leathery ears, stood over a pile of coupons arranged on top of an inventory binder, his elbow and forearm greasy with newspaper ink. This was the only market for several miles, and the customers were either the odd local neighbours or the odd lost tourist, though most tourists had good enough aim of getting lost farther along down the road.

The first woman clucked. "What's wrong? Mister Savei stay a virgin?" They were standing in a row, their hair-sprayed up-dos and prosthetic eyelashes towering over the top of the aisle. They busily filled a basket with Revlon nail polish.

"Goddamn trannies," Saveliy said under his breath.

"Aww." The third Candelario cooed. "Papa's got his panties in a twist 'cause we're bangin' his door, and not bangin'—"

"Say, why don't you ladies go sell yourselves?" Saveliy snapped open a newspaper.

"How you think we get the cash for come shop your junk superette?" said the second Candelario. The other two laughed as they moved to the feminine hygiene aisle.

Saveliy looked up. "What the hell do you need that for?"

The first Candelario held up two boxes and the sisters, heads cocked to one side, shrugged, signalling her to drop both cartons into the basket as the bell rang with a new customer. She was slightly sunburned and kind of bruised, which made for an irregular combination on her skin—under normal circumstances, a mute sienna; that, and her scalp seemed to be bleeding onto her shirt, adding brighter splotches to what might have been older and dried-up instants of other such splotches, or mud. She looked as if she'd been through a washing machine, but her clothes were dry and not especially clean. Saveliy and the three women paused to look at her. Chandel ignored them and headed for the liquor, trailing sand.

The third Candelario resumed a conversation that seemed to have been going on for quite some time now. "I don't care how much work he's had done, or how messed-up his nose looks, I'd sit on his face." They were closer to the register now, each poised over respective copies of *People* Magazine's Sexiest Man of The Year. Chandel stood with a focused stance before the glassed fridge.

"I don't know, I'd have to be pretty strung-out, myself," said the second Candelario, turning her neck, long and stubbled, with the other Candelarios, to the woman contemplating the alcohol at the back of the store.

Saveliy glanced up over the rim of his round-frame glasses. "You read it, you buy it. This ain't a library."

The third Candelario huffed, her laughter suddenly low in pitch. "Does it look like this tita can read?"

The first Candelario tossed her hibiscus-print lava-lava over one shoulder, and the second tossed back her hair—all three delicately replacing their magazines as Chandel slipped a 26oz. bottle of SKYY vodka between the cotton of her underwear and the wide elastic band of her pants.

"That'll be $28.66," said Saveliy.

"Bumbye," said the Candelarios. The women lined up to consolidate their funds, their purses filling the counter and forcing Saveliy to move his newspaper coupons to one side. He didn't notice the audible crunch of Chandel's pockets holding two packages of dried ika and a bag of li-hing mui candy, nor the bell for the shop as she exited, her shirt a little more filled out and angular with a bottle of mouthwash and the last three boxes of lime Jell-O.

"Must be Gigi's new tits," said the second Candelario, arching her left painted-on eyebrow in the direction of the third Candelario, as the other two searched the bottom of their bags for the last sixteen cents. "Sava here distracted, letting that chronic just up and run off with his alcohol."

Saveliy felt himself blush, processing the intolerable thought he'd let a thief get by. He dropped the cash in the register and flung it closed, bolting from behind the counter out the door.

"Thanks for the discount!" yelled the first Candelario.

Each extended a long dark arm to a stand of Dum-Dum lollipops next to the register.

The second Candelario concurred, leaning forward over the counter. "That Savei there ain't so bad, you know."

Their eyes followed him out past the store window, where he had paused at the edge of the parking, scanning both ways. They unwrapped the suckers and popped them in their mouths.

The third Candelario sighed. "Poor virgin."

Although it had been no more than a minute since he had been robbed, by the time Saveliy made it past the stand of plumeria enfolding the entrance of the shop, he found himself at a clear disadvantage—very nearly out of breath, with the thief out of sight. He was hardly accustomed to coming this far down the valley, much less out to the highway. He had spent much of the past eight years in that three mile-radius, moving from his house to the shop, and it had been so long since he'd been to the beach or the harbour, for good reason. As he liked to tell himself, it was the age of retreat for a man of his status, or at the very least, years.

But now he was running, his gut flopping heavily, his neck hair gathering sweat, overcome with the inexplicable feeling he was on an important mission. He flushed with a new vitality, even as he felt he would surely die if he did not stop for breath, at which exact moment, heaving with his hands on his 58-year-old thighs, he looked up in time to see that net of black hair from the superette disappearing over the crest of the valley at the end of the black-grit road.

"You bitch! My shit!"

The mass of black hair continued without missing a beat. "Knees up, old man."

He coughed, and with feigned energy sprinted down the hill. The bobbing net of hair rounded the second bend in the black-grit road to where it met up with the highway and then dived in a parallel curve by the shore. He pumped his legs harder than ever. His side burned and his teeth ached. The tree trunks narrowed and zipped past, and the ground rose up as his boots kicked up a storm of dirt and pine needles but he knew, just a few more steps and he would reach out and snatch the thief by that net of hair, a few more steps, a few more breaths, and he would have justice. But instead, as he cleared the entrance to the beach, fully ready to lay hold of her, he stopped cold and nearly collapsed in fright.

The ocean was gone.

Saveliy shook and pulled back, then instinctively called out to the woman he'd been chasing, who was now climbing through the window of her car, which looked as if it had been tossed off a cliff.

He stammered, tried again, and screamed. "Wait!"

She didn't seem to hear him. He took one last look at the beach, then turned and hurried back to his shop.

By nightfall the entire town had moved out of the valley to the mountain. The highway slowed and thickened, as if the road had halfway through the day melted into a parking lot. People fled, abandoning their cars at odd places in order to escape up the trail. Although it hardly made sense to run from something that was not even there, the town was more afraid of what they could not see, the unknown.

The air was dryer, thinner, and cooler at this height, although the mountain was hardly a mountain by any means—more like a semi-formidable hill. But neither was the town really a town. It did not possess a post office or restaurant, and the two commercial enterprises, a gas station and convenience store, were little more than converted houses themselves.

The town spent a restless evening watching the newly-formed canyon, listening for news of the disappeared ocean. But no one on the radio was reporting. And as the night grew longer, and the shadows of the sea-less canyon grew darker and deeper and steadily more tedious, the sparsely-pined ridge resonated with the laboured snoring of the makeshift campsite.

By dawn the ocean was back.

The campsite discovered this gradually. With no news on the radio, most of the residents slept in, which was easier to do now that the sun had taken an extra six hours to rise. Not even the roosters had crowed. Many people awoke during the night, but attributed their restless sleeping to the distressing events of the previous day, and promptly returned to unconsciousness.

The only one who seemed to have rested soundly throughout the night was Saveliy. He awoke from an uncharacteristically deep and restful slumber, on his side, as custom, facing the direction of the sun—or so he thought. But when he opened his eyes he found himself in an unusual position, instead facing the mountain. He stretched, yawned, and rolled over, but when he rubbed his eyes he found himself, inexplicably, once again facing the mountain. He flipped back and gaped in horror.

A wall of water, the height and breadth of the mountain to which the town had fled, and at some distance from the coast, stood poised over the valley like a sneeze awaiting release, or perhaps a tsunami posing for a photograph. Many of the townsfolk had, in fact, pulled out their cameras. The wind was still, the sun just barely visible over the lip of the ocean.

"It's just like that movie." Saveliy heard the town, now climbing atop their cars, rousing as he pulled on a flannel coat and stumbled from his truck.

The wave loomed like a rug on the point of its being flung, threatening the townsfolk with utter annihilation. Fortunately, it was as if some benevolent force had intervened to hold the torrent back, and at a polite distance of about a hundred yards from the shore. The surface of the water stood as flat vertically as it once lay horizontally, as if drawn up behind a giant panel of glass to frame a world-class aquarium.

One can imagine how, after some initial stage of shock, the more perceptive or business-minded types might have even entertained such commercial potential, for it would have been absolutely mesmerising during a later time of day, when a certain angle of light might shine through and illuminate an underwater universe. Unfortunately, at this point, there was no such illumination: only a five-hundred-foot shadow the ocean cast like a curse.

Saveliy thought he heard a small child ask someone if they were in fact dead. Then, naturally, everyone began to panic.

"Where are the planes? Where are the helicopters?" Not getting an answer to their queries, they would then repeat themselves. "The planes! The helicopters!"

Some of the townspeople ran back to the highway in a misguided effort to salvage things from their homes, while others grabbed at them, urging them not to go, lest the wave arbitrarily crash and flood the roads. The ones who went anyway were soon stuck in traffic, while those persuaded to change their minds to remain were soon calculating in sober and detached agreement that were the wave to drop they would all drown anyway, which sent everyone back into a fit of absolute terror, instigating yet another round of panic. The cycle of fretting was fortuitously interrupted by the sound of a familiar bell.

"It's the Sorcerer." The first Candelario gathered in the nearby refugees.

Elbow to elbow on top of a rusted Volvo, the sisters—in matching black pantsuits—stood together regally, the copper bell from Saveliy's Superette dangling from the middle one's extended manicured fingernail. Saveliy wondered just how much they had confiscated from his shop, but before he could call out, the crowd pushed ahead, and the orators continued.

"Or the Sea Witch," added the second, filing away at a nail.

"Whichever one He/She wishes to go by," yawned the third.

Perched above the crowd, the Candelarios, in their five-inch heels, seemed imbued with an air of authority on the matter. Either it was that or their impeccable make-up and perfectly-styled hair, now straightened out into heavy bangs and long tresses—extra-notable after an evening spent outside in the uncivilised patches of mountain wilderness.

Saveliy, less daunted by the sight of the triplet transsexuals, was the first to pose a question. "What does He/She want exactly?"

The second Candelario shrugged. The other two scratched at their noses.

"The Witch? She comes around every so often. But then—" The second Candelario paused as her sisters joined her in unison—"She's kind of unpredictable."

"What should we do?" said someone in the crowd.

"How much time do we have?" said someone else.

"Why has no one come to help us?" said another.

"These are all good questions." The first Candelario smiled. "Why don't we ask the Sorcerer?"

Just then a voice resounded from the bottom of the mountain, or within it, or above it. It was hard to tell because the sound seemed to fill the space all around them. It was a beautiful voice, feminine and rich and unmistakably Hispanic in origin.

"My dear," reverberated the voice, but in that lovely Spanish way.

Saveliy, instantly entranced, and confident of addressing the Sea Witch as such, climbed onto the roof of a dented Corolla. It was strange, but he felt as if he knew Her, perhaps from a past life. It was as if every woman he had ever loved and forgotten were calling out to him in that voice. And though Saveliy had long since abandoned any mystical notions, it was an impossible thought to ignore. He craned his neck, surveying the valley for a sight of the lovely sorceress, who he imagined as forcefully tall, with rapid dark hair crashing in a devastating flourish at her bone-slim ankles—skin the colour of seashells and eyes literally magnetic, flecked with gems—a body of precious metal and ancient ore.

"Goddess," he exhaled, but did not get a chance to complete the thought, as he was knocked from the roof of the car by a powerful wind, a force that somehow missed the rest of the townspeople gathered round in expectation.

The Candelarios, non-plussed, their hair unperturbed, assumed a mutual expression of seasoned disinterest, and everyone followed suit.

The wind then scooped up Saveliy, bringing him down past the valley, beyond the elongated beach, until he was right over the edge of a 210-foot drop of exposed and craggy sea floor. His arms waved, as if he were flying.

The crowd watched in open curiosity as he grew tiny, now so far away as to appear like nothing more than a speck of dust, before falling silently into the canyon. No one gasped as he was picked up, with his top half seeming to hang lower than his bottom, and dropped once more. Neither did they cower away in fear as he was lifted, half of him now as loose as a rubber band, and dropped again. Nor did they cover their mouths or hide their eyes as he, or at least part of him, was retrieved from the canyon in slow motion, and dropped for the very last time. No one asked aloud or privately wondered why it was Saveliy, of all townspeople, to be swept away and then pulverised like a flower.

The air felt easy with completion and peace. The pines blew wistfully. Everyone felt safe in the presence of the Sorcerer Sea Witch, who, from the sound of crackling branches, was just now emerging into the clearing from the trail.

✎

The mountain of water remained, enclosing the valley village. Many of the townspeople moved on, anticipating a tremendous flood, though some simply sought a freer and more exciting life, as all who stayed had to have their goods flown into the valley. Some tourists flew in, as well as journalists for National Geographic, but over time it became more and more difficult to find the valley, and eventually it was omitted from the map altogether.

There was nothing of special note here, but for a small movie-house called Chandel's Cinema, in which nightly (and nights lasted a lot longer here, with the mountainous horizon obscuring much of the sun's path), the movie-house's namesake would set up a pro-jector at the edge of the cavern, pointing the lens at the curtain of sea. The few inhabitants would take a late dinner and stroll, Spanish-style, through the canyon—which had bloomed into half-desert, half-botanical garden—stopping to rest with their blankets and arms around one another to watch the show. The wonderful thing about it was that wherever you happened to be sitting, whether on the mountain, or on the desert floor, or even in the valley somewhere on your lanai, the curve of the ocean made it seem as if the film were be-ing projected just for you.

ABOUT AILIA HOPKINS
Ailia has lived in Louisiana and Oʻahu and New England, yet tends to find herself anywhere there's karaoke. Although this is her first pub-lished story, in 2011 her Kafkaesque take on a classic campfire snack earned Honourable Mention in an edible literature contest. You can probably guess the recipe behind the Meta-S'mores-Phosis, or just hit her up on Facebook www.facebook.com/ailia.hopkins.

KITSUNE

KZ Morano

~ Japan ~

I woke up with a cold sensation on my chest where the warmth of her fur had been. The curtains ballooned and shrank in a ghostly dance. I inhaled the perfumed cloud that she had left behind and stared into the empty darkness of my room until my eyes hurt.

I padded towards the window just in time to catch one last glimpse of her, silhouetted against the black watery sky, her face turned towards the moon. I shut the window then jumped into bed, placing a pillow on my ears to muffle the haunting echoes of her ululations until they were diminished to a mere phantom of a sound.

I knew she did it on purpose… waited for me to wake up and watch her leave… I knew too that come morning, some guy's gonna end up in the news—dead, disemboweled. Jealousy filled me. I couldn't bear the thought of another man providing her with a kind of pleasure I could never give. I should've listened to my father. "Choose your wife well. You might end up with a vixen clothed in woman's skin." Wise words from a wise old man.

Memories pervaded the air—still damp and heavy with the scent of her passion. We met in the small village. I had been younger then—awkward and completely unremarkable. But she was a different thing. Walking barefooted on the rice fields, she smiled at me, turning the full force of her feral beauty on me. A 'hello' stuck itself somewhere in my throat. But she flipped her hair, so rich and red and rare, and asked if I was going to offer her a ride. Barely waiting for an answer, she hopped into my car in her typical fox-like grace.

She studied me with such unabashed curiosity. When the car vibrated into motion, she smiled. A fang gleamed... smooth, pearlescent... I asked her why she was out there walking all alone. And she said she'd been waiting for me all along. My face reddened. And she giggled prettily, the sound rolling from her throat like bubbles. And just like that, I knew I wanted her in my life. I asked her to marry me that same spring. She laughed and said 'yes' in her sweet straightforward fashion. We kissed and the ponderous limbs of cherry blossoms wept, their fragrant pink tears falling on our heads.

She loved with a kind of fierce intensity that I would often find myself wondering if it wasn't just some elaborate trick. Sometimes, I would catch her staring at the moon as if it were the face of some old lover. At the back of my skull, there was this nagging terror that someday, she'll wonder why she had allowed herself to be tamed and drawn into the impeccable monotony that was my life. There were times when I wondered if I should've just taken a good village woman for a wife.

They say everything gets weary with time. And that spring, no matter how lovely, will eventually seek respite from its opulence and beg for the cold barren relief of winter to arrive. People change. My dreams got bigger. And just as she had willingly settled into a life of bucolic banality, I had begun aching for the city.

So I took her here, though she had at first begged me not to. The city swallowed her whole. Its sights, sounds, and the sheer hugeness of it all frightened her. The city was no place for a fox. I, on the other hand, revelled in its mad diversity... its curves and corners that I tirelessly explored as if it were my mistress.

Lost in my own pursuit of success, I failed her. One night, it became too much for her to bear and something inside her just broke. That was the night that she left, leaping out the window and out of my life with a kind of desperate desire. I ran after her, a thousand promises bursting forth from my lips. But she only looked at me through eyes bearing the wisdom of hundreds of years, her face as cryptic as the moon that she loved so much. People change... Reluctantly, I let her go. Every night, Tokyo's city lights would wink at me like fireflies' sex lanterns. And it would dawn upon me how lonely I am. And that I'm now free. But not really. I'll always be bound to her just as she'll always be bound to me.

I pushed the image of her away... Visions of her standing by the window... her delicate vulpine features illuminated by the moon, her tails—all nine of them—fanned behind her back in flaming tongues of red and tangerine. A tail for each century she had lived... a tail for each century she had waited in the fields... Nine centuries of waiting for love to come her way... Nine centuries of waiting to become human... And after a few years of marriage, I turned her into this...

I'm the monster. Not her.

I tried my best not to miss her. Because that's the only time when she would come... It's been a while since she last snuck into our apartment and slept in my arms. During those moments, I would cling to her and inhale her out-breaths as if it were the last air on earth. Salty sweat and damp fur and the coppery smell of someone's blood—a scent that was uniquely hers.

She would sob, remorseful... trembling with self-loathing... I would hold her in my arms, telling her that it's alright... that we could start again. We would make love and I would taste them on her skin... her men. Sometimes, I'd wish that she'd just do to me what she did to them.

At times, I worry that she might never come back... But then she spent nine lifetimes waiting for me. So I figured, I should wait for her a little longer. *Kitsune... come to me.*

ABOUT KZ MORANO

KZ Morano is a writer, a beach bum, and a chocolate addict. She writes anything from romance and erotica to horror and dark fantasy. Her first published story is "The Baobab" in *Popcorn Horror Presents* published in August 2013 by Popcorn Horror. Her recent works include "The Other Child" in *Ugly Babies: the Anthology* by JWK Fiction in October 2013 (reprinted in *Blood Reign Literary Magazine* December 2013), "Wooden Lips" in *Cellar Door: Words of Beauty Tales of Terror Volume II*, "Fireworks" in *Off the KUF Volume II* and "The Old Man's Tree" in *Blood Reign Lit Mag* issue #1. Several of her stories will also be appearing in various forthcoming anthologies such as *Bones II* by JWK Fiction, Dark *Fairytales Revisited* by Horrified Press and *High End Flash Fiction Anthology* by Leodegraunce.

She blogs at theeclecticeccentricshopaholic.wordpress.com

Twitter: @kzmorano

THE VOLUNTEER

TR Napper

~ Vietnam, Thailand ~

"[Kill them. Kill them all.]" The voice whispered in his ear, insistent.

Aran murmured his reply. "Soon."

He lay prone on the boulder, high on a ridge overlooking the deep green jungle. One side of the ridge fell sharply to the ocean below. The sun pulsed from a cloudless azure sky, the air thick with heat. Sweat trickled down his forehead, into his eye. Aran blinked it away. He should have worn his environment mask. Too late now, the target was well within range; Aran couldn't move and give away his position. Fortunately his chillcloak was functioning, absorbing the heat and releasing cooled air onto his body, keeping him conscious.

The group straggled in a line down the narrow beach below, half a mile away. Seven of them, their outlines hazy in the shimmering heat. They looked like just another Vietnamese refugee family fleeing the conflict in the north. But Aran's regiment was hidden in the valley beyond, and command didn't want any witnesses.

He whispered. "They don't look like combatants."

The voice—metallic, rasping. "[They are *Viet Minh*.]"

"One looks like a grandmother walking on a cane."

"[They are an espionage unit.]"

"They're using grandmothers now? I guess that's some sort of close-combat pulse cane?"

"[Just follow your orders, corporal.]"

The Cochlear-Glyph implant behind his ear went silent. But he knew they were there, waiting for him to act, monitoring his vital signs and movements. Listening to his orders, looking for any unorthodox chatter between him and his squad.

The scout squad of five was spread amongst the boulders. Behind them the regiment was preparing for a surprise push into the south. Three thousand shock troops, one hundred mobile rail-cannons, even a plasma array. It was a bold manoeuvre, along the beaches of Da Nang and into Hoi An. His squad was linked together through their implants, able to hear every word, every murmur, every expletive each other made. They weren't given wider comms access than that. Command didn't trust the volunteer squadrons, they thought they'd warn the enemy or send out the truth about the war onto the freewave.

Aran aimed his rifle, tightened his gloved finger around the steel trigger. He looked over the group again through the sight and chose the most combatant-looking of the seven: a young man holding a machete, leading the refugees. He wore a large conical bamboo hat, reflective sunglasses, a singlet and long shorts. And that's all. How the boy didn't pass out from the maddening heat was beyond him. They must be desperate, walking in the sunlight.

Aran had been a reservist, back home, so he'd been promoted to corporal immediately. But he'd never fired at another human being before. He aimed at the boy's shoulder. Maybe he could just wound him. "Ready men. Wait until I fire. I'll take the lead combatant." Four voices, more or less, grunted in response.

He focused the sight, licked the sweat from his top lip.

Aran sighed. He pulled the trigger.

The arm tore from the torso. Blood sprayed as the young man staggered back a few steps and stared, mouth open, at the spreading stain where his arm used to be. The refugee directly behind—an elderly man—fell to his knees, clutching his chest. The nano-hardened shell had punched clean through the boy's shoulder. The rest of the refugees were being taken apart, bodies and limbs shattering under the unerringly accurate fusillade. Blood soaked the bone white sand, turned the foam at the edge of the water a cruel pink. The young boy walked a few jagged steps away from the group and fell forward into the thin undergrowth at the edge of the beach.

The shooting ended. The grandmother alone stood, looking down at the bodies. Her mouth was open, a soundless scream into the searing white.

Aran looked away, closing his eyes. His hand shook as he tried to wipe the sweat from his brow. "Okay, okay, we're done here."

Again, the whisper. "[The whole squad, Corporal.]"

"Huh? It's done."

"[Not all.]"

"The old woman? You're kidding me."

"[Your orders.]"

"Fuck you and your orders."

"[Are you disobeying a direc…]"

Static.

Then the world caught fire.

Whitelight whiteheat bloomed behind him. Aran shut his eyes instinctively against the incandescence, covered his face with his forearm. Wind started to pick up, rushing past him, faster and faster back towards the source of the light. His throat closed up as the oxygen was sucked out of the atmosphere. He reached over his shoulder and put his hand into his backpack, grasping for his environment mask. He tried to scream an obscenity as he yanked at the mask, but no sound would come from his mouth in the dying air. His lungs burned.

Aran shrugged off one of the straps of his backpack and started to tug at the second, when the wind dragged him along the top of the boulder. He slid from the edge, landing heavily on the hard earth below. The world started to dim.

He felt an object wedged under his shoulder. He moved his hand to it and touched something smooth, almost slick. The environment mask, dislodged by the fall. He pushed it against his face and immediately the straps wrapped themselves around his head, the intelligent PVC moulding itself around his face and skull. The processor at the mouth of the mask started extracting oxygen from the thin air. He breathed in deeply, the burning in his throat receding.

Aran struggled to one knee and looked back down the valley. The Regiment was gone. The jungle was gone. The valley was gone. A crater, perhaps a mile in diameter remained, the raw earth glowing a soft red. The jungle beyond was blackened, shrunken, for as far as he could see.

The wind died down.

He gasped. "Was that a nova bomb? How the hell did the Vietnamese get that?"

Courtesy of the nanos attached to his optic nerves, a small, glowing green name appeared on the inside of his retina, identifying the squad member speaking, KRIT: "[I heard they were dealing with the Californians. It must be true. That's the only place they could get one.]"

"Shit." He slowly got to his feet. "Well, we need to move. This has to be the start of a counter-attack in this area. Everyone come to my position."

After a couple of minutes a lone solider approached him. He wore a green chillcloak and an environment mask, the lifeless gold-reflective lenses staring back at Aran.

"Where's the rest?"

"[They weren't wearing environment masks. You said they weren't required. They're all dead.]"

Aran winced and looked away, down at the glowing crater. He winced again as he realised he was relieved that only Krit remained. Not only was he smart, he was the only one in the team not a common criminal. Krit was some sort of political dissident. Aran hadn't taken much notice when Krit explained his reasons for opposing the war, he was just glad to have one person in his squad unlikely to stab him if he gave unpopular orders.

Still, Aran was pretty sure Krit didn't much approve of him. He had a way of squinting at Aran out of the corner of his eyes like he was waiting, just waiting, for him to say something stupid.

"Okay, we need to move," Aran said, "the locators on our c-glyphs will be disrupted in this area. We'll be off the radar and assumed dead. Now's our chance to get to the Laos border and out of this war."

Krit removed his mask, hunkered down in the shade underneath the boulder. He shook his gaunt face slowly. "[Laos isn't even a tributary state like Thailand. It's part of the Chinese Economic Union. Even if we could make it that far, which we won't, they'd lock us up as soon as we crossed the border. The best option is to make it to the rear command base. Let them know what happened. It's probably a day's walk. We'll live if we keep on our cloaks and masks.]" Krit spoke Thai; Aran only English. His c-glyph translated the words directly into his eardrum, but it was always a couple of seconds behind. It made Krit look like he was in one of those ancient, badly dubbed spaghetti westerns.

An icon in the corner of his retina told him sufficient oxygen had returned to his immediate surroundings. Aran removed his mask as well. "Why not take our chances here? It's better than being cannon fodder in the Chinese Army."

Krit squinted towards the crater. "[There is no *here* here, corporal. Every town for two hundred kilometres has been bombed into oblivion. No food sources either. The Chinese air-force dropped genetic-scramblers on all the major crop formations. The whole area is crawling with either *Viet Minh* or Chinese army regulars. The first will shoot you on sight; the second will imprison you for desertion, make you confess your crimes on the freewave, and then shoot you. It is fifty degrees out here during the day and thirty-five in the evening. If a bullet or starvation doesn't kill you, then the sun will.]" Krit looked over at him. "[There's nothing here to take a chance on. This is the end.]"

Aran rested his head against the warm boulder, looking out at the desolation. The great crater crackled gently in the distance. Lines of sweat ran down his neck. "I shouldn't even be here." He looked over at Krit. "Haven't they learned from the Vietnam War? The one the Americans fought—when was it—nearly a hundred years ago?"

Krit smiled a small smile. "[The Chinese invaded Vietnam dozens of times over the past three thousand years. Unlike the Americans they won a few of those wars and occupied this land, from time to time. They see this as a tributary state, at the minimum.]"

"No one lives here? None at all?"

"[No. Not any more. Except a handful of the people of the sort we… encountered today, just passing through the wasteland.]"

Aran pulled at a small tube at the neck of his cloak and drank from it. His chillcloak gathered moisture that was in the air through synthetic pores, absorbing it into a small reserve built into the cloak. The water was warm. He drank deeply.

He choked, water sprayed from his mouth. He bent forward, his body taut as he coughed.

"[You okay?]" Krit was patting him on the back "[Water went down the wrong way?]"

Aran sat back. Face flushed. "Yeah," he breathed deeply. "Fuck." He blinked at the sunlight and sighed. He could do with a cool beer and a spliff. Right now that would almost feel as good as a ticket home.

He turned back to Krit and sighed. "You're right."

The small man sat in the shade, watching Aran through squinted eyes.

Aran grabbed his mask. "Let's move."

Aran and Krit stood on a low stage in front of the Thai and Chinese dignitaries. The medal presentation was in one of the gleaming function rooms of the Banyan Tree Hotel in central Bangkok. Red-and-yellow bunting shone in the bright lights, bottles of Johnny Walker Black stood at each table, efficient Thai waitresses glided around the room with steaming plates of noodles and tempeh and vegetables. At some of the tables near the front it looked and—suspiciously, tantalisingly—smelled like they were serving meat. Directly in front of Aran he noticed a vaguely familiar figure with an impressive bouffant of hair and a gleaming traditional collarless shirt, watching them from a glitter of Chinese generals. Krit whispered in his ear that it was the Thai prince.

The low buzz of conversation in the room halted as the medal ceremony began. The faces all turned towards him, remaining impassive as the medal was placed around his neck. An announcer to one side spoke of their bravery in the face of an attack with weaponry prohibited under the Hong Kong Accords. A Chinese media team filmed the proceedings, no doubt to be cut and re-cut for broadcast onto the freewave. Inspiring music would underlay the ceremony, pictures of soldiers who had fallen in the battle would intersperse the vision of Krit and Aran, as would some product placements of the latest military hardware being paraded through grey Beijing streets. Pictures of the military eating real meat would of course need to be cut, as would the prince knocking over drinks while trying to pull a waitress onto his lap.

Aran stepped up to the podium and began the short speech his minders had made him memorise. The usual pap: the four bonds of the Union, the generosity of the Chinese empire, something about greatness. They had been angry at first when they discovered he could not speak Mandarin. But he was from the West, so that could be used both an excuse and a publicity coup. Aran blinked in the glare of lights, trying to remember the closing lines.

"This is not freedom..." he blinked again and looked out at the audience. In silence they watched. Even the prince had put down his glass for a moment, looking up at the stage with dull watery eyes. The camera crew loitered nearby. Aran wiped at the sweat beading under his bottom lip, trying to recall the line. "I mean: this is not a jungle war, but a struggle for stability and freedom on every activity... on every front of human activity."

The colonel who had awarded the medals walked from the side of the low stage clapping. The crowd took the cue and began applauding, while Krit and Aran were ushered away.

Aran consoled himself with the knowledge that his verbal stumbling would be edited down to something coherent. The Chinese were desperate to spin the losses of Da Nang into a positive. To hold up Krit and Aran as heroes, as volunteers fighting for China, the only ones who'd inflicted any casualties during an overwhelming defeat. Aran tried to tell them during the debriefing that the espionage squad was probably refugees, but they wouldn't listen.

Aran looked down at his medal. The Third Order of Mao. The Chairman, in bronze, looking resolute towards the horizon. It felt heavy around his neck. Aran thought about booming rifle fire and pink foam in the sea. He ran a hand through his hair, trying to blink out the memories. He needed a drink.

They'd been given a nights leave. The freewave would no doubt show them celebrating before 'voluntarily' deciding to head back into the war. He wandered past the tables of dignitaries eating and drinking. No-one paid him any heed. When he got to the bar he noticed a row of expensive single malt whiskies on the top shelf. Rare, unavailable for most of the population. He doubted he'd have a chance to drink something this good again.

One of the Thai waitresses behind the bar saw him staring and reached for one of the bottles. She smiled as she poured, flashing small white teeth from a small round face. She wore a white collarless shirt pressed tight against her breasts.

He took the glass. "Thanks."

"You're welcome." She put the bottle down, glanced around to see if anyone was standing nearby, and spoke quietly, "You are quite famous Corporal. You have been on the news service for many days."

Aran smiled. "Really?"

She nodded.

"Please, call me Aran."

She smiled, brighter this time, her head bowing as she blushed.

"Your English is very good."

"Thank you. I take night courses." She tilted her head to one side, eyes fixed on his. "Do you speak Thai?

He grimaced. "No, sorry."

"Oh. Strange."

"Strange?"

She blushed again.

Aran shrugged. "Don't worry—most people just assume that I do. My family left here when I was very young." He sipped his scotch, savouring the honey and peat of the single malt, the warmth of it in his chest. "Anyway." He smiled, trying to approximate some charm. "I have the rest of tonight free before they send us back."

She watched him, waiting.

Aran took a longer chug of the scotch. He coughed into his hand. "I mean... I'm sure we'd be allowed to have a drink together when this function is over."

"You're staying here?"

"Yes. I have a room right at the top of the hotel. Fiftieth floor—a luxury suite. Three rooms, latest model *Tai* screen, marble everywhere. Um, have you eaten?"

She shook her head. "Staff are not allowed to eat here."

Aran nodded, "Sure. I understand." He finished his scotch, gave the glass to her so she could pour another. "Well, I don't have to stay here much longer, now that the presentation is done. I'm allowed anywhere in the hotel. We could go now, order some dinner. They wouldn't know it was you in my room. We could get some more drinks, download the latest holofilm." He held his glass high. "All courtesy of the Government of China."

She shook her head. "No. I cannot leave with you. Come through the staff door." She motioned with her eyes to a plain white door on one side of the room, her voice low. "Two hours. I know a way to your room where we will not be seen."

❧

The corridor was dark. Slats of light shone sideways from a handful of doors left ajar down the long corridor, function rooms, or kitchens, or bathrooms beyond. The *thrum thrum thrum* of music from a bar somewhere in the building echoing down the corridor. Aran followed the service entrance the waitress had shown him. It continued for some time, away from the function room. He swayed as he walked, head light and feet numb from the alcohol.

He'd probably been seen, but it didn't matter. The hotel was in lock-down: bioscans, ballistic detectors; the electromagnetic deflector had even been switched on for the prince and the generals. Squads of security personnel in polished black storm armour walked the perimeter, peering at passing river traffic through rifle scopes. There was no way in or out.

"Hi."

Aran started. The waitress was there, in the shadow of the doorway, a few meters further down the hallway. He peered into the darkness. "I didn't see you there."

Her small teeth glittered in the shadows. "This way, we will go by the freight elevator."

"[Wait.]"

Aran started a second time. He turned, the sudden movement making his head spin. He put a hand out on the wall to steady himself. He looked up to see Krit behind him, silhouetted in an open door.

"Oh Krit, hi, um, I've a…" Aran winked, pointed a thumb back at the waitress, "I've got something to attend to."

"[Aran you need to get out]'

"Get out? What do you mean?"

Krit took a step forward, the light falling directly on his face. His voice was quiet. "[I've got a way out of here. Tonight. I know people who can remove the control core in your c-glyph, destroy the locater completely.]"

The waitress moved next to Aran. She looked up at him, "What is going on?"

Aran waved her away. "It's nothing, I'll be with you in a minute." She looked at Krit, then nodded and backed away until she stood out of earshot.

Krit glanced at the waitress, then back at Aran. "[You don't belong here, foreigner. Time to go home.]"

"How would I do that?"

Krit pointed down the corridor. "[The basement. Behind the hydrogen generator there's a grate that's been removed, the pulse field around it deactivated. You can get through to the basement of the hotel next door, and from there back to the streets. We only have an hour's window before it switches back on, any longer and it'll be picked up in the hotel's internal scans. This is your last chance.]"

Aran nodded. "I'll be there."

Krit squinted at him. "[You better be. One more hour and you'll be chattel, a promotional tool for an illegal war.]"

Aran didn't know what chattel meant, but he assumed it wasn't a good thing. He held his hands up. "Please. I'll be there Krit."

Krit squinted for a moment longer, then walked past him down the corridor.

The waitress waited until Krit was out of sight before moving to Aran's side. He reached out and grabbed her hand. She pulled it away, took a step back. "What was he talking about? Don't you want to fight for the Chinese? I thought you were a war hero?"

Aran held out his palms. "Yes, yes, of course baby."

"Why is he talking about 'getting out'?"

Aran cleared his throat. A slender beam of light fell across her face, accentuating the smooth skin, the small mouth, the delicate ears. Her eyes were in shadow. She was pretty and Aran was feeling expansive from the expensive scotch he'd been downing all night. "Krit is a criminal, drafted into the Chinese forces. He's been looking for a way out since we walked into the jungle a few weeks ago. I told him I'd meet him later just to get rid of him."

Aran moved closer to the woman, grabbed her around the waist and pulled her towards him. She let him. He looked down into her dark brown eyes. "What I really want is to be with you. Now let's get out of here, okay?"

She put a hand on his chest. "So you are a volunteer? You want to fight for the Chinese?"

He felt the heat rising on his neck. "Um, yeah. Of course."

She smiled a small smile. "Good. I have a surprise for you."

❧

Aran was completely naked, sitting on the large plush bed in the centre of his suite. With the alcohol and the kissing and the game of getting him undressed, he wasn't sure how long he'd been in the room. Maybe thirty minutes, give or take. Through the haze of single malt and lust he felt his stomach knotting. Krit was waiting in the basement to help him get out of this mess, and here he was in his hotel room wondering what sort of panties this woman was wearing.

Aran rubbed his eyes with thumb and forefinger, whispered to himself. "Idiot." He shook his head and looked up at the woman. "What are you doing?"

The waitress was setting up a *Tai* recording unit—a small bronze stand with a light blue crystal lens—on the dresser, pointing it at the bed. It would capture perfect three dimensional images of the room. She spoke over her shoulder, "Recording it."

He held his hands down over his groin. "Why?

"For a—what's the word in English? A memento."

"Really?"

She turned and smiled, running her eyes over his slender torso and abdomen.

He blushed. "Um, babe, I hate to rush things now, when it's all getting so interesting, but is this going to take long?"

She raised her eyebrows. "In a hurry?"

"I have to meet someone," he winked, "but I'll be back of course."

She ran her hand down her shirt before hooking her thumb in her belt. Her pale slender fingers hung near the zip of her pants. "Don't worry, I will make it quick."

Aran smiled. It had been a long time since he'd been with a woman. Quick he could certainly do.

The waitress had undone a few buttons down the front of her shirt, hinting at a white bra underneath. Aran looked down at his hands. "I'm naked here. When am I going to see you?"

She tilted her head to one side, gave him a coy smile. "Now. Close your eyes."

He did so. He could hear her fiddling with something near the set of drawers, perhaps aligning the camera.

"You promise to keep them closed?"

"Promise." As Aran said the word he opened his left eye a slit.

She was coming towards him, something in her hand. She raised her arm. Aran saw the expression on her face then. Hate. That's what it was. Hatred, undiluted. He opened his eyes wide, bringing up his arms as she brought down hers.

"What the—" the loud snap of an electrical discharge sounded. Pain shot down his right arm, cutting through the haze of alcohol. Aran rolled sideways, falling off the bed. He pushed backwards along the floor away from the woman, then staggered to his feet. His arm dangled limp at his side, covered in blood. The smell of ozone hung in the air. The adrenalin had cleared his vision, he felt his good hand shaking.

She stood before him, watching. In her right hand was a pulse blade. Blue lines of electricity danced along its edges. "What is my name?" her voice seemed different, changed; tinged now with malice and blood.

"Huh?"

She took a step forward. "What's my name, war criminal?"

"War criminal? What?" He stepped back, his legs brushing the side table next to the bed.

"You never asked my name. That's no way to seduce a lady now, is it? We often like it when men care enough to ask our names." The knife hummed in her hand. "Names. Do you know the names of the Thai citizens forced to fight and die in the war against Vietnam?" She took another step forward. "Do you know the names of the innocent Vietnamese burned in nova strikes and paralysed by nerve sirens?"

Aran, wide-eyed, said nothing.

"Names. So many names. And men like you do not know a single one." She held the blade up, in front of her face, looking through the hissing blue air into his eyes. She switched to Thai "[A present for you from the Thai resistance.]" She turned her head slightly, perhaps to make sure the camera had a profile of her mouth when she spoke. "[This is what happens to collaborators.]"

"Wait!" Aran held up his left hand. He couldn't feel his right arm at all any more. "Why don't you stab a fucking general? They're the ones doing all the killing."

She let the blade dip slightly. "No one knows who they are, not the ones in this hotel, anyway. How many thousands of generals are there in this war? But everyone knows you, don't they? The foreigner, the Thai—"

"But I'm not Thai. I just—I just wanted to get laid. I shouldn't even be—"

"—the *traitor*. The butcher." She stepped forward again, speaking over him. Aran leaned back against the side table, the bedside lamp pressing into his buttocks. He reached down, grasped it as the waitress stepped forward, and hurled it. She moved her head to one side, but it wouldn't have hit: his aim left-handed was terrible. The lamp struck the dresser instead, shattering on impact, knocking over the recording unit. The woman was startled for a moment, and Aran, fuelled by the fumes of whisky and death, ran at her screaming. She brought her knife arm back for the strike, but too late, his shoulder striking her across the forehead. She staggered back and crumpled into the wall next to the chest of drawers, dropping the knife to the floor. It hit blade first, setting off a charge that sparked and smoked against the carpet.

Aran ran towards the hotel room door. His scream turned into a yell as his bare foot came down on broken lamp. He staggered, falling into the door head first, splattering blood on the white wood. He pushed himself up to his knees and looked behind. His foot was a bloody mess. He leaned against the door, breathing heavily.

The waitress moaned. She was getting to her feet, blood flowing from a split on her forehead. She looked around the room for a moment, eyes glazed, until she saw him. Her face seemed to clear. She reached down for the blade.

After dragging himself up, Aran turned the handle, and threw himself out into the corridor. He heard a buzz and crackle behind him as the woman slashed the air where he had been standing.

Aran shouted down the corridor, toward the elevators, where two guards in storm armour were posted. "Help!" He backed away from the bedroom door. "Help—someone's trying to kill me."

The woman burst from the room as the two black-sheathed figures began to move down the corridor.

Aran turned and ran in the other direction, back towards to the freight elevator the waitress had shown him. He heard her screaming, "Stop, stop, stop!" Each exhortation higher and louder than the one before. Heedless he ran down the thick green carpeted corridors, splattering them red as he turned the corners, left then right, then left. There were shouts behind him, followed by the distinctive percussion and echo of shots fired. Aran ran faster, taking corners wide, slamming into walls with his shoulders. He got to the freight elevator, pounded the button for down, leaving bloody handprints across the control panel. He leaned forward against the clean steel doors, breathing heavily, head cocked to the direction he had come from. There were yells and the stomping of heavy boots. They were coming.

"Come on," he grunted, hitting the control panel again. Aran looked at his hand. It was shaking. He clenched his fist. A dull pain came from his lacerated foot. Blood was still trickling down his limp forearm. Aran banged his head once against the door, left his head resting against the cool steel. "I shouldn't even be here."

The heavy footfalls were getting louder. People were yelling in Mandarin. He wasn't getting out of this one.

Aran looked up at the doors. "Please, I'll do anything. I'll..."

PING.

The elevator opened smoothly. He stepped inside, hit the button marked B. The doors were closing as the yells echoed through his c-glyph. "[Stop. You are ordered to stop immedia...]"

He leaned back and gave out a long ragged breath. The elevator fell rapidly, barrelling towards the basement below.

PING.

Aran emerged in the twilight heat of the basement. Large, anonymous machines groaned and hummed. The dull plascrete floor warm against his feet. He padded through the shadows of the machinery, looking in the dusk for the hydrogen fuel cell generator. Belatedly he realised he had no idea what one looked like. The elevator pinged somewhere behind him and he knew it was streaking back to the floors above to pick up a delivery of black-armoured men and women. Women and men coming for him with blunt-nosed machine guns and force rods and the power over life and death. He ran.

After a few minutes he realised the basement was too big. It stretched out into the dusk in every direction. He was dizzy, stumbling as he ran. He didn't know where the 'back' of it was. He wasn't even sure if his hour was up yet, whether the pulse field around the grill was reconnected.

He came to a halt near an old plastic stool sitting in the shadows against a dirty steel wall. Aran slumped down in it, looking back in the direction from which he'd come. Blood shone against the surface of the floor, one bloody right footprint repeated every meter or so. He leaned back against the warm machine and laughed softly. Not the hardest fugitive to track down.

Aran wondered if Krit was still waiting. "Krit?" He whispered.

Nothing.

He repeated the name, softly at first, then louder, over and over, until he was yelling. "Krit, Krit, KRIT!?"

The name echoed briefly, but was soon swallowed by the noise of the machines. He sighed and leaned back, wiping the sweat from his face. Neat lettering was printed in both Thai and Chinese on a steel plate riveted into the wall in front of him. Aran stared at the plaque, thinking about what would happen when he was recaptured. Prison, death, or back to the war. He wasn't sure which one he would prefer.

The c-glyph interpreted his stare as a request for translation. After s few seconds the nanos on his optic nerves activated. A translation visible only to his eyes appeared in the air in neat glowing red script about three feet away:

HYDROGEN FUEL CELL GENERATOR
100MW CAPACITY
DO NOT OPEN CONTROL PANEL WHILE GENERATOR IS IN OPERATION

Aran sat up straight. "Fuck."

A small, dark alley opened at the right of the machine. He staggered to his feet and down into the darkness. Soon he saw the dull gleam of a plascrete wall ahead. Behind the machine a grate sat on the ground, a black hole above it. He didn't care any more whether the pulse field was active. He threw himself in.

✎

Aran ran alongside the canal through the rain, slipping on the smooth slick stones from time to time. His knees battered, hands scraped, the wound on his foot opened up and bleeding. His right arm dangling uselessly by his side, bouncing in time to his balls as he ran through the dark and the wet.

They would be getting in boats now, coming down the canal, following his locater chip. But sanctuary was nearby. Home was nearby. He banged on the gates of the embassy, screaming, until a burly Australian in a military uniform came to the gate. The buttons on the shirt across the man's broad chest strained against the fabric.

Aran pushed his arm through the bars, imploring the guard. "I'm Australian."

The man looked down at Aran standing there, shivering and bloody and naked, then back down the canal. Sirens were flashing in the night on a series of craft racing out from the hotel dock. The guard nodded. "Better come in then, mate."

✎

White room. Black, plasteel table. Mirrored window against one wall.

Aran sat on an uncomfortable chair, staring at a young man in a grey suit standing across from him. Aran had on some crumpled tracksuit pants and a tee shirt they'd found for him. The shirt had the words, 'I've been to Bali, too' printed across the front. His arm was in a white sling—the wounds had been healed with a medical nano-spray, but the numbing effect of the pulse knife had yet to wear off.

The man in the grey suit was holding a palm screen, looking at its contents. "Aran Sintawichai?"

"Yes."

He looked up, gave a small smile. "I am John Borthwick, the consular officer here at the embassy." His speech was crisp, unaccented. Aran knew the type. He had worked in IT support for a while, for a company that serviced the Australian foreign affairs building. Aran had heard the young man's way of speaking there among the other diplomats. It was the sort of speech that formed after a dozen years at fenced-in international schools and a thousand conversations with diplomats from California and Northern Europe and India. The bumps and divots of cadence and tone buffed and smoothed to an unaffected sheen.

Aran got up, walked around the table and held out his good hand. "When can I go home?"

Borthwick grasped his hand for a moment. His grip was weak, his fingers soft. "I'm afraid I have some bad news."

Aran lowered his hand slowly. "What?"

The man cleared his throat. "How can I put this? It's quite delicate. I guess I should be straight with you, Mr Sintawichai. In light of you aiding another country in an illegal military action, Canberra has decided to revoke your citizenship."

"What?"

Borthwick held up the palm screen. "This decision came straight from the Minister."

"What?" Aran didn't feel quite right. He couldn't focus on the young man.

"Sorry. But this is from the top. You understand."

Aran shook his head slowly. "But I'm not Thai, I'm Australian. We moved there a few months after I was born. During the Tribute Crisis."

"You have *dual*-citizenship. And according to our records—and several recent, very popular Chinese freewave broadcasts—you've rather unfortunately been fighting for an enemy of Australia."

Aran shook his head again, more definitively. His eyes began to refocus. "They press-gang prisoners and homeless people into service to meet the volunteers quota imposed on Thailand, you moron. I was in lockup overnight for being caught with weed at a full-moon party. I'm a tourist."

"Hmm." Borthwick looked down at the small screen in his hand, "I see the Chinese gave you a medal for bravery during a fire fight with some Vietnamese troops."

Aran rubbed his temple with two fingers. "I didn't do anything to deserve it. I just killed... I think they were refugees."

Borthwick raised an eyebrow. "You're telling me you committed a war crime?"

"No... I..."

"Because that's what shooting unarmed refugees amounts to."

Aran put his hand down on the smooth black desk, his legs felt tired. His voice was soft. "You lecture me. You lecture me when Australia hasn't accepted refugees for a decade."

Borthwick pursed his lips. "I don't understand your point. We do have the sovereign right to determine the circumstances in which people come to Australia. We don't have the right to butcher innocent civilians."

"I didn't have a choice. I was following orders. If you don't follow orders in the Chinese army-"

Borthwick interrupted, shaking his head. "That's the Nuremberg defence Mr Sintawichai. You should know that historically," he smiled a pained smile, "it was not a successful one."

"You're following orders, aren't you?"

Borthwick paused. "I don't know what you mean."

He straightened, took a step closer. "What do you think is going to happen to me out there, arsehole? I'll be put back in the war. I'll be a dead man."

Borthwick waved away the suggestion with the flick of his fingers, "Orders or not, the point is moot, Mr Sintawichai." He drew in a deep breath, then smiled again. "Now, because of your links with Australia..."

"Links?" Aran felt himself going red, his good hand started to shake.

Borthwick held up one finger. "Because of your links with Australia, we have provided you with an explanation as to why you are no longer welcome in our country. We've given you first aid for your injuries. More than could be expected, really. But you're not Australian any more, Mr Sintawichai, and this," he pointed downwards, "is Australian land. It's time you left."

Aran did the only reasonable thing there was left to do. He kicked Borthwick in the balls. The man collapsed with a groan, eyes wide, holding himself. His palmscreen clattered on the clean white floor.

Aran stood over him. "Links? What are your links?" His voice was shaking, "You don't even have an accent, motherfucker. What are your fucking links?"

Borthwick responded with a groan.

He'd started yelling again when the burly Australian entered the room. The big man shook his head, a sad smile on his face. "Sorry about this mate."

The force rod came down.

Darkness fell.

❦

They stood on the baking airfield, waiting to board.

"[Sergeant Sintawichai, what's our destination?]"

Aran turned, looking down at the thin volunteer. "Da Nang."

"[What's there?]"

Aran looked off into the shimmering horizon. "Home."

ABOUT TR NAPPER

TR Napper worked as an international aid worker for ten years. He lived for several years in both Mongolia and Lao PDR. He has also worked in Papua New Guinea, Myanmar, and Indonesia. He currently resides in Hanoi, Vietnam. Over the past five years he has had numerous articles published at *The Guardian*, Australian Broadcasting Corporation's *The Drum*, *New Matilda*, and others. TR Napper has also had fiction published at OMNI Reboot. You can find him online at: www.nappertime.com, and follow him on Twitter here: @_Ruijin_

Bright Student

Terence Toh

~ Malaysia ~

The boy with the scorpion tattoo threw back his head and laughed.

It put Yi Ling in mind of the cry of a raven.

"The one thing my shop *doesn't* have!" he said. "And that's what you want!"

This is getting surreal, Yi Ling thought. She caught sight of her reflection staring back from the glass jars on the shelves all around her: it was almost hilarious how nervous she looked.

"What exactly do you need ginseng for?" the boy asked.

Yi Ling hesitated before answering.

"It improves your memory, right? I've got a big exam coming up, and I need all the brainpower I can get."

"Oh, is that so?" The boy smiled. "I have something far better for that."

He looked right into her eyes: he was a cobra, staring down its prey. Yi Ling was shocked at how green his eyes were.

"Imagine having a brain as swift as quicksilver, a memory as powerful as a mammoth's. Imagine if you could answer any question put forth to you, whether as trivial as a baby's name or as complex as the dance of the stars in the sky," he said. "I have something that can supercharge your brain. It's an old recipe given to me by my ancestors. You'll never have to worry about tests or any kind of academic challenge ever again. And all I ask in return is something simple."

Yi Ling shivered.

"It's not… my soul is it?"

The boy laughed again. "What would I want with a soul? Do I look like the devil or something? No, my dear. All I want is your shadow." He smiled.

"Excuse me?" Yi Ling thought she had misheard.

"Your shadow."

"But why?"

"We have our uses for it," the boy said. "Bottle it maybe, weave it into a cloak, or pickle it and serve it with rice and sambal. You'll be amazed what you can do with a shadow."

Sensing her hesitation, the boy spoke again.

"It's not like you really need it, right? What good has your shadow ever done for you? Seriously, when was the last time you even noticed it was there?"

Yi Ling had to admit that he had a point.

*

Five hours ago, everything had been normal.

A double period of Tort law lectures. Ugh. Yi Ling hated those. Two hours of Mr Ong droning on and on, his flat monotone turning the most sordid cases of harm and human injury into agonising exercises in staying awake.

She had gotten last week's Negligence assignment back. A bright red 'D-' was scrawled at the top of her paper, together with '*Poorly written,*' and '*Out of topic*' scrawled in her lecturer's messy handwriting underneath.

Yi Ling had wanted to cry. Five nights she had spent on this essay. All those long hours poring over textbooks and course materials, all wasted!

The results put her in a funk, and she had little mood for the day's lecture, which was on Vicarious Liability.

She should have copied off Kenny's paper, Yi Ling reflected sadly. It would have been the easiest thing to do. Kenny, the class swot, who lived and breathed the law, a man whose idea of fun was an evening in the library with a statute book and a mug of coffee. He also didn't go out much: one little smile, and he would have bent over backwards to help her score.

But no, she *had* to listen to Amira. Sweet, sanctimonious, Saint Amira of Petaling Jaya, always doing the honourable thing. "You should be ashamed of yourself!" she had lectured Yi Ling. "If you don't use your own effort, you might as well not try at all!" How they were best friends, Yi Ling sometimes couldn't understand.

It was easy for Amira to say, Yi Ling reflected bitterly. Amira was blessed with a quick brain and a marvellous memory. She also sported an impressive co-curricular résumé that would give any university recruiter a hard-on: the girl was a state debater and swimmer, for goodness sake. She would have no problem finding a scholarship.

Yi Ling, on the other hand, was getting seriously worried. That assignment had contributed 30% of her grade. She did some mental calculations: with her marks, she would need at least a B+ on the final paper to be accepted into a good university.

Fail that, and she could kiss her current lifestyle goodbye. Farewell to the bustling metropolis of Subang Jaya, with its clubs and bars, and hello again to the coffee shops and paddy fields of Alor Setar, her hometown. Her parents would put her in some God-forsaken university in the middle of nowhere with an oppressive dress code and dreary lecturers.

And she would rather kill herself than let that happen.

There has to be another way, she thought.

Yi Ling closed her eyes, and imagined sleeping with her lecturer.

It wouldn't be that bad, would it? Mr Ong, all 220 pounds of him, with his food-flecked beard and sweaty palms. She imagined lying beneath his colossal weight, pretending to climax as he huffed and puffed from the physical exertion: the man perspired walking from one end of the classroom to the other, for God's sake!

And that's if they even got to there. Mr Ong had probably never been laid in his life: would he even know what to do? Yi Ling wondered if her lecturer would be able to find his penis beneath all his rolls of fat. Or who knew, perhaps it had shrivelled up and dropped off, after decades of disuse. Grown a pair of wings and flown away, maybe.

The thought made her giggle.

Her laughter broke the silence: in the front of the classroom, Mr Ong stopped speaking. He glared at her momentarily before going back to his lecture.

Oh damn, that's not a good start, Yi Ling smiled.

She suddenly felt disgusted with herself. Three years ago, Yi Ling knew she would never even have contemplated anything like this.

But that had been before the days of the law degree. Before the days of the endless lectures, the ultra-competitive coursemates, the never-ending assignments and the death of her social life. Law school was the ultimate vampire. It drained everything from you: your finances, your time, your dignity, and peace of mind.

She needed to study harder, she told herself. Exams were in a week, and painstaking analysis of past year papers over the last seven years showed that examiners seemed to have a hard-on for questions on vicarious liability. Why, her seniors told her that in 2005, there had been *two* questions on the topic for Paper 3, which had thrown the entire class into disarray: most of them had expected occupier's liability and the rule of *Rylands v Fletcher.*

Law exams were tricky bastards.

Yi Ling was thankful when the lecture ended. She made sure to make an impression on Mr Ong on her way out: a flirty smile, laughter at his jokes, 'accidentally' brushing against his tremendous girth as she left the room.

Every little bit counts, she told herself.

Her housemate did not even look up at her as Yi Ling entered their apartment.

"Hey girl," Kumar said, his eyes not moving from his laptop.

He was tall, dark and scrawny, and had not shaved for days. Her housemate was seated on the sofa, a huge stack of files piled up by him. Thick textbooks formed a small tower on the table nearby, next to a steaming mug.

The television was on: a news channel on mute.

"Yo, Kumar," Yi Ling slumped next to him. "How's the project going?"

"Awful," he muttered. "Can't figure out this bloody diagram."

Oh. Well that meant she couldn't borrow his laptop then. Hers was in a shop in Digital Mall, having crashed two days ago.

Yi Ling glanced at Kumar's work.

...the fundamental thermodynamic relation is generally expressed as an infinitesimal change in internal energy in terms of infinitesimal changes in entropy...

She shuddered.

Kumar was in second year engineering. Being a Humanities student, Yi Ling didn't know what he actually studied, but knew he had a workload just as heavy as hers, believe it or not.

"I've been up all night trying to understand this," Kumar sighed. "Entropic theory. What the hell, man."

"Maybe you need a break," Yi Ling said. "Seriously, dude, your eye-bags are nasty."

"My pills are finished already," Kumar said. "I need to go to the clinic later."

Kumar had been taking sleeping pills since he was nineteen. It had all started during his A-Levels: his financially-strapped family had put a lot of stress on him to get a scholarship, and he had developed insomnia in the process.

After weeks of restless nights, Kumar had gone to the doctor, who first prescribed him pills called Lexotan. Kumar had tried them for a month, only to grow resistant: images of him flunking everything had been more powerful than the pill's sedative powers.

Now he was on Ativan, a stronger drug that Kumar said worked wonders. Yeah, he probably hadn't had a natural night's sleep in years. But that was the price you had to pay for academic excellence.

It was better that than end up like her ex-secondary school classmate Fiona. An image swam into Yi Ling's head: a sallow-faced, wiry-haired girl, with a scar on her face.

Fiona had been extremely driven. She had few friends, constantly barricading herself in the library with her textbooks, studying for up to 16 hours a day, as the rumours said.

For her School Certificate exam, she had scored 10 As… and a D.

The day after the results were announced, Fiona leapt off the top floor of a condominium. There had been an article in the paper.

Yi Ling shuddered at the memory. She would never get to that stage, she reassured herself. No matter how bad things got.

But she really needed a break: Yi Ling had not been anywhere other than classes or home for the past week now and every cell in her body cried out for deliverance.

Retail therapy. I need it now more than ever.

She left Kumar, and went to her room to change. After that, she picked up her phone, and called Amira.

Petaling Street. Kuala Lumpur's Chinatown. A hustling, bustling street, packed with traders of every conceivable shape and size, all peddling wares ranging from bootleg Hollywood blockbusters to imitation Italian handbags.

Amira and Yi Ling chatted as they walked beneath the prominent green arch that marked the street's entrance, and headed towards a row of stalls selling accessories.

Red lanterns marked with Chinese characters hung on strings from lamp posts. A grey-bearded man peddled wooden handicrafts from his wheelchair, while two Bangladeshi-looking fellows walked around with novelty pens and torchlights.

A Chinese man with spiked hair shouted at them in Cantonese from his pirated DVD stall: "*Ham tai, ham tai! Veli cheap!*"

Beside him, an elderly Malay woman stretched her hand over the clothes she was selling. Genuine Kalvin Cleins underwear.

In the air, the delicious smell of roasted peanuts mingled with the foul stench of an exposed drain.

There were many tourists, many of them haggling with vendors or taking photographs: an Australian man was smiling as he snapped a selfie with a pretty young handbag seller.

"Ooh, check that out!" Amira giggled as they passed a stall selling brooches. She wore a black t-shirt and jeans, matched with a blue headscarf. "A genuine Mockingjay pin!"

"How much?" she asked the elderly woman keeping shop.

"Forty ringgit," the woman replied in Malay.

"What?" Amira was shocked. "That's ridiculous!"

There was a small argument: Yi Ling watched in amusement as the woman haggled with her friend, eventually bringing down the price to 25 ringgit.

"And that's the way you do it," Amira said proudly as they both walked away.

"Whatever lah," Yi Ling smiled.

It was while they were walking past a row of Chinese food stalls that Yi Ling noticed something strange in an alleyway nearby.

There was a boy. He was pale, with brown wavy hair, and dressed in a black shirt and jeans. There was a large tattoo of a scorpion on his well-developed left biceps.

He smiled at Yi Ling.

And suddenly, he vanished.

Yi Ling blinked in amazement.

"Did you see that?" she asked Amira.

"See what?"

"That boy."

"Ooh. Was he cute?"

"Kinda." Yi Ling was hesitant. "Hey, uh, I'm just going to check out those stalls over there, okay?"

"Yeah sure," Amira said. "Knock yourself out. I'm getting some *char kuay teow*."

With that, Yi Ling walked nervously into the alley, which was dim and deserted. The only thing stirring were two or three feral cats, who miaowed in suspicion at Yi Ling as she passed.

Yi Ling shuddered.

The place stank. Piles and piles of old newspapers and scrap metal, next to overturned dustbins loaded with rotten food. What looked like human faeces was clogging up a drain. Graffiti was scribbled on the metal grilles and doors of the back of the shophouses forming the alley—most of it profane or political.

Why was she here? Yi Ling couldn't explain it. All she knew was she was suddenly filled with a morbid curiosity. There was something about that boy that intrigued her, and she knew she would not be at peace until she saw him again.

One of the feral cats hissed and arched its back. Yi Ling noticed it had only one hideous yellow eye. It clawed savagely at the empty air.

There was suddenly a voice. "Can I help you, miss?"

Yi Ling jumped: she whirled around to see the boy from earlier, standing at the tinted-glass doors of a shop.

But that shop wasn't there before! She could have sworn!

The boy smiled.

"Why don't you come in? There may be something here you're looking for."

The boy's shop was dusty and crammed, filled mostly with rows and rows of shelves. A stuffed eagle hung from the ceiling, while a medieval suit of armour stood in one corner.

Their contents of the jars on the shelves were unusual. One seemed to contain a shrunken head, while another held a wrinkled hand with six fingers. Another was labelled: 'The Tears of Your Lover upon Learning of Your Death.' Still another had what appeared to be a stillborn foetus submersed in a clear milky liquid. To Yi Ling's horror, it seemed to be moving.

Yi Ling had listened, half-bemused, half-scared, as the boy gave her a very strange offer.

"But… how are you going to take my shadow? Can you?" she asked.

"All you need to do is drink a special tea. It's a bit sour: it is made from some very rare herbs, after all. Old *Orang Bunian* recipe. You heard of them?" the boy asked.

Yi Ling nodded. The *Orang Bunian,* or 'Hidden People,' were right out of Malay folklore. They were a race of supernatural beings said to reside deep within the Malaysian jungle. Like the elves of Western legend, they were said to look like unnaturally beautiful humans, with access to magical powers beyond mortal understanding.

She had heard stories about them as a kid from her old housekeeper back in Alor Setar. Mak Cik Fatimah, grey-haired, snaggle-toothed, saronged, had used them as bogeymen to influence her behaviour. According to her, the *Bunian* were a race of tricksters, who liked nothing more than causing havoc.

"*Adik,* don't go out too late," Yi Ling remembered Mak Cik Fatimah telling her in Malay. "Or the *Orang Bunian* will catch you, and make you their slave!"

Yi Ling had always thought of the *Orang Bunian* as a myth.

Seeing this shop and its strange wares, however, she wasn't so sure any more.

The boy reached under the counter—he seemed to have an entire world down there—and pulled out an ancient-looking copper teapot, and a glass mug.

He poured a murky brew into the mug. It smelled of smoke and old leaves.

"How do I know this is safe?" Yi Ling asked. "How do I know you haven't drugged it?"

"You have my word that it is perfectly safe. All it will do is make you lose your shadow, and nothing more," the boy said.

"What about the getting smarter part?"

"That will happen. In a matter of days, you will be the brightest student in the class. You have the word of the *Bunian.*"

"Losing my shadow… it won't hurt me, will it?" Yi Ling asked.

The boy sighed. "What, do you think you're going to get shadow cancer or something?"

To her embarrassment, Yi Ling found her hands shaking as she picked up the mug. She pressed it to her lips, and said a silent prayer.

Part of her wanted to fling the mug into the boy's face, accuse him of scamming her. What he was suggesting was impossible! A violation of physics and biology and logic! Who knew what his real intentions were?

But Yi Ling was desperate. What did she have to lose, anyway?

She closed her eyes as she gulped down the brew. It was sour and burnt her throat, and Yi Ling forced herself not to throw up.

The boy smiled as she slammed the empty mug on the table with a loud *thunk.*

"That was awful," Yi Ling said. "Do you have any water?"

She stopped. For there was a hideous pain throbbing in her temples.

Yi Ling tried to speak, but her words were stuck in her throat. There was vertigo, and her knees were suddenly weak. Her vision blurred, before suddenly snapping back into focus. There was an unnatural brightness to the world that warped her senses and made her want to throw up.

Her head started to ache. Yi Ling clutched the counter for support.

"I thought you said—"

Yi Ling screamed. Her feet started to burn: it felt as if her heels were being forcibly ground by sandpaper.

The boy grinned. In her vertigo, his features twisted. No longer was he very handsome; instead, with his slit eyes, overly pointed chin and gnarled forehead, he resembled a crone from a medieval painting.

Yi Ling screamed in agony. Tears poured down her cheeks, smudging her makeup.

She was suddenly aware of a dark shape forming behind her. A strange cloud of nothingness—*how was it possible for nothing to have a shape?*—which billowed into a human silhouette.

Even through the burning pain in her feet, Yi Ling recognised the figure's faint outline.

It was *her.*

The boy now had a small plastic jar. He raised it and shouted some foreign words, and the shadow grew ill-defined, losing its features as it turned into a cloud that floated, like smoke in the wind, into the jar.

"You're going to do very well in your studies, Yi Ling," the boy laughed. "You're certainly going to shine."

That was the last thing Yi Ling remembered before she blacked out.

❧

"Hey. Hey, girl. Are you alright?"

There was a stinging pain. Someone had struck her on the cheek!

Yi Ling opened her eyes, blinking at the sudden infusion of light.

Amira was standing before her, her brow furrowed, panic in her eyes.

"Oh my God," she said. "I thought you were dead!"

"What the hell happened?"

"I don't know! I suddenly see you lying on the ground, muttering like *kena rasuk*, I was so scared—"

She was lying on a bench. How she had got there, she had no idea. The last thing she remembered was a good-looking boy with a scorpion tattoo and a strange column of smoke...

Holy shit.

Instinctively, she glanced at the dark alley she had been to earlier—it was no longer there. The space where Yi Ling had walked earlier was blocked (or replaced?) by a wall.

Somehow, she was not surprised.

Yi Ling forced herself to get up.

She was still in Petaling Street, on the road by the Chinese food stalls, where Amira had gone after she bought her Mockingjay pin. There were about a dozen curious onlookers nearby, all staring at them with a mixture of fear and amusement. A middle-aged Malay man in a football jersey was taking photos of her with his phone.

"Let's get out of here," Yi Ling said, self-conscious.

"Should we see a doctor?" Amira took her friend's hand. "You don't look good. Maybe we should—"

"No," Yi Ling said. "Let's go home. I have an assignment to finish."

And at that, they walked away.

❧

Seeing as the fainted girl was okay, the bystanders dispersed.

The Malay man with the camera phone smiled as he went through his shots. *They were both kinda pretty*, he thought. *Damn, I should have stepped in to help, got them indebted to me. Then ask them both out on a date, romance, threesome!*

As he went through his pictures, however, he noticed something peculiar.

It was a bright sunny day: his shots had been very clear.

The sunlight meant there were a lot of shadows. They were easy to spot: there was the shadow of the Malay girl on the ground. An Indian man and his son cast twin shadows on the nearby wall, with the shadow of a car nearby.

The girl who had just fainted, however, did not cast one. On the patch of road beside her, where her shadow should have been, there was nothing.

✎

That night, Kumar came home to a strange sight.

Yi Ling was sitting by the table in the hall, a huge stack of files before her.

She was furiously scribbling on a test-pad, her wrist moving so fast it was almost a blur. Sheets of paper were strewn all over the floor, all covered in Yi Ling's semi-cursive writing.

"Damn girl," Kumar said. "You alright?"

Yi Ling did not answer. Her eyes were glazed. Her lips were moving; she appeared to be muttering under her breath.

"…*acceptance*," she said, her voice a flat monotone. "*In the case of Jaran v Gorsby, it was established that if consideration is adequate yet not sufficient—*"

She did not stop writing.

"Yi Ling," Kumar said. "Can you hear me?"

"*…the person making the offer must then revoke his—*"

"Shit girl, snap out of it!"

Desperate, Kumar shook Yi Ling by the shoulders. Her body was unusually warm, and she was passive. Indeed, she didn't even seem to realise she was being shaken. Her wrists kept moving even after they had been forced off the paper.

Kumar was about to call an ambulance when she suddenly snapped back into life. The haze in her eyes disappeared, and her wrists fell limp.

"What just happened?" Yi Ling asked, dazed.

"You were in some kind of trance!" Kumar said. "Damn, girl, do you know how scary that was? Seeing you saying all that mumbo-jumbo like that—"

Yi Ling however, was not paying any attention.

She picked up the scattered papers on the floor, and slowly read them.

A wide smile broke out on her face.

"This is amazing!" she exclaimed, waving the papers in Kumar's face. "This is bloody amazing!"

"What is?" a baffled Kumar asked, but Yi Ling was in her own little world.

"It worked!" she screamed.

Kumar watched, bemused, as Yi Ling did a little dance for joy. He had no idea what was going on, but humoured her as she pulled him into an impromptu tango.

"Girl be crazy," he muttered as he retreated to his room. He had no time for this, he still had three more Physics chapters to cover, damn it!

After finally running out of energy, the beaming Yi Ling opened the window, and took a deep breath.

There was a full moon tonight.

And in its silvery light, Yi Ling practically *glowed.*

❧

"You wanted to see me, sir?" Yi Ling asked as she stepped into Mr Ong's office.

It had been a week since her visit to Petaling Street.

"Yes, I did," her lecturer nodded.

His desk was extremely messy, with empty pizza boxes and plastic drink cartons nestled amongst kitsch travel souvenirs and half-marked assignments.

Even with the window open, the room felt stuffy in the sweltering heat.

"Will this be long, sir?" she asked. "I need to go home soon, I'm not feeling very well—"

"Sit down, Yi Ling," Mr Ong said, motioning her to the seat in front of him.

"I just want to commend you on what a great job you've been doing," he said.

He held up a test paper: Yi Ling recognised it as an assignment she had completed two days ago.

"In all my five years of teaching, this is one of the best papers I have ever read," Mr Ong said. "Not only do you mention all the relevant cases, but your arguments are mature and well-presented. Seriously, there's a lot of stuff in here that's PhD material."

He cleared his throat.

"Indeed, the paper was so well-written that well… how do I put this… at first, I thought you might have been… cheating," Mr Ong's voice trailed off. "But after checking with Turnitin, and some other sources, I came to the conclusion that you couldn't have. A lot of your insight is fresh and completely original! No textbook in the world has them!"

Mr Ong stared at her briefly, before quickly turning away. He blinked in discomfort.

"Please excuse me for a while. I have sensitive eyes," he said.

He opened his drawer and took out a bottle of eye drops, which he quickly applied.

"Right then, where was I?" her lecturer said. "Oh yes."

He cleared his throat again.

"I'll be frank: before this, I'd almost given up hope in you. You didn't seem to be taking the course seriously… I mean, honestly, you were coming in late and sleeping! I figured you for one those spoilt rich kids, you know? The kind who cruise by courses on their parents' money… I was getting ready to put your name down for my re-sit classes!"

It was difficult to pay attention. Yi Ling's head was spinning, and her body was burning with a terrible fever. But she forced herself to look interested.

"Thank you for proving me wrong," Mr Ong said. "It seems that academically, you're a bit of a late bloomer, but when you do bloom, you bloom brightly. I have absolutely no doubt that you will do great in the exam, but I'll wish you all the best anyway. And remember, should you want a letter of recommendation for a university or anything, I'll be more than willing to write you one."

They shook hands.

"Anyway," Mr Ong said. "Forgive me for being rude, but… how do I put this? Have you done something with your skin?"

"What?"

"You seem… fairer. And your complexion… there's something about it that I can't explain," he struggled to find the words.

"I don't know what you're talking about," Yi Ling said.

She left the office, not even bothering to smile or wave goodbye. One, she was feeling unwell, and two, with her new brains, it's not like she needed to be nice to him any more.

The last week had been crazy.

Academically, Yi Ling had been excelling.

Her lecturers had all been extremely impressed at the sudden increase in quality of her legal arguments. Indeed, during a recent Jurispudence lecture, one of her answers had apparently been so magnificent that her teacher had taken notes. It was remarkable!

Her sudden boost of intelligence had been noticed by her classmates, who typically, had started sucking up to her. Yi Ling had to turn down countless requests to lend them her lecture notes or go with them for study group. Even Kenny was asking for her help, for God's sake!

She wouldn't have been able to help them anyway. How could she tell them that the secret of her success was supernatural, that the answers just 'magically' popped into her head?

Even more amazingly, Yi Ling found she was able to solve Kumar's physics assignments.

She was careful, however, not to let Kumar know this. Again, how would she explain it?

And so, Yi Ling had tried to be subtle. Tried hinting to Kumar he was going about this the wrong way, he had misunderstood a crucial theorem, maybe he should try different calculations, but her friend did not seem to get it at all. His dull wits frustrated her. How was he so *stupid?*

She was thankful for her sudden new talents. Exams started tomorrow, and she was not stressed. And all it had cost her had been her shadow. Which absolutely no one had noticed was missing.

Best deal ever.

Yi Ling worried, however, that she was falling ill.

It had started two days ago. She had been playing badminton with Amira when she suddenly felt an odd sensation in her chest. It had been bright and sunny at the time.

It had started off mild; a slight tingling. Yi Ling had shrugged it off at first. *Maybe my sports bra shrunk in the wash or something,* she thought. She hadn't had the luxury of free time in ages, and it felt good to be active again.

But the pain had slowly intensified, to the point where she collapsed in tears. Her entire body felt like it was on fire. A concerned Amira had brought her home. A thermometer revealed she had a high fever.

Yi Ling had barricaded herself in her room with chicken soup and copious amounts of water.

The next morning, she felt fine. But the burning pain returned periodically. Sometimes it was her chest, sometimes her head, her legs, her lower body, sometimes her entire being. It was as if someone had lit up a furnace in her soul, which was slowly roasting all her insides.

Today, there was extra agony. The heat was almost unbearable. Not to mention the nausea and discomfort. Yi Ling had taken three aspirins, to no avail. She wondered if she had caught some sort of flu. Oddly, there was no sweat; Yi Ling remained as dry as a bone, which she wasn't sure was good or not.

She staggered out of the college.

A friend waved at her, oblivious to her suffering. She did not have enough strength to reply. Yi Ling was glad she had not brought her backpack today. God knows if she could carry it.

She would not be able to make the walk back to her place. That she was sure. Especially not in the hot weather.

Yi Ling had never been what the Malays called a *puteri lilin*, or 'candle princess', a girl scared of heat, but given how she was feeling, she had to get out of the heat quickly.

She hailed a taxi, begging the driver to turn the air conditioning up as high as possible.

*

"Keep the change," Yi Ling tossed a 50-ringgit note at the driver, as she rushed back to her apartment.

It took every ounce of strength she had not to pass out. Normally, Yi Ling would take the stairs, but today, she headed straight to the elevator.

Her apartment was empty; Kumar had gone to a tutorial. Desperate, she pulled off her clothes and rushed to the bathroom, where she turned on the shower. Yi Ling closed her eyes and felt the water cascading all over her, delighting at the coolness.

It was almost orgasmic. *Hydrogasmic.* That really should be a word, she thought.

Her relief, however, was short-lived. After five minutes or so, despite the deluge of icy water washing all over her at full pressure, the overwhelming heat returned.

To make things worse, there was suddenly steam in the bathroom. It was perplexing; Yi Ling looked around for a while, before realising it was coming from her.

The water was boiling as it touched her skin!

"WHAT THE FUCK?" she screamed.

Trying not to pass out, Yi Ling rushed to the hall, where she turned on both the fan and air-conditioning. She thought about getting dressed, but decided not to. Yi Ling drew the curtains, and sat naked in the darkness. The cool air against her skin was refreshing.

She pulled up Kumar's laptop.

Too much heat in the body, she typed frantically into Google.

A million results; Yi Ling scrolled through eight or nine pages. Most of them were references to ancient Chinese medicine. Apparently heat was caused by too much *yin* energy in the body or something. She did not know how relevant all this was, but copied them down.

Just then, the door opened, and Kumar walked in.

"Holy shit!" Yi Ling screamed.

Quickly, she grabbed the sofa cushions nearby to cover herself. Kumar yelled and covered his eyes.

"What the hell?" Kumar turned to face the wall as Yi Ling ran to her room. "What did you do to yourself, girl?"

"I... I was hot, alright?" Yi Ling had thrown on a bikini, with a thin sheet over herself for extra modesty. Even that, however, felt stifling. "I didn't know you'd be home!"

"Tutorial cancelled," Kumar muttered. "If I'd known I'd have stayed for the show."

"I'm decent already, by the way!" Yi Ling shouted as Kumar headed to the couch, his hands still over his eyes. "You can stop doing that now!"

"No, girl," Kumar said. "I... I can't look at you!"

"What?" an indignant Yi Ling screamed, hitting him on the shoulder. "Look, I have been working on my diet, alright, and I know—"

"No, no!" Kumar protested, covering his eyes even tighter. "You're... you're shining!"

"What?" Yi Ling was perplexed.

"I don't know what you've been doing, girl, but it's not natural," Kumar said. He sat down on the sofa, facing away from her. "You're glowing in the dark! It's like fucking *Twilight*!"

"What do you mean?"

"Look." Kumar took out his phone, and snapped a picture of her.

"Make sure you delete that photo after this, I don't want you saving it in your Wank Bank or something," Yi Ling said.

She looked at the screen, and gasped.

The room had been in near darkness; the photo, however, looked as though it had been taken during a solar flare. It was badly overexposed. In its centre, Yi Ling's body was literally glowing with an intense white light. It was so bright that it obscured all her features, making her look barely human.

The picture reminded Yi Ling of pictures of saints she had seen when going to church with her mother in her youth, except for one crucial difference. While the people in those pictures had the light surround their figures, like an aura, in this picture, the light seemed to originate from the centre of her body, growing dimmer as it radiated outward.

"Holy shit." Yi Ling almost dropped the phone in shock.

"What have you been doing to yourself, girl?" Kumar asked. "Are you on drugs?"

"No," Yi Ling said, trying hard not to lose her breath. "This... this is different."

She told him what had happened. Kumar was shocked, especially after Yi Ling turned on the lights to reveal her missing shadow.

"Impossible," he said. "You can't remove shadows! They aren't even... things! They're just... just..."

He struggled for words, before throwing his hands in the air.

"I'll look it up on Wikipedia."

He went to his laptop.

"There! 'A shadow is an area where direct light from a light source cannot reach due to obstruction by an object,'" he quoted. "It's an area! How do you take away an area?"

"Well, that guy certainly managed to," Yi Ling said. "I think it was magic or something."

"Magic? You think this is Harry Potter?" Kumar was incredulous.

"Well, what does your precious science say about this, Mr Engineer? Can it explain why I'm suddenly missing a shadow, and why the hell I'm suddenly feeling this stupid heat?" Yi Ling was trying hard not to scream.

"Well," Kumar paused. "I'm slightly baffled on the first question. But as for the second... when light is blocked by an object, it forms a shadow. Since you can't form a shadow, the light has to go somewhere else…" He snapped his fingers. "It goes into you!"

"What?" Yi Ling was shocked.

"Can't you see, girl? You're absorbing all the light! That's why you're glowing like a lightbulb! That's why you're feeling so hot! The light that hits you cannot be converted into shadow, so it stays in your body!"

"Is that possible?" Yi Ling felt even more faint.

"I have to admit, it doesn't make sense scientifically," Kumar said. "But I think science went out the window long ago. Anyway, we better get this checked out. What's happening to you really can't be safe. I think you should go back to the shop. Get the guy to reverse this."

"I don't know," Yi Ling said. "The shop kinda… disappeared after I took the drink."

Kumar's eyebrows raised. "Seriously? Like in a horror movie?"

She nodded.

"The fact we can see the glow means the light must be in one of the upper layers of your skin," Kumar said, stroking his chin. "Probably the epidermis. But since we've only noticed this recently, maybe the light was first stored deeper inside you, and then slowly accumulated 'til… oh my God, this is crazy!" He decided to try another tactic. "Okay. So you can answer any question put to you, right? Have you tried… I don't know… asking yourself how to solve this problem?"

"It was the first thing I thought of! But it didn't work," Yi Ling said.

"Shit. Well, maybe you should get to a doctor." Kumar picked up his phone. "I know this guy you could try. I had a lecture with him once. He's this German expat that specialises in odd scientific phenomenon. He lives in Bangsar. We can drop by tomorrow, and—"

"Not tomorrow," Yi Ling said.

"What? Why?"

"It's the Tort paper! It starts at noon, and I really can't afford to—"

"Your exam? Is that all you can think of now?" Kumar was incredulous again.

"I can't miss it! My parents would skin me alive!" Yi Ling said.

She stared at Kumar. "Would you risk missing your final exam for something like this?"

Kumar barely took ten seconds to make his reply.

"Fair point," he said. "But immediately after the exam, we'll go, alright?"

He put his hand on Yi Ling's shoulder. "In the meantime, you take care of yourself. Keep away from bright lights."

Yi Ling laughed.

"Oh come on, Kumar, I know how to take care of myself."

❧

It was noisy outside the Weaver's College Multi Purpose Hall the next afternoon.

Students clustered in groups, many sleepy-eyed. Most carried textbooks or iPads with lecture notes. A tall Indian boy was chugging a flask of coffee, not caring about manners or decorum as brown streams of liquid flowed down his neck and soaked his shirt. Near the bathroom, about ten students were in a circle, eyes closed, head bowed in prayer; next to them, a boy was panicking. Apparently he had confused what paper it was today.

Yi Ling paid little notice to all of this. Her chest felt like it was on fire, and her heart was pounding so hard she feared it would burst.

A number of students instinctively turned to stare at her as she walked by, only to look away, blinking and rubbing their eyes.

Yi Ling had taken another picture of herself this morning. She was still shining, although thankfully she was slightly dimmer now. The glow was less noticeable in bright surroundings, although it apparently still irritated the eyes. She hoped the person sitting behind her had brought sunglasses.

It was a warm day. There were few clouds in the sky, and the sun was out in full glory. Yi Ling had worn the lightest clothing she could find: a spaghetti strap top and a cotton skirt. She had awoken an hour earlier to lather her skin with sunblock, and was carrying an umbrella.

Despite all that, she was already feeling faint.

Three hours. Just get through these three hours. That's all it takes. Soon, this nightmare will be over.

As she put her bag in the holding room nearby, Yi Ling noticed something unusual.

The edges of her bag's strap were singed.

Yi Ling forced it out of her mind as she entered the exam hall.

❧

Their seating positions were announced on a paper stuck to the hall's door.

Yi Ling noticed, to her dismay, that she would be sitting next to a window.

She went to the invigilator—a grumpy-looking Chinese man with horn-rimmed spectacles—and asked if she could change seats.

"I'm afraid not," he said. "The seating positions have all been fixed."

"But I have sensitive skin!" Yi Ling said. "I'll fall sick if I get too much sun."

"Do you have a medical certificate?" the invigilator asked.

And that was the end of that.

Yi Ling sighed. *It is only three hours*, she told herself.

She took her seat with the hundreds of other students, and listened to the exam briefing. The papers were soon passed out, face down. When the invigilator gave the signal, Yi Ling turned it over, and smiled.

Negligence! Defamation! *Donughue v Stevenson*! Nuisance!

And not a single question on Vicarious Liability!

Yi Ling smiled to see the reactions of her fellow candidates.

Three rows from her, Amira looked as though she was going to cry. One boy was just staring at the paper resignedly. Another was asleep, his head resting on his hands, apparently given up all hope.

The possibility of re-sits was looking extremely certain for them.

As strange as things turned out, it's lucky I took that bargain, Yi Ling thought.

She started to write.

Donughue v Stevenson is a landmark case which gave rise to an entirely new branch of law, namely, the law of tort. It all started when two women decided to purchase a bottle of ginger beer from a café in Paisley, Renfrewshire, only to discover...

Her pen sped across the paper at near-supersonic speed. Facts, cases, statutes, all these tumbled out of Yi Ling's mind so quickly she hardly had time to process them as they turned from thought to words on paper. In barely ten minutes, she had written two pages already.

Outside, the sun shone on.

✒

Two hours into the exam, students noticed a strange smell in the exam hall.

The rough odour of flesh and fire; the scent of meat left too long on the barbecue.

It started off subtle—a mere suggestion in the air, noticeable only if you took a whiff. Soon, however, it had intensified into a strangling, suffocating smell; a putrid odour that brought upon coughing and wheezing.

Some students took out handkerchiefs and tissues. Some covered their noses and mouths with their shirts and blouses. A boy in the third row coughed loudly as he rushed to the toilet. The sound of his puking was audible even from within the hall.

A vast majority of the students kept on writing, forcing themselves to ignore the smell. Come what may, they would finish the exam.

The invigilators searched all over the hall for the source of the smell. One of them—a young woman in a kebaya—was poking at the bottom of the walls with a plastic ruler, hoping to find a dead rat or something of the sort.

In her seat by the window, Yi Ling kept on writing.

Twelve sheets of paper already. And that was for the first two questions!

One more question to go. The rule in *Rylands v Fletcher*. Ooh, that had always been her favourite chapter!

Her head was starting to spin, and the burning sensation in her abdomen was almost unbearable. Her wrist and palm were starting to throb. But Yi Ling gritted her teeth. There was still so much to write! She wouldn't have been able to leave even if she wanted to. Her legs felt like lead, and her arm did not feel part of her any more—it was writing with a mind of its own, her brain spilling out facts like a faucet.

She barely noticed the discomfort of the students around her.

Just then, the invigilator from before, the one she had talked to, walked by her desk as he attempted to track down the scent.

He sniffed loudly by her, and did a double take.

The smell was coming from her!

A pretty girl, deathly, unnaturally pale, in a writing frenzy. But what was this? There were wafts of smoke rising from her arms and neck!

"Miss," the invigilator said. "Is everything alright?"

His voice broke the silence of the auditorium. Students from all over the hall craned their necks to look.

Yi Ling did not respond, so wrapped up in her work.

"Miss, I think you should come with me."

The invigilator placed his hand kindly on her shoulder.

There was an intense pain, and he let out a scream as he jerked his hand back. It was like touching a boiling kettle! The invigilator stared in shock at the bright red burn that had formed on his palm.

In five years of his invigilating, he never had anything like this.

The smell was beginning to get worse. At the front, the young lady invigilator had collapsed, and had to be brought out for air.

And Yi Ling kept scribbling on.

The invigilator knew that desperate steps had to be taken. He wrapped his hand in the sleeve of his jacket. Bracing himself, he grabbed the sheets of paper the girl was writing on.

"Young lady—"

"Give that back!"

Yi Ling screamed. She lashed out at the examiner, snatching the paper again.

Suddenly, there was an intense agony; Yi Ling screamed, and stared at her arm in shock. The sudden movement had caused her arm to literally *catch fire.*

Students started screaming.

Yi Ling screamed in agony as she beat her arms against her table, the wall, the window, hoping to extinguish the flames. This movement, however, only seemed to make things worse; the fire was spreading to her entire body. The heat was excruciating; so hot, it almost seemed cold. Her clothes were slowly consumed by the enveloping heat, and her skin blackened as if it were being roasted.

As agonising as the pain was, however, she saw something that really filled her heart with anguish.

A spark had spread to her exam papers, which were now ablaze.

"My papers!" she screamed. "Not my *fucking* papers!"

Around her, students were panicking. Many of them were running in terror, although one or two of them produced camera phones to record the incident. A loud fire alarm blared.

"Where is the bloody fire extinguisher?" the grumpy invigilator screamed.

Just then, he gave a strangled cry. He nearly wet himself as he saw the burning girl walk up to him. The smell of burnt flesh was overwhelming. There was barely any skin left on her, her face was a bloody mess of bone and tissue, and her hair was gone.

She shouldn't still be alive! And yet, she moved towards him.

There were a bunch of charred papers in her hands.

"I'm done, sir," Yi Ling said. "I hope I pass."

The flames had lessened. There was little pain; most of her nerves had already been burnt away.

Yi Ling pressed the papers into his trembling hands, and collapsed. Her body was almost completely blackened bone.

The invigilator screamed. His knees wobbling, he staggered to his feet and fled the hall.

His shadow was long and crooked against the walls.

LANGUAGE TRANSLATION
char kuay teow - a popular local rice noodle dish
kena rasuk - Malay for 'gotten possessed'

ABOUT TERENCE TOH

Terence Toh writes newspaper and magazine articles by day, and fiction by night. He is a merry wanderer of the night, constantly searching the world for fulfilment, inspiration and affordable plates of pasta. His short plays have been performed at the Short and Sweet Theatre and Musical festivals in Kuala Lumpur and Penang. Most recently, his short stories have been featured in the *KL Noir White* anthology published by Fixi Novo, and read on BFM Radio.

No Name Islands

Kawika Guillermo

~ Indonesia ~

The cargo ship in the bay was covered in such a heavy grey rain that it appeared like a whale, hovering still and alone, barely visible except in the occasional flash of lightening.

My sister Putri and I stood on the docks, waiting. We were used to the rain, having worked for over two years on that unnamed island, one of many privately owned islands in the Casr archipelago of northern Indonesia, a free economic zone where companies constructed biome plumes that produced weather catered to certain crops or animals. On the island of rain, the clouds unleashed a perpetual torrent of rainfall that grew enhanced stalks of rice like monsters swelling in pride. For two agonising years Putri and I worked on those rice terraces, high above the plains, high enough to see the smoke plumes linking to the sky like chains.

The man from the cruise ship arrived. Rain puttered on his wide yellow hood. "The captain will let you on," he said. "You can cook, right?"

I nodded.

The man looked to Putri. Her dark hair covered her eyes from beneath a transparent umbrella. "And her. Your friend. She can wash dishes?"

"She's my sister," I said.

"Really?" The man turned toward Putri, and then back to me, and my much lighter complexion. We had already given him nearly all of our two-year savings, so I saw no harm in placing some extra rupiah in his pocket.

He shrugged. "Whatever you say, chef."

❧

On the ship Putri and I shared a cabin with a large window to the ocean. The janitors and deckhands stared at us, marking their suspicions with turned eyebrows. It was obvious by our skin and hair that we were not really brother and sister, though she called me Ar-ta, "brother" in her native tongue. Thankfully, our lives were hidden behind the iron walls that separated the kitchen staff from the rest of the ship.

The cruise ship turned out to be the best gig Putri and I had since our expulsion from the island Aoro, Putri's native homeland. Like all the islands of the Casr archipelago, Aoro was set to be terraformed for a new crop, but first had to be scorched with clouds that rained fire to clear it of unwanted ecology. I was not supposed to be on the island. I was a light-skinned tourist with a penchant for traveling to unknown places, claiming land with every camera flash.

Aoro Journal Entry:
Day 1

Success! I'm off the map! Lovely island by the way, pristine and untouched. To think I'll be one of the last people ever to see Aoro in its primitive state.

Day 2

Hiked the red mountain today. Beautiful, but all the while heard loudspeakers warning "TERRAFORMING IN THREE DAYS. EVACUATE NOW."

Day 3

Some native people still on the island. Do they not understand the loudspeakers?

Day 4

One day left and there are A LOT of natives still here. They refuse to leave their homes. Will the company still go through with it?

Day 5

I left Day five blank. How do you describe when a strange man begs you to take his sister, and then disappears into the jungle? What do you think when you find yourself standing in line for the last boat off the island, holding the hand of a thirteen year old girl in a long yellow dress, whose name you do not even know?

After my shift in the kitchen I joined Putri on the upper deck of the cargo ship and felt the cool, dry air of a nearby desert island where biome plumes created a cloudless dry sky, perfect for growing enhanced tomatoes and cucumbers.

"I've never breathed air so thin," Putri said. "Like I'm not breathing at all. Makes me wanna spit."

"It's just like in Vel City," I responded. "Where I was born."

"If they ever let foreigners in Vel City, maybe I'll see it one day." She let spit bubble from her lips before spewing it into the ocean. "You know, the managers here won't buy our story much longer, *Ar-ta.*"

"There are other islands," I said. "Other jobs."

"What if we got married?" She wiped her mouth. "I'm old enough now." She tilted her head slightly, her dark brown eyes slightly dilated from the night's darkness. "I keep thinking. What if that's why my brother—my *real* brother—asked you to save me? For my people, who once worshipped the red mountain, lineage is all that matters. Pass on the seed, and we will never die." She spat again, perhaps in disgust. "Why else would he give me away to a young, male foreigner?"

For the first time I felt something pent up inside me as I observed her lithe figure in the darkness. Part of me, it seemed, had always, and would always, dream of her, with all the love I couldn't hold.

The next morning, grey clouds crawled towards the window of our cabin. I woke with Putri in my arms, still nude, to the bright white pallor of an island covered entirely in snow and ice. A great glacier was at its centre, and its shores were frozen over. Ice extended far into the horizon. A line of workers dressed in heavy coats unloaded metal that would be used to process canned fish.

"Ar-ta! Ar-ta!" Putri screeched, her face locked in a scream that would not come out. I saw what she saw. The jagged rock encased in ice that was once a waterfall. The plain of clean snow that was once a forest. The glacier that was once a red coloured mountain.

On the bed, Putri stood up, legs splayed, nude. She opened the window, letting that rush of freezing dry air envelope her naked body, shiver her skin, toss her hair wide.

"Come get it!" she screamed, throwing her fists like a boxer. "Come try me! I will never, ever die! I will never die! I will never die!"

ABOUT KAWIKA GUILLERMO

Kawika is a gender-confused lover, a gasoline-and-fire mixture of Irish, Chinese and Filipino, and a heathen with just enough faith to keep writing fiction. His work has appeared or is forthcoming in JMWW, Smokelong Quarterly, Annalemma, and The Monarch Review. He spends his days endlessly revising his novel in Nanjing, China, where he also teaches multicultural literature and edits for *decomP*. Visit his website at http://kawikaguillermo.com and follow him on twitter @kawikaguillermo.

THE DEAD OF THE NIGHT

Barry Rosenberg

~ Australia ~

An excited Peter drove at the speed limit from Gympie back to Nambour. The Council had asked *Paranormal Inc* to investigate a property. One sniff and Peter suspected vampires. He could hardly wait to tell Simone. They hadn't done battle with vampires for ages.

As he arrived home, thick clouds began to mass in the blue sky. He parked and hurried into the house. Simone, dark skin aglow, greeted Peter with a kiss.

"How'd it go?" she asked.

"Excellent." Peter opened his laptop. "Listen to this. Dimitri Romanesceau arrived in Gympie about eighteen-seventy for the gold rush. The other miners avoided him, accusing him of doing black magic. But guess what?"

"He found gold."

"He found gold." Peter tapped the laptop. "After scraping around for a few years, he found a seam."

"And became rich and happy ever after?"

"Not exactly." Peter had an angular jaw and sharp cheekbones. A tall stringy man of twenty-eight, he had a friendly face. It could harden and acquire sharp edges but that was a face rarely seen. When on a story, though, he was like a dog with a bone. "He had a cave-in. Apparently, that happened a lot to miners who weren't liked."

"Ones who found gold?"

"Yes. Anyway, two days after he was pronounced dead..."

"Did they find his body?" Simone asked.

"No. And they made sure no one dug him out. Whatever air he had down there, it wouldn't have lasted more'n an hour or so. Conveniently, the miners had a strike, or something." Peter shrugged. "No normal person would've survived two days."

"But?" Simone's eyes gleamed. She liked a good story. She loved a scary one.

"Two days later and there was a hole in the cave-in. A hole dug from the inside."

"Oh!" Simone shivered. "And the miners?"

"Two were there overnight. Supposedly to keep guard. They were found dead in the morning. Dead and bled."

"A vampire?" Simone's eyes gleamed with a touch of cold silver. "And? Anything else?"

"Dimitri had a property south of the mine. He'd built a ramshackle house on it. The miners say he dug himself a grave and lived in that. They didn't see him again and no more miners died."

"But?" Simone knew when there was more to tell.

"The occasional bushie disappeared. So did quite a few cats and dogs. After that, it went quiet. Well, the gold petered out and there were fewer vagrants. It was reckoned that he lived on raw roos and other wildlife."

Simone rested her elbows on the table. "This Dimitri sounds too cheap for a vampire, a half-bite, perhaps. Still, that's over a hundred years ago. What about now?"

"Well, the Council now own the property but no one will live there. There are bad smells and scary sounds. The rumour is that the vampire is still around."

"Really?" Simone went to the window. The Queensland sky was dark and ready to unleash dark torrents of tropical rain. "Still alive? But that now suggests a fully-fledged vampire." She turned around. "This is beginning to sound really strange."

Peter's angular face lit with a crooked smile. "It's said that he travelled through Java and dabbled in black magic. Their rituals also involved the use of blood."

"Really?" Simone repeated. "And so the Council wants us to deal with their problem?"

"That's our job."

"Vampires are tricky." Simone studied the threatening sky. "So, when do we start?"

"Not today." Peter referred to his laptop. "I said we'd start tomorrow."

Simone, nodding, glanced around their living room. They had an odd collection of objects. Shining skulls rested on desks, silver daggers hung on the walls, and books of magic filled the bookshelves. These objects, however, were not just for decoration. These were their working tools.

"Uh-huh." Simone headed for the bookcase. "I'd better work on my pronunciation for spells against vampires."

"Pronunciation is certainly important," Peter said. "That's why my parents shortened our name." He made a face. "Mind you, you think they would have done better than choosing Pan."

"Peter Pan." Simone shrugged her slim shoulders. "They weren't to know—a different culture and all that."

That afternoon, they decided to go to the beach. When Peter backed out of the driveway, though, he had an odd illusion. The walls of the garage shimmered and, instead, he saw a rundown shack. With a shiver, he shook his head. But though the image faded, a sense of disquiet remained. It was, he knew, a premonition. The house in Gympie was going to be a problem.

Pulling away from the kerb, they were soon on the road from Alexandra Headland to Mooloolaba Beach. Simone, catching glimpses of the sea, began to click her fingers. But her left eye silvered, causing her to stop humming and to concentrate instead on the view. What should have been bright sun and sand was hidden by a smoky veil.

It's the house in Gympie, she thought. *It won't be like anything we've seen before.*

At Mooloolaba, they stopped for coffee. Across the road, the ocean was blue and clear. Yet Simone still had the impression of smoke and haze.

"So," She put down her cup, "tell me more about Gympie."

This, she knew, must be the correct question for the sense of smoke immediately increased and she could feel her left eye change again. Peter also noticed the silvery glint and his scalp tingled. For Simone, trouble was a girl's best friend.

"Here are the old Gympie mines." Peter pointed to a map on his laptop. "On a couple of acres to the south is Dimitri's old shack. It's been bought and sold a few times but no one will stay. They simply pass it on at the best price. The Council wants us to deal with it."

Simone shivered as icy smoke ran along her spine. "It's full moon tomorrow and so the effect is probably at its strongest then."

"That's what the real estate agent said."

Simone switched from the map to a Word document. "Built by Dimitri Romanesceau. Romanesceau... Romanesceau..." she murmured. "Obviously from Romania."

"From Transylvania itself, home of Count Drac."

"Oh!" Simone's left eye flashed silver. "So we're back to vampires again."

On the following day, with a packed 4WD, they left at three for Gympie. In only fifty minutes, they were just south of the small town. Turning onto a minor road, they entered an outer suburb of rundown properties. The houses, made of timber, were set among dry grasses and tall gum trees. A few cows gathered around a trough on one property. At a second, a lone horse pressed against a fence. At a third, chickens pecked on the hard-packed earth. They didn't see any people. The farms didn't pay and their owners had to go to the seaside resorts to find work.

Further on, the scrub became taller and wilder. The road turned into a dirt track and the high wheels of the 4WD were needed for passing over rocky outgrowths. Where the track ended, they stopped at a weathered wooden gate that hung at an angle from rusted hinges. Though it was just mid-afternoon, shadows and smoke hid the clouds and the sky.

"This is it." Peter drew on thick gloves and took hold of the gate. As he scraped it across the gravel, spiders and beetles ran from the rotting wood. "We'd better watch out for snakes." He'd no sooner spoken than a dark shape, as long as Peter was tall, slithered into the grass. He watched it, ready to run but it quickly disappeared.

With the gate open, Peter drove further towards the house. Usually, one of them would close the gate but this time, they kept it open. So far all they could see were ragged wattles, palms with broken fronds and the stumps of rotten gum trees. Peter nudged the car up a slight rise until they spotted the remains of a hut. Tennis court-distance away, it lay below them in a slight dip.

Simone put her head out of the car window. "Something's here." She shivered though her eyes glinted.

Peter drove down a little into the dip. "Hardly anything is growing." He killed the engine. "Just withered grass and skinny trees."

From the back of the 4WD, Peter took out a long silver sword plus a gun that fired silver bullets. As he added a holster and sheath to his belt, it seemed as if cobwebs were sticking to the back of his mind. He turned. And jumped! A huge figure was reaching out for him. Then, heart pounding, he realised that it was only the shadow of frayed branches from a rotten gum.

Peter lightly massaged his chest. "Something's here all right." They walked down the dip and stopped near the door. Then, in case a living someone was in the hut, Peter called out, "Hello. Anyone around?"

He waited but there were no replies. No audible replies, anyway. But there were vicious vibrations in his head. Vibrations that wanted to push him back. Vibrations that snarled, *Go away! Go away!* As chills ran up and down his spine, he looked at Simone. She was leaning forward as if fighting against a wind. She was getting the vibrations as well.

Peter stepped closer. The walls were made of grey planks, warped and rotten with age. The roof was made of corrugated iron, so rusted that dark flakes, red as blood drifted down from it. Where he stood, the absence of two planks in the wall made enough space to serve as a doorway. Rectangular holes on either side formed the windows. They seemed like the two eyes on the opposite sides of a nose. Peter wiped away a cold sweat. The house was watching them. No wonder, no one could live here.

On the top of the house, a cylinder of corrugated iron formed a rough chimney. Further back, sprouting out from the sparse scrub, was the outhouse. A box of grey planks, it probably just covered a deep hole.

Peter nodded at it. "The dunny."

"The toilet," Simone said, her left eye shimmering. She toed the cracked soil. "It's completely dry. Everything's dry, virtually dead."

Peter knelt and bent a blade of grass. It snapped. He scuffed the ground and unearthed particles as white as bone. "Killing fields?" He looked up enquiringly. "I bet the grass was once lush and green." He rose, unholstered the gun and unsheathed the silver sword. The withered trees sucked the light out of the afternoon and the inside of the ruined house was a mess of moving shadows.

Simone withdrew a large torch from a shoulder bag.

"Keep the light on my feet," Peter said and stepped through the doorway.

To his wife watching, it was as if he'd stepped through the nose of a broken skull.

Moving slowly, Peter could see that warped planks formed the floor. They were also rotten so that he tested them with the sword before shuffling forward. In some spots the wood gave, showing joists that rested on packed earth. The remains of a single iron bed occupied one corner. A broken fireplace with ancient ashes was set in the middle of one of the walls. One pile of wood suggested a chair. Another suggested a table.

Peter twitched his nostrils. "I smell rot and… corruption… and psychic decay." He made a face. "It's pretty foul."

"Take care."

Knowing the rotten spots, Peter again slowly explored the room. This time he held the sword parallel to the ground as he dowsed for psychic impressions. "Vampires live for a long time," he said. "Especially if they can sleep in soil from their homeland." But the blade didn't move. "Strange, nothing. I expected the silver to react."

"You think there's a cellar?" Simone watched from the doorway. "Perhaps he's buried under the planks?"

"Could be." Peter, taking small safe steps, left the room for the weary grass. "But I don't think so." He sheathed the silver sword. "I don't know what we've got here."

"But we'll find out at midnight." Simone gripped his arm. As usual, fear and excitement were giving her strength. One eye was as black as obsidian. The other was speckled with silver.

"We've still got a few hours then." Peter holstered his gun. "Let's eat."

They drove into town and over a long meal, they browsed the Internet.

Simone suddenly sat upright. "What's this?" She pointed to a photo of a skeleton. A number of tools were also scattered around its shallow grave. She read from the website. "A miner was murdered, apparently for his gold. But there's a note; the body was strangely desiccated."

Peter studied the image. "Yep, Dimitri's work." He glanced out of the window. The moon was visible behind a veil of ragged clouds. "Let's go back." He rose and his face was grim. "I hope we can handle this."

Simone shivered. "I hope so, too. But it feels quite different from anything we've ever met before."

When they returned, the shallow dip that held the shack was as dark as a bowl of ink. Walking down to the house left trails of inky smoke that clung to the two, clutching fingers that tried to hold them back.

Peter rubbed his arms. "Getting colder."

The inky black flowed in, out of, and around his body. The moon was a bleached white so that the timber walls gleamed as bright as an ancient skull.

Simone shone her torchlight through the doorway. "The chill is coming from inside."

Peter put a finger to his lips. He could hear a *thump-thump, thump-thump*. His heart echoed the sound and it took all of his control not to run away.

Go away! the house warned them. *Go away!*

In Peter's mind, the words were an inky, icy smoke dripping like blood. The air was deathly silent. No wind rustled the spare trees. No owls hooted. No night creatures disturbed the withered grass. Other creatures had shown more sense than they. The animals had heeded the warning and left.

Peter looked at his watch. "It's almost the witching hour."

"Vampire time." Simone poised on the verge of change. "You think we'll really see a vampire?"

"I don't know." Peter touched the scabbard. "The sword didn't react."

"Yes!" Simone clenched her fists and abruptly faced to the cloud-tossed sky. "Vampire, come! Vampire! Vampire!" Her eyes were silver orbs.

Peter, retaining more control, looked around. Despite the impression of being in an inky well, the white moon was still bright enough to show the green of the 4WD and the bone-white of the shack. Eyes half-closed, he lent against the vehicle's bonnet and let his other senses take over. After an unknown time, he pointed towards the shack.

"Look," he said. "Look but not with eyes alone."

They both moved forward. A black shape was slithering out of the doorway.

"The python?" Simone said.

"It's longer, bigger." Peter dropped his hand to touch the comfort of the silver sword. "It's almost like smoke, flowing smoke."

"Shall we go in?"

"Not yet." Peter shook his head. "Let's wait and see."

He held the sword, his hand shaking slightly. A storm cloud covered the moon and slowly moved aside. A howl came from somewhere—perhaps from the house—and his hair stood on end. There was a movement inside the shack. Peter swallowed but forced his hand to hold steady. Then a dark shape, unexpected despite his expectations, filled the doorway and Peter gasped.

This was no movie vampire. It was not slicked back hair and carefully tailored fangs. This thing would never have won any awards for looks. Human in shape, its form was constantly shifting as if it truly were made of smoke. The top of its head was flat but the front extended slightly into a snout. Its hair was thick, almost a kind of fur. The smoke-formed eyes did not change as rapidly as the body but maintained a bilious glow that gleamed with malicious intelligence. The creature opened its mouth and the white moon reflected from viciously curved fangs.

Unconsciously, Peter and Simone backed away.

Consciously, they stepped forward.

"Take the sword!" Peter passed it across. Then he took the safety off the gun. The vampire howled and waves of chill rode over Peter. "That head!" He cried through chattering teeth. "That's dingo or fruit bat."

"Or both."

The creature sidled towards them. It started slowly as if the doorway that framed it also held it. Peter stared. From its smoky shape, thin and cobwebby strands of smoke attached it to the wood. For one step... two steps... three steps... the vampire-thing struggled forward. Then it was free and, with a surge like wind blowing over a forest fire, it rushed forward.

Peter braced himself. Simone raised the sword. He fired the gun. The flash of light headed straight for the body. But it had no effect. He fired again and again. Yet the silver bullets had no effect. At the last moment, he threw himself to the side. Simone swung the sword and cut the creature in half. But it refused to be cut. The sword flowed through smoke and the shape reformed.

The vampire fought towards them as they struggled to step back.

At the top of the dip, the creature halted. It had reached a boundary and could go no further. Peter and Simone stumbled further away, struggling for breath. They recovered to see that the vampire was still trying to get at them. It was like a wild dog at the end of its tether. Its human part cursed them, a strange tongue piercing their eardrums.

"We had no effect on it." Simone was panting as if she'd just run a race. "What the hell is it?"

"What the hell, indeed. It's so… so insubstantial. It's almost like a… like a…"

"Like a what?!"

Suddenly, Peter bent, grabbed a handful of dirt and threw it at the creature. The dirt touched, almost. Almost and then they came flying back.

"Look!" Peter cried. "Our silver just goes through him. His bites and nails just go through us. But you saw what happened to those leaves and dirt. They came straight back. So what do you reckon?"

"It's not real?" Simone spoke slowly. So slowly, she came to a stop. "It's vampiric but not a vampire. It is not a vampire, it's a… It's a ghost of a vampire!"

"Yes! What we're seeing—no, not seeing but sensing—is poltergeist activity." Peter raced back to the 4WD. "He's psychically sensitive to us and we're psychically sensitive to him. Non-sensitives would get the chill and the dread, all right. They'd run but they wouldn't see what we see."

"So, we're really in the shit!" Simone laughed wildly. "He's like a very old teenage poltergeist. What the hell do we do?"

"You know what we have to do."

"Yes, but it's been a while…" Simone stopped speaking.

"And it's bloody dangerous."

Simone released another laugh, wild but not hysterical. "That's what I'm here for. That's what me ol' granpa raised me for."

"Okay." Peter took a deep breath. "Then show me your face before you were born."

"Corny, Peter, corny." Simone laughed again, a sound that made the vampire fight even harder to get at them.

Peter, however, ignored the creature's howls. He stayed very still and dived deep within. Subtle changes began to take place. Soon, Peter Pan was no more but Pieter Pantrowski resurfaced. This was not a person who might stay forever young. Indeed, the hardness of his face suggested that he had never been young. This was the face of a warrior. This was a Pieter who did not back down. This was his face before he'd been born.

Simone had also transformed. It began with her eyes: one becoming obsidian and the other again turning silver. Next, she'd stripped and wrapped a loincloth around her waist. Over her bare breasts, she drew lines using mud taken from the sacred part of her garden. Dots and swirls went over her face. This was what her granpa had taught her. This was dreamtime for warriors.

Simone took a spear from the back of the 4WD. Strange symbols were carved into its length. Curious hangings clacked and clapped to make disturbing noises. As she stamped her feet, she repeatedly thrust the spear at the vampire. Both of them were chanting magic incantations—Simone using high frequencies, Pieter using low.

More than human, they advanced towards the Dimitri-thing. He/it tried to sink his fangs into them. But this was no longer a physical attempt. The creature now knew that he needed to sink his psychic venom into their minds, into their spirits.

With his mixture of European and Javanese witchcraft, Dimitri had so far always been victorious. Yet these two kept changing their attack. First Pieter dominated with his European roots; roots that matched those of Dimitri. Then Simone dominated and her indigenous roots were older, deeper, and far more powerful.

As the battle was fought, the vampire's smoky form went from black to deep blue and then to brown. It started to retreat. Snarling and spitting, it backed into the skull-like house. The place that was its sanctuary and that also was its coffin.

Pieter and Simone pushed at it, slowly but inexorably. At the doorway, the snout jaw opened wide and its fangs bit down towards Pieter's shoulder. But it was held at bay by the spear penetrating its wispy flesh. The two continued with their purifying incantations and, finally, entered the house. The smoky figure howled and became even more insubstantial. They walked the whole of the room with their fierce chant. The wispy grey smoke was almost transparent. Then, under the purifying pressure of their chants, it burst into flames until it had completely vanished.

The room slowly lost its foul smell and chill. Yet still they continued. They maintained the exorcism until the first blush of pink touched the gathering of clouds. When, at last, they stopped, they heard a miracle. A bird landed on a branch of one of the dying trees and sang. A magpie hopped into the doorway and regarded them with curiosity. For the first time in a hundred years, birds flew around the shack.

Weary to the bone, they walked out and into the brightening day. After a few steps, they turned to look back. The shack no longer looked like a skull.

"It's gone." Simone's eyes had lost their silver sheen.

"Moved on." Tiny changes returned Pieter's face to the soft features of Peter. "I thought we'd meet a vampire. I never thought we'd meet the ghost of one."

"The ghost of a vampire."

Simone looked at the trees. Their branches no longer seemed like the gnarled and reaching hands of the dead. They seemed like they might once more be ready to come alive.

ABOUT BARRY ROSENBERG

Barry was born in London but moved to Canberra, Australia, after completing a PhD in visual information processing. Becoming involved in meditation, he left research to concentrate on tai chi and meditation. Nowadays, Barry lives on the Sunshine Coast, Queensland, where he combines writing with woodwork. He began writing poetry in 1975. Since the 1990s, he has been writing speculative fiction. In the past few years, Barry has had 3 novels published by small publishing companies and a dozen short stories.

YAMADA'S ARMADA

Eeleen Lee

~ Singapore ~

Nicky's memories were stained red long after the incident on Rig-One. But on that morning Nicky had no idea when he stood on the Double-Helix Bridge, squinting up at the linked hotel towers that loomed over Marina Bay, Singapore. He was just the new intern for the lifestyle magazine, *Neo Haven*, sent to interview the reclusive celebrity chef Hiro Yamada.

Nicky had the same amount of information about Hiro Yamada as most people living in Malaysia and Singapore—not much at all. After the Three Year Southeast Asian Firewall-Siege, these countries relaxed their myriad cyber-fortifications. Foreign news access was cut off in that time, although some internet connection had trickled in via pirate satellite relay. When the attacks finally ceased new regulations were implemented to ease strain on the fragile infrastructure.

In order to gain internet access and other communication privileges you had to earn them per month, along with your basic wage. Unlimited access became reserved for Movers or Shakers. Movers had to display social mobility or business acumen, whereas Shakers were Movers who later became famous. The famous few, like Hiro Yamada, were granted tax shelter and permanent residency in Malaysia and Singapore. The celebrity circus of Movers and Shakers was dubbed "The Game" in the definitive by its active players, whereas spectators inserted an expletive of their choice between the words.

The Game showed signs of missing one of its key players. Nicky had poured over his notes about Hiro Yamada the previous night: reclusive celebrity chef, dubbed with the epithet "Sugar Samurai" after his signature trick of spinning threads of sucrose so fine they split when dropped onto a blade of a katana.

After a series of world tours and talk-show appearances, Yamada was diagnosed with throat cancer, and retired to live at sea on his houseboat. He re-emerged into the gastronomic world after a three year hiatus, apparently fully recovered. What Yamada allegedly lacked in gustatory sense he made up for in visual and tactile innovation, drawing on his background as a biochemist. He opened a chain of concept 'candy bars' in Tokyo, New York, and Singapore. Glow-in-the-dark sorbets (using extracts from luminous sea algae), 'pearls' of white chocolate and wasabi made by dipping them into liquid nitrogen. Grenadine was one of Yamada's favourite ingredients, but just another word to Nicky, who sipped his algae tea and subsisted on glass noodles as he did his research.

The azure water beckoned to Nicky to take a swim as he leant on the chromed handrail of the Helix Bridge. Nothing lived in the water down there except for nanobots, tailored microbes and other synthetic scavengers. They sanitised the seawater to neutralise any lingering pathogens and odours and changed colour according to atmospheric conditions. Tonight the sea was programmed to turn silver in celebration of the Mid-Autumn Festival.

Nicky entered the hotel lobby, polished and lit to such extreme brightness he had to wear his sunglasses indoors. The press and media pass freshly tattooed in yellow and black ink onto his forearm still stung, as the lift sensors hummed and scanned his body for weapons and hitchhiking microbes.

The lift stopped at the SkyPark on the roof of the hotel. Nicky did not know what to expect since his last visit to the hotel when he was a boy, before it added two more blocks and a subterranean park. Is the high tea buffet still open to members of the public? Do domesticated Mekong River dolphins still frolic with hotel guests in the extended infinity pool?

A foreshortened slab of undulating scarlet water greets Nicky when he gets out from the lift—no dolphins or people are in the swimming pool today. As Nicky made his way out into the sun, the pool's sheer length is enhanced by the levitating sun loungers and potted travellers palms lining the edge.

Nicky walked halfway along the two-hundred and fifty metre pool before he squatted down to plunge his hand into the red water. In spite of the colour it felt like any other public pool—warm water undercut by cool currents. Nicky licked his fingertip and recognised a gamut of flavours from his early childhood. Sour tang then sweet aftertaste as it slipped to the back of his throat. Cranberry. The real stuff, not a cocktail of lab-developed simulants derived from seed bank extracts. The mixture was laced with preservatives to keep it from going off under the sun.

So, the social underground media rumours were confirmed—Yamada's sponsors paid for a new pool in any hotel he stayed and filled up its swimming pool with any sweet liquid of his choice. This extravagance was both publicity stunt and corporate rivalry. Who was footing the bill for this latest display?

A skinny Eurasian girl in a gun-metal grey sheath dress descended from her perch on a nearby levitating sun lounger and strode towards Nicky with trademark PR impatience. She held out her left hand for Nicky to shake, perpetually crooked at the wrist from always checking the time.

"Hi, I'm Chelsea. Congratulations, you've passed the test."

Nicky looked back from where he emerged from the transparent lift doors, checking for scanners or biometric equipment.

"You dipped your hand into the pool," explained Chelsea. "Mr Yamada refuses to speak to journalists who don't possess an innate sense of curiosity."

Chelsea remained on the edge of the pool to show Nicky that she will not lead him to Yamada's executive suite. "Mr Yamada will see you on Rig-One tomorrow morning."

"Non-Movers aren't allowed on Rig-One."

"The Game moves as you play it." Chelsea the publicist recited the catchphrase, but she could not resist a pointed glance at Nicky's media tattoo, a mere temporary pass.

"Any questions before you meet Hiro Yamada?"

Nicky wipes his hand on his trousers, "How'd you get so much cranberry cordial to fill up the pool?"

"Grenadine." Chelsea corrected him and rolled her eyes at Nicky's faux pas. She took her leave of him, but not before turning around and putting a finger to her lips, "Trade secret."

Chelsea left Nicky smarting from her aside by the grenadine-filled pool. He glimpsed his reflection dissolving in the red water. Enough to make cocktails for his neighbourhood in the Jurong West Sprawl, where his family lived inside the husk of an old shopping mall. The pool gave the illusion that the water extended to the horizon. In reality, the water spilt over the edge into a catchment area below and was then pumped back into the pool.

In his ear stud, Nicky's recording software entity beeped to indicate Nicky had left it online since he entered the hotel. Hence, all live audio recordings were auto-uploaded to a cloud.

If he pulls off the Yamada interview the powers-that-be may offer him a better room than he is working in now, and Nicky will afford the deposit on the studio apartment in the Green Lace Aquatecture Belt along the old Sungei Buloh wetlands. The e-brochures offered artists' impressions of cascading blue steel—frozen wavelike platforms, apartments and walkways suspended over the former mangrove swamps.

Nicky looked off into the distance, and saw the Marina Financial District barricaded behind the Tide Barrier, overlooking the harbour. He went to the District twice when he was still fresh out of college but failed both job interviews.

❦

Rig-One stood in the Singapore Strait, between Changi and Marina Bay. Nicky arrived early at the pier. Floating steel modules interlinked to form a floating covered walkway extended from Marina South Pier to Rig-One. The armed guards and police officers at the checkpoint admitted Nicky after he showed them his upgraded media tattoo. They reminded him to limit his RSE to audio recording setting at the guardpost.

As Nicky strolled inside the modules, the support struts gave him the impression of walking inside the ribs of a gargantuan sea serpent. He peered out between ribs at the harbour scene beyond the tempered glass—no signs of sharks or other large fish. But there were long dark shapes attached to the underside of the walkway, visible through the glass floor, waving like prayer flags in the water. Nicky pressed his ear to the surface of the glass and listened to the rhythms of Marina South—clankings of construction accented by foghorn blasts of distant freighters.

Nicky did not stop at the shopping arcade. He saw no reason to take in the monastic ambience, the place was empty except for cleaners and service staff. But the RSE was going into overload as it picked up humming, buzzing, and emanations of piezoelectronics in the cool dry arcade. The jagged coral outcrop replicas emanated menace while unnecessary signs floated around, warning non-existent shoppers not to touch the merchandise unless they intended to purchase it. Nicky wanted a bottle of distilled water. Perhaps being in the middle of the over-saturated sea has triggered his thirst.

The shopping arcade was empty—tourists never ventured outside of Rig-One. Holographic light displays of scarlet twist in curlicues in front of Nicky. It is the symbol for Rig-One's medical tourism, the hermaphroditic sea-slug known as the Spanish dancer. Nicky tried not to laugh; perhaps Hiro Yamada would announce a sex-change during his interview?

Nicky progressed further inside another module, moved along by an extensive travellator that sloped downwards. The sea was murky outside the glass, but Nicky was disappointed to see nothing swimming in this area. Most seafood was harvested in designated catchment areas off Chek Jawa. More black pennants were attached to the base of Rig-One and it is suddenly clear to Nicky that Rig-One, like many marine artificial structures, is not what it seems.

Rig-One was not based on standard oil rig design—an offshore platform built on top of legs secured to the seafloor. The pioneering headquarters of Malaysia and Singapore's medical tourism industry was a compliant tower: a framed structure extending from the seabed to a position above the surface. The hospital and living quarters were distributed throughout the structure's levels. If the tower should sway about its base in response to environmental forces, the rest of the structure would feel little movement.

Alighting from the travellator, Nicky saw more compliant towers through the windows. There were more rigs, numbered from Two to Nine, were arranged in the distance like an approaching fleet of ships.

Along the corridor were pockets of seaweed and algae arranged in neat glass displays. Nicky reached the visitor's centre, which housed a ten-foot aquarium tank in the wall behind the reception. He recognised the scarlet fronds hidden among the coral as the hermaphrodite sea slugs called Spanish Dancers. Most medical tourists still flocked to Rig-One—the place for major operations and gender reassignment.

The receptionist looked up from filing her nails, although she didn't have real nails as Nicky saw chrome-plated talons. He showed her his media tattoo and the receptionist held a scanner over it to verify Nicky's security clearance.

"No need for that, he's with me." Nicky suddenly heard Chelsea behind him. Chelsea, donning a pair of fetching spiked earrings and a stretched smile, was accompanied by two men in white boiler suits. Both men were so tanned that their skins took on a purplish hue under the fluorescent light. One man had long scars scoured around his mouth whereas the other had neck tattoos creeping over the collar.

"Hi again." Nicky waved at Chelsea, "Are these two with you?"

"Yes." Chelsea pointed to Tattoo Neck, "They are Badjao. South China Sea gypsies. Mr Yamada believes in equal work opportunities."

Nicky reached behind his right ear to mute his RSE.

"Keep your RSE on. You're in luck. My boss is in the mood for an long interview today." Chelsea ushered Nicky into a lift, followed by the two bodyguards. She swiped her hand over the palm reader and the lift began its ascent.

The lift opened into a sparse suite with a window overlooking Marina South. Chelsea took up her position on a sofa near a window and began tapping away on her tablet.

Nicky expected the hunched-over posture of a reclusive celebrity invalid, ready to fence with the questions. Yet the man at the bar looked more sunburnt and fit than his recent publicity shots. Hiro Yamada stood tall for his stature, enhanced by his gauntness after cancer treatments. Nicky tried not to look at Yamada's neck but he smiled, as if it was the first time someone had tried to peek at the scar circumventing his throat. Nicky did a waist-level bow in return.

"Drink." said Yamada, not as an offer but a command. He slid a cocktail glass containing deep red liquid along the counter towards Nicky, Western-style.

Nicky caught the drink just before it fell off the end of the counter. The glass stuck to his fingers and the liquid sloshed over the rim.

"Cheers." Yamada raised his glass. As Nicky placed his lips to the the rim of his glass he discovered sweetness and sourness clashing at the tip of his tongue.

Nicky hazarded a guess, "Grenadine?"

Yamada nodded while Chelsea raised a trimmed eyebrow at Nicky.

"The glass is made out of sugar. A 'Candy Bar' favourite. It'd cost you $1300 at the Candy Bar on Sentosa. Triple that in Tokyo."

Nicky took a tentative lick at the sucrose coating his lips.

"When a man who makes wonders with sugar wants to give you something sweet for free, you better listen." said Yamada.

Nicky unclipped the stud from behind his ear and set the device on the counter. He readied his list of questions. ("Ask Yamada if he remembers our interview back in 2018!" Nicky's editor had emailed him last night.)

Yamada leant over the bar to talk to Nicky, and the spontaneous conspiratorial intimacy unnerved him.

"This is my last interview."

Over on the sofa Chelsea gasped and ceased tapping on her tablet.

"You're bowing out of the spotlight? Again? Has your cancer gone into remission" asked Nicky, trying to stay focused.

"I never had throat cancer," admitted Yamada, pointing at his throat, "I've been living with the Badjao for three years."

Nicky heard Chelsea's tablet clatter to the floor before she raised her voice. "The interview is now over!"

Yamada looked over at Chelsea as if she had barged in, "We agreed to what I would say during the interview, but now I've decided not to conduct an interview. This is a confession."

Chelsea now stood in the middle of the room, caught between Nicky's confusion and Yamada's about-face. Nicky reached out to retrieve his ear stud but Yamada caught his hand. Nicky asked Yamada if he wanted to go off-record from this point onwards. Yamada then tightened his grip on Nicky.

"Don't you want my story for that editor bitch at your magazine, boy? Your first big break so that you can afford a shoebox on a floating habitat no better than the families in a Phuket sea ghetto? You and several thousand others eating shit recycled from the sea, while drugged up to your scalps with immunisations against the latest waterborne disease or marine parasites?"

Yamada had a surprisingly strong grip for a recovering invalid. Nicky felt the tower sway, or he now felt weak.

"Listen." Chelsea said, the tower slightly swayed in the other direction while Nicky heard muffled thuds in the levels below.

"The Badjao," Yamada declared, "are ahead of schedule. Typical sea pirates."

Chelsea turned on Yamada, "This was not the plan! You said you could get amnesty for those who are now your bodyguards in Singapore or Malaysia. Don't forget that I forged all those bodyguard permits!"

Nicky listened out for more thuds above Chelsea's raised voice and recalled what little he knew about South China Sea pirates, referred to by the sterile abbreviation 'SCSPs' by the media. SCSPs were still considered a distant threat, unlike the Straits of Malacca pirates recently repelled by the Malacca Straits Barrier Reef, not a natural wonder like the former Great Barrier Reef, but a mine-laden one created for maritime security.

When Chelsea ran out of accusations, Yamada resumed his story: "The Badjao came at night when we were off the Anambas Islands." Yamada looked far out of the window, beyond the horizon, "Just three boats and their mother vessel, a dozen men with machine guns."

Nicky noticed Tattoo Neck at the door, his index fingers permanently crooked from pulling triggers on many pre-loved AK-47s.

"So we waited. The nearby governments wouldn't intervene, and Japan was on tsunami alert again. My story got lost."

"Did the Badjao know who you are?" asked Nicky.

"My creations were so delicious that one American critic declared 'It's like an angel peeing on your tongue!'." Yamada gestured towards imaginary awards mounted on the wall behind him, "Fame counts for nothing out at sea. No, the Badjao spared my wife and I because I made 'magic jelly' for them."

Chelsea was holding her face in her hands, as if to plead, 'Mr Yamada please don't go there!' But Nicky could not stop listening if he wanted to.

"On my houseboat I experimented with flavours and micro-organisms, long used for food preparation processes, like yeast cultures for production of bread, alcohol, or cheese. I discovered the wonderful uses of the bacterium Xylinum. In a solution, it turns sugar into a cellulose-fibre—paper produced by bacteria!"

Yamada produced a whisky glass from under the bar. Nicky saw a thin film that looked like beige papier-mâché clinging to the insides of the glass.

"One day at sea I was so hungry I ate my xylinum cultures without getting sick. I discovered xylinum is so pure that if placed inside the human body, it is accepted by the body. The cellulose generated binds a lot of water. When the Badjao ate my 'magic jelly' they never felt thirsty and rarely hungry."

"What happened to your wife?" asked Nicky.

"A stray bullet from a faulty machine-gun hit her—here." Yamada pressed his ring finger so hard onto the centre of Nicky's forehead that it left an indentation.

"So, I'm not sick." Yamada said.

"Physically—you look well." Nicky conceded. "But you are profit-eering. Are your latest 'sponsors' the various pirate groups you've be-friended?"

Yamada laughed, "How could I join them? Not that I lacked offers. Imagine; 'Yamada's Armada' ruling the waves! The Badjao and other sea gypsies powered by Yamada's magic jelly. Could your agency put a better spin on it, Chelsea?"

Nicky picked up his ear stud and declared, "This interview is over."

A shiny object flew past Chelsea with a dry whooshing sound and hit Yamada. Upon impact, Nicky saw the machete embedded in Ya-mada's chest.

Nicky grabbed Chelsea and both ran into the lift as Tattoo Neck and Scarmouth went to the bar to make sure Yamada was dead. As the lift doors shut, Chelsea was too shocked to scream, and instead blurted out, "What is this shit?"

"Mutiny," replied Nicky. "The Game has moved on; the Badjao are taking over Rig-One."

Nicky and Chelsea ran down the blood-smeared corridor, hoping to es-cape through the travellator that led out to the connecting steel mod-ule. The staff were screaming, pursued by several more sunburnt men with bigger scars and tattoos. They were wielding machetes and ma-chine guns under their grey boiler suits. Yamada's murder created some confusion amongst the Badjao, and gifted Nicky and Chelsea with at least fifteen minutes to get off Rig-One. Pressing with the full force of her weight, Chelsea snapped off the wooden leg of an over-turned chair to use as a club.

Nicky gave her a quizzical look, "Have you spent time in Johor Bahru?"

"Not quite. My dad left my mum and me in Woodlands, to shack up with a Mover. Who dumped him for a bigger Shaker." Chelsea shrugged as she embedded her spiked earrings into the business end of her wooden club. Impressed, Nicky planned to ask her out for Siberian coffee if they ever got off Rig-One.

The steel module still held strong as Nicky distracted one Badjao while Chelsea clubbed him on the head. Both continued to run along the module, but Nicky felt weak.

"Don't stop." Chelsea said. "I'm sure you know the emergency action that happens should Rig-One get threatened."

Nicky did not know but he gathered from a massive metallic yawn sounding from the direction they had come, the sound of metal buckling and glass shattering pane by pane. The steel module walkway had been programmed to detach from Rig-One, and contract like an accordion.

"Get to the arcades!" yelled Nicky.

"No difference!"

Nicky dragged Chelsea with him, "They won't destroy the shops! Think of all the lawsuits!"

Chelsea dropped her makeshift club and sprinted down the walkway with Nicky as they heard a fresh series of explosions threaten to catch up with them.

"Yamada told me once," Chelsea said to Nicky when they reached safety in the arcades, "Grenadine comes from the French word for 'pomegranate', and it later gave its name to the explosive device."

Nicky nodded and accepted the fact but his memories were already saturated—not just with the sound but also the colour. But not the red of blood or wine, yet the shade was just as dark and specific. It went by the more explosive name of grenadine. As teams of armed guards ran past them, Nicky turned to Chelsea and asked her out for coffee when this whole mess has blown over.

"Sugar-free coffee, please." said Chelsea and tossed her makeshift club onto the floor of the arcade.

ABOUT EELEEN LEE

Eeleen Lee was born in London, UK, during the year punk rock exploded and throughout the following decade. As a result, her Spotify playlists are full of two-minute protest songs and synth-pop classics. Her fiction and non-fiction has been published by Mammoth Books UK, Intellect UK, Monsoon Books Singapore, Fixi Novo, and Esquire Magazine (Malaysia). She tweets at https://twitter.com/EeleenLee.

LOVE AND STATUES

Jax Goss

~ New Zealand ~

It is just before dawn, and they have walked all night. The sun is coming up. Or it would be if it weren't for the low bank of cloud sitting just above the horizon. It glows orange, for a few glorious minutes, bathing the world in warm fuzzy magic, and then goes grey again. The air is moist, and they are both wrapped in coats, bundled up, except for their hands which at some point in the walk have found each other.

They stop at the railway station.

"They say it's the second most photographed building in the South-ern Hemisphere, after the Opera House."

She smiles. "How do you measure something like that?"

He shrugs and turns to take her other hand. The moisture is sitting on her fringe in tiny droplets, and her cheeks are red from the cold. He thinks for an instant that she is the most beautiful thing he's ever seen, and then laughs inwardly at his own silly romance. She's just a girl, after all. A girl who is leaving.

She sees something pass across his face, and cocks her head, smil-ing. "What was that?"

He shakes his head, shy, and she laughs. They start walking up Stu-art St, talking quietly, laughing. Small talk, they call it. Little tiny con-fidences that add up to intimacy. When they get to the Octagon, she goes and stands at the feet of the Robbie Burns statue.

"Did you know," he says, eager to enchant her with his hometown, secretly hoping she'll stay, even though he knows she won't, "when they built Dunedin, they built it with plans from Edinburgh? The centre of town is a replica. The names are even basically the same. They both mean Town of Edin, or something like that. That's why the Octagon is on this ridiculous hill."

She traces a hand along Robbie's foot. "Is that true?"

"I don't know," he laughs. "But I heard it."

She turns to him then, and there is something new in her eyes. "I'll tell you something about this town you may not know. Something true."

He cocks his head at that. He's lived here his whole life. She's been here a couple of weeks. This should be good. "What's that?"

She moves closer like she's telling him a secret. "The statues are alive."

He looks up at the old familiar face of Robbie Burns, mildly uneasy, but mostly amused. "You mean, like, Doctor Who Weeping Angels alive?"

She laughs again. She laughs a lot. He likes that. "Of course not, silly. They're not monsters. But sometimes they come alive. I know, I've seen them."

He raises an eyebrow. "You've seen the statues come to life?"

She nods.

"It was late one night. I was in the Gardens. The gates were closed and I shouldn't have been there, but I'd stayed after closing time, and had curled up in that, you know, the stage by the playground? I was out of the wind there, you see. Anyway, there are those statues of Peter Pan and Wendy and the other characters from that book? And they came alive. I saw them. They moved, and danced, all totally silent. But they looked like they were laughing. Having a good time."

He decides to humour her. "Maybe it's just those ones. Peter Pan is magic after all."

She shakes her head, and places a hand on Robbie again. "He was there too. Sitting in the midst of them, residing like some kind of benevolent patriarch. I sat very still and quiet, and they never knew I was there. And I watched them dance."

Her voice has genuine wonder in it, and for half a moment he believes her. Then he chuckles. She glances sharply at him. "You think I'm making it up?"

"Well, come on? Dancing statues?"

She looks at him for a long, long moment. Then she sighs and shakes her head. He can see her moving away from him, even though she's not moving.

"What...? Are you serious? You seriously expect me to believe that the statues in Dunedin come alive and dance around the Gardens at night?"

She shrugs. "No. I guess not." Her voice drips disappointment and it's like a punch in his gut. Like he hasn't lived up to something. He reacts with anger.

"You're crazy."

The look she gives him this time is one of shock and hurt. And then he sees her face change. All that warmth drains away. Her mouth sets itself in a firm line. Her voice when she speaks is cold and glittering.

"I guess maybe I am."

And then she walks away. He is already regretting his anger, and he calls to her to stop. She turns and looks at him, arms folded.

"I'm sorry."

She shakes her head. "People have called me crazy my whole life. But I know what I know. I thought you were different. Maybe I am crazy, maybe you're right. You and everyone else. Or maybe I just see what's in the world, instead of what I expect to see. Either way. I have a bus to catch."

And like that, she is gone. He knows her name, and that she comes from a small town in Germany. He does not remember the name of the town. And now she's gone.

It is less than a week after she leaves that he waits in the gardens after closing time. He knows nothing is going to happen. He knows. But he is there anyway. The night is slightly warmer. Spring is coming. Still, he is wrapped in coats and blankets in the same place she said she saw them dance.

He waits. And nothing happens.

And then he wakes from dozing off, and thinks to himself, *this is ridiculous, go home.* He stands up quickly, in irritation and looks up.

They all stand perfectly still for one moment, staring at him, and then they scatter, gone back to their pedestals. Robbie gives him a long sad look, and trundles off.

There, in the night, he stands, his belly filled with regret.

ABOUT JAX GOSS

Jax Goss is a wandering South African who has settled in New Zealand. She lives in Dunedin, where she is currently employed full time as the mother of a very small human, and writes on the side. She expects this situation to stay the same for a while, but she has long ago learnt that nothing ever goes the way she expects.

She edited Solarwyrm Press's inaugural anthology *Fae Fatales: A Fantasy Noir Anthology* which also contains her story "Lady Isabel and the Elf Knight." She won a Highly Commended Prize in the Commonwealth Short Story Writing Competition for her short story "Icarus" in 2011. She has a book published called *The Edge of the Map* which is available on Amazon and Smashwords. She was also published in *Idol Meanderings*, also available on Amazon.

Her website is: jaxgoss.wordpress.com, and you can follow her on Twitter: @belgatherial.

GONE FISHING

Jo Thomas

~ Pacific Ocean ~

Grace and Maui O'Malley sat on one of Halcyon's two docks. The oncoming sail was barely working with only a breath of wind to push the boat along.

"A pacific day," Maui said with a grin.

Grace swung her feet slowly in the ocean's waters. Had they actually expected to catch anything on the fishing lines they pretended to watch, she wouldn't have moved at all. Resources were scarce and unfarmed fish were rarely this close to the sea steading.

"Research vessel," she said quietly and Maui nodded in agreement. "Wonder what they're following."

It couldn't be anything else with the old-fashioned rigging and the small, sleek shape that time and nearness would resolve into a cat or a tri. Like all such boats, it would carry a small team of scientists following marine life or something else they thought worth studying. They shouldn't be a threat, they shouldn't be here to steal, but they might not realise the value of anything they wanted from the Halcyon.

Maui shrugged his big shoulders. "Brought 'em a long way out from Jo'burg's reach, anyway."

Grace lifted the large, floppy brim of her hat so she could look over her shoulder at the people busy working on Halcyon. Only a handful of them were as fair-skinned as she was. Only one or two looked as obviously Māori as Maui. Most were somewhere in between.

"No news for us to tell," she said, "Except for another bunch of teen-agers shipped off to Jo'burg for naval service."

Maui nodded. "Nearest place from that direction is Lotus. Might have some good news from there. A stronger alliance or a chance of trade, perhaps."

As if there was anything available to trade: sea water, fish, people.

"I guess it's possible," Grace said, "But I'd've thought Fair Isle or Titokowaru are more likely with the current."

The boat came closer and, just ahead of it, a distinctive fin broke the water.

"*Mako!*" breathed Maui, unconsciously sending the message over his brain-jack.

Grace smiled at his reliance on technology as she lifted her feet out of the water. They had only just completed their own naval service and were finding civilian life as different as the steaders had warned they would.

"Be careful," Grace said quietly, "It's not a good idea to show-off just how Commonwealth we are so far from Jo'burg. Especially if this bunch've been to Fair Isle or Titokowaru."

She named their nearest, anti-Commonwealth opponents but Maui only nodded absent-mindedly. His attention was on the approaching fins—another had now joined the first—and he watched with the intense interest of an apex predator watching competition. More distant enemies held no interest for him at the moment.

Grace laughed and stood up, untangling herself from him.

"Relax, *maki*," she said, tapping the stylised orca on his shoulder.

Something in what the steaders were doing, perhaps the sounds of metal structures being put together, had already drawn the sharks' attention. The two great grey and white fish moved close enough for their markings to be clearly seen, their distinctive dorsal fins breaking the ocean's surface repeatedly. The larger raised its head from the water and then raised itself on its tail for a good view of Grace and Maui.

"Very clever," Grace said to it as if it could understand.

"You follow any kind of *mako*, man, or just these?" called Maui to the researchers, now close enough to hail by voice alone.

Two, Grace noted, male and female with the steady gaze that came of a long time at sea and so tanned their dark skin almost was black. The two of them exchanged looks before the man responded in the clipped, precise tones of a Jo'burg Patrician. He was a long way from home.

"They're great whites, not *mako*."

"All sharks are *mako* here," said Grace with a shrug, "We use it as a general term."

She watched the couple look the whole steading up and down, taking in the mix of skin colour. Their eyes caught on and widened at the *moko* displayed by frayed cut-offs and flapping shirts. The designs were not wholly traditional and were confined to shoulders, torsos and thighs as facial markings didn't mix with naval service. Halcyon was Commonwealth, and proud to give its young to the service for the reward of arms, technology and food, but it was also Māori.

"This is the Halcyon sea steading?"

"We're that obvious?" Maui asked with a lazy grin.

The man stiffened. "We have a good chart."

There was something about the researcher's tone that put Grace to wondering if she could find a market for his little craft. It would have to be a steading the researchers hadn't been to for plausible deniability.

"Please, come aboard and welcome."

Grace was careful to extend her hospitality in English. Using any other terms from the steading's mixed heritage would be too binding in this pair's company.

"I think I'd rather have the *mako* in," muttered Maui.

Grace agreed. "The meat would certainly be more useful."

"We could always eat the researchers."

"We don't know what they're carrying," she said.

The two great whites hung around, which meant that the disagreeable researchers also had to stay in the area. While the sharks moved with ease, the humans kept to their pitiful little cat. The researchers' dark skins got more grey and drawn with each hour the sharks stayed in the area.

"Something wrong?" Grace asked after the second day.

They stuttered and spluttered their way through nonsense thinly disguised as science before retreating to their cat in a hurry. These two had to have done something.

"Get someone looking at the systems, Maui," Grace ordered.

On the third day, she went to talk to the sharks again.

"With all respect, *mako*," Grace said, "Swim off. You are eating my few wild fish and I'd rather you didn't."

One of the sharks regarded her for a moment, holding an eye out of the water as it swam lazily about the dock. If it was paying attention it was only because she was a stranger to it, not because it understood her words.

"She's not listening to you," said Maui, joining her on the dock walkway.

"There are *maki* that come here," Grace said to the shark, "A pod of orca that will eat you if they see you."

The shark flicked its tail as if in disdain.

"If I see you again, I will eat you," Grace swore.

Maui laughed at her.

"You sure no one ever trained a shark for military purposes?" she asked him.

Maui shook his head. "Why would they want to serve humans? Anyway, it's the researchers that follow them that've broken Commonwealth law. A worm in the weapons systems."

"We caught it?"

"No. Not yet. The eyes and turrets are dead. It doesn't seem to have a taste for brain-jacks and it hasn't got to the *Connaught*, yet. We've isolated the ship's systems."

Grace felt both sick and excited. Sick that another senseless battle in the Steadings War was about to start and excited about the chance to fight, to flex muscles, to prove herself.

"Who're we looking at? It's got to be an opportunist strike."

She tried not to think about what it cost to get a worm, in food or people or materials.

"Piripi said the worm tastes Wa-ry," Maui said with a shrug.

"Bloody Titokowarus," said Grace with weary anger, "Have Sean keep the main eyes on their heading—in case we get the eyes back on line—but keep the low levels going all around. Everyone's to take watch shifts with bins. Don't want to get snuck up on."

"Weapons?"

Grace looked around at the Halcyon steaders. "Cutlasses. No firearms until we see something to hit. Can't afford to lose the bullets. Keep the turrets down as if they're dead. If we get them back on-line, they can react fast enough if the Wa-ries follow their worm for it to be safe. I don't think they're rich enough to be much of a threat without the worm."

It still wasn't enough to settle the sickness or the excitement.

"We breaking out the *Connaught*?"

"Give me half an hour," she answered, "Then we'll go hunt the hunters."

☙

The researchers jumped when she stepped into the cabin of their little cat.

"Nice place," she said with affected carelessness, "Bit small."

The male stood as if to warn her off—"You can't—"—and stopped when he clocked the Commonwealth combats.

Grace smiled and wished she was still allowed to carry the old Jack on her left arm. It was unlikely that these two would realise the lack made her less than official. She had some authority as the head of the steading but that that only extended half a mile out on the ocean. All the researchers needed to do was get away from the steading and she would be breaking the Commonwealth law that Halcyon was pledged to uphold.

"Oh, I think you'll find it's physically possible for me to board your... vessel," she said.

They blinked at her, silent. They were probably exchanging comments over their brain-jacks. She didn't care. They had brought this on themselves. This was their fault.

"You've attacked the Commonwealth state of Halcyon in an act of war," Grace said evenly, keeping her fury over the attack to herself, "Have you anything to say in your defence?"

"An act of war?" the female demanded, "We haven't done anything like that! We just—"

"Shut up!" the male cut in.

"You brought invasive software from another steading," Grace explained as if to a slow child, "Another state."

The female laughed dismissively. "But rivalries between steadings are nothing to do with Commonwealth law!"

"Wrong," replied Grace, "The Sea Steadings War still rumbles on and Titokowaru, the rival steading you did this for, is not a member of the Commonwealth. Therefore, it is an act of war."

The female shrugged. "We didn't do anything. They've attacked us just as much as you. They infected the cat's dry-brain and we're down to manual."

"So you knowingly entered another state with infected systems and didn't declare it?" Grace asked sweetly.

"We didn't do anything," the female insisted.

"You can't do anything!" the male said at the same time, "We're citizens of Jo'burg!"

"Who are Halcyon's allies as we are both Commonwealth states. Now, if you would just come onto the dock, we can proceed through the legalities."

Grace gestured towards the hatch and, wordlessly, the two researchers did as they were bid. Their body language spoke of anger with a small amount of fear. They didn't like the gun and cutlass she carried but hadn't touched, fearing the backwater nature of the sea steadings. Coming from a more settled state made them trust the uniform and the goodwill of the Commonwealth.

They were also convinced they had a basic right to life without trying for it, a belief that no steader would ever hold. Anyone who was familiar with steading life or living this far away from full Commonwealth control would have known to flee.

When they were on the dock, Grace managed to manoeuvre them so that their backs were to the artificial reef without them realising. This business would be easy to conclude. She put on her best captain's voice to begin their sentencing.

"Lacking the resources to try and sentence you here—"

"Well, at least you're civilised enough not to just kill us outright," the female said in a cutting tone. She didn't truly believe she was in any danger of being killed, despite her fear of weapons.

Grace smiled and continued smoothly, "Means we also lack the resources to take you to somewhere else that might. The nearest settlement of any size is on North Island. And there's nothing to say they can deal with you, either."

She hadn't thought it possible for their skin to go any greyer. They looked as if they were seriously ill and the beading sweat on their brows did nothing to dispel the image.

"The Commonwealth treaty says that, in such circumstances, we can deal with outsiders who break the law as we would our own."

With a swift movement, she drew her cutlass and swept it across their necks. The force of contact, so unexpected, had the bodies falling into the artificial reef even as the last remnants of life clutched at their throats and tried to prevent the blood spurting. The surprised looks disappeared under the blue Pacific waters.

"Dinner is served," Grace said to the fish inside Halcyon's artificial reef. They seemed excited about it. It was a while since they'd had blood and flesh to feed on.

In the dock, on the outside of the reef, the larger shark raised itself on its tail again. Grace was unsure whether it saw two sources of blood it wanted to get to or two people it recognised dying. It was hard to say how any *mako* felt about humans.

"Maui," she called out across the docks, "We need to line up a buyer for a standard two-man cat."

It wasn't like they could afford to keep it or patch it, even if it weren't identifiable.

"Right-o!" she heard him call back.

Now it was time to get the idiots who had thought to hook a sweet fish with their digital worm and caught themselves something much more dangerous instead.

"Kawa? An old war canoe?" Maui asked with an incredulous tone.

"Like we're any better with just the *Connaught*," Grace said, thinking of the ships they'd had before their last campaign, and of the damaged ships they'd won and had to trade for new fish and plant stocks to replace the resources raided when that last campaign had started.

But Maui wasn't thinking of things like that. He laughed, deep and from the belly. "Maybe we should paddle their arses and send them home for stealing our culture."

She leant over the side of the *Connaught*. It didn't look as if the Titokowaru warriors had noticed them or, if they had, recognised the ex-patrol ship for what it was. Nor had they seen the two *mako* that had decided to follow her. That said, the distinctive dorsal fins would be very small points from this distance.

"Do we need to have olive skin to be Māori, now?" she asked with a raised auburn eyebrow. "Aren't we Māori because it's our way?"

The crew laughed and Maui flushed. "They just look—"

"As if they should be in something dragon-prowed and beating on shields," Grace said, grateful there wasn't enough readily available iron to supply that sort of low technology culture among the steadings.

"We need to conserve ammo," she said, "So it's good they are as they are. We could get away with one shell to dazzle them and then an old-fashioned boarding."

It might be another twelve months before they could get to a proper Commonwealth naval base to trade ammunition for more service. A fight with cutlasses was better than a shoot-out.

"Or we could go round them and take their steading," said Maui, "Let those left behind take care of these Wa-ries."

Every adult on Halcyon had seen naval service. Everyone left behind was capable of defending themselves.

"But the best fighters are here," said Grace, unwilling to leave what was probably the harder battle to the worm-ridden Halcyon.

"So?"

"And these are bound to be the best of the Wa-ries fighters," she said.

Maui frowned. "Their steading's resources will be worth more to us and Halcyon should be able to cope with these... losers."

"There are three types of steading," Grace intoned in the same voice her father had used to teach them their history and then added in a more normal voice, "And they're the wrong type."

She'd known Titokawara was poor, of course. They all had. They'd even known the Wa-ries were weird for their perceived history. But this was a bit more than she'd expected.

Maui crossed his arms. "Enlighten me, oh great captain."

Grace raised her eyebrows. She could feel the others in the crew pausing in their jobs to watch. If she didn't come up with an understandable, acceptable reason not to follow Maui's advice, she could end up watching them sail for Titokowaru steading anyway. Even though the ruins of that other steading wouldn't actually do them any good.

She held up three fingers and marked the first finger off with her other hand, "Former financial enterprises like Halcyon."

The plans had been submitted by Grace and Maui's shared O'Malley ancestor some two centuries ago, shortly before the ice age hit the Northern Hemisphere. Building had started even as the first influx of refugees hit Aotearoa. As other pressures came into play, it had become a home not just a business. All residents were shareholders although the O'Malley descendants held a greater share. Which was why there was a chance Grace's decision would be ignored.

"Sea steadings such as Halcyon," continued Grace, "Are usually pro-Commonwealth because we were businesses first. We need global alliances in order to secure trade and survive."

Maui made a "move on" gesture. The crew leant forward.

"Then there are the resettlement steadings."

Some of them started even as Halcyon and its ilk were being constructed, as Aotearoa and neighbouring Australia struggled to find places for the flood of refugees.

"Those who still identify with their deceased parent nation are generally pro-Commonwealth," said Maui, "Yes, I know. What's this got to do with the Wa-ries?"

"Third kind," Grace said firmly.

"What?"

"You remember the history lessons," she nudged, "The people who lost the land grab when the nations collapsed."

Maui stared at the distant canoes.

"They're in a canoe because that's what they can afford," said Grace.

Although even that much was arguably of value in the harsh world of the sea steadings—where almost everything but their basic food and the next generation had to come from elsewhere. The easiest way was to take it from another steading too weak to hold on to what they had. Only the Wa-ries knew where they'd found enough wood to build a canoe.

"So the worm they sent...?" Maui asked.

She sighed. "They probably spent all they had on getting a program they were assured would disable an enemy. Maybe they sold their own into indentured servitude or tricked someone richer into sharing it. But it worked. Commonwealth grade defences don't mean a thing if—"

"They ain't got that swing?"

✦

"Of course," Grace added some time later as their boarding party faced the welcoming committee over the rail of the *Connaught*, "They're likely to dress their poverty up as something else."

"You mean like a fanatical return to the pre-Westernised culture?" Maui asked.

They watched the Titokowaru warriors' *peruperu* for a further heartbeat before he allowed his frustration to get the better of him.

"Seriously, people, I do not have time for this," he shouted, "Either shut up and fight or shove off!"

Grace shrugged and unholstered her side-arm. As the leader of the group started another insult in pure *te reo*, she re-homed a single bullet in his temple. The Titokowaru warriors froze and she spoke into the resulting silence before the panic started.

"You have a choice. You can leave and we will not follow you—"

One of the warriors shouted "Never!" in *te reo* and was echoed by the rest. They were wide-eyed and edged away from the corpse of their leader, though. Whatever psychological benefit the *peruperu* had been giving them was gone, just as she'd hoped.

Grace continued as if she had not been interrupted, "Or you can surrender and we w—"

"We keep to the old ways, *tauiwi*, we do not surrender."

"You don't know your own history is what you don't," Maui growled.

"That makes no sense," Grace threw at him before returning to the Titokowaru warriors' choice, "You can surrender and we will accept you as members of our *iwi*. We always welcome strong men and women among us."

Her crew flicked a look at her but she gave a little shake of her head. They would speed the steading's return to full strength. Grace would ensure they were welcomed but they wouldn't be included as shareholders—at least not until they'd proven themselves.

"Or you can fight and die."

The self-designated leader laughed, a crow of derision, "We will not die to warriors who bring their women along. Warriors who let their women speak for them are not warriors at all."

Grace would bet there was nothing but women and children left at Titokowara. She would have to collect them—peacefully—in the near future. Without warriors, neighbours would find them easy pickings and sell them on for more valuable resources.

"We're not warriors," said Maui, "We're marines."

The crew of the *Connaught* laughed.

"And I am Grace O'Malley," Grace said, "And I'm not in the habit of letting my enemies live."

She holstered her gun, her hand already on the rail to vault over onto the wooden canoe. A deep breath, forget the past and the future, focus on the fight.

"No prisoners. Cutlass only. Don't waste bullets on them. Don't feed any of them to the *mako*. Time to fight!"

Grace drew her own cutlass as soon as her feet made contact—to draw before meant she risked cutting her own legs off if her landing went badly—and it flashed out in a heavy swing. It made contact with a short but heavy club, changing the course of her momentum as she moved, ducking away from another club that had been aimed at her temple. A quick reverse of cut caught the first club's wielder on the arm and Grace moved on to the second, content that the first would not be able to attack again and that someone behind her would finish him off.

The *Connaught* was slow going back. It was difficult hauling back the wooden hulk that was almost as long as they were and intent on being directionless. Grace wasn't quite sure what she'd do with the wood, wherever it had originally come from, but she still had a use for the bodies.

The two great whites continued to circle them. Grace had had one of the corpses—out of thirty-four dead warriors, in all—thrown to the fish as a sort of "thank you" for bringing the Halcyon steaders a prize, no matter how small. The rest would be fed to Halcyon's artificial reef. She wondered if they could smell the blood from her crew's wounds and their own dead. Three Halcyon marines would never fight again.

"So we continue to advance the Commonwealth's interests," said Maui as he adjusted the ropes that held the canoe.

Grace smiled, a tight hunter's smile. "Well, we've got rid of thirty four men who disagreed with their policies."

"World peace and wealth for all!"

She took one of the rope ends and leant back with all her weight so Maui could tie off the adjustment.

"I wouldn't go that far," she said, "But I might add the point about population control."

"We're just making room for more of ours," Maui said with a grin and kissed her quickly, between tasks.

"We'll go back for their families when we're sure the worm is cleaned out," she said, "When we can afford to give them the time they need to be won over."

"So much for population control."

"I'm not leaving them to starve or be captured. We're better than that!"

Maui shrugged. "They can buy their way on to Halcyon with whatever resources we can break Titokowara down to. I'll make sure we have shareholder support."

Grace turned and looked out to sea. She squinted, uncertain, and then smiled as she watched another type of distinctive dorsal fin approaching from the distance.

"Look! *Mako!*" she broadcast to the whole crew through her brain-jack, "Looks like the mako will be paying us back for those fish they stole."

They all stopped and looked as seven fins broke the surface again, a little nearer than when Grace had first spotted them.

"Let's get one of the *mako* for ourselves," suggested Maui, "I wouldn't mind some of that liver."

ABOUT JO THOMAS

Jo Thomas is a part-time writer hiding in a full-time worker's life. She is occasionally allowed out to play for historical fencing and the odd speculative fiction convention. She can be found at http://www.journeymouse.net and as @Journeymouse on Twitter.

SHADOWS OF AN ANCIENT BATTLE

Daniel A. Kelin, II

~ Hawai'i ~

A pale red sun caresses lava-coloured streets, echoes of the island's birth. Towering edifices shimmer in the dwindling light. Long shadows slowly reach toward volcanic mountains. In a time before time, volcano goddess Pele once laid claim to the blackened rocks and burnt trees where shadows hid, unseen in the dark of the night. In a time called now, two bent figures scurry along the parched sidewalk past rows of peeling grey apartment boxes.

Street lights wink, hum and glimmer. In the humid stillness of twilight, where even mosquitoes battle sluggishly with the thick air, a phantom forest appears. The aged two hurry toward home through the translucent forest, their calabashes heavy with kalo and sweet potato picked from a nearby community garden. Their silhouettes stretch behind them, tugged reluctantly from the deepening darkness. Had the passing jogger given them more than a glance, it might have appeared as those the old women were trying to outrun the night.

Heads bowed, the two whisper incessantly, glancing sharply about. Dark clouds meander in above the two. The women tuck in tight, ready to protect themselves from the threatened rain. A lone truck shifts gears, echoing the sky's sudden deep rumble. Long palm leaves clack in the wind. Drops of rain pelt the lone pedestrians. Wrapping their grey heads with wrinkled clothing, the two women hasten their steps.

The blackness thickens. The streetlight above flickers and winks out with a brief flash of light. The hurried two glimpse a dim, human-like silhouette rising from the shadows, a kihei of black skin dangling over its dark shoulder. A man, maybe. An animal, possibly. A threatening attitude, most definitely. He waits patiently for them.

"Hiding in the dark," one old woman whispers, fear lining her angry voice.

"Lurking," echoes the second.

"But we know when you appear."

"We always know," the second chuckles lightly.

"That snort of breathing."

"Grunting," says the second.

Small red slits glimmer from that dim shadow of a mostly man as he breathes a rumble in response. A dull *thump-thump-thump* escapes the tightly shut windows of a passing car.

The two bent figures turn quickly, stumbling over spiky shards of street-coloured lava. Despite the dusky light, the shadowy maybe man steps easily through a tangle of brittle charcoaled tree branches, barring the women's path. Squeezing out their fear, the aged, bent two draw themselves up taller than any eyewitness might imagine possible. "Let us pass," one softly demands. From close by, the sound of a door clicking shut.

"Ancients trespassing on ancient ground," breathes the mostly man, and repeats, "Trespassing." A distant siren punctuates his threat.

The malingering sunlight feeds the illusion of two twisted silhouettes unfurling to match the strange man-beast's height. "We wish to pass," the second says. "Go."

"Go on."

"Nuisance."

"You don't belong."

The red eyes stare unblinking as the two now erect women stand their ground. "Not here," one says, as the second finishes, "not in this place. Not in this now time."

In the brief silence, the roar of the ocean echoes as if a long forgotten memory.

"You two," rumbles the dark one. "You've trapped yourself in this shadow of a world that has no roots. You've lost power, lost the place you say is of you. Lost your very reason for being! Scat."

"This is our land, our water. We come from, came out of this place. And *belong*," the first woman replies. "Move aside."

"Not for your kind," the dark one responds.

"Invader," hisses the first woman.

"Destroyer," the second squeaks.

The first spits in anger. "Pua'a!"

A noise escapes the throat of the darkened man, something between a snort and a chortle.

The sun hides. In the absence of shadows and dim light, two bodies suddenly and unexpectedly brush past the red-eyed beast of a threat.

"*Kama*pua'a!" snarls the dark one, "A pig as certainly as you are but shadows of women. *Mo'o*."

The dark clouds flash with a rumble of thunder. A great pig with sharp tusks leaps out of that silhouette of a man. Lowering his bristly, wrinkled head, the hogman lunges at the thin, grey ladies.

The two gape helplessly as the ancient creature charges them. A single, eternal moment passes. A car alarm erupts. A lone baby's cry. A heavy roar rolls out of the hogman as he quickly crosses the empty space between his ancient enemies and himself. In the next moment, calabashes shatter on the broken lava. Two mo'o scatter free of those bent grey shadowy forms, wriggling into a crack in the ground. The hoofs of the great black pig trample the kalo and potatoes, but touch neither the women nor their mo'o selves.

Kamapua'a grunts and relentlessly pounds the hardened lava. He slams his snout into a widening crack, but sees only wriggling tails as the mo'o burrow deeper into the crevice. Kamapua'a snarls and paws, rooting out great blocks of lava, but just as his tusks near them the mo'o seep further into the black rock mocking the pig with their lizard grunts. His eyes flaming, Kamapua'a digs so deep so quickly an underground stream gushes into his wrinkled snout, choking the giant pig. The mo'o, dragons of the sea, squeak out a laugh and swim quickly off in the buried waters.

The shadowy hogman roars at the night, tearing up trees both wooden and metallic. He quickly turns the offending ground into a pile of rubble. Breathing shallow and hard, the hogman's eyes and ears slowly survey the area. Not a sound, not a sight. Just a tiny gecko crawling over the dark picture of a walking man. Kamapua'a smashes it; eats it. He grunts a humourless laugh, then slowly disappears back into the darkness.

As his grunts fade, the ancient dragons re-emerge from the rubble under a flashing light that warns vehicles of a torn-up street. The pale glow of an open garage washes over two women bent with age as they scamper down the empty street, giggling quietly.

A passing radio murmurs news of burst pipes and flooded streets. The car abruptly swerves. The weary driver swears. "People should cage their pigs at night."

HAWAIIAN
Pele - Polynesian volcano goddess
calabash - bowl
kalo - taro
kihei - cape
pua'a - pig
Kamapua'a - Hawaiian trickster hog god
mo'o - large, magical lizards

ABOUT DANIEL A. KELIN, II

Daniel A. Kelin, II is an actor, director, playwright, educator, author and avid traveller. He has designed and implemented programs across the US, in the Marshall Islands, India, American Samoa, Pohnpei, and Guam. Dan's work with Pacific Island youth is profiled in *Performing Democracy* and *The Arts and Bilingual Youth*. Under a Rockefeller Foundation grant he developed and toured a play based on the songs, dance and folk stories of the Marshall Islands. Throughout that time, he worked with storytellers which resulted in a book of those stories, *Marshall Islands Legends and Stories*. Other writing has appeared in *Parabola*, *Teaching Tolerance*, *Hawaii Review*, the *Indian Folklore Journal*, *Tinfish*, and the *Eclectic Literary Forum*. He has also penned profiles of Pacific and Asian youth for Highlights for Children and Hopscotch for Girls. Kidz Book Hub, Australia, will publish one he wrote on a young actor from India.

In Memoriam

Fadzlishah Johanabas

~ Malaysia ~

Friday
February 29, 2036
16:37 hours

Alia couldn't remember much what exactly happened, but she clearly remembered being lifted into the air as her car spun, and the sudden jerk when it landed with a thud, roof kissing the road. She also remembered white foam bursting out of the steering wheel and congealing around her. She had always wondered how it worked.

Despite the ringing in her ears, Alia could hear the song the classic radio channel was playing. "Someone Like You" by Adele. She used to hear it looped on her iPhone back in college. Maybe it was because of the rush of blood in her head that she giggled. Tariq always rolled his eyes whenever she described to him the concept of touchscreens and tablets. They're bothersome, he'd say. Ever since Apple collapsed almost ten years ago after a massive lawsuit, Korean technology took over the mobile industry, and six years ago they came up with cranial implants.

Why was she thinking of trivia when she was hanging upside-down, surrounded by gooey foam?

Tariq.

Wednesday
July 15, 2037
09:10 hours

As the orderlies and nurses wheeled her gurney into the operating theatre, all Alia could think of was how white the square room was, so white. Making a stark contrast was a band of black that ran all along the four walls two meters off the floor, with a blue glow making endless circuits along its track. Alia was convinced the low hum came from the light. She turned her neck from side to side and made a quick inventory of her surroundings. In the middle sat a large chair, bigger than a dentist's, upholstered in faux leather, also white. A man in scrubs stood facing a counter that stood against a corner of the far wall, and a screensaver of amorphous shades of white and grey filled the rest of the wall right up to the band of black. Two nurses, also in white scrubs, wheeled in trolleys with unopened sterile packages.

Alia also noticed that there was not a single hint of metal in the operating theatre.

"Why is everything so white?" she heard herself mumble.

Doctor Bashkar, her surgeon, stopped beside her gurney and adjusted his cap. He looked good in shirt-and-tie, but in scrubs, he was the image of a hero in old Hindustani movies her mother loved. Hazel eyes, a dimpled chin, and just the right amount of chest and forearm hair.

"Because," he said, "we don't want distractions when you concentrate on the screen." He flashed her a smile, displaying a row of teeth whiter than the theatre.

During her first consultation, he had said that they were of the same age, but he looked much younger than forty-one.

"You have no idea how difficult it is to clean this place," said one of the nurses who wheeled her in. She rolled her eyes at Doctor Bashkar, and he laughed.

Alia felt her fears dissipate. She was in good hands.

Why, then, did she feel this lingering doubt?

Friday
February 29, 2036
15:12 hours

"I want you to know this is bothersome."

Tariq's fingers were rapidly tapping the air in front of him, but Alia knew he was talking to her. She didn't remember ever teaching her fourteen-year-old son the phrase, but he'd come home from school a few weeks ago and started saying "this is bothersome" to everything she asked him to do. He must have learned it from his friends. Teenagers.

"Stop surfing and help me with these, will you?" Alia said.

Tariq dropped his hands from the virtual keyboard only he could see and focused his eyes on her. "I wish the Koreans will come up with mind-activated commands instead of virtual keyboards and voice-activation. At least then you can't tell if I'm paying attention or not."

"I thought we don't get any reception here."

"Barely," Tariq said. "One bar. I don't know why this stupid supermarket isn't rigged with its own wifi."

"Maybe," Alia said, turning her right hand slightly to the right to instruct the half-filled cart in front of her to move, "The owner wants us to buy groceries instead of getting lost in our heads. Now go and look for candles, will you?"

"I told you I don't want a party. Parties are for kids."

"And miss a once-every-four-years birthday party?" Alia said. "I don't think so, kiddo. Now scoot."

"This is bothersome," Tariq grumbled as he turned, shoulders slumped, toward the far end of the supermarket.

Wednesday
July 15, 2037
09:21 hours

"Are you comfortable, Puan Alia?" asked the anaesthesiologist. He had introduced himself as Doctor Shafik before hiding his face behind a white mask that left only his eyes and eyebrows exposed. He had deep laugh lines that complemented his kind eyes.

"Are these straps necessary? I can barely move a muscle."

"They're not too tight, are they?" he asked, readjusting the strap that secured her left forearm.

Alia squirmed in her seat a little. "No, it's fine. This just feels like a scene in a horror movie."

Everyone in the operating theatre laughed.

"I know what you mean," Doctor Shafik said. "The straps are a necessary precaution. Sometimes patients react violently, and we cannot afford to have them move even a single centimetre. We try to avoid muscle relaxants if possible."

With her head and neck the only parts of her body left unbound, Alia kept her gaze locked on the anaesthesiologist and craned her neck to catch glimpses at the medications he was preparing into several syringes. Of the two largest ones, he filled the first with murky yellow liquid and the other with something thick and white. Then he placed all the syringes on a small tray and sauntered to her side. He checked the intravenous access he had inserted at the back of her right hand earlier that morning. He had surely noticed the fine scars when he searched her hand for a good vein to use, but he did not show any signs that he did. Alia wondered if he talked about the scars and where they could have come from with his colleagues behind her back.

"I'm giving you some dormicum, which is an anxiolytic," he said, showing a syringe filled with clear liquid. "Then there is co-tatrim, a seventh generation cephalosporin, which is an antibiotic." She showed her the murky yellow liquid-filled syringe.

Alia gave a nervous laugh. "I don't understand anything you just told me."

Doctor Shafik grinned behind his mask. She assumed he did, because the mask shifted upward. "I have to inform you of everything I'm administering. Medico-legal stuff. The first one is to keep you calm, and the second is antibiotic cover for the surgery."

Alia nodded.

"And then there's this baby," he said, showing her the syringe containing the white cream. "This is a selective substance P antagonist, which basically blocks all the pain receptors throughout your body, both physical and anticipatory."

She wasn't interested in the medications. "What's the hum?"

"You'll get used to it. See the black band? It's the fMRI machine. If you want details, you have to ask the surgeon. What I do know," Doctor Shafik added as he glanced at his workstation monitor, "is that you are slightly tachycardic. Relax, this procedure is safe."

This doctor sure loved his medical jargons. Alia didn't know what "tachycardic" meant, but she assumed the anaesthesiologist was referring to her fluttering heart. He was wrong about one thing, though. She was not afraid of the surgery; at least, not that much.

Was she doing the right thing?

Friday
February 29, 2036
15:45 hours

Alia waited in line and adjusted her hijab. The supermarket was cool with ambient air-conditioning, but outside the sun was scorching the land. Despite the cumulous clouds creeping behind the glass-walled skyscrapers, it didn't look like it was going to rain anytime soon. One of the widgets that were constantly displayed at the far left corner of her visual field showed the temperature of Kuala Lumpur that evening, which was 45.2°C. Wearing a black long-sleeved blouse was definitely a big mistake.

Tariq stood beside her, oblivious to his surroundings. He was almost as tall as she was, but the boy had a habit of slouching, something she was still struggling to break. From the way his body tensed up and the repetitive movements of his fingers, he was playing one of his online games. She had stopped playing online games since she started working. Back then she had to lug around her laptop everywhere and had to depend on wifi hotspots to go online. Alia chuckled to herself and wondered how she had survived without cranial implants.

Alia tapped the air in front of her and accessed Bernama, the local news channel. Instead of news, however, the channel was airing an advertisement.

"Dongnam Group Medical Centre offers the first memory-cleaner service in Malaysia," said a fair-skinned Indian model in a form-fitting white suit that accented her curvaceous body. She showed a hospital lobby that looked more like a hotel's. "Want to leave your past behind and start over with a clean slate? We can do it for you. Register now and enjoy a great discount!"

She had such perfect white teeth, Alia suspected they were manufactured, which was the latest trend. Rid yourself of unsightly natural teeth and implant your gum with bioengineered ones. Alia had saved enough to let Tariq undergo the procedure before he entered university in a few years' time. Even though she knew she was not at fault, she was plagued by a mother's guilt over Tariq's jutting upper canines and crowded front teeth. Besides, she didn't have anyone to impress other than her husband, and Basri loved her just the way she was. At least that was what he kept telling her every time she considered repairing parts of her body.

"Kiddo," she asked absently. "If you can forget something, what would it be?"

Tariq's fingers didn't stop moving, but he cocked his head slightly toward Alia. "This party you're throwing, Ma. My friends will think I'm such a freakasaur."

Freakasaur. That was another of his favourite phrases.

Wednesday
July 15, 2037
09:40 hours

"Tell me if you feel any pain or pressure," said Doctor Bashkar as he tightened a screw that secured a framework that kept her head immobile.

"Which you won't," Doctor Shafik chimed in.

"Don't mind him," said Doctor Bashkar. "He thinks that the substance P antagonist is a medical miracle. Do you feel anything?"

"No," Alia said. She could not move her head even a fraction. "What's that trickling down my scalp?"

"Just a bit of blood, nothing to worry about."

Alia felt the gentlest of touch as the surgeon wiped her scalp with a clean gauze.

"Since you wear the hijab, I'm not worried about your public appearance. I hope your husband won't mind, though. It's going to take some time before your hair grows back."

She had known before the surgery that they would have to shave her head as they had to cut open both sides of her scalp. Doctor Bashkar had even illustrated the incision lines and the underlying skull opening with the help of a holographic model of the head. Both Alia and Basri had been carefully explained the details of the surgery. Her husband wasn't happy, but her psychiatrist, Doctor Cynthia Khoo, conceded that this surgery was one of the best treatment options for Alia. She was the one who referred Alia to Doctor Bashkar after months of treatment.

It was one thing to see whole lengths of her hair floating down. Even though Alia wore the hijab, which covered her head and neck, hair is a woman's crown. She had another concern. "Will I have scars?"

Doctor Bashkar gave the frame a gentle shake to ensure it was fixed, then leaned down to meet Alia's eyes. "Can you believe that even with advanced robotic technology, I still have to do the initial incision by hand? Since I have to cut right down to the base layer, it'll disrupt the regenerative cells and that part will be replaced by scar tissue. Fortunately for everyone, we're advanced enough to ensure the scars won't show, and hair surrounding the scars will adequately cover them.

"We will do a test run of the MRI," Doctor Bashkar continued, "and then we'll scrub in and start the surgery. Don't worry when you hear the hum getting louder; it's the MRI working. Just relax. You're in safe hands."

Alia nodded by reflex, but her head wouldn't budge. "Okay, doc." She closed her eyes and whispered "Bismillah" under her breath. *In the name of Allah.*

The hum grew steadily louder, and the blue glow sped faster along the black band. Within minutes, coloured cross-sectional cuts of her head replaced the screensaver on the wall she was facing, with a revolving 3D image of her brain dominating the top right corner. The images were so detailed, she felt nauseous. Alia had not expected to witness the insides of her body, up to the pulsating vessels that riddled the multitude of folds of her brain. She could even see the titanium personal communicator cranial implant resting above her right ear, which was certified to be MRI-safe. It had to be switched off as to prevent interference, and for the first time in years, Alia's visual field was devoid of anything virtual.

"Beautiful, isn't it?" said Doctor Bashkar.

"Tell me if you feel like vomiting," offered Doctor Shafik. "I can give you some anti-emetics."

Behind her, Alia could hear sounds of packages being opened. She assumed the nurses were laying down all the surgical tools on their trolleys. From the corner of her eyes she could see Doctor Bashkar exiting the operating theatre, followed by the sounds of a pipe churning out water that lasted several minutes. Doctor Bashkar returned with both hands lifted in front of him, the dark hairs on his forearm plastered on his skin.

"Doctor," Alia whispered. "I think I'm going to need that anti-vomiting medication."

Friday
February 29, 2036
16:00 hours

Alia swiped her card on the screen at the corner of her parking lot to pay the parking fee and the cost of charging her car, and unplugged the charger from the insulated socket. Her late father used to complain about the ever-increasing price of petrol. Now Tariq only read about petroleum in history books. She wondered if her son realised how difficult life was in the early 2000s, and if he appreciated his privileged life. Alia sighed and studied Tariq, who was loading the groceries into the car. He'd only call her a freakasaur for reminiscing on the past.

"What?" Tariq asked.

"What what?"

"You're staring at me."

Alia grinned and ruffled his hair, which was awkward now that he was much taller than he used to be. "You're fourteen today, kiddo. I don't know when puberty is going to hit you—"

"Ma!" Tariq snapped. His ears were red.

"Fine, maybe you have reached puberty. Your Papa never said—"

"Ma!"

Alia laughed. "I'm embarrassing you, aren't I? Don't tell me your friends are online, listening."

"I would have clamped your mouth long ago if they were." He clearly did not share her amusement.

Alia kept her hand on Tariq's head, playing with his hair. He had his father's curls. He would need a haircut soon, though, judging on how deep her fingers were buried in his hair. He had not pulled away, which was always a good sign. They stayed awhile like that, mother and son, and she wished that moment would last forever. Her little boy was growing much too fast for her liking.

"Happy Birthday, kiddo."

Tariq huffed. "Come on, let's get this over with. Promise me this is the last leap-year birthday party you'll throw, okay?"

"You'll change your mind in four years, trust me."

Wednesday
July 15, 2037
10:15 hours

Alia found the stench of burnt flesh disconcerting. What was worse, the smell reminded her of barbecued meat, and her stomach growled. She hoped no one would notice it, what with the humming of the MRI and the loud whirr of drilling. The frame surrounding her head was covered with three layers of white cloths, leaving a window for her to look at the screen. By now, she actually found the image of her brain fascinating.

A clock blinked at the bottom corner of the screen, but Alia lost track of time. Instead, she concentrated on the songs playing in the background. She recognised the tracks. Maroon 5. Doctor Bashkar wasn't lying when he told her that he was of her age. She couldn't understand how Tariq loved listening to mind-trance using synthesised voices. The singers weren't even real people!

"Okay, Puan Alia," said Doctor Bashkar from somewhere behind her. "I've exposed both hemispheres of your brain. Don't be alarmed if parts of your body suddenly move. We'll try not to touch the motor strip. Now we'll use the fMRI to record the desired parts for the robotic arm to target its laser ablation."

Doctor Bashkar had explained all this to her during their second clinic appointment. She and Basri held hands as they listened to the surgeon's explanations, and Basri had asked detailed questions. Would there be permanent damage? What were the complications? What if the robotic arm fired at the wrong places? What was the percentage of success? For that 'unfortunate' zero-point-eight percent, what were the damages? They spent over two hours in the clinic, and when they reached home, Basri tried to talk her out of it.

But Alia had made up her mind. There was no turning back.

In the operating theatre, the music stopped. All noises ceased, except for the low hum of the MRI. A series of random images started playing in rapid succession. A ball, clouds, a car, birds, a holographic mind-trance idol, phrases and so on.

"Puan Alia," Doctor Bashkar said, his voice hushed. "I need you to concentrate on the images. Don't think about anything else. Just the images. Look at them, register what they are, but don't make any personal connections if possible."

The hum of the MRI became louder, but Alia ignored the sound. She concentrated on the images. Some of them reminded her of—

No. She must concentrate on the images alone.

The images stopped, and the rotating 3D projection of her brain took over the main screen. Only, there were now patches of colours in shades between red and blue that dominated the back of her brain, and smaller patches by the side at the front, more on the left compared to the right.

"Do you see the colours, Puan Alia?"

"Yes."

"The functional-MRI captures parts of your brain that's most active during the image capture. You see the colours at the back? Those are your occipital lobes, where your vision is processed. The ones at the front are your frontal eye fields. You have a beautiful brain, Puan Alia."

Trust a neurosurgeon to say that.

"Now," Doctor Bashkar continued, "I want you to close your eyes. I know it's going to be hard for you, but I want you to remember everything you can about your son. Can you do that?"

Alia had been preparing for this for over a week. She inhaled, deep. "Yes, doc."

She had done her best to suppress memories of Tariq, but now she had to willingly conjure images of him in her mind. She felt warm tears flowing as she remembered a wrinkly baby barely longer than her forearm wriggling against her, searching for her breast on instinct. She remembered a baby crying whenever he was left alone, tears coming and going at will. She remembered that same baby taking his first tentative steps, and his giggles as he ambled toward her open arms. She remembered a toddler showering her with kisses, bringing home an ebook filled with artwork he did at kindergarten, usually for her, and only on occasion for his father. She remembered her first argument with a little boy who came home with muddy clothes. She remembered coaxing the little boy to eat his vegetables, and finally resorting to threats.

She remembered him screaming, "Ma!"

Friday
February 29, 2036
16:29 hours

"Ma!" Tariq screamed.

Alia never liked distractions when she drove, but Tariq's voice was filled with urgency, and, above all, fear. She turned, but instead of seeing him, her eyes were fixed beyond him.

She should have looked at him. She should have looked at only him.

A deafening *bang*!

The trailer rammed against the car, sending it flying, turning, turning. Alia felt her neck whip about, and air rushed out of her lungs. She couldn't breathe. Strangely, after the initial noise, the whole world went quiet, even as air became land, land became air, and air became land again. The steering wheel burst and sent forth white foam that engulfed her, coalescing and pinning her against her seat. Before she knew what was happening, her vision was filled with white with flecks of black and red.

The car creaked and grated against the road, and she hung upside down. Adele was singing on the radio, but her voice was wrong, discordant. Alia's chest hurt. Breathing hurt. Her abdomen felt crushed; every small movement brought searing pain throughout her body. But she wasn't thinking about her pain.

"Tariq," she croaked. She choked on her own bile and saliva, and she coughed, which brought more pain. "Tariq."

Only Adele answered her. Alia remembered the lyrics; she used to sing along to the song. She would occasionally sing songs by Adele to lull Tariq to sleep.

"Tariq, *sayang*. Are you all right?"

Silence.

The foam slowly dissipated, collapsing into itself, leaving Alia free to move again. She was pinned close to the roof, but she could still twist in her seat. The passenger door had been crushed inward, and Tariq hung in his seat, drenched in blood. The dashboard on his side had been crushed, and the foam had not been released.

His arms fell limp, bloody.

Alia screamed.

Wednesday
July 15, 2037
10:32 hours

"Puan Alia," Doctor Bashkar said, "you can open your eyes now."

Alia opened her eyes and had to blink away tears before she could concentrate on the screen. Half her brain bloomed with bright patches of colours. Now she saw what her surgeon meant by her brain being beautiful.

"These are your memories of your son."

Half her brain. The entirety of her life.

Saturday
March 1, 2036
09:05 hours

Alia bathed whatever was left of her son for the last time. She held him gently, caressed him. She barely heard family and friends gathered in and out of her house reciting the *Yaasin.*

Tariq was no longer there.

Neither was she.

Wednesday
April 9, 2036
20:20 hours

Alia had left the food Basri bought for her untouched. Again. She sat on Tariq's unmade bed and counted the discarded clothes and socks on the floor. Everything was in place; no one had touched anything. Tariq had always hated it when she cleaned his room.

Monday
May 12, 2036

When Basri came back from work near midnight, Alia was sitting at the edge of Tariq's bed in darkness. She had not even bothered to turn on the light. She had not bothered to do anything, really. Bothersome. Tariq loved saying it.

June 30, 2036

The semiconductor company Alia worked for had to call Basri to inform him that they had to let her go. She had not come to work since the accident, but she had not replied to any of their mail.

Alia had turned off her cranial implant for months now.

July, 2036

Basri came home late again. This time, he found her lying on the carpeted floor at the foot of Tariq's bed, with a pool of congealed blood around her slashed wrist. On the bed was an opened album, a scrapbook, filled with pictures of Tariq. Alia had torn off everyone else from the pictures, including herself.

The doctors said she was lucky she had been too weak from malnutrition, and that the cuts were not deep. The next day, Doctor Cynthia

Khoo walked into the single-bedded hospital room. Alia was lying, unmoving, her wrists and ankles tied to the sides of the bed.

September, 2036

Doctor Cynthia Khoo assured Basri that they were making progress. In truth, Alia had tuned her out.

November, 2036

January, 2037

February, 2037

Alia spoke for the first time in months, but her words made her husband cry.

"Tariq's fifteen," she said. "My son's growing up so fast."

May, 2037

"What are you suggesting?" Alia asked Doctor Cynthia Khoo. "Do you really think I'll be better then?"

Her psychiatrist walked across the room, her steps heavy. She stopped in front of Alia and sat opposite her. "Nothing else is working. I think this is your best hope."

Wednesday
July 15, 2037
10:45 hours

"I need you to do one last thing for me, Puan Alia."

Images and videos of Tariq started playing in rapid succession. Everything she had recorded of him, she had given to Doctor Bashkar before she deleted the files from her cranial implant, as required as part of the treatment. Alia felt her breath catch.

"We will subtract the previous imaging, including our preliminary scans last week, and localise memories of Tariq. I need you to concentrate on these images and videos, and don't hold back on experiencing the emotions they bring. The fMRI will be active while the robotic arm ablates the targeted areas."

Alia did as she was told.

She had never done anything more difficult in her life. Giving birth to Tariq was nowhere near this painful. She had no choice. She had to erase all memories of Tariq if she were to live again.

Again, she concentrated on the images, and thought about the moments they captured. Tariq had patted his birthday cake right after she shot him blowing the candles. Tariq had fallen down the first time he rode an electrobike. She had shot the video, but in the chaos, she dropped the camera. Tariq argued with his father right after a Raya picture with Alia's side of the family. Tariq hugged her and told her he loved her. He was twelve. He hadn't told her that he loved her after that. He said he was too big for that, and it was bothersome.

Bit by bit, the coloured areas dissipated as the robotic arm did its job.

Tariq avoided family pictures. They were bothersome.

Where half her brain was filled with Tariq's memories, only half of that remained lit.

Tariq called her a freakasaur, but he was grinning ear to ear when he said that.

The lit portions became smaller and smaller.

Tariq screamed her name for the last time. His face was a blur.

"Stop! Stop!" Alia was crying in earnest, and she spluttered the word over and over again. "Stop!"

The recording stopped, and an image of her cradling baby Tariq in her arms dominated the main screen. The hum of the MRI subsided to a background noise. The operating theatre came alive with confused murmurs.

"Puan Alia," Doctor Bashkar said, his voice tentative. "Are you all right?"

"I can't lose him. I can't. Please, stop."

Thursday
July 18, 2037
00:28 hours

For two days after the surgery, the doctors kept Alia sedated. Whenever she was awake, she was inconsolable, and alternated between sobs and coos as she caressed the picture album she had brought along to the hospital. The album was a breach of protocol; she was not supposed to print out pictures of her son. She was supposed to delete all evidence of his existence.

Alia kept repeating Tariq's name, and kept asking for forgiveness. She refused to let go of the album, even when she was asleep. She clutched the only thing she had left of her son close to her heart.

That night, in her drugged sleep, Alia dreamt of Tariq.

He was fourteen, and he wore the same clothes he did the day he passed away. He was grinning. He hadn't smiled that bright in over a year. His teeth looked perfect the way they were, jutting canines and all.

"Kiddo?" Alia asked.

A blanket of mist covered everything. Darkness surrounded them, but somehow Tariq was aglow, illuminated by an invisible light source. He held his hands toward her, palms up. Alia reached for him. His hands were still small, and warm. So very warm.

"Where are you taking me, *sayang*?"

Tariq shook his head. Instead, he enveloped her in a tight hug. She did not remember him being this strong. Alia hugged him back and inhaled the scent of kiwifruit from his hair. He had refused to try other shampoos.

"I love you, Ma," Tariq whispered against her chest.

Friday
July 19, 2037
14:45 hours

Alia adjusted her hijab in front of the bathroom mirror as Basri packed her bag. Her surgical wounds were healing well, and Doctor Bashkar had promised almost non-visible scarring. She liked him. He was honest enough to not promise a scar-free healing.

"Ready?" Basri asked.

"Let's go home, *sayang*," Alia said.

He kissed her forehead, then squeezed her hand and led her out of the room. Doctor Bashkar met them near the nurses' counter; he was just completing his afternoon rounds. His smile was warm when he greeted them.

"Well, Puan Alia," he said. "I don't know if stopping the procedure was good for you or not, but I'm glad there is no permanent loss."

"Me too," said Alia. "Thank you so much, doc."

Basri shook hands with Doctor Bashkar and mumbled his gratitude. The doctor excused himself to continue with his rounds. Basri slung his arm across Alia's shoulder and guided her toward the lift. The lift was about to close when a young nurse came running toward them.

"Puan," she said, panting. "You forgot this."

The photo album. Alia took it, gently, and caressed the plain peach cover. "Thank you, dear."

Then she returned the album to the nurse.

Both Basri and the nurse stared at her, wide-eyed.

"He's a beautiful boy," Alia said, smiling. "His mother must love him so much, the way the pictures were taken. It's a good idea, putting such albums in patients' rooms. A good way to calm the nerves."

As the doors of the lift slid closed, Alia was still smiling at the gaping nurse. She did not give the album a second glance.

ABOUT FADZLISHAH JOHANABAS

Hailing from Kuala Lumpur, Malaysia, Neurosurgery Resident Fadzlishah Johanabas has published short stories, both speculative and contemporary fictions, in over 25 venues, both locally and internationally. In Memoriam was the first story he wrote after a major road-traffic accident that he still wishes never happened, that he still wishes he can forget. You can find him at http://www.fadzjohanabas.com, and he tweets as @Fadz_Johanabas.

Lola's Lessons

Shenoa Carroll-Bradd

~ Philippines ~

I grew up in a small village in the Philippines, at a time when the world was at war with itself. I don't remember the war, but I do remember the soldiers, and the day that my grandmother, my Lola, was taken.

We had gone out early in the morning with baskets slung on our backs to see if the mango trees along the river were ready to be plucked. I used to go by myself, scrambling up the trees, nimble as a monkey, but ever since the Japanese soldiers started haunting our streets and jungle, my Lola insisted on accompanying me.

We made it out of the village without being disturbed, and Lola told me stories of the many beasts who inhabited the jungle beyond. She told me of the aswang, and quizzed me on how to spot a manananggal, to see how well I'd listened to her tale the day before. We walked nearly all the way to the mango grove before three soldiers emerged from a nearby thicket and motioned us over. They wore huge guns at their sides, and belts of shiny brass bullets.

My Lola leaned down and whispered in my ear that I should be like a little mouse, and say nothing to attract the attention of such cats.

They surrounded us, prodding at our baskets, asking where we were headed so early in the day.

My Lola told them, and they scoffed.

"There aren't enough mangoes in that grove to fill a single basket," one growled.

"Maybe they're spies," another said. "Running off to sell their secrets."

The third pushed my Lola with his gun. "Do you even have any secrets left, old woman?"

Lola kept her nearly-toothless mouth shut, and her eyes down.

I couldn't understand why she let them speak to her that way. Around our house and throughout the village, lolas were always treated with respect. I glared up at the soldiers with their guns. These strangers had no manners.

The third man, the one who'd spoken last, caught my gaze, and frowned. "What are you looking at, little rat?" He spat between my bare feet.

I didn't answer him, but it didn't matter.

The soldier raised the butt of his gun above my head, ready to bring it crashing down.

Lola stepped in front of me and raised her arm, catching the full weight of the rifle between her wrist and elbow. Her arm cracked like a fresh bough, and dropped limp at her side. She staggered back a step, reaching around to push me behind her, so that all I could see was the mango basket slung across her back like a tortoise shell.

I ducked my head when I heard the soldier swing again, and Lola fell back against me. I held my hands up as far as I could, trying to brace her, trying to hold up my world. The day was warming already, but I remember that the sweat pouring off me felt cold and slick, like tree frog slime.

After that last blow, the soldiers let us pass, laughing and mocking as they went. Lola and I resumed our walk. Her left eye swelled and darkened like a passionfruit.

My stomach hurt worse than any hunger pains whenever I looked at her eye, or her dangling arm.

My Lola said nothing. She didn't even whimper.

"Maybe they were aswangs in human form," I said, hoping to distract her.

She shook her head slowly. "No, my little love. They were just men. Though sometimes, that can be just as bad."

We lapsed into silence. I wanted to say I didn't feel well, and suggest that we go back home, but how could I, after that? Hot tears tracked down my cheeks.

When Lola heard me sniffling, she stopped, and bent to face me at my level. Up close, her eye looked even worse, like purple liver under raw chicken skin. "Stop crying," she told me, though her speech seemed a little slurred, and one corner of her mouth didn't match the other. "If you don't stop crying, the aswang will come to take you away, and leave behind only a pile of sticks."

I wiped at my face with both hands, but the tears kept coming.

"Hush, my baby." She reached out with her good arm and stroked my hair. "Nothing calls monsters faster than tears, whether it's the monsters with guns, or the ones without."

I sniffed hard and nodded, fighting to banish the tears and snot.

Lola stood again, slowly, and we continued along.

When we reached the grove, I was disappointed to see that not many of the mangoes were ripe yet.

On better days, Lola had teased that she could sniff the mangoes out, like a little fruit bat in a dress, and would direct me from beneath the tree. We used to joke and play as we worked, but that day, she stared up between the branches and said nothing.

I set my basket by her feet and shimmied up the trunk, keeping an eye out for tree snakes and tarantulas. I did my best to show her what I'd learned, picking the ripest of the meagre harvest and dropping them into the basket below.

Lola settled onto the gnarled roots beneath my tree, and she stayed there even after I moved on to the next.

I said nothing, wanting to impress her with my skill and speed, to show her the extent of my independence. The mangoes kept me distracted, and didn't let me dwell on the soldiers or their cruelty, but the same was not true for Lola. Through the rustling leaves, I heard the soft sound of her weeping. She clearly didn't want me to know, so I pretended I didn't hear. I focused on the smooth mangoes, and tried to pretend that there was nothing else in the world but reaching out and plucking them down.

After a few minutes, I got the feeling of being watched. I assumed Lola had moved over to the base of my tree, and would soon start calling out directions, guiding me to the sweeter fruits, as it should be. But when I looked around, she had not moved, and I saw no one else in the grove. From my perch, I would have been able to spot anyone approaching, so I felt safe. I could watch over Lola, and let her have a little rest.

When I gathered all I could from my tree/lookout post, I slid down the trunk, skinning my brown knees against the bark as I descended. I dropped to the ground and grabbed my basket, then turned to check on Lola.

A man stood over her. A stranger.

My heart leapt, and I squeezed the basket tight.

He didn't look like a soldier. He wore no uniform, no gun, but I just couldn't understand how he'd gotten there without being spotted. He bent over her while she leaned against the tree trunk, eyes closed, just as she had been when I left her. His lips were moving, and as I drew closer, I saw that one long hand rested on her slumped shoulder.

I saw that her chest still rose and fell, easing some of my fright.

The stranger looked up at my approach, and took his hand away.

I hurried to my Lola's side, not making eye contact with the stranger, too afraid after all the trouble I'd caused with the soldiers. "Lola?" I gently took her good arm and shook it. "Lola, wake up."

She murmured something and began to stir.

I felt the stranger's gaze on me, and recognised it as the same weight of eyes from earlier. I steeled myself before glancing up at the stranger.

His dark, bloodshot eyes bored into mine, and I saw something there that made me feel like I was dreaming. My reflection was upside down in his eyes, as if I stood on my head.

Lola sat up, blinking and looking around.

"Good," the stranger said, bending to lift a long bundle of sticks all wrapped up in a brightly patterned blanket and tied with vines. "I only stopped to offer this lovely lady my assistance."

The timbre of his voice made my skin prickle. It was like wind and stone, and the creak of trees scraping against each other.

"We're fine, thank you." I stepped closer to Lola. "She's just fine, and we're heading back home now, so she can rest properly." I grabbed her hand, just to make sure. The stranger hoisted his parcel onto his shoulder and looked me up and down for a moment, as if trying to guess my weight. At last, he inclined his head. "Very well. I won't keep you." He turned and walked past us, through the grove and into the deeper jungle, vanishing into the sea of green.

Even after he disappeared, my skin stayed rife with goose bumps, despite the heat.

I turned my attention back to Lola, watching her carefully. "Did he hurt you? What did he say?"

She shook her head slowly and said nothing.

I glanced again in the direction the stranger had disappeared, but I saw no one and no longer felt the press of eyes. We were alone. "Why don't we go home early?" I suggested. "We have enough mangoes for today."

Lola nodded. Her eyes seemed flat and far away, but at least my reflection stood right-side up between her lashes.

I took the heavier basket and helped get hers settled across her back, careful not to brush or bump her arm. It had turned a terrible colour, like her eye. I took her good hand in mine, and we returned to our village. She walked slower than usual, lethargic and quiet, and her eye finally swelled shut. She seemed crushed beneath the weight of her years, and her wrinkled brown skin felt as rough and dry as papery bark.

*

My mother, my Nanay, did not cry when she saw the extent of Lola's injuries, though her eyes filled with sparkling tears that she refused to let fall. She washed Lola's face, and did her best to set the arm with her limited knowledge of local herbs.

Lola did not say a word to any of us, and when the midday meal came, she refused to even stir the contents of her bowl.

We all ate quietly, trying not to dwell on the day's darkness. After a while, my Nanay laid a hand on Lola's good arm. "Please," she said, "You need to eat. It will help you heal faster."

Lola did not respond. She stared into her bowl, head down, and would have seemed asleep, had her eyes not been open.

My Nanay shook her shoulder gently. "Please? Just a few bites, and then you can rest."

Lola did not respond, and when my Nanay shook her harder, she went completely limp and slumped sideways out of her chair, toppling to the floor. When she struck the ground, my Lola didn't sound like a woman any more. She rattled like the stranger's parcel.

My Nanay screamed as Lola split apart on impact. Her dry, wrinkled brown skin shattered, leaving behind a bundle of twigs and branches in a dress. A face stared up at us from the pile, hastily sketched in dark, dry blood.

*

I am old now, older than Lola was, and the soldiers have gone. When I was old enough to join our local militia, I did, even though the war was over. Day by day, soldier by soldier, I spread my influence throughout our militia and made sure no man raised a hand against lolas, or children.

I no longer wear the uniform or carry a gun, as I am now too tired to bear their monstrous weight. But I tell my tribe of grandchildren all the stories I know, all the warnings of the aswang and the manananggal, and they listen well. Each one carries a bulb of garlic and a packet of salt, and each one knows to look a stranger straight in the eyes.

I've often dreamed of meeting the aswang again, and of what I'd do differently this time. It is too late for all that now, but perhaps my Lola's lessons can keep my grandchildren safe, and reflected right side up. Because of her, I have taught them to find something to laugh about, no matter how sad, or scared, or lost they feel. Because of her, their tears will never call to monsters.

ABOUT SHENOA CARROLL-BRADD
Shenoa lives in Southern California and writes whatever catches her fancy, whether it's horror, fantasy, or anything in between. Say hello on Twitter @ShenoaSays or join her fan page at www.facebook.com/sbcbfiction.

WHEN THE RICE WAS GONE

Dominica Malcolm

~ South Korea ~

Rugged up in thermal underwear, a long-sleeved blouse, jeggings, and a winter coat, Song Ae-jung walked into the bathroom-sized freezer and made her way directly to the only shelf on which frozen vegetables remained. She knew exactly what was in each clear plastic zip-locked bag—zucchini, cucumber, spinach, white radishes, soybean sprouts, and *doraji*. After placing each bag into the basket she held in her left hand, she headed back to the freezer door. As she turned around, she looked back in at the now empty room and closed her eyes. She took a deep breath, allowing the cool air to fill her lungs, before opening her eyes again and shutting the door behind her.

Ae-jung placed the basket onto the counter, then removed her coat and placed it over the back of a wooden chair. While waiting for the the food to thaw, Ae-jung moved to a nearby cupboard to pull out a package of *gim*, sealed in an aluminium vacuum-pack for freshness, and the last clay pot of white rice. She looked inside and estimated about two cups remained; just enough for herself and her companions.

As Ae-jung poured the rice into a saucepan, Deangelo Freeman walked into the military base's large kitchen, carrying a four-litre bottle of water.

"I still can't tell if it's a good or bad thing that we've still got so much water, but we're down to the last of our food," he said.

Ae-jung turned around, stood on her tiptoes, and kissed Deangelo's dark cheek. "I don't care what it is," she said. "I'm sick of this place and can't wait to get out." She handed Deangelo a measuring cup. "Now please fill this up and get the rice started. I'm going to go check on Ki."

She found her husband, Ki-ryong, snug beneath a half-dozen blankets and laying on several pillows spread over the stone-cold floor. Kneeling down next to him, Ae-jung placed the back of her hand over his forehead and felt the heat sear up through her skin. She frowned thoughtfully, and hoped the meal she and Deangelo were preparing would help take some of the fever away. The last thing she wanted was to lose him the way so many others had perished, deep beneath the city of Seoul.

Her mother was the first person she knew to go, when Ae-jung was only ten. That was a quarter of a century ago now. She was orphaned after that, as her father had remained above ground to help with the battle against the North. Once the US base lost contact with the outside world, they were on lockdown. No one went in or out. But that was about to change.

✦

"Bibimbap's ready," Ae-jung said, bringing in a tray with three bowls of rice topped with julienne vegetables, each ingredient separate from the others.

Ki-ryong sat up and let his blankets fall off his shoulders as he took the bowl in his hands. He inhaled deeply and savoured the scent of the cooked vegetables and rice before Deangelo handed him a set of chopsticks and a long-handled spoon.

"This looks so good, Ae," Deangelo said as he took his own bowl and kneeled down on a cushion at the table that was placed inside a hole in the ground.

Ae-jung sat down next to him, placing her feet in the hole. Deangelo picked up the bottle of sauvignon, which he claimed to have found in some long-dead army official's quarters, and had been saving for such an occasion as this.

He poured the wine into each of the glasses in front of them, and turned to Ae-jung. "Do you wanna make a toast?"

Lifting up her glass, Ae-jung said, "To our last meal in this hell-hole. May whatever is left above ground not be as shit as this."

"Hear, hear!" the men agreed, lifting their glasses, too.

They clinked together, and then moved immediately to mix their bibimbap. The meal was enjoyed in silence so that they could remember every taste that crossed their lips, not knowing if this meal would be their last ever upon the Earth.

⌀

The trio stood at a metal ladder that reached two floors above them, and led to a manhole cover. Time had not been well kept in the last couple of years, with more important survival issues to deal with, so they had no idea what month it was or what the weather would be like outside, if it was even habitable. Each of them were dressed in as many clothes as they could find in case it was winter, and therefore colder in the sun than underground, and carried a backpack full of various equipment they considered they might need.

Deangelo stood nearest to the ladder. "Let me go first," he said. "My Pa trained me to deal with anything when I was young. He didn't want me to be just another civilian."

Ae-jung and Ki-ryong had heard the story countless times of Deangelo's army-trained father getting stuck inside during the lockdown and wanting to make himself useful. He didn't just train Deangelo, but several other children born of military parents, no matter their age. They didn't interrupt him, however, as they both knew how important it was for Deangelo to keep his father's memory alive through the repetition.

"Stay down here until I know it's safe, okay?"

The Koreans nodded.

"In case I don't come back," Deangelo added, "know that I love you both."

He kissed them both firmly on the lips: Ae-jung first, followed by Ki-ryong.

"I love you," Ki-ryong mouthed, having lost his voice to illness.

Ae-jung simply held in a breath and tried not to cry, not wanting to consider the possibility of Deangelo not coming back.

⌀

Secured to the ladder with climbing equipment, Deangelo pounded a sledgehammer against the manhole several times until he finally pushed through. Pieces of rubble fell to the ground beneath him, and he was glad he couldn't see his companions below. As he pulled himself through the hole, it took Deangelo a few blinks before he could see anything. It hadn't occurred to him that it might be nighttime, what with having just finished lunch, unless there was some other reason for there to be no sun. The lack of heat from the sky thus made Deangelo glad he was wearing a ski suit, though there had not been as much as a speck of snow on the ground.

The second thing Deangelo noticed, after the absence of light, was how still everything seemed. It was eerily quiet, with not even a hint of insects chirping. In the short distance that was visible to him in the dark, he could see weeds and shrubs growing over building ruins. He suspected he could even see a cherry tree further out, and felt inexplicably drawn to it. Each shallow step closer he took, the more it felt like someone's spirit was drawing him to it. His mother's?

A memory of springtime in one of Seoul's beautiful gardens came to him. His mother, a short Japanese woman, picking a cherry blossom from a low-hanging branch, and placing it in the short, tight curls atop his head. She kissed him on the cheek and called him "Prince." Two weeks after that, Deangelo was told she'd been shot dead by a North Korean spy because of his father's position in the US Army.

When he reached the tree, Deangelo felt a feminine-sounding whisper in his ear. It sounded like, "Save them."

He turned around, but he couldn't see anyone. If there had been even a light breeze, he could've blamed the whisper on that, but there was none. It was definitely not his mother's voice, though.

Deangelo, they need you.

This time the voice sounded more like it was inside his head rather than a whisper in his ear.

"Who are you?" Deangelo asked the voice, feeling rather foolish. "Who do I need to save?"

The Songs.

"How do you…?" he started to ask, but hesitated. "This is ridiculous," he said to himself. "I've just been underground too long. And now I'm talking to myself."

Deangelo shut himself up and turned back to the cherry tree, picking a bud from the nearest branch. He decided that if there was life like this here, there couldn't be much nuclear fallout remaining, if indeed there had been at all.

✎

Ae-jung and Ki-ryong were curled up on a tarnished brown leather couch when Deangelo returned.

"There's no one out there," Deangelo said, "but it looks safe enough."

Ki-ryong coughed in reply, and Ae-jung added, "We have no other choice."

Deangelo agreed and held out a hand to Ki-ryong. As he pulled Ki-ryong to his feet, Deangelo asked, "Are you going to be alright to climb to the surface on your own?"

A shrug was all Ki-ryong could muster.

"He'll manage," Ae-jung said, standing up and putting her arm around her husband's shoulder. "But if not, we can tether him to you, and you can go first."

With a nod, Deangelo agreed, and added, "There's just one more thing. There's no sun, at least not right now."

"So what do we do? Wait until it's light?" Ae-jung's brow was raised, but there was not enough skin on her forehead to furrow.

"I don't think so. We can find somewhere to hide in the dark without disturbing anything, and wait. See if anyone else is around then." Deangelo's thumb rested on his five o'clock shadow while he scratched his nose, then added, "Sound good?"

✐

When they reached the still air, the sky seemed darker to Deangelo. From a pocket in his backpack, he pulled out a flashlight, compass, and map of Seoul. With the bombed buildings that surrounded them, he knew he wasn't necessarily going to be able to get his bearings so well, and his memory of the city from when he was a boy of eleven—the age he was when he entered the lockdown—was rather shaky.

"I think we should head north," Deangelo said, "away from the river." He was referring to the river that separated Old Seoul from New Seoul. "I want to try and find out just how much damage the North did here."

With Ki-ryong's condition, the journey to Gyeongbokgung from Itaewon-ro took several hours, but still the sun did not rise in that time. Many of the buildings they passed were in ruins, and empty cars with blown out windows littered the streets.

"It looks like there's not a soul left in Seoul," Deangelo joked, trying to lift their spirits rather than focus on the negatives of possibly being the last people alive, but the others didn't laugh.

One notable structure that remained standing was a Buddhist temple, where they temporarily stayed to allow Ki-ryong to catch his breath.

Deangelo explored the temple grounds while the others rested, and came across the skeleton of a monk. The only way he could tell who the body belonged to was the orange cloth that covered the bones. After his eyes could no longer focus on it, he returned to his partners.

"Let's go," he said. "We can't stay here."

"Ki still needs time," Ae-jung said, watching Ki-ryong's short intakes of breath.

Deangelo handed her his backpack. "Carry this," he said, "and I'll carry Ki."

Ae-jung did as she was asked, and Ki-ryong climbed atop Deangelo's back, wrapping his puffy-coat covered arms loosely around Deangelo's neck. Deangelo checked the map and his compass in the light of his flashlight, and continued navigating them to the north.

When they reached the ancient palace and took in the features of Gyeongbokgung, there was not an eye that did not water. The red paint had faded due to lack of care, but the dark-green roofs were there, and the whole place looked untouched.

"I guess the North didn't have a complete disregard for our history," Ae-jung said, once she was able to lift her jaw up from her chest.

From Deangelo's back, Ki-ryong dropped down to the large stone field that stood between the palace walls and the palace gate that they had just walked through. The emotion that overwhelmed his entire being came out in a passionate kiss for both his wife and Deangelo. He then pulled them both close to him on either side of his body.

"It doesn't make sense, though." Ae-jung looked between her husband and lover. "Not from everything we've been told about the North. Why would they have saved this place?"

They got their answer when they made their way through to the double-roofed Geunjeongjeon Hall. As they climbed the steps to the building that was once home to the king's throne, an acrid stench began to fill their noses. It was too dark for them to yet see what was causing the smell, but they had to know.

"Let me go first," Deangelo said, but Ae-jung shook her head.

"No. This is my country, my history..." Ae-jung trailed off, not wanting to say too much that may offend the American, because it had been his home, too, for most of his life. Skin-tone didn't change that,

186

and Deangelo had felt like part of her family for the last couple of years. "Follow close behind me," she added. "Catch me if I fall."

Ki-ryong looked at her with sad, questioning eyes. She shook her head at him, too.

"Please stay here," she said to her husband. "You're too sickly, and I don't know if we'll find something that can kill you."

Ki-ryong nodded and slowly climbed back down to the bottom of the steps, and sat on the second from last of them, with his feet flat on the ground. Ae-jung turned to Deangelo and grabbed his hand so he could hold hers in it, making her feel more protected. Together they climbed the remaining steps, and when they reached the top, they couldn't believe their eyes.

Through the wide open doors immediately before them was an enormous pile of human remains. The bodies were at various stages of decomposition, which made Deangelo wonder if the war was still going on, or if the North had just used some kind of chemical to partially embalm the bodies and intentionally sicken anyone who should happen across them. Of those that had faces, they all looked feminine.

When Ae-jung caught sight of a child's wide-eyed, horrified face on the body of a skeleton, she closed her eyes, took a large intake of air through her mouth, and turned around to rest her head on Deangelo's chest.

"Let's go," he said. "We can't stay here."

Back to the river.

The soothing woman's voice from the cherry tree had returned to Deangelo's mind, but he shook it out of his head, not wanting to start calling himself crazy. The river would be a terrible idea.

"But where can we go?" Ae-jung asked, looking up at Deangelo's dark eyes. "There were so few habitable buildings on our way here, and it could be light soon. Ki isn't even fit to keep going."

"Then we'll keep going, check the Queen's Quarters, the King's Quarters, all of the other buildings here if we have to, to see if any are empty." Deangelo said. "At least so we'll have somewhere to stay during the light. We can move on again after the next sundown."

"I don't think I can handle any more bodies," Ae-jung said, taking Deangelo's hand and leading him back down the stairs. "I'll stay here with Ki while you go find us somewhere to stay, okay?"

Deangelo briefly kissed her lips and agreed. "I'll be back soon."

The three of them ended up staying in a room at the old Folk Museum after Deangelo informed them that the rest of the palace buildings were much like the throne hall. When the sun finally rose, they were curled up together on a carpeted floor, next to an old cart encased in glass. Ki-ryong was in the middle, with Ae-jung resting her head on his chest, and Deangelo's right arm wrapped around his waist. The windowless room hid the sunlight, allowing them to sleep.

Ae-jung was the first to wake, but she did not wish to rouse the others. She walked through the hallway to the entrance of the building, passing the broken glass doors which were once automatic, and sat down on the stone steps to watch the sunset. Splashes of pink and purple painted the sky to her right.

Her body jumped a little, startled, when Deangelo came and sat down beside her.

"I don't think it's a good idea for us to make Ki walk again tonight," he told her. "I want you to stay here with him while I try and hunt down some food, or medicine. Both, if I can manage it. I think it'll be easiest to do on my own."

Ae-jung simply nodded, and watched as Deangelo stood and took out his map, compass, and flashlight before heading east. She stayed there until the sun was lost to the night, and returned to her husband in the museum.

Ki-ryong was awake, then, staring at the cart in the dark. He didn't even flinch when Ae-jung entered the room, just asked in a husky voice, "Do you remember..." but he trailed off, unable to use his larynx further.

"Do I remember what?" Ae-jung asked, and came down to his level, looked in his eyes and tried to determine his meaning. "Anything from before the lockdown?"

He nodded, and Ae-jung took his head in her hands, and brushed his fringe out of his eyes. "I remember my mother's calming touch," she said, and kissed him on his forehead. "I remember how much she loved me, and wanted for me." She took Ki-ryong's hands in hers now. "How she wished I'd been born in another time, or another country."

Ae-jung noticed a tear in the corner of her husband's left eye, so she wiped it away with her thumb.

"But I think about what that would've meant for me, and not in a good way. I wouldn't have met you." She kissed him on the lips. "Or Deangelo. Maybe you two wouldn't have even met without me." She brushed her fingers through Ki-ryong's hair. "Do you remember when I introduced you?"

A smirk of a smile crossed his face, and Ae-jung knew he was picturing it. It wasn't the most sane introduction, but somehow the line, "Ki, I found you some manmeat, Deangelo," always brought a smirk to both men's faces. She had actually meant to say, "Ki, I found you a man, meet Deangelo," but had stumbled over her words.

Prior to that meeting had been a discussion between Ae-jung and Ki-ryong. Ae-jung recounted her memory of it for Ki-ryong, trying to keep his brain occupied while they waited for Deangelo to return.

"At first I didn't know what to think," she said, "when you first told me you liked men. I felt betrayed, like you married the wrong person. I thought it meant you wanted to leave me, like it would be easy for me to move on and find someone else in what was already a small underground community by then. But then you told me it didn't mean you loved me any less. It took me weeks to figure out you meant it, because I didn't want to share the bed with you at first."

Ki-ryong moved around behind her, and wrapped an arm around her waist.

"And just like that," she said, "you did this, and I knew. You still wanted me. You just also needed to experience the touch of a man."

Ae-jung began to remove her coat, and hoped their body heat could keep them warm. If they only had one more night together, she wanted Ki-ryong to be able to remember it into the afterlife.

§

It was near dawn when Deangelo finally returned. He'd had to scour much of what was left of the north of Old Seoul, but had managed to bring back some bags of dried noodles.

"All the drug stores have been picked clean," he told them, looking sorrowfully at Ki-ryong.

Ki-ryong embraced the dark-skinned man and kissed him so Deangelo would know he appreciated the effort. When Ae-jung joined them, hands and fingers tore at clothes, then lips and mouths were added to the mix to explore their bodies. The temperature in the room rose, and sweat pooled on Deangelo's back more than it did for the Koreans. Their exertion wore them out and brought them to sleep, so they wouldn't have to worry about facing the day once the sun rose.

When it was about midday, Ae-jung began to feel restless. She grabbed her clothes and rugged up, leaving her men with Ki-ryong laying his head on Deangelo's naked chest.

Walking out the broken glass doors, Ae-jung felt an overwhelming sense of solitude. She didn't know why Deangelo was so worried about them wandering around in the day. There was no one left in Seoul. He might have thought he was making a stupid pun joke the night they left the military base, but he was right. There were no souls left in Seoul. Deangelo surely couldn't have found food if there had been.

With the light of the sun on her side, she decided to let her men rest and see what she could find in the next few hours. She didn't bother to take Deangelo's map or compass with her, since she planned to walk in one direction only, and then straight back again.

What Ae-jung didn't expect was getting smacked in the back of her head with a blunt object only an hour into her journey, and falling to the pavement beneath her feet.

When she came to, her nose felt of dried blood, and someone was pulling her hair. It looked like she was inside some kind of warehouse. Her hands were bound behind her back.

"*Nǐ hǎo*," a voice said, and then added a bunch of other words she didn't understand as the voice's owner dragged her to her feet.

"I don't speak Chinese, asshole," Ae-jung spat, spraying saliva on his face.

"Ah, then you must be South Korean," the stranger said with a thick Chinese accent, "choosing English as your second tongue."

Ae-jung didn't reply, trying to figure out what he meant by that. The North had learned Chinese? The North had China on their side?

He observed her with his hands firmly on her upper arms. "How did you get here?" he asked.

"I could ask you the same thing."

The man shook his head. "I'm the one asking the questions."

"I've lived here my whole life," she spat. "This is my home. It's not for you, or the northern scum. What are you anyway, just some scavenger?"

He didn't answer her. For a moment his whole face went blank, and Ae-jung thought it could be her chance to escape. His arms fell limp at his sides, and she cautiously stepped backwards, hoping any movement wouldn't re-capture his attention.

Ae-jung heard him whisper, "What do you want me to do?"

She watched his face contort, back to the man who asked the questions, then to something more menacing. Ae-jung turned and ran for her life, but before she could reach the door, he'd grabbed her head. Before she could gasp, he swiftly twisted her neck until she fell to the ground, lifeless.

Deangelo woke up with a start, in turn frighting Ki-ryong awake, who was still lying on his chest. They both looked around the room, and then back at each other with horrified expressions.

"Where's Ae?" Deangelo asked.

The river.

That voice from the cherry tree was back, whispering in his mind.

"Why would she be at the river?"

Ki-ryong just looked at him with the most confused look. Then he heard it too.

The river.

Choking and then coughing, Ki-ryong found as much strength as he could manage and started dressing himself. Deangelo followed suit. They both ran out the broken glass doors, leaving most of their belongings behind. Deangelo had his bearings now, and took hold of Ki-ryong's hand, pulling him south as they ran in the light of the moon.

After about an hour, they stopped at an intersection and jumped inside a car to sit down and catch their breaths.

"What are we doing, Ki?" Deangelo asked, knowing well that Ki-ryong wouldn't be able to give him much of an answer. "We're listening to a voice in our heads, that's what. We're going crazy." He placed his hand on Ki-ryong's beside him. "Was it Ae who kept us sane?"

Ki-ryong shook his head and pointed in the direction they were headed.

"The river?" Deangelo asked.

Ki-ryong shook his head again.

"The military base?"

A nod this time.

"You think we're losing our marbles because we left it?" Deangelo offered, and got another nod in reply. "So, what, the atmosphere here is polluted with something that makes us lose it?"

A shrug.

"I find it hard to believe the North had that kind of tech," Deangelo said.

And then he heard Ae-jung's voice in his mind, calling. *Deangelo. Deangelo, where am I?*

He looked at Ki-ryong and asked, "Did you hear that?"

Again, some confusion from Ki-ryong, but then his eyes open wide. "Ae," he mouths.

"We don't know where you are," Deangelo said aloud. "Where did you go? Why can we hear you in our heads?"

I… I remember… a Chinese man.

Ki-ryong and Deangelo looked at each other, trying to figure out what she meant.

A warehouse.

"Are you there now?" Deangelo asked. "I saw some when I was out last night."

No. Water.

And then as if saying that word in their heads made her acknowledge her predicament, Ae-jung gasped, and said no more.

"The river," Deangelo said, and Ki-ryong mouthed at the same time.

They pushed the car doors open and continued their journey south, at a quicker pace than they had before. Somehow hearing Ae-jung had helped give them strength as they worried for her safety.

When they reached the river, the crossed a bridge halfway and looked in both directions. It felt hopeless. Ae-jung could be anywhere.

Suddenly they heard a splash in the opposite direction, and another gasp. Deangelo ran to the east side of the bridge first and saw her.

"Ae," he yelled, and then Ki-ryong was at his side.

Deangelo dived into the water, his ski coat keeping the cold from penetrating his chest, but his legs were freezing. When he got about a metre away from her, arms outstretched, ready to pull her close and save her, something pulled him under, and soon he was fighting for his life, thrashing about. As he was dragged under, he noticed a pink fish tail with yellow fins at the end had replaced Ae-jung's legs. As shock overcame him, he looked down and saw the face of a pale-skinned woman. The cause of his demise. She, too, had a fish tail, but hers was blue. His last, wide-eyed thought was, *Mermaids?*

When Deangelo didn't come back up, Ki-ryong dived in after him.

Given the choice of his sole survival between the three of them, which likely wouldn't last anyway, given his illness, and possible death now, it didn't even need to be asked.

When he locked eyes with Ae-jung, he felt her sorrow throughout his body. She met him halfway, kissed his mouth, and pulled him under.

It's done, Li Qiang. Now come, be rewarded.

The words permeated the Chinese man's mind, and an image of its owner followed. A naked white woman he'd met by the river when he was fishing one night.

As he followed her instruction, heading south, his mind fell to the memory of that meeting.

She was sitting on some rocks, or rubble, he couldn't specifically remember.

"Help me," she called to him.

He walked straight up to her and asked, "Are you real?"

In the four months he'd been in Seoul, he hadn't seen another human. He'd been sent there by his government to see if there was anything they could salvage from the remains of the city, and then abandoned when he lost his communications device. Li Qiang presumed they thought him dead. Seeing the foreign woman had him wondering if they were right.

The woman nodded. "Come here and touch me if you don't believe it," she said.

As he reached out to her, she grabbed his hands and placed them on her breasts.

"How... how can I help you?" he asked, pulling his hands back.

"There is a Korean woman here, somewhere in this city. I want you," she said, placing a finger to his chest, "to find her."

"What then?"

"Keep her until further instruction."

"And what will I get in return?" he asked.

She stood up, took one of his hands, placed it on her buttocks, and kissed him firmly on the lips. "More of that, taken to the next level."

He watched her, dumbstruck, as she then walked toward the river, and disappeared.

It wasn't until he found the Korean woman that Li Qiang realised it was not a dream. He tried to keep the memory of holding her captive from entering his mind next, but the woman's words filled his mind.

Kill her.

Inside the warehouse, when the Korean woman came around, he got curious. He wanted to know where she'd come from; why he hadn't seen her before. But it wasn't to be. The white woman had other plans.

Kill her now, while you still can.

Her voice continued to echo in his head, even now, and he wondered why he was returning to a woman who would make him do this. A woman who could put thoughts in his mind.

Then he stopped in his tracks. This was not what he wanted. He lifted one foot and twisted to go back the way he'd come, but as soon as that foot hit the ground, a song filled his head. He entered a trance as the song drew him back toward the river.

As torturous as the words sounded—incongruous with the soothing tune—he could not stop himself from walking.

> *Come to the river*
> *You are the last man in Seoul*
> *All Koreans gone*
> *Come to the river*
> *Where lay the men from the war*
> *Victims of my song*
> *Come to the river*
> *Meet your beautiful lady*
> *Take me on a date*
> *Come to the river*
> *Receive me at my best, and*
> *Meet Mr Kim's fate*

Though Li Qiang knew Kim was probably the most common Korean name, somehow hearing it in his head like this made him realise she was referring to the North's former dictator. Had this fair songstress controlled him, too?

For a moment, the song paused, long enough for the woman to whisper in his head, *Yes.*

He could see the river by now, and—hoping it could buy him some time—asked, "But why?"

I was murdered by my Korean lover, when his wife discovered us.

But Li Qiang wasn't listening too closely to her, trying to figure out any possible escape route. Before he could turn and run, she began repeating the song, the trance returned, and he walked on. Then he saw her, standing naked in the middle of a bridge. He could see her mouth moving in time with her lyrics, but they remained in his head instead of escaping her mouth, until he was three metres away from her.

"Wha— What do you want from me?" Li Qiang asked, when she had finished her song and taken hold of both his lower arms. He had to look up at her, as she had about fifteen centimetres on him. "What *else*, I mean?"

"Do you not wish to make love to me?" she asked with sultry eyes.

He was too fearful about what that would mean for him now, so he slowly shook his head.

Then you die sooner. Her words penetrated the deepest recesses of his mind in a painful manner he'd never felt with her words previously. It was enough of a distraction that she was then able to drag him over the edge of the bridge, where she dived into the river. As the pain receded in his head, he saw her legs morph into a tail. All too late did he discover the truth.

Seoul was destroyed by a vengeful, genocidal mermaid.

ABOUT DOMINICA MALCOLM

Dominica Malcolm is the author of *Adrift*, a speculative fiction novel that follows pirate Jaclyn Rousseau in the 17th and 21st centuries. As with her novel, her writing tends towards pirates and/or mermaids, though she also writes dystopias. Look her up on Goodreads to find other anthologies she's been published in.

Though born in Western Australia, Dominica holds citizenship in both Australia and the USA, and currently lives in Malaysia with her husband and two children. She travels a lot, having been to over 30 countries in 6 continents around the world, which inspires some of her writing. She has a Bachelor of Science in Internet Computing, and a Graduate Diploma in Media Production. Checking out her web site (http://dominica.malcolm.id.au) will lead you to music videos and short films she's worked on, as well as sample stand-up comedy, artwork, and writing.

THE HEALER

Aashika Nair

~ India ~

Apple extract and mint – a task for secrets.
Raspberry juice and cinnamon – love potion.
Lemon juice, anise and a splash of strawberry – to forget.

Sonal ran through the list in her head, closing her eyes as she sat in the city park. The faint pink-and-orange blossoms from the tree fell gently as the wind scooped them from the branches and laid them on the ground with the softest landing possible. It was an evening of sorts; calm and cool on the exterior but maybe, behind the clouds, a plan was brewing. Sonal's fingers moved slightly, as if she were coming awake from a coma.

Her thoughts shifted to her present life circumstances, and she wondered again if she had chosen the right path. After all, the Head Mistress had carefully elucidated her two options, her tone expressing her preference.

And Sonal had picked to continue her life as a Young Mistress here. On Earth. In this very town of Manipal.

The Head Mistress, though blatantly disapproving, allowed her wish to be granted—Sonal was not the first, and neither would she be the last to make that choice. So, Sonal quietly packed her necessities, rented a cosy little apartment across the crystal rivulets on the west side of town, and minded her own business.

Three months had since disappeared. She sighed inwardly and stirred, as did the fallen leaves in hushed whispers.

That's when she felt the shift in the weight of the bench and a pained panting. Her eyes darted left.

The boy had piercing eyes, but she had no time to register its details.

He had been pierced.

He didn't respond at first, seeing her but not quite seeing her too. Angry puce blotches bloomed across his red shirt and tattered shorts, and his bony kneecaps jutted out at an almost obscene angle.

"Gang fight… knife… after me," he wheezed out. Then, he trailed off and promptly collapsed into her lap head-first.

Sonal didn't know who he was, or the truth. But the wound looked deadly, and it was time to show she could do she was did best after years of training. She threw his arm over her left shoulder and brought him back to her apartment in small, quick steps.

Lightning forked the warm grey sky.

⌁

The boy had been sleeping deeply on her bed since yesterday evening. Sonal had slowly spooned in a mixture of peach tea with crushed poppy seeds, to heal his internal tissues and wounded organs throughout the night. Amidst his feeble, half-delirious attempts to brush her off, she applied the avocado-saffron paste to his right abdominal region. She couldn't help but stare at his ribcage as she thumbed the paste across the deep wound—his bones were arranged as if on display for a counting game.

Sonal felt slightly uneasy, as if the boy had known who she was—what she was—and came to her for help, of all the people in the park. Who was he? She herself had never tended to a male before. In her world, the healing mistresses were all females, and so were most of their patients—only a select few, out of dire necessity, were male.

She picked up a change in breathing noise. The boy had awoken. He sat up slowly, scanning the small room. She noted how quietly he breathed.

"Thank you," he said, his voice surprisingly crisp and clear.

She sat at the edge of the bedside, checking his pulse and wounds.

"How are you feeling?"

He smiled shyly, and she caught a glimpse of his teeth. *Perfect for a scrawny thing like him*, she thought enviously and briefly remembered how her mother used to rub neem leaves on her teeth to whiten them.

"Much better... I'm Aditya." He stuck out his hand, oddly formal for someone who looked only a couple of years younger than she was. She took it up.

"I'm Sonal. Wait here, I'll get your lunch." She slipped into her kitchen to spoon the soup and bring the food tray to the bed. He ate with gusto, yet she could tell he was savouring the consistency and taste of the broth. A comfortable silence washed over the little scene.

"You're very beautiful. The girls where I live don't look like you do!"

She blushed at his sudden words; obviously this wasn't one kid who filtered his thoughts first. It had been a long time since she heard the compliment without feeling icky, under the obsidian glare of drunken men in dark alleyways. Her mother used to tell her that, until she reached eighteen. Then, she had told Sonal, "Show me that your skill and courage match that beauty of yours." That was also the last time Sonal saw her mother.

"So... you want to tell me how you ended up with a knife through your ribs?"

He grinned and burst into his adventure animatedly.

❧

Two months passed. Aditya came to live with her, having decided to permanently leave his 'god-awful' orphanage. "No wonder Lord Krishna doesn't come when they pray to him!"

He took a helper's job at the local market, and often brought her back tasty snacks—some of which he pilfered. Though the living-in arrangement drew no attention, she wouldn't have bothered about it—*she wasn't exactly one of them, was she?* She was fairly certain he was head over heels in love with her; she herself had become terribly fond of him.

His wit and humour belied someone his age, and he never failed to make her laugh every day. "You're too serious. If you never smile, you'd only have me to marry!" he'd tell her, eliciting a giggle. *Mating? Yes. Marrying? Heck no.*

Sonal watched him often, thinking about the deception. *Here he is telling me everything about him; his friends, his shoddy school. His dreams, his poor literacy skills. His secrets. So naïve, so trusting.*

She wished she could reciprocate that. *But he mustn't know. He cannot know. Our world is a world of secrets.* She'd recite the warning forcefully in her mind, as if clamping down a restraint on a mad dog.

His eyes were a mystery to her—a clear sable, flecked with tiny strokes of grey on their tranquil surface upon closer inspection. They were so familiar, like fragments of an old song in one's mind, but never loud enough for one to catch the lyrics. *I bet Diya would know, she knew everything about anything!*

Thinking about Mistress Nindiya aroused the old feelings of missing her companions. *I wonder what they felt when I left—Nindiya wasn't thrilled with my decision.* And neither were the other women, really.

Aditya would have to leave soon. The Head Mistress always had her spies, and sometimes took up observations herself through the veil between this world and her own. If anything happened—meaning if Sonal broke their rules—she was sure the Head Mistress would pay her a 'kindly visit', austere eyes and all.

It was a Saturday night in charming Manipal when the boy, having turned fifteen, hugged her tight and kissed her chastely on her cheek.

"I would've died without you that day." And he fell asleep.

Sonal's heart broke a little. What would she do now?

That's when the woman in red appeared behind her. Startled momentarily, Sonal recovered quickly in this parallel dimension she'd transcended into and gave a little bow.

"Hello, Mother."

The Head Mistress studied her daughter. To see Sonal in the flesh was a joy, but one she chose to suppress.

"You have to stop this. That boy has to go. Or you have to come back." She stared at Sonal sternly, her clear brown eyes seeming to solidify in tandem with her tone.

"I know, but—Why?" Suddenly, she registered that phrase in her mind. "Why does he 'have to go'? Why would you say that?" Sonal worked up some defiance.

Silence.

"There are secrets and reasons in this world—yes, as ever there will be in our world—that is better left unknown. Just do as I say, please," came the authoritative command.

Something is very wrong with this picture.

"You can't tell me that and expect me to simply drop everything. I deserve to know why! I rescued the boy! I kept him alive!" She trailed off, tears threatening to spill over as she tried to choke back a sob. "I'm healing him."

She poured her frustration and anger, accumulated over the years at her mother's reticence and, sometimes, barely maternal attitude. One salty droplet escaped her eyes.

More silence from the Head Mistress.

Sonal wasn't sure how much time slowed down. Was it, too, waiting for something to be revealed, or did it already know as much?

"Because... because, he is your brother."

And time stood still.

"Boys and men aren't allowed in the arcane, ancient world of female healers... our interests at heart are towards women, first and foremost. I made the grave mistake of falling in love with a male I never saw again after I became pregnant. So I gave this boy up for adoption and refused to continue our female bloodline—I couldn't risk having another boy.

"The nature of my job demands that I protect the strands of our realm from fraying at its edges. I protect our maligned, oppressed female kind. What we do, Sonal, is delicate and healers are only gifted with abilities from special lineages, like ours. I cannot have you coming to love him, the way you should a younger sibling, because he jeopardises everything you stand for as a healing mistress, trained to take over my position someday. You may hate me, but there is a greater good in why I do this. Please..."

That was the first time, through her glassy vision, that Sonal saw her mother lapse into emotional vulnerability.

To carry out your duty.

Sonal could finally understand at least a fraction of the gravity of the word.

Moments came and ran within their time stream, and finally when she gained some self-control, the Head Mistress kissed Sonal's forehead.

She had to do it.

The next day broke into a crisp October morning. Sonal was cheerful, and gave Aditya a glass of her specially-created tea, taking him for a walk in the city park.

The tea of lemon juice, anise and a splash of strawberry.
To forget.

ABOUT AASHIKA NAIR

Always nervous yet excited for new beginnings in life, the soon-to-be-18 Aashika can be a paradox at times. Difficult, but simple really, is how she feels one should view life. With music's lifelong warm embrace and the written word's true companionship, she enjoys critical thinking and solid relationships, not necessarily with the nitty-gritty aspect! Besides, with huge support and guidance from loved ones, she and her personality feel ready to pave their paths on this earth.

CAVES OF NOBLE TRUTH AND DANGEROUS KNOWLEDGE

Celeste A. Peters

~ China ~

Twelve-year-old Wáng Zhēn ducked behind the nearest workbench. Wide-eyed, she watched as shards of scrap metal whizzed past the drill press, the lathe, the milling machine and her head.

She'd never seen Grandpa so furious. He'd just stormed into his workshop and started throwing things around the cave. He hadn't even seen her in the corner. Grandpa had taught her many things, including how to remain calm when upset. Now he was exploding like Spring Festival fireworks.

Had Grandpa gone mad? Zhēn saw no one around who might have angered him. None of his inventions were missing or damaged.

When his temper fit ended, Zhēn stood. Genuine surprise showed in Grandpa's zitan-brown eyes as he grabbed and held her tight.

Zhēn grinned. He might be one chopstick short, but she loved him dearly. She gently jabbed his upper arm. "You scared me!" A beat passed then she asked, "So, what's wrong?"

Grandpa's fist came down hard on the prone carcass of a steam-powered camel prototype. "That puffed up rooster! He just offered me a bribe to destroy the archive!"

"What?" Grandpa was an honourable man. He had spent his whole life protecting the family's archive. No wonder he was angry! But who wanted it destroyed? "Who's rooster?"

"Professor Cecil Fletcher." Grandpa's jaw clenched as tight as his fists.

"You mean the Englishman with the fuzzy, grey bird's nest on each side of his face?"

"Ha! Yes!" Grandpa spit on the dirt floor. "He's supposed to be a scholar and teacher at a big school in England; 'Oxford' I think he calls it."

"But that's stupid. Why would a scholar want to destroy the archive? Most people want to steal it."

"I don't know, Zhēnzhēn. But I *do* know the archive is our ancestors' gift to the future. It's our family's duty and honour to guard it, so I will."

"Hoooot!" The whistle at the archive cave!

Grandpa sprang to his feet and ran outside. Zhēn followed, her long, black pigtails bouncing and waving. Her eyes winced in the harsh midday sunlight as they sprinted along the base of a cliff dotted with hundreds of ancient caves.

Zhēn arrived breathless at a pagoda framed hole in the rock face. Inside, a tunnel led to a large cave housing a seated Buddha statue and a smaller cave containing the family archive.

Zhēn headed straight into the tunnel. Grandpa grabbed her from behind, pulled her to her knees and pinned her flush with the wall, just in time. Steam blasted across the passage from the mouth of a brass laughing Buddha perched atop the lintel of the archive's entrance.

Startled but curious, Zhēn took a deep breath and leaned forward, peeking into the archive cave. Two scowling men, a middle-aged Brit and a massive young Asian man, were inside pinned beneath heavy chain netting.

"Aha! My trap worked," beamed Grandpa.

Zhēn saw Grandpa press his right palm into a shallow wall indent. The steam Buddha stopped bellowing but the net remained on the two intruders.

Zhēn and Grandpa approached the captives. Zhēn sniffed the air and nodded at a can clutched in the Brit's pinned right hand.

Grandpa said, "I see you took matters into your own hands, Professor Cecil Fletcher. And you brought along your Shànghǎi body guard, Zhòu Lì, to help out."

Lì barked, "Release us right now, Old Head!"

Ignoring Lì, Grandpa towered over Fletcher, "You've made a big mistake."

"No, Sir," Fletcher snapped back. "You have. The only thing in this can is fuel for my lamp. You can't prove otherwise. And if anything happens to me, my government will demand severe punishment."

Grandpa appeared unmoved by Fletcher's threat.

The Englishman's eyes darted about. Then he smiled sweetly. "Will you release us if we promise not to return, Sir?"

Zhēn held her breath. Surely Grandpa wouldn't consider such a foolish move.

"Do I have your word?" asked Grandpa.

"As a scholar and gentleman, yes," replied Fletcher.

"If you come back, I'll turn *you* over to the authorities. Understand?"

"Yes."

Grandpa put his thumb under a link and lifted the net, having first engaged its counterweight with a flick of his foot.

"No!" Zhēn cried in disbelief.

Fletcher rose to his feet and popped a dent out of his brown derby. Then, nose in the air, he marched for the exit. Lì followed, casting a sneer at Zhēn.

"Why did you do that, Grandpa?"

"There might have been truth in his threat, Zhēnzhēn."

"But you trust him to stay away?"

"A Chinese scholar would keep his word. I'd like to believe a British one would too."

Zhēn, remembering the attempted bribe, doubted it. She wondered if Grandpa was thinking properly after all.

❦

Zhēn was on edge for days afterward, watching for any hint of the Englishman's return. Late one morning a note arrived at the workshop by messenger. Grandpa, busy at the lathe, asked Zhēn to read it aloud.

She unfolded the delicate paper on which the note was written.

"'Sir: An explosive will go off in the archive at precisely noon today. Should you decide to risk your life seeking it, the outcome will be on your head, not mine. You are duly warned. Vacate your workshop, too. Another explosive will go off in it at the same time. Sincerely, Prof. C. Fletcher, MA, DLitt'"

"What?" How had he gotten past the archive's guard devices? "Your workshop, too, Grandpa!"

Zhēn loved Grandpa's inventions. Most were based on knowledge he'd found in the archive's scrolls and several of these scrolls lay about the workshop next to unfinished projects. To imagine the archive *and* the workshop destroyed...

Zhēn cleared the tears welling in her eyes so she could read the face of the geared clepsydra standing in the corner. "It's nearly noon!"

Grandpa was already handing her the nearest scroll. "Here. Take this. Gather up as many as you can in the next five minutes. Then *get out of here*, Zhēn! Do you understand?"

"Yes, but..."

"I'm going to the archive."

"But you'll be blown up!"

"Don't worry about me, Zhēn. I'm depending on you. Save what you can here but, above all, get out before *this* cave blows or my heart will be too broken to mend." And Grandpa vanished.

"He *has* gone crazy!" feared Zhēn as she ran from workbench to workbench gathering scrolls, sketches and Grandpa's steam-powered nutcracker. Did she have time for the wind-up messenger pigeon too? Glancing over at the clock, she stopped short.

Zhòu Lì stood in the doorway and, like Zhēn, he held something in his arms—something big.

"Dog Fart! You're not supposed to be here!" he shouted.

"And neither are you." Zhēn's heart pounded its way up her throat. "You haven't set the explosive yet? So that was just a lie to get us out of the workshop."

"Your weak brain is overheating, girl. Take it outside to cool off."

"And leave you to destroy Grandpa's inventions? Uh, uh." Keeping her eyes on Lì, Zhēn bent down and placed her precious cargo on a shelf below the nearest workbench.

Lì likewise crouched down and unloaded his burden onto the floor. "I gave you a chance to leave, but if..."

Like a graceful mountain lion, Zhēn leapt high over a workbench and grabbed onto the closest ceiling support beam. Swinging around it she rammed her feet into the side of Lì's head. He staggered, stunned.

Zhēn dropped to the floor, disappointed the blow hadn't knocked him out. She needed a more powerful move. How about the dim mak strike Grandpa had taught her?

It could kill. He'd said to use it only if her life were in danger. But was it? Nothing was stopping her from leaving the cave—nothing but wanting to save Grandpa's workshop at all costs.

Zhēn ran at Lì, her right hand pinched to a point and aimed at the side of his neck. As she threw all her strength into the jab, Lì's left hand came up and grabbed her arm in mid strike. Her calmness training quickly forgotten, Zhēn screamed in pain and anger as he held her at arm's length, her free arm chopping at nothing but air.

Lì threw her to the ground and put his right foot on her stomach. Wrenching a leather drive belt from a milling machine, he tied up Zhēn's hands and feet then hung her from a pulley hook descending from the ceiling grid. She had no choice but to watch, horrified, as Lì set the explosive device's geared timer.

Grandpa saw the power source for his guard devices, a boiler hidden outside the tunnel entrance, had been disabled so he entered the family's archive with careful haste. Inside, Fletcher was kneeling over an explosive amid piles of dusty scrolls.

"Stop!"

Interrupted, Fletcher rose. "So you have decided not to heed my warning."

"No honourable man would. Do you not understand the value of these scrolls? What they mean to me and my people?"

"Of course I do. But do *you*, Sir, understand what they mean to me and my people in Great Britain?"

Grandpa edged a few feet closer to Fletcher, wary but curious. "I suspect you could use their wisdom to your advantage. So why do you want to destroy them?"

The old man narrowed the gap a few feet more.

"You have a lot to learn about us Brits, Sir. For example, we pride ourselves on being the most technologically advanced and moral civilisation on Earth.

"I, personally, have built an excellent reputation and popular following in London by giving public lectures based on my travels. And do you know why?"

Grandpa continued his slow advance.

"Because I demonstrate the superiority of British ingenuity and technology over the primitive efforts of low-lifes like you."

Grandpa lunged at Fletcher, but the professor deftly reached beneath his jacket and pulled a revolver from his trouser waistline.

Grandpa stopped with a jerk.

"I truly do not wish to use this, Sir, but I will if I must."

Eyes fixed on the pistol, Grandpa said, "Now I see. Your name would be dishonoured if other Englishmen learned of the knowledge contained in these scrolls."

"Bravo, Sir!"

"You brag about British morals, yet you value your reputation above scholarship and truth. You're truly a dishonourable man."

Kablam! The shockwave from a nearby explosion rocked the archive. Scrolls crashed to the floor raising a cloud of dust.

Zhēn! The workshop!

Heartbroken and furious, Grandpa kicked high and knocked the revolver from Fletcher's hand. Fletcher scrambled for it but Grandpa grabbed him by the neck and tossed him into the air. Then, lightening fast, he reached into his apron and flung a bayonet-sharp scraper tool at the surprised man.

Blowing sand from nearby dunes wailed as Lì dragged Zhēn, still bound, toward the archive's entrance. Her head hung low, weighted by shame. She'd failed to save Grandpa's workshop and the precious scrolls inside.

But on entering Zhēn cried, "Ha!"

Grandpa was climbing out over piles of fallen scrolls while Fletcher, pinned to a ceiling beam by the collar of his tight-fitting jacket, struggled high above.

Zhēn saw Lì gasp and acted fast. Falling, she twisted and swung her body around, knocking Lì's legs out from beneath him. In unison, Grandpa whipped another scraper from his apron and sent it flying at Lì. The tool's rounded wooden handle struck him mid-forehead, knocking him out.

Grandpa untied Zhēn and they hugged hard, each relieved to see the other alive. Then Grandpa gently pushed Zhēn aside and, arms extended, moved his palms over Lì's body.

"What are you doing, Grandpa?"

"Ensuring nothing can move but his head. I'll teach you how some day."

"Okay…" Grandpa could do that?

Lì awoke and struggled to move. Zhēn saw panic in his eyes. He addressed Grandpa with a shaky voice. "Who *are* you?"

"My name is Wáng Jié," Grandpa said.

Lì's eyes opened wide. "The Wǔshù Master? The one who fought off an attack on the Daoguang Emperor? Alone?"

"Yes."

With new respect, Lì bowed his head toward Grandpa then looked up and sneered at Fletcher.

Zhēn's eyes opened wide, too. So Grandpa wasn't crazy! He was smart and famous. *And I am his student,* she beamed.

❧

Grandpa tied up the two men and handed them over to local villagers who had rushed to the caves concerned about the blast.

Over the next few months, Grandpa and Zhēn talked with the villagers about how best to protect the archive. After much arguing, they decided to hide its entrance beneath sand.

Convicted of their crimes, Fletcher and Lì were, likewise, buried in jail.

Factoid: In 1900 Wáng Yuanlu, guardian of the Mògāo Caves near Dūnhuáng, discovered an archive hidden by sand. Decades later, British scholar Joseph Needham, in his work Science and Civilisation in China, *used material from the archive to prove the Chinese were the true inventors of several technological advances previously claimed by the West.*

ABOUT CELESTE A. PETERS

Celeste A. Peters is an author of seven published non-fiction books who is trying her hand at fiction. Her short story "Without Blemish" was published last year in Edge Science Fiction and Fantasy's *Urban Green Man* anthology, and her story "A Fable for Those Who Would Mess with Fate" received Honourable Mention in the 2011 Robyn Herrington Memorial Short Story Contest. Celeste's website is www.celestepeters.com and you can follow her on Twitter @CelesteAPeters.

THE SEVENTH MONTH

Agnes Ong

~ Malaysia ~

Staring danger in the eye always made me feel more alive than ever. A firm grip on the handle of my cleaver, the sole of my left shoe scrapping the dirt on the ground, muscles tensed, eyes on the target, I saw my present, no past, no future, just frozen in time. Someone shouted and all hell broke loose.

The cleaver was one with my body now, moving with my thoughts fluidly. It went where my eyes fell and cut up flesh like paper. Blood splashed onto my face and soaked into my shirt; warmed my heart and I caught myself smiling. No one was ever going to get past me without getting a taste of my blade. After all, I needed to preserve my reputation as the most notorious gangster in Old Town, Maniac Butcher, they called me.

It was another typical day at work for me, a gang fight at a deserted corner of an oil palm plantation in the outskirts of Selangor. That was how we settled our differences among the gangs, whether it was territorial, women or money. We let the fist, steel pipes, knives, cleavers and *parangs* do the talking. Guns, you say? It was too risky to use them then as the police had been cracking down on weapons smuggling syndicates in the country lately. So, no guns for now, back to the old days of fighting with real weapons and not just a piece of metal with a trigger which any sissy can wield and call himself a hero. These weapons that we used drew blood, broke bones, severed limbs and scarred faces. If you survived, you carried the mementos to show your heroic deed, just the way I liked it.

I was flying through the crowd, driven by adrenalin like jet fuel. All the faces I passed were a blur. Their screams of agony gave me pleasure. I was unstoppable. Sensing an imminent attack from my right, I swung my cleaver around to block my enemy's advance but my arm stayed limp. I looked to find my cleaver lying on the ground, shimmering red in blood. It was only then that I saw blood oozing out from my right sleeve.

My enemies were no fools. They could smell an easy prey from miles away and I was standing before them, stunned from my injury. Within seconds, three opposing gang members zoomed in on me and pounced!

Reaching for my cleaver with my left hand, I felt a dagger digging into my lower back. Swinging around to fend off my attacker, I missed. Another guy took advantage of my blind spot and dealt me a blow in the head with a steel pipe. I doubled over in pain. Simultaneously, a skinny lad gave me a boot and sent me crashing to the ground.

This was how it ends for a guy like me. When the strong fell, the weak swarmed in to feed on the remains like a pack of hyenas. I had no fear as I surrendered to Death, my vision turning red, grey and fading to nothingness.

A sharp stab to my back woke me. I sprang up, thinking that I was still in the battlefield, only to find myself drenched in sweat, panting like a dog at Death's door. As I surveyed my surroundings, a blinding pain shot up my shoulder causing me to see stars and collapsed onto my pillow.

"Easy. The doctor said you need to rest."

I recognised Ming Chai's voice. It was a sign that I was alive and safe.

"What happened?"

"Ma Ko saved you. We won the fight. Now, the eight-hundred-and-eight members will not cross over to our territory any more."

My boss had saved me yet again. But then, we never kept count of these things. As his right-hand man, it was my duty to protect him but we always had each other's back, no matter what.

So, we succeeded in securing our territory, and I asked the same question I always did after each fight, "What's the head count?"

"Three dead, ten injured."

The score was not bad at all considering our gang was out-numbered in the first place.

"Have you collected the money for the dead from the other members?"

"Ah Mun will take care of that."

The pain on my shoulder had subsided and I opened my eyes. Ming Chai was sitting beside me on a stool, examining my wound. He looked skinnier than I remembered but he had always been skinny since the day I met him.

It had been five years since I found Ming Chai in a back alley lying in the cold rain. He was 13 years old then, trying to make a living on the streets picking pockets. He was a terrible thief. That night, I found him half dead after he was beaten up for getting caught. I guessed I grew fond of him after I found out that he was abandoned by his parents just like me. He was also grateful to me for saving him. Naturally, he followed me everywhere after that and became my shadow man.

"Eat this. It will stop the pain," Ming Chai gave me two yellow pills, "The doctor will not be coming again, so I suggest you stay in bed and don't get your wounds infected."

For gangsters like us, going to the hospital to treat our injuries was never an option. That would be like walking into a lion's den to be eaten alive. With our record, the police would be all over us the minute we stepped into a hospital. So, we had to rely on illegal doctors to do the job but they were not always available.

"How many days was I out?"

"Three."

"What!"

"Don't worry, I have informed Sue."

"What did you tell her?"

"I told her you were away on business."

I breathed a sigh of relief. Keeping such bad news from Sue was of utmost importance to me. She was the love of my life and I would never do anything to hurt her.

You find this strange coming from a ruthless killer like me? Well, every man has his weakness, and Sue was mine.

I grew up in an orphanage where love, like food, was never enough. Being a scrawny kid then made me an easy target for bullying. That was where I trained to be a fighter. At age 15, I ran away and ended up working as a runner in one of the many pubs owned by Ma Ko. I was tough, fearless and loyal. By the time I was 18, I rose through the ranks and earned Ma Ko's trust to let me manage one of his pubs.

Sue came into my life when I turned 21. The pub was crowded with gamblers and drinkers who were betting on the football matches of the night. It was a rowdy group but nothing I could not handle. In the middle of an intense match, this petite girl entered the pub and she immediately caught my attention. Girl looking for boyfriend, perhaps, I remembered thinking then.

From the corner of my eye, I watched her squeeze through the crowd and moved towards a middle-aged man sitting at a table in the corner. He was obviously not into the game as he just sat there staring at his empty beer bottles. I was intrigued.

The girl sat beside the man and started talking to him. At first, he did not respond. Then he began to cry. She continued talking, rubbing his back to soothe him. The man was becoming more and more upset. He started to shout and pushed her away roughly. A few other guys standing nearby tried to interfere and ended up starting a brawl.

To minimise the damage, a few of my handlers and I broke up the fight. Then, we chased the man and the girl out of the pub. There was no exchange of words. As soon as I left them out on the curb, I turned to go back inside when she said, "Thank you."

Those two words sounded so foreign to me that it made me stop in my tracks. Why would a perfect stranger thank me for throwing her out so unceremoniously? I nodded without turning around.

Just as I was about to take another step, she asked, "Could you help us get a taxi? My father is really drunk and I can't manage him alone."

This time I turned around and surveyed the situation. The man was lying, half passed out, on the pavement, unaware that his daughter was left to fend for herself alone. Then, I looked at the girl for the first time.

Under the yellow street lights, her features were sad. The big round eyes were bloodshot and her shoulders sagged under an invincible burden. Her dark hair which shone in the light seemed to envelop her face in a sort of halo. But, make no mistake, she stood tall and strong despite her slight frame. There was no fear in her face.

As a gangster, I have seen many girls and women, most of them were sluts or gold diggers. There were also the other girls and women who avoided people like us, they were usually afraid to look us in the eye because we had the tattoos, street swagger and reek of trouble. The girl standing before me that night was different. This made me curious and I wanted to get to know her.

We ended up sitting by the roadside for almost an hour. She did most of the talking. She told me that the man was her father, a butcher. He was upset because her mother had run away with another man. As she told me her story, there were no tears, just strength and dignity in her voice, telling it as it was. I remembered thinking that I admired her for her courage and calmness. After she left in the taxi that night, I could not stop thinking about her.

Realistically, I knew that a girl like Sue was out of my league, so I put her at the back of my mind. Then, two days later, she surprised me by turning up at the pub to thank me personally, again, and this time with homemade curry puffs. That was when our relationship began.

Unlike other people, Sue saw me as a person and not a gangster. After spending some time with me, she was aware of what I did but she did not shy away. She continuously persuaded me to turn over a new leaf and she never gave up no matter what I did. Ironically, I found this trait of hers annoying yet endearing at the same time. I guessed it made me realise there was still some good left in me that only Sue could see, and that made me feel more connected to humanity than I have ever felt.

Unfortunately, Sue's father did not share the same sentiment. He was against our friendship from the start. Whenever I went to his shop, he would threaten to kill me with his butcher knife but he never had the guts to do it. Even though she tried not to show it, I knew that Sue was troubled by her father's objection. Somehow, her old man's blessings still meant a lot to her. So, I stopped going to his shop and we would meet outside her work place instead.

The thought of Sue made me want to touch her face, smell her citrus perfume and feel her baby-soft skin even more. I could not lie there any longer. Despite the pain, I got up and headed out.

"Where are you going?"

"I have to go see Sue."

"But…"

Ming Chai took one look at me and he knew it was pointless to argue.

It was just after dusk when I reached our usual meeting spot under a large mango tree beside the corner shop lot where Sue worked as a tuition teacher. Her classes usually ended at 8pm, so I waited, leaning against the tree.

At 8.15pm after a throng of students left the centre, I eyed the door of the shop eagerly. Sure enough, five minutes late, a petite figure appeared.

"Sue!"

She froze, then, turned to my direction. The blank expression on her face turned to recognition and a smile lit up her face like the morning sun. She ran towards me and hugged me fiercely.

"Urgh!"

"What happened to you? Are you hurt?"

Sue opened the jacket and saw the bandages on my shoulder and arm. She gasped.

"It's no big deal," I said as I tried to grab her hand. The movement sent pain shooting up my arm again, making me a little faint.

I must have gone really pale at that moment as I saw the horror in Sue's eyes. Immediately, she put my good arm around her narrow shoulders and said, "We are going back to your place now."

Just like that, she took charge and we moved forward. I liked that in a woman, particularly Sue.

As we walked back to my house, she talked, telling me about her work. She never asked about my injuries. That's another thing I loved about her, she never asked questions to answers she already knew and she never questioned what I did even though she made it very clear that she disagreed with my 'business'.

By that time, the evening sky had darkened. Several people had laid out various fruits and food and were burning joss sticks and paper money by the roadside. Such a scene was not uncommon since it was the seventh month of the Lunar calendar, also known as the Ghost Festival. The Chinese believe that this was the month in a year where the gates of hell were opened and the spirits were allowed to roam freely among the living.

During this month, the superstitious lot would not leave their homes after dusk as they believe that the spirits were most active from dusk until dawn. Those who were out in the night during that time, and especially those who were down on their luck, could be easily possessed by the roaming spirits.

It was also in this month that many would note an increase in the number of road accidents and suicides. They reasoned that these cases were the deeds of malevolent spirits who were out to seek vengeance or simply to find a replacement so that their souls would be set free.

Our gang members often joked that when we walked the streets during the wee hours of the day in the seventh month, we would most likely meet some of the enemies which we had killed in battles. Then, we would send them our best wishes and watch them disappear into thin air. Secretly, I would watch the empty streets during this time and hoped to see my father who died in a road accident from driving drunk and tell him how much I hated him for ruining my life, but none of that ever happened. But then again, I never believed in ghosts.

As we walked past some of the people making offerings to appease the roaming spirits, a few of them cast suspicious glances at us while others simply avoided any eye contact for fear that they would see what they feared most. I didn't care and neither did Sue. In fact, I rather enjoyed the scent of the joss sticks, which had a calming effect on me. Sue continued chatting until we reached my house.

I was exhausted by then from all the walking. With the help of Ming Chai, Sue laid me down on my bed. She stayed by my side, caressing my face. Then, she started to cry. Her tears surprised me as that was the first time I had seen her weep.

"Baby, it's all right, I am here," I said trying to hug her with my good arm.

"NO!" Sue pushed me away, hurting me, "You've got to stop doing what you're doing. You're going to get yourself killed."

It was not the first time we had this discussion and every time, I would make excuses, dismiss her or change the topic.

"I am fine, baby. I'm here..." I began.

But Sue cut me off, "Stop! Or I'll leave you!"

For a long time, no one had dared to threaten me. I was speechless. The threat did not sound real to me, so I started to change the topic.

Without another word, Sue got up and started to leave. Stunned, I moved too quickly, hurting my wounds again, and I moaned. This caught Sue's attention and she turned back to me, worried look on her face. She still loved me very much after all.

"I will consider, my love," I said after catching my breath.

My answer seemed to satisfy Sue and she smiled, putting me in cloud nine. Everything was going to be all right, I thought.

For the next couple of days, I slept for most of the day but no amount of rest could make me feel better. Food did not agree with me too as I threw up much of what I ate. The only thing that kept me going was cigarettes. The smell of tobacco made me lightheaded, took the edge off my pain and I almost felt good again.

During the evening, Sue would come to see me after work. She told her father she was staying with a girlfriend who had just gone through a breakup. The excuse was lame to me but it did not matter as long as she was with me. During the night, I watched her as she slept beside me, drinking in her scent, which soothed my pain.

On the third day, I seemed to have regained a little of my strength and I decided to go out of the house to meet Sue at the gate. Just as I reached the gate, I saw her slender figure appearing at the bend of the road leading to my place. She smiled when she saw me and quickened her pace. However, my eyes were not on her, but on a man about 10 feet behind her.

The old man did not move any closer. He just stood there, eyes staring in my direction, unwavering. As I made eye contact, I felt a force radiating from the man even though he was quite far away from me. I tried to break away from his stare but found myself frozen in the spot. A crushing sensation began to develop around my chest which I knew was caused by this invisible energy, making it hard to breathe.

Then Sue reached me and hugged me. I gasped. Her touch must have broken the spell. I bent down to kiss her and took in her scent which made me feel better instantly.

"Who's that old man behind you?" I asked.

"What old man?" Sue replied.

We both looked behind Sue but the road was empty.

"He must have left," I said, trying not to make a big deal out of it.

That night, I watched Sue sleeping by my side but I did not feel at ease. All I could think of was the old man. I knew he had followed Sue to my place. Who was he? What did he want? Why?

I had dealt with many nasty characters before but this was the first time I felt intimidated. I could not figure out the reason behind my fear but it was real and it started to consume me. By morning, I was totally exhausted by the chaos in my mind that I slept fitfully throughout the day after Sue left for work.

"Wake up! You have to leave now!"

Ming Chai was shaking me as I opened my eyes, still fuzzy from sleep.

"Quick! There's not much time left."

Then, I heard the commotion outside. A woman was wailing and screaming at the same time, and there was a man shouting gruffly. As I listened, it became clear to me the woman was Sue.

At once, I pushed Ming Chai aside and ran out of my room. I swung the door open and saw the old man standing at the gate with his eyes closed. Behind him, Sue was trying to break free from her father.

"Get out, Ah Seng, now!" Sue yelled as soon as she saw me, her voice hoarse from crying.

The moment the old man heard Sue screaming my name, his eyes flew open. His stare pierced me and I was at once enveloped by the suffocating energy again. His lips began to move, speaking in a strange tongue, slowly at first then speeding up. As the chants accelerated, it grew louder, filling my ears, penetrating my mind and impaling me with agony. I felt the life being sucked out of my body as I crumbled to the ground, paralysed.

My flesh began to discolour in blotches of rancid grey. I was frightened by the sight. The odour from the rotting flesh was making me sick. At that point, I had lost control of my limbs but I was fully aware that I was floating out of my body. And I was soon hovering over myself.

"No! NO!" Ming Chai was shouting beside me.

He then ran to the gate and yelled at the old man, "What have you done?"

"Son, you know what you did was wrong. He has to return to where he belongs," the old man replied calmly.

Sue's father had released her by then. She rushed to my body and began sobbing. I wanted to comfort her but my fingers ran through her like evening mist. I sensed a shift of energy in Sue as my fingers ran through her body. Another life was beating inside her. It was then that I realised she was with child. My heart ached for my wife and unborn child but it was too late.

My surroundings began to dim. Everyone else was frozen in their spot. The only movement was the beating of their hearts in their chest which were now visible to me.

"It's time to leave," a deep voice said behind me.

Turning around, I saw two huge creatures dressed in ancient Chinese warrior's costumes. Standing with animal legs, they towered above me. The one with the bull's head held a forked spear while the other with a horse's head was armed with a long spear. They were the infamous soldiers of the God of Hell who came to claim the souls of the dead. I stood before them, fearful yet mesmerised by their unworldly beauty.

Without another word, the bull face warrior pointed at me with his forked spear. A translucent lasso shot out from its tip and bounded itself tightly around my wrist. I felt electricity running through my entire being and became irresistibly drawn towards the creatures even though none of them was holding the lasso.

The creatures took a step and the scene around us changed instantly. We were walking on the street towards the mango tree in the night. The roadside was intermittently lined with offerings and burning joss sticks. There were some spirits crowding around these offerings but as soon as the creatures walked past them, they stood up to follow. A few others who were slow to get in line were electrocuted, emitting a stench of burning flesh.

Soon, our little procession had grown into a large crowd. We were all heading to the same destination, pale faces, limbs like tendrils of smoke, only dark patches on our transparent bodies mark the spot of Death's kiss. The dead were returning to hell on the last day of the seventh month.

The mango tree opened up into a burning gate of fire, the heat so intense that I could see myself begin to evaporate. At that moment, I realised that this was how it really ends for the likes of me, a life full of regrets and condemned to an eternity in the inferno of hell.

Perhaps I would return to visit Sue on the next seventh month.

ABOUT AGNES ONG

A freelance web content writer and novelist in the making, Agnes is also an occasional blogger at Angie Creative Ink (www.angiecreativeink. com). Coping with an unknown nerve condition all her life has presented many challenges and it is through writing that she found solace, escape and revelation. She hopes that her work will continue to console, excite, delight and inspire many people from all walks of life to pursue their passion in life no matter who they are or where they are. Success achieved through many struggles is definitely much sweeter.

AND THEN IT RAINED

Rebecca Freeman

~ Australia ~

Toby mumbles in his sleep and I hold my breath as I watch him change positions. The mat gives a little protection from the dirt, but the rock is hard and I wonder how he can even fall asleep. But he's four, and can sleep anywhere.

I think about his youthful resilience, so I don't have to think about the fever. I have been putting off a trip into the Town for three days, in the hopes he'll improve. I lie back down underneath the shade-cloth and look at the clouds through the tiny holes. There is a breeze and I can smell rain. Here, on the edge of the desert, that's usually as good as we get, but maybe today will be different.

The change in atmosphere wakes Toby.

"Serena?"

I'm at his side before he begins to panic. The delirium takes over sometimes, in that space between sleep and wake.

"I'm hungry."

I brush his dark hair back from his forehead.

"Want some biltong?"

He screws his face up. I don't blame him; I hate the stuff, too, but it's the only reliable protein we can get and I need to try and get him stronger so we can make the crossing. The Nullarbor used to be so easy. Nowadays, we gamble with the dry and the heat, and try to ignore the bones bleached white by the side of the road. I've made the crossing three times, practically a veteran, but that was before Toby, and it's a whole lot different with a child on the back.

"Hey," I say, "want to come into the Town with me? The greengrocer might be there."

"She wasn't there last time."

Toby had sulked for days from the lack of fresh fruit. He tips his head back to look at me, dark eyes squinting.

"Come on," I say. "You never know, there might be some other children."

We both know that's unlikely. All those in the Town are at least in their early twenties, and nobody ever talks about their own children, if they have them. It is as if he were the only one of his species. It's one of the reasons I want to leave. I don't trust most of the people here, and they don't trust me. It has been getting more and more difficult to trade with them over the past weeks, and it's making me uneasy. Best to go, even if we don't have as much money as I would have hoped to raise.

I hold out my arms and he crawls into them. I want to cry and tell him I'm sorry. Sorry that he's ill, sorry that we have so little, sorry for this shitty world. I hug him tighter and close my eyes.

"I'll get the bike ready."

He nods against my shoulder. I pass him a piece of dried mango, the last one we have, and he takes it without complaint, even though it's all he's eaten recently.

The bike starts on the first try. I want to take it as a good omen, but chances are there will be nothing to buy. And that the guy who sells cigarettes and chocolate in the small lean-to next to the drinking tent won't be there. If I tell myself this enough, I won't be disappointed if it turns out to be true. I check that I've got the book to return to him, and Toby appears at my hip.

"Okay, let's go."

Toby holds on tightly, arms almost all the way around my middle. *He's getting bigger*, I think, and I push off and guide the bike down the rocky trail to the main track, and we jolt and judder for the next forty minutes, sweating underneath the bandannas which cover our noses and mouths from the dust.

The gunner nods at us from his makeshift watch tower, as I park up and remove the key. I get the feeling he'd be friendlier if we lived in the Town, but that goes for most of the people here. I give him a smile anyway.

As expected, there are only a few tables with anything worth buying, but I'm almost stupidly excited at the sight of melons and tomatoes. Toby sees them at the same time as I do, and we grin at each other.

Suspicious though they are, the people still need to barter, and I have what they want: tobacco, sugar, salt. I've brought a good amount to trade. We get two melons, which I sling in a string bag over my shoulder, and seven tomatoes, still attached to their vine. They smell incredible. I guess that they've been grown in the vegetable patch behind the greengrocer's tent. How she keeps it going, and with what water, I don't know, but I feel lucky to have so much fruit at once.

"I just need to see if I can get something else," I say to Toby, casually.

The lean-to looks like it's been knocked about a bit recently—too many drunks stumbling out of the tent next door, I imagine. I hold Toby's hand tighter and put purpose to my stride.

The cigarette guy is sitting back in his chair, but as I walk over, he stands and waves to us.

"Haven't seen you for a while," he says, nodding at Toby. "Was getting a bit worried."

"I brought your book back," I say.

He takes it, and there's warmth in his smile.

"You got anything for me? We had a trader on Friday but he was all out of smokes."

"Got some loose," I offer. "And some papers."

"Papers? Where you get this stuff..." he laughs and shakes his head. "I guess... I can do a hundred papers for... a hundred grams of chocolate?"

He winks at Toby, who blushes.

"He's not been so well. I'm not sure chocolate..."

Toby tugs on my hand and I sigh, and relent.

"Sure. Chocolate would be great."

"And the loose?"

I open my mouth to suggest something, but he interrupts.

"I see you've got some of Glenda's tomatoes there. Come and see what I have."

He motions under the counter, and beckons us over.

I'm hesitant, but it's the middle of the day. Of course it's safe. He opens a bag and holds it up to my face. I step back, not sure what he's trying to do, and he laughs.

"Go on, smell it!"

I take a breath. It's almost bitter; it smells like freshly-cut grass, or pepper, and it seems so familiar, but I can't place it.

"It's basil! Remember basil?"

I take another breath and this time, I smile, too. The smell is taking me back to when there was winter and cold and you actually had a chance to miss the sun, back to promises of shared meals and long evenings and wine and laughter.

"I'll do you a deal. You both look like you never eat. Give me four sticks of loose, and I'll come out and cook for you."

I hesitate, but the thought has taken root: hot food, and perhaps some adult conversation with an actual adult. An adult who reads books, and smiles at me.

"Okay. I can't fit you on our bike, though…"

He waves my concerns away.

"I've got my own. Scooter I rebuilt when I got here two years ago. Doesn't go that fast—"

"What does, on these tracks?"

He laughs.

"Exactly. Meet you up front?"

I nod, turning before the blush hits my ears. I have to stop myself from dragging Toby straight back to our bike, reminding myself that I still need to see if the chemist has something for his fever. She is just shutting up her stall, but graciously agrees to see us, and refuses all barter for the tea she gives us.

"One cup, three times a day," she tells me. "If he's not better in three days, come back. I'm expecting another trader through any day now, and I could have something better. I'm sorry…"

Her eyes are tired, and sad, and she looks from Toby's face to mine.

"I'm sorry I don't have anything else."

I thank her and she puts her hand gently on Toby's head, and we nod our goodbyes.

When we get to our bike, the guy is waiting with his scooter.

"I don't think I ever told you my name," he says, a little too quickly.

I get the feeling he's rehearsed the line in his mind while we were getting Toby's tea.

"Serena," I say, smiling a little.

"Calvin." He laughs.

I hold my hand out, and he takes it briefly. I can't tell if the nerves in my belly are from fear or desire. Whichever, I need to keep a lid on it.

"We should get going."

"Lead the way," he says, swinging his bag over his shoulder.

It's getting late, and I set off at a steady pace. Despite the scooter's size, it keeps up, and we make good time, just as the sun begins to set behind the clouds, which are still building into thunderheads in the west.

"Nice setup you've got here," he says, untying his scarf from around his face.

"It's okay for now."

He's just being polite; I know it's rudimentary at best. But it helps us keep our independence, which is worth enough.

He kneels in front of our upturned tea chest, and unpacks his backpack. There is pasta and basil, as well as a bottle of wine, and some oil.

"You have salt, I guess?" He grins.

I give him the small pouch I took to the Town with me, then stoke the fire and blow on it a little. With a little more wood, it soon begins to warm the hotplate, and I put two saucepans out for him to use.

"I just need some water—and some tomatoes," he says, pulling out a small, sharp knife.

I hand him the bucket, and take Toby over to the entrance of the cave. We sit down to talk about what we saw in the Town. It's a chance to practise memory games, and maths. He's getting to kindergarten age, but I guess I'm as good a teacher as any to prepare him for the real world.

"Who'd like some food?" Calvin calls out.

Toby almost falls over his feet to get to the tea chest, and I smile at his enthusiasm.

"Should I be offended that you're looking forward to Calvin's cooking so much more than mine?"

He is already eating, ignoring me, but Calvin grins, and hands me my bowl.

"I wasn't sure if you drink?"

He holds up the bottle.

"Sure, I'll have little."

He pours me more than I want, and I sit with my bowl, and take a bite of pasta. The combination of flavours is divine. It is the best food I have tasted in months, maybe years, and I let out a small groan.

"Oh, that's really good. Wow, it's really good!"

He laughs, blushes a little at the praise. I raise my glass in a silent toast, and he does the same. It's almost like real life. Or like life, as it used to be.

Afterwards, I prepare Toby's tea, and he drinks it quickly. He's tired, and paler than before. I sigh, tucking a thin blanket around his shoulders as he lies on his mat. Hopefully, tomorrow will see his fever break.

Calvin is standing at the cave entrance, and I look over. If there's a moon, it's nowhere to be seen, and the air feels charged. We're in for a thunderstorm.

"The wind's picking up," I say.

"I guess I should head off," he says. "I don't want to get caught in it."

I frown at the gusts whipping up the dust at the bottom of the track.

"It'll be a rough ride," I say. "If you've something you can use as a swag, you're welcome to stay the night."

It must be the wine talking, because I can't believe I've just offered an almost-stranger to stay. But now it can't be unsaid, and he accepts with thanks, and walks over to fetch a jacket from the scooter.

I make coffee. Calvin comes in as I'm pushing down the plunger.

"Coffee, too?!"

"No milk, of course," I say, "but I have sugar."

"Sugar would be great. Thanks."

I hand him his mug, and we walk back over to the entrance of the cave, sitting down to watch the sky.

"Hey, I have something to show you."

I turn to look and he holds in his hand a jar. There is no label, and there is nothing on the lid, so I take a guess at what's inside. It looks like homemade jam, and I say so.

He laughs.

"Yeah, it's jam. But take a look at the lid. The edge of it."

He gives it to me and it's heavy and cool in my hand. I squint a little at the writing: 14 Dec 2020.

"A... best-before? A best-before date? Where did you find this?!"

He grins. Giddy.

"One of the drunks fell asleep outside my shop the other night. I had a chance to... well, let's just say he left with fewer treasures than he came."

"This must be... I can't remember the last time I saw something with a best-before. I mean, as a child, maybe?"

"I know. Blows your mind, right?"

"Yeah," I nod. "Yeah, it really does."

I hand the jar back to him and he returns it to his bag. We sit quietly for a minute. I wonder if, like me, he's travelled back in time, in his mind. I think about breakfasts and my mother and inevitably, I wonder where my sister is. I haven't thought about her in weeks. Toby doesn't ask about her as often as he did, and so I'm not reminded as often. Back a couple of years, or maybe more, I used to think about her everyday. Pull her memory out and play with it, like a doll. Imagine her there in front of me as if she were a hologram or a ghost. But she belongs in the past, like mass-produced food and best-before dates. I can't hope she'll suddenly turn up again, and I don't even know what I would do if she did. For sure, I wouldn't give her Toby back. Not this time. He's mine, now.

I suppress the annoyance I've managed to work up, and try for conversation with Calvin. He's my guest; I should be polite.

"So, how did you end up in the Town?"

"Heh. The question. I was just looking for a lift over east. There were some sandstorms and I got stuck waiting. Had some cigarettes and a few boxes of stuff I stole back in Perth, and people were bartering for them, so I figured I could make a go of it."

"So you'll stay around here for a bit?" I ask.

"It's... there's a bit of community, I guess. You're not, then?"

I shrug.

"I'd like to move on. No great hurry, though."

He holds my gaze for a moment too long, and I feel I've said the wrong thing.

"You could stay," he says, gently.

I smile, and in response, he puts a hand on mine, and his mouth on mine is garlic and warmth and sweet coffee. I pull back a little. This is risky.

"I'm sorry, I mis-read..."

He pulls back, and blushes.

"No, it's fine."

I put my hand on his.

"It's fine, really. It's just... it's been me on my own for so long. Just looking out for myself, and for Toby, you know? I... oh, what the hey, let's just go inside."

He laughs and stands up and pulls me up beside him, and there is another kiss, and I feel my belly flip, that old familiar excitement. I feel myself blushing, too, and I try to keep my head focused while my body is responding in all the ways I thought it had forgotten.

I pull him by the hand to my sleeping mat. Outside, the wind is whipping the tarpaulins as the first rains for years begin to fall. We half-tumble onto the blankets, pulling at each others' clothing, the sense of urgency infusing our fingers and tongues and as I put my hand on the small of his back, he murmurs something into my neck.

"What was that?" I say, turning my head, and startle, as I feel something cold and flat against my throat.

"I said, I told the others I would be able to screw you over, and they didn't believe me."

He turns the blade slightly and I can feel the point digging in under my jawbone. There is another thud in my belly, but this time, I'm not confused about what I'm feeling. I stare at him and wonder where the warmth in his eyes went. How could I have so misjudged him?

"All you needed was a little wine and the promise of a fuck."

He smiles and presses the blade in deeper. I can feel it cutting into my skin, and a scream lurks in the back of my mouth. I hold my breath deep it inside me.

"I'll be quick," he says softly, lips close to my ear, "that way, your boy won't know you're gone until tomorrow. No point in waking him, right?"

My mind is foggy with desire and I struggle to focus. *Clarity*, I tell myself. *Breathe.*

I smile, keeping my eyes as cold as his, and slide my hand out from my back pocket.

"No point at all," I say.

The stiletto is so sharp, I don't think he even feels it until it is deep his groin, but suddenly, he gasps, pulls back, looks down.

"What... what..."

His knife falls from his fingers as he holds his hands up in some gesture of disbelief or horror.

"You..."

"Shhh," I whisper. "Relax. It won't take long."

I wipe my own blade and return it to its sheath, get to my feet and straighten my clothing. He sits back on his heels, silent, looking at his bloodied fingers, and his face begins to lose its colour.

I put my back to him and begin to stuff my coat in my backpack, and behind me, he slumps heavily against the cave wall. I feel tight around my heart.

I prioritise what we can carry. The wine will spoil, so I pour it out. My stash of barter-goods is already packed up, but I have a little space. I slip Toby's tea into a side-pocket. I take a last look at Calvin, or the body that used to be him, and check through his bag. The jam is still there. I pick it up, weighing it in my hand. Sweet nostalgia, but that's all it is. In a practical sense, the jar could break and it's too heavy. Plus who wants to eat jam that's over a decade old?

I load the bags onto the bike, and siphon the fuel from Calvin's scooter into a bottle, then start the bike. I leave it running while I go to wake Toby.

"It's time to go," I tell him quietly.

He's groggy, but he wraps his arms around my neck and I carry him to the bike, sitting him in front of me. The rain is steady, which will make the tracks slippery until we get to sealed roads, but it will also cool the night, as we put hours between ourselves and Calvin's body, and the Town. They might not even bother coming after us. Everyone's dispensable nowadays. I rub at the pain in my chest and feel a sob in my throat as I hold Toby close to me. I give the bike more throttle, and we head up the hill. I don't even know why I'm crying, or why I can't stop, but the rain washes the blood and salt from my face, and we ride east, to start again.

ABOUT REBECCA FREEMAN

Rebecca Freeman grew up on a farm surrounded by sheep, bushland and huge skies, which was as amazing and interesting as it sounds (she even had a pet kangaroo for a time). She then went to boarding school in the city, which was not at all as amazing and interesting as any of the stories promised it would be. Rebecca always wanted to be a writer, but she put it off for years, because procrastination is what she does best. Now that she has a partner, four small children, many pets and a garden to which to devote herself, she finally finds the time to write. Rebecca lives with her family on the south coast of Western Australia, and blogs almost-weekly at thisclimbingbean.wordpress.com.

WHERE THE FIREFLIES GO

NJ Magas

~ Japan ~

At a quarter to eleven, the master died. Outside, Tanuki turned away from his vigil at the window, hefted up his bulk, and climbed down off the gas meter. His ceramic feet clicked hard on the pebbles at the side of the house as he dropped the final few centimetres. He winced, but no sound came from inside—no lights turned on and Shizuho didn't come to the window to investigate. Tanuki let out his breath slowly. What would he have done if she had come to the window? He could freeze himself up of course, but that would raise all sorts of questions as to how the ceramic *tanuki* from the front door managed to get all the way to the side of the house. Subterfuge was no activity for short, round creatures—even those endowed with supernatural mobility.

As carefully as he could he picked his way along the pebble path with his walking stick in hand, and only allowed himself to make any more noise when he finally arrived in the back garden. There, the chirping crickets overpowered nearly all other sounds. It was an awful racket, but it allowed him to walk with ease. A fine thing too; the cramps in his legs made walking gingerly difficult.

The backyard was a mess. It had been a lovely garden once, but had given up on itself in the absence of care. A sagging juniper leaned half of its weight on a mouldering crutch and the rest over the cement blocks of the eastern wall. The mosses were balding and crow pecked, and ravens had carried off several of the smooth, white pebbles that comprised the rock garden. If there were any koi left in the pond adjacent to it, they couldn't be seen under the thick green coat of algae.

Tanuki leaned against a mossy pagoda and pulled his straw hat down off of his ears to fan his face. It should have been one of the Shisa twins running these kinds of errands. Four legs were better than two in any case, and the lion-dogs had made it clear enough over the years that their speed and agility was far superior to Tanuki's own. He cast his gaze across the garden to where the rubble of the eastern Shisa should have been, but it couldn't be seen through all the weeds. How pitiable that for all that speed, a twelve year-old boy could end them with one wicked push.

"Well?" The word rattled down the roof tiles, fell into the clogged eaves and spilled out the side.

"A moment, please," Tanuki wheezed and carefully eased his bottom down to the warm grass under him. "It's not so easy any more, getting from one side of the house to the other."

"Perhaps you should consider a life less stationary," the disembodied voice offered.

"Well I'm sorry I don't get out and patrol the garden every night! Some people don't have a roof they can run up and down on whenever they please." Of all the nerve. Who had been sitting outside the window all night, risking detection? Certainly not that ugly gargoyle on the roof. He didn't even have the decency to come down and greet his friend face to face.

"Forgiveness. I spoke without care."

"Of course you did," Tanuki muttered, but couldn't stay angry with his friend. Onigawara hadn't been built to be soft and sentimental. A sentry of hard angles and wild glares could be forgiven for an excessively blunt comment now and again.

"Give me a moment, I'll come down."

"Take your time."

And it would take time. Onigawara couldn't simply animate like the rest of them. He had to physically pull himself out of his roof tile—a square barely big enough to frame his scowling, horned head. For a creature whose job it was to protect the house, it was a laughably slow process. Then again, he'd had the Shisa twins in to hound and distract any intruders in the past.

At last Onigawara sat on the edge of the eaves with his tiny stone feet barely extending past the gutters.

"Do your legs get cramped, spending so much time squeezed into that little tile?" Tanuki asked.

"Tell me of the master," the gargoyle grunted in reply.

"The master has died." Tanuki stopped fanning his face, and let his hat hang still in his paws. The two shared a moment of silence.

"Was anyone with him?" Onigawara asked at last.

"Yes, his daughter Shizuho. She was with him all night, and gave him his last water before he passed. I don't think she'll leave his side until Kentaro arrives."

Onigawara dropped a second grunt off the roof. "And what of young master Kentaro? Why was he not here to witness his father's last hours?"

Tanuki scowled and snapped his jaws, sending his jowls jiggling up to his ears. "He will arrive tomorrow morning. Business, he said, keeps him away, or so I understood from Shizuho's side of the conversation this afternoon."

"I overheard parts of that conversation. Shizuho seemed upset."

"Of course she's upset! He means to have this place torn down before the master is even cremated! Everything will go with it. All of the master's possessions, everything she ever loved from her childhood. All of it. Gone." Tanuki slapped his hat against the base of the pagoda and then placed it firmly back onto his head. "That man has no respect. Do you remember how he kicked me over when he was a boy? He called me ugly and laughed when I hit the gate. I still have a hole in my tail. It lets in all sorts of horrible breezes and—"

"Hush! Something approaches." Onigawara stood and drew his sword, which thankfully was a process much quicker than removing himself from the roof tile. Tanuki had no interest in playing the distraction, however. He pointed a grin up to the moon and froze back into a two-foot statue.

"It is impolite to call a person 'thing', you know," a new voice said. A pair of dark triangle ears preceded a small pink nose only by virtue of being taller than the weeds in the garden. The cat they were attached to stepped delicately into sight on its hind legs moments later, looking—as cats are wont to do—arrogant and self-important. With its eyes mostly closed, it stood in stillness and silence to take in the garden, or perhaps to give the garden a moment to take in it. Secretly impressed by the cat's grandness, Tanuki nevertheless didn't move until it hit him so hard on the snout that he was forced to extend a leg or risk tipping over.

"Ow!"

"Neko-mata," Onigawara greeted and sheathed his sword. Tanuki would have liked the reassurance of it out in the open, if only to remind Neko-mata that demons—even minor demons—were unwelcome.

Neko-mata smiled. "Why such dour expressions on so fine an evening? The crickets sing, the fireflies dance, and the scent of death is so delightfully thick in the air I could smell it all the way from the graveyard."

Onigawara growled. "It is our master who has died. Keep your distance."

The demon raised its paws in surrender, though its smirk remained.

His smarting snout held in his paws, Tanuki added, "His son means to have our home demolished, and we will likely go with it."

The cat swished its forked tail through the tall grass thoughtfully.

"I see. That is a problem. I can't imagine you'd be able to escape the humans' machines; small tile legs couldn't possibly move very fast. And you," he said, casting a disdainful look at Tanuki, "dragging along the bulk of so many years reclining on the door step."

"That is where the master set me and so that is where I have stayed!" Tanuki barked back.

Neko-mata smiled, but it went no further than his whiskers. "Well, you could come away with me, if you like. I know of some places that could use another pair of eyes to watch over them. New apartments that aren't in danger of being torn down for many more years, but have no guardians to speak of."

"Absolutely not." Onigawara stood upon the very edge of the roof, planted his feet and crossed his arms. "I will remain here till I be cracked in half."

Tanuki hesitated a moment, but finally nodded his agreement.

The demon's tails changed the direction in which they swished. "I could raise him for you. Then you would be masterless no more."

Onigawara's sword was in his hand again with such speed that it might have been conjured there for all the motion that Tanuki saw.

"You may try, and I shall have you cleaved in half."

Neko-mata didn't move and neither did Onigawara. In fact, the only things moving in the garden were the small, flickering trails of the fireflies, which seemed indifferent to the sudden tension.

Eventually, Neko-mata shrugged and turned away from the door.

"Have it your way," it said. "There is nothing I can do for you." It brushed past Tanuki with its nose in the air and stepped onto the path that wound around the house.

They owed the demon something at least for its consideration of their troubles—impractical though they had been. As the cat reached the corner of the porch Tanuki called out, "Thank you for your time all the same. Shizuho was cooking *kara'age* earlier. There might still be some oil in the fryer if you want it." Neko-mata didn't answer, and the upward flick of its tails could have been acceptance or dismissal, Tanuki couldn't tell. The demon disappeared around the side of the house and no more was heard from it that night.

The sound of stone sliding against stone drew Tanuki's eyes upward again. Onigawara had sheathed his sword, and sat once more on the eaves, looking out over the garden.

"Suppose… that we *did* go with him." Tanuki offered after a time.

"No."

"But supposing we did—"

"No."

It was useless to press the issue. Onigawara seemed determined to go to his fate, and as much as Tanuki didn't want to lose this—the humid summer nights in the garden, the friendly banter, and the ease and comfort of having a home and a master to belong to—there was no escaping the inevitable.

The old ways were fading. What humans once feared no longer affected them today. No one worried about angry weather *kami* any more. Ghosts had become the stuff of children's playtime stories and demons the outdated legends of the dark ages. What preyed on the hearts and minds of humans these days couldn't be warded off by a gargoyle with a sword: who has the most expensive car, the biggest house, the most plastic surgery; whose child has been accepted to which prestigious private school and how many sleepless nights it took to get there. These woes even a *tanuki* struggled to solve for people who no longer believed a cheap ceramic raccoon-dog had any power at all. For those like Onigawara who still fought against the things that go bump in the night, the lack of faith from those whom he protected must be particularly hard.

The two friends sat in pessimistic silence, watching the fireflies wink on and off. Nostalgically, Tanuki said, "I count four by the pond."

"There are three in the juniper," Onigawara answered flatly. Tanuki could add no more. There had been a time many years ago when this game could continue for hours. Fireflies had filled the garden then, and the darting lights whizzed by so fast that even in the space of an entire night it was impossible to count them all. This year there seemed to be only seven undulating pulses of light—roughly half of what there had been the year before.

"Perhaps we will go where the fireflies go," Tanuki said sadly.

He lifted a paw for one of the glowing lights, but it vanished before it could settle on his small black pad. One by one the fireflies turned out their lights; in the quiet, lifeless garden, the pall of death was more tangible than ever.

"Do you think the master's spirit will be alright without us?"

"He is not without us." Onigawara stood and paced the eaves.

"But he will be, soon."

"What happens in the future we cannot control. But we can still protect him now." Facing east, he paused. "If Neko-Mata smelled death from as far away as the graveyard, then I fear to think what else may have smelled it."

"What else? You mean, something worse that a cat demon?"

"Yes. Death calls to unclean things. We must keep them away."

"We? What do we even have to fight with?"

"I have my sword and you have your stick. Fear not, I have done this before, when the mistress passed away. I can do it again."

"You had the Shisa twins then."

"I can do it again." Onigawara stood tall on the edge of the roof, his mouth firm and something that might have been determination or madness in his eyes. Tanuki didn't want to guess which it was.

"Fine. Fine, but if you get us both killed in this I'll... I... I shall never forgive you!"

"If I get us both killed tonight, then we have nothing to fear for tomorrow, do we?"

There was a disturbing logic in Onigawara's words and surprisingly, a good deal of comfort. If he died, at least he wouldn't go alone. Then again, the gargoyle was confidence incarnate; perhaps they had nothing to fear at all.

Tanuki stood and began pacing the garden as Onigawara paced the roof, but they remained undisturbed until well past midnight.

It started with bells. The ringing was faint at first, and Tanuki might have passed it off as the chime of the night watch had Onigawara not suddenly stopped above him.

"What? What is it? A demon?"

"*Odokuro!*" Onigawara hissed.

"*Odokuro*? What's that? Is it bad?" His friend's sudden quiet was unsettling, and fear began to crawl over Tanuki once more.

"It is a bone demon. It rises out of decay and neglect to eat the flesh of the living and dead alike—then it takes the bones to add to its skeletal body."

Tanuki gaped up at Onigawara. "It'll devour the master and Shizuho both!"

"Yes, unless we stop it."

"Is it—can we stop it?" The question, once forced out, carried on it all of Tanuki's fragile courage, and hung it in the air between them.

"Yes, but I will need your help."

"Of course. I'll run to the shrine—gather a few talismans, maybe even persuade an inari or two to come and help."

"No, I need you with me. There isn't much time. Come, man the eastern wall with me."

"How do you know it will come from the east?"

Onigawara was already off the roof and half way across the weather worn top of the cement wall, making tiny *clip-clop* noises with his smooth stone feet. "Because that is the direction of the graveyard. That is where it will draw up the bulk of its body."

Entirely out of his element, Tanuki nonetheless crossed the garden to the eastern wall. The juniper was his best choice for climbing up; several of its branches hung untrimmed and low. He pulled himself up onto one of the large rocks under it. The stone wobbled unsteadily, and when Tanuki looked down to check his footing, the open-mouth snarl of the fallen eastern Shisa stared back up at him.

Already unsettled enough for one night, Tanuki put the image from his mind and climbed the tree. The height was dizzying, but there was no time to orient himself. The *odokuro*—all seven feet of its clattering bone composite body, topped with an enormous skull—came around a bend in the alley and fixed the blue glow in its empty eye sockets directly at their garden.

"*Amatsukami* protect us." Tanuki gasped in awe.

"There are no *kami* here." Onigawara growled and swung his sword in warning before the demon. "Go back whence you came. You'll take no bones from here."

"Bones..." it rasped. *"Give... me... bones."* Crossing the alley swiftly on long legs, the demon grasped the wall with both skeletal hands and heaved itself up as if no opposition stood in its way.

"Away!" screeched Tanuki. "This is our house. Away with you!" He lifted his walking stick over his head and brought it down as hard as he could on an exposed collarbone. The demon didn't seem to notice. It teetered on the wall a moment and then leaned forward, stretching an arm down to the earth on the other side.

If Onigawara was perturbed at all by the *odokuro*'s indifference he didn't show it. He swung his sword down hard on the outstretched limb and severed it from the rest of the demon in a single blow. The demon gave no sign of pain, but the loss of the limb unbalanced it, and it tipped over the wall and into the juniper, knocking Tanuki down with it.

For a brief, terrifying moment the ground rushed up at him. His long life outside the front door flashed before his eyes as he made peace with the world—Onigawara included. Then, just as suddenly as it had started, his fall was halted by a well-placed branch of juniper, which snagged in the hole in the back of his tail.

"Thank you Kentaro," he gasped. "Your cruelty has saved me tonight."

The *odokuro* thrashed in the tree above him, stuck temporarily in the overgrowth of needles and branches that caught in the crevices of its bone body. The tree wouldn't hold forever though, and as the demon twisted, the branches creaked and snapped and gave way, piece by piece.

Tanuki reached for the tree trunk to free himself, but the juniper swung so violently he couldn't get a handhold. The monster above him loomed closer. Unable to pull itself back up on one arm alone, it snapped off the branches trapping it instead, grinding them to mulch between its teeth. One misplaced bite could easily take Tanuki's lower half with it.

Tanuki stretched himself out as far as he could, but the needles of the branch nearest to him danced just out of reach. He tried twisting his tail around but it only lodged the branch deeper in his hollow cavity. He'd about made up his mind to chance rocking back and forth when the branch he was caught on gave a sudden, violent lurch. It tipped him downward and sent him spinning the last few centimetres to the ground, where he finally came to a stop when he collided with the pile of bones sloughed off by Onigawara.

But rather than scatter lifelessly into the garden, the pile clapped and rattled as if laughing at him. Wide-eyed, Tanuki pulled himself to his feet and backed away, jostled and bumped as the scraps of demon collected together again. The bucking bones grew so lively that the ground beneath Tanuki's feet vibrated with their drumming, and before his horrified eyes they reassembled the severed arm—as whole and complete as if it'd suffered no damage at all.

"The other hand!" Tanuki cried up to his friend, but Onigawara gave no sign that he heard.

The arm seemed to have no designs for Tanuki. It propelled itself instead on its fingers back toward the demon it belonged to.

With no time to consider the danger, Tanuki threw himself onto the tailing arm and wedged the end of his walking stick between the bones of its wrist. The tip of the stick dug deep into the ground, staking the limb to the earth and the arm—having stuck itself back together again—couldn't disassemble away from the foreign object, nor could it lift itself high enough to free itself.

"Onigawara! The hand! The hand!" Tanuki yelled again, but the gargoyle was out of sight.

The *odokuro* howled its frustration, drowning out Tanuki's shouts of alarm in a screaming clang of bells. Even if he could raise his voice over the cacophony, the thrashing of the limb under him made holding on a difficult enough task.

"Onigawara!"

Without warning the disembodied limb bucked up and threw Tanuki clear into the air.

Time around him seemed to slow to a crawl.

Higher than the juniper, the wall—even higher than the roof—Tanuki had never been so high in his life. The view was amazing. The bright red pillars of the shrine down the street were visible, even with the lights of the three-story shopping centre framing it from behind. In the distance there were even a few green points of light—fireflies—moving on for the season to the secret place of gods and *kami*.

How different things were when looking down, rather than up. This must be how Onigawara saw the world—stretched out before him in humbling vastness. Tanuki's life might have been very different if he'd sat with his friend on the roof, even once. He could have, if he'd tried.

He could have climbed the juniper and walked the wall. He could have—

Time snapped out of its slow motion drift. Tail-first, Tanuki slammed onto the edge of the roof and spun down through the air before shattering on the flagstone steps in front of the porch. The mournful crash of a jolly piece of pottery was swallowed up by the clacks of scattering bones as Onigawara made the final blow on the *odokuro*'s left shoulder. The demon howled but defenceless, it could do little else.

Onigawara wasted no time.

Climbing over twisting vertebrae he hooked his feet into the back of the demon's skull and hacked away at its neck. The demon screeched and thrashed but Onigawara could not be dislodged; with a final, terrible blow, he cut the head from the *odokuro*.

A bell tolled and echoed over the wall. The skull and all its stolen bones disappeared, and Onigawara was thrown head over heels through the garden. He lost an arm at the base of the juniper, and both legs on the stones of the koi pond where inertia bounced him up and dropped him into the endless green.

*

Kentaro arrived at seven twenty-four the next morning in a crisp black suit and matching tie. Armed with a briefcase full of paperwork he faced the home of his late father and in his head drew figures and calculations and projections of the worth of the land without the antique building that sat on it.

In the garden he did the same; he took notes of the property lines and the meterage, inspected the alley behind the half collapsed eastern wall and kicked aside the broken pottery that might trip the brokers who would come to view the house.

Half of a plump *tanuki* face spun off into the weeds, its wide grin belying its pitiable state.

"This place is a death trap. I don't know how it didn't kill my father years ago."

Mounting the steps to the porch, he slid open the door and trod on the tail of a cat napping in a patch of morning sunlight. It screeched and hissed but before it could escape, Kentaro had it by its nape.

"Goddamnit, Shizuho. Stop taking in strays," he muttered and evicted it out the door.

Offended, the cat sat in front of the porch, refusing to be rushed, and passed its tongue fourteen times over its left paw and six times over its right. Its point made, it stood and followed the trail of stressed and crushed weeds to the cheerful, skyward smile of the broken *tanuki.* "That man, indeed, has no respect," it said and swished its tail thoughtfully westward.

"Let's go," it said at last, and picking up the shard of pottery, it mounted the fallen juniper before disappearing over the crumbled wall.

A solitary firefly winked once in agreement and followed after it.

ABOUT NJ MAGAS

Born and raised in Canada, NJ Magas now lives in Kyoto, Japan with a dog, a bird, a tortoise, and her spouse. She writes when she should be sleeping, walks when she should be writing, and practices Japanese fencing when she needs something else to do. She's not sure that she's ever seen a ceramic tanuki come to life, but is convinced that if it's going to happen it'll be at the temple behind her house where she spends a lot of time observing, thinking, and coffee drinking. NJ Magas reviews the books she reads on her blog, http://njmagas.wordpress.com/ among other things. You can also follow her on Twitter @njmagas.

THE KING OF FLOTSAMLAND

Tom Barlow

~ North Pacific Gyre~

When I heard the *butter butter butter* of a helicopter approaching from the east, I dropped the fish netting I'd been untangling and strolled over to Baggie Beach. The previous afternoon, Koo, worried, had tipped me that Midas Recycling was sending out a consultant to find out why she and her harvester crew had failed to meet their monthly production quota. Again.

I was hoping the consultant would haul her and the rest of the crew back to the mainland for their winter furlough. Once the harvester was abandoned until spring, I would be free to leave Flotsamland myself and return to San Diego. My monthly resupply flight from the Fair Share Gaea group was due on Sunday, and I could hitch a ride home with them.

The Sikorsky settled onto the deck of the cargo ship a thousand yards from my floating trash-pile kingdom. That ship was already half-full of pieces of the island, chewed away by the harvester in August, while I was incapacitated by an infected cut on my foot. Mr Pepsodent, the largest of the neighbourhood sharks that hung around hoping for a taste of Harry (I'm Harry), swam by on his way to check out the noise.

I lifted the binoculars I'd found in a month before in the hatch of a half-a-sailboat just as the helicopter door swung open. A tall, cadaverous man in safety-orange coveralls jumped to the deck. He appeared to be about my age, mid-thirties, with extremely long legs and a long face, like a wax model left in the sun. He scowled at Koo as she approached, the rest of her crew trailing several paces behind. Two of them were wheeling their sea chests, just in case.

Cadaver Man and Koo immediately started to argue, she on her tip-toes, arms crossed. Anger can ruin some women's looks, but she was as fetching as ever. The man brushed her aside, though, and strode to the superstructure, then up the outside ladder to the bridge. Koo followed, still carping at him.

To my dismay, the Sikorsky took off again a short time later, carrying no passengers. It disappeared over the eastern horizon, taking with it at least a month of my winter vacation.

That evening I was walking the three-mile perimeter of my island nation to see what new, interesting trash had arrived courtesy of the North Pacific Gyre when Koo paddled out of the twilight. I followed as she circled the mainland to dock on the western shore, out of sight of the cargo ship.

"Passport, please," I said as she heaved herself out of the kayak onto the dock I'd built with aluminium cans.

"Funny man," she replied. She'd never visited the Flotsamland mainland before, except in my dreams, but she'd spent many hours talking with me from her kayak as I kept myself interposed between the harvester and the shoreline it was supposed to devour. She wasn't the most loyal of Midas employees, thankfully.

Her skin shone like eggplant. She was taller than I'd thought, and her PFD had been concealing a curvaceous torso. Her face was cute, in a kewpie way—wide eyes, button nose, small mouth under spiky black hair.

"We need to talk," she said.

"Come up to the office." I pointed to my shack, perched atop Mount Détritus.

She followed me up the twenty-foot hill. We made ourselves comfortable on the cushions I'd crafted from sailcloth and kapok. "Tea?"

She nodded. I cracked open the valve of one of the dozen propane tanks liberated from an abandoned pontoon boat, lit the jerry-rigged burner, and put on the water kettle.

"Who's the new guy?" I said.

"His name is Goodale. He claims the home office isn't going to pull us out until the cargo hold is full."

I fiddled with the teapot to cover my anxiety. "You can't be serious.

Do they know what the winter's like in the North Pacific?"

She pulled off her sweater. Even a small fire heated up the shack nicely. I'd built it in the shape of a teepee. "Midas has whole cities for processing the waste we harvest from the sea," she said. "If they run out of product, the company goes belly-up."

The currents of the north Pacific circulate clockwise, aided by the prevailing winds, and the trash from surrounding shorelines is pushed toward my island as surely as water is drawn to the drain. It was at the centre of this gyre that Flotsamland had taken form over the last century, a solid disc of trash a mile wide and 100 feet thick. My little pied-á-terre represented a goldmine for a company such as Midas, and they loathed Fair Share Gaea for claiming its riches should be shared with the world's poor.

"Midas has already taken, what, eight-hundred million tons of trash out of the ocean in this area?" I said. "Why don't they look somewhere else? I hear the Marshall Islands are nice and trashy."

The kettle boiled, and I poured the water onto the tea leaves. The smell of bergamot from the Earl Grey was lost on me. When you live on an island made of trash, you learn to block out your sense of smell.

"Stupid question," she said. "The better question is, what will they do to keep their big machines fed?"

"You think I could be in danger?" I handed her tea in my favourite cup, with the logo of the cruise ship, *Bacchanalia.*

"The first thing Goodale asked me was when we could expect the next day with good cloud cover and calm seas."

A CNN satellite had been watching Flotsamland since Fair Share Gaea landed me here in a PR stunt that culminated in the pending UN resolution to declare it a shared world resource. My job was to play chicken with the harvester by keeping my kayak, the *FLS Scumbucket,* interposed between the island and the harvester whenever the weather was calm enough for harvesting. Two years of playing dodge 'em had convinced me that the company was unwilling to risk public condemnation by harming me in front of the cameras.

"I appreciate the warning," I said. "But aren't you taking a risk by telling me?"

"I took this job because nobody was hiring marine biologists," she said. "I thought I could continue my whale research. I had no idea how cutthroat this business is. These are evil people."

"And here we are, fighting over trash. Do you even feel like the world was wearing out?"

She leaned back against a seat cushion I'd harvested from a 2017 Toyota roadster. "I can't speak for the world, but my little piece of it is exhausted."

We sat in companionable silence until she began to snore softly. I woke her just before dawn so she could get back to her ship before first watch.

The next day brought a return of summer weather, clear and temperate. Only the falling water temperature and southerly declination of the sun foreshadowed the approach of winter. As the harvester chugged toward the island, I paddled out to intercept it.

Goodale was at the con. As I spun the *Scumbucket* to face the harvester's three-story-high scoop, he turned off his engines and snatched the microphone from its hook on the bridge.

"You're trespassing on Midas property," he said, "and interfering with our legal business operations. You have ten minutes to get out of my way." His voice was as deep as a humpback's keening, and gravely. It had the forcefulness of a military order.

Which put my hackles up. A military brat, I'd spent my childhood without a home to call my own, surrounded, raised, by order-followers and order-givers.

I picked up my megaphone, made from a highway cone. "Beautiful day, huh? Have you introduced yourself to the TV audience?" I pointed to the sky.

He exited the bridge and walked the narrow catwalk to the upper lip of the scoop, only twenty yards from my boat. I popped open my dry box and pulled out the flare pistol the CNN reporter had given me to draw their attention in the event of a confrontation.

Goodale looked down on me. "How tough do you think you are, kid?"

"Tough enough, I guess," I said, with the bravado that came from confidence that my courage would not be tested.

He leaned against the railing and lifted one foot onto the lower rung. "I bet you have a ten-second pitch for the cameras, right? All you pretty boys talk in sound bites."

The "pretty boy" comment cheered me up a bit. I recited, "The oceans belong to everyone, not just the countries with big guns. The

North Pacific Coalition had no right to sell off the harvesting rights to this latitude. Flotsamland alone is worth billions, and we're here to make sure the poor people of the world get their cut for a change."

"You're an idiot, kid. A dangerous idiot. He stared at me like I was a dog to be cowered. "I didn't come out here to play games. You want to avoid becoming recycled trash yourself, you'll leave as soon as you can."

Although I'd expected him to threaten me, as others had before him, he spoke with that voice of a drill instructor, one that expected immediate and unswerving obedience. Dad had that kind of voice.

The Midas crew and I had long before come to a tacit agreement on ground rules for ocean face-offs; if I could hold my position, they wouldn't assail it. If they could get around me fairly, they could chew on Flotsamland for the rest of the day. None of us believed any more that trash or the cause warranted bloodshed. At least, until now.

"Forecast calls for increasing cloud cover tonight," Goodale said before turning away and returning to the bridge. As the harvester puttered back to the ship, I wondered if I had the guts to face a real assault. If they shipped Koo home, I was pretty sure the answer would be no.

⌀

The clouds did indeed arrive that night, thick and wet, but, as usual, the seas came up, too. The waves were tall and broad enough to toss Flotsamland around like a garbage-can lid in a tornado, and the harvester remained tied up to the cargo ship.

The following morning, I awoke to the unmistakable smell of shit. Dread fell over me as I dressed and stepped outside.

There, on Styrofoam Beach, lay a lifeless 15-foot-long baby humpback whale, a harpoon sticking out of its head like a toothpick from an olive. Its belly had been slit from stem to stern, and guts were spilled across one of my rain collection tarps. A message was painted on its side: "You're next."

Goodale was watching me through binoculars from the ship's superstructure. He waved derisively.

A hundred yards offshore, a pod of humpies circled slowly, each surfacing in turn as it reached the nearest point to the island. The pod stayed there for the next two days before leaving. Each morning Koo paddled out and spent a couple of hours circling and singing along with it.

✒

The Fair Share Gaea copter arrived on schedule that Sunday. Since waves were still percolating the island, it hovered and my usual contact, Pamela, zip-lined down.

"I thought Midas would be gone already," she said as she unclipped from the line.

I explained the situation, wondering if I should have kept the whale to show her, instead of dumping it back into the ocean.

"You can't spend the winter out here," she said, concerned, as she checked out my kingdom. I'd been segregating new trash with the thought of adding some acreage to the western shore—plastic in one pile, then glass bottles, cans and other metal containers, nets, and mile upon mile of monofilament line. A tall stack of driftwood was drying at the foot of Mount Détritus, and my rainwater collection tarps and barrels covered much of the northern plain.

"I'll stay as long as Goodale does," I said, hoping my spoken commitment would bolster my resolve. I could almost hear Dad telling me, for the thousandth time, "Quitters never prosper." In fact, I wasn't sure my sister would even welcome me back on the mainland. She had her own place in San Diego, and my presence was an unwelcome reminder of our loss: both our parents were killed in the Congo War.

"We didn't bring food," Pam said, "or clothes, or anything. We thought we were coming to pick you up." I was taken aback when she confessed that the organisation didn't have the money to make another trip for several months, even if the weather cooperated.

I almost cracked from longing for the convenience of central heat, hot meals, fresh laundry. Electricity. I'd installed solar panels and a wind turbine on Flotsamland to power the fridge I'd found in a crate of appliances, but it had crapped out months earlier and was now a part of the appliance archipelago.

Seeing Koo watching from the ship gave me courage to say, "I'll get by. A case of Korean army rations floated in this spring, enough to hold me for the winter, along with the fish and sea birds I can catch. You haven't lived until you've roasted an Auk."

Pam, resigned to my decision, lowered the few supplies they had brought, mostly magazines, and flew away with the understanding that they would return in April, come hell or high water.

I'd never felt more alone.

I wasn't alone for long, though. That evening the sky cleared and the sea smoothed over. The water was already noticeably cooler, on its way down to its winter temperature of 55 degrees. My feet were beginning to ache from the cold every time I sat in my kayak.

The harvest moon that night was full and almost bright enough to read a magazine by, so I spotted Koo as she pulled up to Baggie Beach and dragged her boat onto shore. She removed a large backpack from the luggage hatch and slowly hiked up Mount Détritus to the shack. Since I had a tarp for a door, she knocked on the eye of the wooden Cyclops, a ship's figurehead, that I'd used to frame the entrance.

"Let me guess," I said. "You want to borrow a cup of sugar."

She stepped into the shack, dropped her bag next to the small fire burning in the fireplace I'd made of an old oven, and squatted, rubbing her hands over the flames. "*Qué onda?*"

She'd lost weight in the short time since her last visit, and there were bags under her eyes. Her hands were cracked and dry, the curse of saltwater.

"*Nada.* You okay?" I said.

She laughed bitterly. "I used to think I could find the good in anyone, but Goodale is dead to me, after he killed that whale. I spent a year in grad school following that pod through their migration. They pass through here twice a year, from Hawai'i to the Alaskan coast and back. I knew that calf's mother."

"I'm sorry," I said. I pointed to her bags. "You're planning to stay?"

"I'm requesting political asylum."

"No problem," I sat upright. "Place your hand on your heart."

She pressed her palm to her bosom.

"Do you promise to uphold the laws and defend the honour of Flotsamland against any and all foes? And obey the monarchy?"

"I do." A slight smile broke through her distress.

"Then I hereby welcome you as a loyal subject of Flotsamland."

"My liege," she said, and curtsied.

"Later that night, she made an assault on the crown. I didn't object.

The weather was boisterous for the next week, and we took the opportunity to repair some of the damage the harvester had made over the summer. When the weather finally settled down enough for Midas to resume its attack, Koo joined in Flotsamland's defence with gusto.

The doubled size of our fleet made it easier to parry Goodale's harvester thrusts. Fortunately, a North Pacific high also stalled over us until almost Christmas, with a cloudless sky that kept us in clear view of the CNN audience. And when the clouds finally returned, so did the waves.

Goodale was indefatigable, though, spending every possible daylight hour at the helm of the harvester, stalking our perimeter like a caged cat. Several times, he sent the rest of the crew in the lifeboat to box us in, but they rowed with the enthusiasm of ill-treated slaves and we easily avoided them

Not all was right in Flotsamland, though, even with our increased population. The supplies adequate for me alone were diminishing quickly when split two ways. The pile of dried driftwood dwindled, and the old saw, which I'd found trapped in one of the logs, was so dull it could barely cut plastic.

Koo and I filled the empty hours getting to know one another. I told her about how I came to volunteer for Fair Share Gaea (pretty girls, too much beer), about my dead-end job pressing tofu, my university days leading to an utterly useless degree in geography, and my boyhood, a different home on a different military base every twelve months.

She described her fieldwork in marine biology. I also learned that she had been a star diver in college, in high school, in grade school, an almost-Olympic talent, thrilling to her parents, who were unhappy unless they were pursing unattainable goals.

Neither of us talked about our old romances. I'd had very few, and handled them badly. Fear of commitment on my part was often cited as the reason for the failure.

On Christmas Day, a smudge of sun far to the south, dim as a 15-watt bulb, backlit thick grey clouds. No satellite coverage, for sure. The sea was mirror-calm.

"This is trouble," I said to Koo. Shaking her awake. I quickly pulled on my clothes and wrapped a wool rug over top like a serape.

Goodale had the harvester headed for Cape Cardboard. We hurriedly launched the fleet and paddled like hell, managing to pull in front of the harvester as it closed to within 50 yards of the mainland.

Goodale was puffing on a cigar the size of a barracuda. He waved us aside, and kept coming. Waved again, kept coming. Koo looked at me, eyebrows raised.

I picked up my speaking tube. "Get out of the way," I shouted to her. "No need for both of us to go in harm's way."

She stuck out her tongue and made a few quick pry strokes to bring her boat closer to mine. Goodale was now only twenty yards away. The knife-edged, stainless-steel screw thread that chewed up the material gathered by the harvester's front-end scoop was already feasting on material floating loose in the waters around our shoreline. Bushels of squid were being pureed.

Ten yards. We back-paddled. Goodale kept coming. We backed up some more. The stern of my boat struck the shore. Goodale kept coming, a smile on his face. The screw thread made a whining sound as it spun.

I chickened out.

"Retreat!" I yelled to Koo as I took three quick strokes, carrying me beyond the machine's scoop.

I turned to make sure Koo had followed, but she hadn't moved. Instead, she gave Goodale the finger as her kayak was dragged into the scoop. The screw grabbed the prow of her boat and remorselessly sucked it in. Her boat was suddenly jerked vertical, catapulting Koo out of the cockpit, still holding on to her paddle, over the scoop and into the ocean.

The awful screech of the harvester as it began to chew up the shoreline drowned out any other noise, but Goodale laughed as I frantically circled the harvester. As soon as I cleared the hopper, I spotted Koo, floating and shivering. I prayed that the commotion would keep Mr Pepsodent away.

To my relief, there was no sign of the shark, but Koo had lost control of her limbs in the cold seawater, and I had to dead-lift her onto my deck. I ripped off her PFD and shirt, as well as my own, threw the rug over both of us and hugged her fiercely.

She stopped shivering after ten minutes, and was finally able to speak. The first thing she said was, "Get me to shore."

"Yeah," I said. "Let's get to a fire."

She shook her head. "Put me there." She pointed to a narrow defile formed by an old lifeguard tower and a pile of deck chairs, twenty yards to one side of the path Goodale was chewing into the island.

"Hurry," she said.

I figured that, once on shore, I could carry/drag Koo to the shack before she caught pneumonia. As soon as I landed where she indicated, though, she crawled out of the boat. She staggered for a few steps before strength returned to her legs.

As I made my way to the bow of the boat and precariously stepped onto land, Koo made a beeline toward the Anchor Alps. There, she grabbed two of the largest plough anchors, forty pounds each. One in each hand, she limped toward the harvester, now ten yards into the mainland and gobbling up more of the island by the minute.

Goodale had turned to watch the digested debris fill the hopper, and didn't see Koo come up alongside the scoop. She dropped one anchor, grabbed the other with both hands, and heaved it into the screw. She picked up the second anchor and repeated the motion, then backed away quickly.

A second later, an ear-piercing screech filled the air. I clapped my hands to my ears as the rear end of the harvester raised slightly, like a bee sucking pollen, then crashed back to the sea. Smoke poured from the engine compartment under the bridge. Goodale stared in disbelief for a moment before killing the engines.

I grabbed Koo in my arms and lifted her off the ground. Straining to find words strong enough to indicate my awe, I said, "God, I love you!"

She hugged me back, but her teeth were chattering too hard to speak.

That night, as I tried to make hot soup out of a can of army rations that might have been dog food, she explained that a section had broken from the leading edge of the screw thread weeks before, leaving a gap they'd intended to repair while in dry dock over the winter. She estimated the damage caused by carefully dropping the anchors into that gap would take months to repair.

✐

Those were the worst months of my life. At first, Koo discounted her sniffles as a cold that would soon pass. However, the weather turned piercingly cold, with a persistent arctic wind and fog, so the damp was unavoidable. At first, I spent my daylight hours filling the bite the harvester had taken out of the island. On the horizon, I could occasionally see the star-like lights of welding torches as Goodale and his people worked to repair the harvester.

When Koo began hacking up yellow sputum, I put aside my work and huddled with her under a thick pile of rugs, sail cloth and awnings, creating our own body-heat sweat lodge. We passed the long nights in intimate conversation. I'd always believed that inside each of us are a few ugly rooms best left unexplored, but I opened mine for her, and she didn't flinch. The memories she was most reluctant to reveal, I found touching.

When she began coughing blood, I did the only thing I could. I paddled out to the cargo ship.

The crew watched from the railing as I approached a steel cliff two stories high.

Goodale let me bob there for a couple of hours, futilely hailing the ship, before finally deigning to appear.

When his head appeared over the rail, I said, "I want to make a trade."

He spat, but the wind took it well clear of my boat. "What do you want?"

"I want antibiotics. Koo is really sick."

"In return for what?"

"The island." My kingdom for a horse.

He rubbed his chin. "But it's not your island to trade, kid."

"Whatever. I won't stand in your way, as long as you leave enough land for us to live on until we can be rescued."

"Nope," he said.

"What do you want?" I said. "Anything."

He smiled. "You got nothing to bargain with, kid. I'm going to get the island whether you like it or not."

I bit back my anger, on Koo's account. "You can't just let her die."

"Is that right? You're the one to tell me what I can and can't do?" He shook his head. "Company medicines aren't for traitors." He pointed toward the horizon. "You best get home. Looks to me like a gale's coming."

❧

I sewed Koo in a cocoon of Tyvek, which claims to be highly water resistant. I weighed her down with a hundred pounds of anchors. Five thousand feet to the sea floor. From there, she'd never be able to witness the destruction of her adopted homeland.

*

I spent the second half of the winter lying in the shack, too dispirited to even build a fire most of the time. Occasionally, I'd screw up enough initiative to dress and walk down to the Bay of Boxes and watch Mr Pepsodent swim back and forth. I wondered how long it would take him to devour me.

*

The harvester repairs were completed just in time for the first overcast, calm day, a harbinger of the spring climbing the latitudes toward us. I was gumming something cloyingly sweet and brown. The packaging, in Chinese, featured a grinning family, but it wasn't bringing me any joy.

I heard the diesels start up a quarter of a mile away, followed quickly by the smell of exhaust. The wind was out of the east.

I threw off my rugs and stood, my joints creaking from the effort. In the moment of clarity that accompanies a sea change, I saw my shack through a stranger's eyes: a hovel of junk, the type of mean existence that presages life at the end of human history.

I found scissors and trimmed my beard as much as possible, then shaved off the rest. I cut my bangs so they didn't hang over my eyes, brushed my teeth, cleaned out my ears. Took a teeth-chattering sponge bath. Ripped open a plastic bag containing a white captain's uniform from a Norwegian Cruise Line ship. The harvester was closing quickly.

I saluted the shack, then descended Mount Détritus. Goodale was headed toward Koo's Cove, but I was able to beat him there, even walking at a funeral pace. I grabbed a plastic deck chair along the way. When I reached the shore, I took a seat, facing the harvester.

Goodale was smoking again. He looked calm, almost bored, altering his course slightly so that I was dead-centre in his path.

I turned to look over my kingdom. Where Goodale saw billions of dollars in plastics and other recyclables, I saw the only real home I'd ever known. The Christmas tree of aluminium foil that Koo and I had erected. The basketball court, fishing net hung from a hoop that once held a wooden barrel together. The Air Mail mailbox I'd fixed to the top of a mast high in the air above my shack.

Until that moment, I never truly understood why my parents had been willing to die for their country.

Mr Pepsodent, prescient, appeared, swimming laps along the shore. Goodale was now so close I could see the gravy stain on his lapel. He obviously had no intention of stopping. I closed my eyes and thought of Koo.

Then the engine sound changed pitch. I opened my eyes to an amazing sight—the harvester rising from the sea. Goodale clung to the ship's wheel as it rose higher, higher, until I could see that it was being carried on the broad white jaws of a pair of humpback whales. At apogee, the whales flicked their heads in unison, tossing the harvester free. It flipped once before smashing into the water, upside down. Immediately, more whales came flying across the surface of the sea, smashing into the harvester with their jaws. A huge hole appeared in the hull and water began to pour in. Again, the harvester was lifted, and this time, as it went flying, Goodale, with a death grip on a life preserver, was tossed free. He landed twenty yards clear of the wreck, which the whales continued to pound.

Goodale looked my way, terror and pleading in his eyes, and began frantically swimming toward Flotsamland.

Mr Pepsodent met him halfway there.

❧

Fair Share Gaea returned two weeks later, just as I'd finished constructing Harvester Harbour from Goodale's wreckage. They came by ship, this time, a small cruise ship, and not alone.

Pamela came ashore first.

"You made it," she said, relieved, and gave me a hug.

"I hope you have good news about our sovereignty," I said. "We have our first martyr." I told her what had happened in her absence.

She put her arm around me in sympathy, then pointed to the ship. The railing was crowded with people. "I'm afraid I have some bad news, Harry. The courts nullified the contract with Midas last Monday, and boy, did we celebrate. We didn't know that the UN had already promised the island away."

My eyes were watering in the ocean wind.

She nodded toward the onlookers. "The NPC took these people's island away to build a wave power collector farm. They demanded another island as compensation, so Flotsamland is what they were given. Some deal, huh?"

I guess the Cherokee wouldn't have been surprised.

"Still," she said, "it's not all bad news. You've done your job, Harry. You get to go home."

So I abdicated the throne, and followed her back to the cruise ship. Later, as we sailed away, I realised that Pam was wrong about one thing.

I wasn't returning home. I was leaving it.

ABOUT TOM BARLOW

Tom Barlow is an Ohio, USA writer. He is the author of the science fiction novel *I'll Meet You Yesterday*, and his work has been featured in anthologies including *Best American Mystery Stories 2013*, *Hard-Boiled Horror*, *Best of Crossed Genres #2*, *Battlespace*, and *Desolate Places*, as well as many magazines including *The Intergalactic Medicine Show*, *Digital Science Fiction*, *Coyote Wild*, and *Encounters*.

www.ingramcontent.com/pod-product-compliance
Lightning Source LLC
Chambersburg PA
CBHW050304110726
47899CB00007B/2104